THEIR SECOND CHANCE MIRACLE

SOPHIE PEMBROKE

REUNION WITH THE BROODING MILLIONAIRE

ELLIE DARKINS

MILLS & BOON

First Published in Great Britain 2022
by Mills & Boon, an imprint of HarperCollins*Publishers* Ltd,
1 London Bridge Street, London, SE1 9GF

www.harpercollins.co.uk

HarperCollins*Publishers*
1st Floor, Watermarque Building,
Ringsend Road, Dublin 4, Ireland

Their Second Chance Miracle © 2022 Sophie Pembroke

Reunion with the Brooding Millionaire © 2022 Ellie Darkins

ISBN: 978-0-263-30213-4

03/22

MIX
Paper from
responsible sources
FSC® C007454

This book is produced from independently certified FSC™ paper
to ensure responsible forest management.
For more information visit www.harpercollins.co.uk/green.

Printed and Bound in Spain using 100% Renewable Electricity
at CPI Black Print, Barcelona

dec...
writer and en...
up romantic proposals, ...
trips to the past with dashing her...
working she can usually be found running arou...
toddler, volunteering at her local library or escaping all o...
the above with a good book and a vanilla latte.

...iniseries

...e by Sophie Pembroke

...and the Rebel Billionaire
...is's Shy Cinderella
...n Seal the Deal

Discover more at millsandboon.co.uk.

THEIR
SECOND CHANCE
MIRACLE

SOPHIE PEMBROKE

MILLS & BOON

For everyone who has lost someone they love
over the last couple of years.
But most especially in memory of Eden Anna.

CHAPTER ONE

IT HAD BEEN a long time since Finn Clifford last walked the cobbled streets of Wishcliffe village on a mission, but he had one now. One final step towards the goal that had driven him for the last decade.

Growing up at Clifford House, less than a mile away, his usual goals in Wishcliffe had to do with hanging out with his best friend Toby Blythe and trying to obtain illegal pints at the King's Arms pub. But he was an adult now—a thirty-something even, as Toby, now his business partner, kept reminding him with a smirk. He had a purpose in life. He was a successful businessman, a force to be reckoned with, a world away from the boy he had been...

But he still winced when he saw the ancient bent form of John Yarrow sitting on his usual bench outside the King's Arms, smoking his pipe.

'Finn Clifford, as I live and breathe,' John called out across the street, his breath misting in the cold air. 'Been a while. Not looking for mischief, I hope?'

'No mischief, sir,' Finn called back. 'I'm on a mission.'

'Are you now?' John's gaze was assessing. 'Sounds like it's going to get you into trouble.'

'Probably,' Finn admitted. 'But it'll be worth it.'

'Hmm.' John sucked on his pipe, then nodded. 'Get on with it, then.'

Finn picked up his pace.

The weak January sun had barely managed to make it above the rooftops of the cotton-candy-coloured cottages that lined the side streets leading down to the sea. In summer, the village would be bustling with locals, tourists and day-trippers from the surrounding towns, all looking for the coastal charm Wishcliffe provided in spades. But today the high street was empty, a number of the shops not even open for the day.

The shop he wanted was, though. From the cross at the centre of the village, where High Street and Water Street met, Finn could see the yellow glow of the lamps in the window and the rusting metal shop sign swaying in the breeze from the sea beyond.

He stalled for a moment, breathing in the salt air until his lungs felt cold. Part of him—not a small part either—wanted to turn around and head back to the tiny car park by the chapel where he'd left his car. But that wouldn't be in keeping with his mission. And he'd come too far over the last few years to give up now, when he was so close.

This was the final stage of a decade-long plan of revenge. He couldn't stop now, even if he wanted to.

Besides, the worst she could say was no, right?

Resolved, Finn headed down Water Street and pushed open the door to Wishcliffe Antiques and Col-

Sophie Pembroke has been dreaming, reading and writing romance ever since she read her first Mills & Boon as part of her English Literature degree at Lancaster University, so getting to write romantic fiction for a living really is a dream come true! Born in Abu Dhabi, Sophie grew up in Wales and now lives in a little Hertfordshire market town with her scientist husband, her incredibly imaginative and creative daughter and her adventurous, adorable little boy. In Sophie's world, happy *is* for ever after, everything stops for tea, and there's always time for one more page…

Ellie Darkins spent her formative years devouring romance novels and, after completing her English degree, decided to make a living from her love of books. As a writer and editor, she finds her work now entails dreaming up romantic proposals, hot dates with alpha males and trips to the past with dashing heroes. When she's not working she can usually be found running around after her toddler, volunteering at her local library or escaping all of the above with a good book and a vanilla latte.

95100000351637

CHAPTER ONE

IT HAD BEEN a long time since Finn Clifford last walked the cobbled streets of Wishcliffe village on a mission, but he had one now. One final step towards the goal that had driven him for the last decade.

Growing up at Clifford House, less than a mile away, his usual goals in Wishcliffe had to do with hanging out with his best friend Toby Blythe and trying to obtain illegal pints at the King's Arms pub. But he was an adult now—a thirty-something even, as Toby, now his business partner, kept reminding him with a smirk. He had a purpose in life. He was a successful businessman, a force to be reckoned with, a world away from the boy he had been…

But he still winced when he saw the ancient bent form of John Yarrow sitting on his usual bench outside the King's Arms, smoking his pipe.

'Finn Clifford, as I live and breathe,' John called out across the street, his breath misting in the cold air. 'Been a while. Not looking for mischief, I hope?'

'No mischief, sir,' Finn called back. 'I'm on a mission.'

'Are you now?' John's gaze was assessing. 'Sounds like it's going to get you into trouble.'

'Probably,' Finn admitted. 'But it'll be worth it.'

'Hmm.' John sucked on his pipe, then nodded. 'Get on with it, then.'

Finn picked up his pace.

The weak January sun had barely managed to make it above the rooftops of the cotton-candy-coloured cottages that lined the side streets leading down to the sea. In summer, the village would be bustling with locals, tourists and day-trippers from the surrounding towns, all looking for the coastal charm Wishcliffe provided in spades. But today the high street was empty, a number of the shops not even open for the day.

The shop he wanted was, though. From the cross at the centre of the village, where High Street and Water Street met, Finn could see the yellow glow of the lamps in the window and the rusting metal shop sign swaying in the breeze from the sea beyond.

He stalled for a moment, breathing in the salt air until his lungs felt cold. Part of him—not a small part either—wanted to turn around and head back to the tiny car park by the chapel where he'd left his car. But that wouldn't be in keeping with his mission. And he'd come too far over the last few years to give up now, when he was so close.

This was the final stage of a decade-long plan of revenge. He couldn't stop now, even if he wanted to.

Besides, the worst she could say was no, right?

Resolved, Finn headed down Water Street and pushed open the door to Wishcliffe Antiques and Collectibles without even pausing to glance through the window first.

Victoria looked up as the bell over the door jingled, and Finn felt a jolt as his heart jumped into his throat. In the yellowing light of the coloured glass lampshades dotted on the shelves around her, she appeared more beautiful than ever.

Her silky dark hair was caught up in a simple pony-tail at the base of her neck, and her severe black jacket and top did nothing to accentuate the gorgeous figure he knew was hidden underneath. She was thinner than he remembered, her eyes a little large in her face, the shadows under them not quite hidden by make-up. But she'd never looked more beautiful to him.

Stop staring, he told himself fiercely. *She's Barn-aby's. She'll always be Barnaby's.*

And because of that he would only ever be able to admire her from a distance, never letting her know how perfect he thought she was. He'd resigned him-self to that years ago, that first summer Toby's older brother Barnaby had brought her home to Wishcliffe after they met at university.

He'd fallen in love—or at least lust—on the spot. And known in that same instance that he could never do anything about it—least of all let Victoria know how he felt. So he hadn't. Not in all the fifteen years that had followed. Barnaby had been like a big brother to Finn too. He would never do anything to betray that.

Not even now he was gone.

'Finn!' Victoria's smile looked forced, but that

wasn't really a surprise. 'How lovely. What can I do for you?'

That was her hostess voice, Finn recognised. The one she'd used as the lady of the manor, Viscountess Wishcliffe, before she was widowed. Before she'd been replaced last September, when Toby came home to inherit his older brother's title as Viscount, and brought his new American bride, Autumn, with him.

She'd never used that tone with him, though. He'd always been family, before now.

'Toby told me you were working here now,' he said, not answering her question. Not yet. 'I had to see it for myself to believe it.'

Victoria bristled at that. 'I have a degree in art history and a master's in art business, plus several years' experience of working at auction houses. What's so incredible about me working at an antiques shop?'

He'd set them off on the wrong foot already, which was sort of par for the course for him with Victoria. He'd never been able to keep his foot out of his mouth around her.

'I'd forgotten about you working up in town.' He hadn't. Finn didn't think he'd forgotten anything about Victoria from the moment they'd met.

She'd commuted into London from Wishcliffe, where she was already living with Barnaby, planning their grand wedding, and only quit after their son, Harry, was born. She'd planned to go back, he knew, but then Toby and Barnaby's father died and Barnaby took up the title, and she'd had more than enough to do as Viscountess, keeping Wishcliffe from going under.

But that was Toby and Autumn's job now, and here Victoria was. Getting back to her roots.

'I wasn't suggesting you weren't qualified to be here,' he said when she stayed silent. 'I'd have thought you were over-qualified, if anything.'

'I've been out of the antiques world a long time.' She sounded faintly mollified. 'This seemed like a good way to ease myself in, and Joanne needed the help in the shop, so it worked out for both of us.'

'That's…good.' Finn perched himself on the corner of an old oak sideboard, until Victoria glared at him and he slid off again, hands in his pockets. 'Actually, it's antiques I came to speak to you about.'

Her eyebrows jumped at that, surprise obvious on her face. 'Antiques? I've seen your London flat, Finn. There's not a thing older than last year in the whole place.'

A slight exaggeration, but he had to admit that he favoured a more modern aesthetic in his London home. 'Ah, but this isn't for the flat. It's for Clifford House.'

Victoria's eyes widened as she leant forward across the desk. 'You really did it then? You bought back Clifford House?'

Nobody had thought he could, not even his closest friends, not really. But Clifford House was his by rights—by birth, by history, by inheritance. It had been passed down to the eldest son in the Clifford line for so many generations that they'd run out of room on the family tree. It was the place he'd been born, the place he'd grown up, the place that he'd always known would come to him.

The last place he'd seen his mother alive. The only place he had happy childhood memories with her.

Clifford House belonged to him, and he belonged to it. And now, finally, that was official in the eyes of the law again.

Pride filled him as he nodded. 'I really did.' It had taken him a decade to earn the money and orchestrate the sale. Ten years since the day he'd learned that his own father had sold his heritage, his home, purely to keep it from ever falling into Finn's hands. Not just Clifford House itself, or the grounds that surrounded it, but every heirloom, every keepsake, every stick of furniture that went with it. 'But that's just the start.'

Because if his father's aim had been to stop Finn from ever being Lord at Clifford House after his death, then he had failed. And Finn had every intention of rubbing his nose in that failure.

'The start?' Victoria asked. 'What's next?'

'Next, I have to buy back all the heirlooms and antiques to fill the place. And that's where you come in.'

Victoria stared at Finn, taking in the smirk on his lips and the fire in his eyes.

Of course. He'd only come to find her because he needed her help. That made sense.

Or maybe Toby had put him up to it—had him come up with a pity job to keep Poor Victoria busy now she'd handed the estate over to him and Autumn. Never mind that she'd *wanted* to leave.

She'd stayed on at Wishcliffe for a full year after the horrific sailing accident that took her husband and son from her. She'd lived in that big house full of all its memories, and she'd followed the plans that she and Barnaby had made together, to try and make the estate solvent. She'd given Toby the time he needed to tie up his business loose ends—and to get to a mental place where he was ready to take on the job as Viscount, something he'd never thought would fall to him.

Victoria had done everything she could and then she'd stepped back gracefully to let Autumn take her rightful place as Viscountess, while she'd helped and supported her from the sidelines. And when they were settled up at Wishcliffe House she'd moved out—even if it was only as far as her little cottage on the outskirts of the village, by the sea. She'd found herself a new job. She'd stepped into a new life. A quieter, safer, softer life than the one she'd thought she'd be living with Barnaby and Harry, but *her* life all the same.

She'd done everything properly. Everything right. Thinking of others all the way.

But that wasn't enough, apparently. Toby and Autumn still insisted on dragging her back to the main house for dinner every week, still fretted that she wasn't happy, that she needed more in her life. More people, more adventure, more challenge.

What none of them seemed to understand was that she'd *had* all that. She'd had true love, the fairy-tale prince—well, viscount in her case—the perfect family, the happily-ever-after.

It just seemed that 'ever after' didn't last as long as it used to, that was all.

Victoria knew that her life had been blessed—from

the moment she'd met Barnaby until the moment she'd lost him and their son at sea. She'd had all her good fortune and used it up fast. All she hoped for now was a quiet, settled, content existence, doing things she was good at. Was that so much to ask?

Apparently so, because now here was Finn, with a huge project that he just *had* to have her help for—as if there weren't a hundred antiques dealers in London who would jump at the chance to take it on.

'Toby put you up to this, didn't he?' she said accusingly.

Finn looked honestly taken aback. 'No. I haven't actually spoken to him about it yet—he's meeting me at Clifford House later. I wanted to get you on board first.'

'You really expect me to believe that after a year away you've come back completely without prompting to ask me to take on your little revenge shopping trip?'

'It's not a revenge shopping trip,' Finn said with distaste. Victoria raised her eyebrows. 'Fine, it is. But can we at least call it something else? Like a Heritage Restoration Project?'

He didn't mention the year away. Victoria wasn't surprised. He wasn't the only friend who'd dropped out of her life once her circumstances changed. People weren't sure how to deal with a thirty-three-year-old widow who'd lost not just her husband but her only child as well. It was too sad for them, so they stayed away.

Joanne, who owned the antiques shop, had helped her come to terms with that. She'd lost her husband in her late forties and moved to Wishcliffe to get away from the pitying looks and the blind date set-ups.

'People start to panic that you'll be on your own, you see,' she'd said when Victoria had wandered in one day, three months after the funeral, looking for a distraction. *'You're an aberration. So they try to fix you. To find you a new life, before you've finished saying goodbye to your old one. Either that or they stay away, like what happened to you might be catching. They're scared is all, and they're thinking of themselves instead of you. You take your time, do what you need to do, and ignore all the rest, okay?'*

Joanne had become a friend, long before she'd been her boss. Victoria credited her with helping her find her feet. Her own path towards what she wanted the rest of her life to be.

Peaceful mostly, she'd decided.

Finn Clifford's life, Victoria knew, was anything but peaceful.

Even before his father had upped and sold Clifford House and all its contents, just to stop it falling into the hands of a son he regularly described as 'degenerate', the people of Wishcliffe and the surrounding area had all known of the drama playing out in the family. From Finn's mother walking out when he was a child—only to die a year later in a car crash with her lover—to the knockdown, drag-out fights between father and son that had required the police to be called more than once, Finn's life was definitely dramatic.

And that was something that Victoria wanted no part of.

'It'll be fun,' he cajoled, obviously sensing he was about to get rejected. 'Like a treasure hunt. That's what we should call it! My Heritage Treasure Hunt. Buying back all the things my father sold and shoving our successes in his face. It'll be great!'

'For you, maybe.' Victoria shook her head. 'Do you even realise what you're asking, Finn? It'll be months of research, travel, work… I'm not up for that. And besides, I don't think this focus on revenge is good for you. You've bought the house. Isn't that enough?'

His whole adult life, that was what he'd been focused on, as far as Victoria could see. Being successful enough, earning enough, to buy back Clifford House after his father sold it when Finn was away at Oxford, in his last year of university.

And now he'd done it. Shouldn't that be enough?

'No,' Finn said, his voice cold. 'It's not enough. But I need your help for the rest. Please, Victoria.'

The please almost broke her. That and the idea of being needed again. Having a purpose beyond living out her quiet, safe days.

But that wasn't her plan for her future.

'I'm sorry, Finn. I can't.' She shrugged apologetically. 'I have obligations here, working for Joanne, apart from anything else. I can't just up and run away on a treasure hunt with you.'

Even if a part of her wanted to. A small, secret part of her that had been quiet for such a long time, and was now stirring again at the thought of a new adventure.

His disappointment was clear on his face, but he didn't press her any further.

'I understand.' Finn reached across the counter to place a palm against her shoulder. 'Take care of yourself, Victoria. And let me know if you change your mind.' He turned and walked away, back out into Water Street, heading for the cross.

'I won't,' she whispered to herself as the door closed behind him.

'I love what you haven't done with the place, Finn.'

Finn started as his best friend's voice echoed through the empty rooms of Clifford House. Turning away from the window, he gave Toby a wry smile as he joined him in what had always been the ballroom, a vast open space with wooden floors and huge windows leading out onto the terrace. Finn vaguely remembered a ball being held there once, but that must have been long before his mother had left, and he didn't have so many memories left from that time. Just the impression of swirling dresses and music and staying up past his bedtime.

Most of his memories of Clifford House weren't the happiest. But they were his, just like the house. And some of them, the earliest ones…

Sitting with his mother in her favourite garden, making up fairy tales together. Baking mince pies with her at Christmas. Curling up beside the fire after playing in the snow while she made him hot chocolate, and knowing that he was loved.

Those memories were what he forced himself to remember when he looked around Clifford House now. Not the others. *They* were the reason this place mattered.

Something else he wouldn't let his father take away from him.

'Well, you wanted to see it.' Finn spread his arms wide to encompass the vast emptiness of the old Georgian-style manor house. 'Here it is.'

'Not *quite* as I remember it,' Toby observed. 'I seem to remember there being, oh, furniture, maybe?'

'I'm working on it. Come on, I've got the kitchen up and running at least.'

He led Toby through the warren of corridors to the kitchen, ignoring the empty space where the old farmhouse table used to sit and directing him to one of the folding chairs beside a rickety picnic table instead. 'Coffee? Or beer?'

'Coffee's fine,' Toby replied, gazing around at the space. 'So, what's first on your agenda here?'

Finn flipped on the kettle. He really needed to get a proper coffee-maker set up in here. Coffee, then furniture, that was the actual plan—but probably not what Toby was asking.

'That depends,' he said. 'I got lucky in that the most recent owners only got as far as making the place good and painting it all white before they ran out of funds and had to sell. Apparently this place has been a money pit for at least three other families since my father sold it.'

'So you've got a blank canvas. You can really make this place your own.' Toby sounded approving of that—maybe even a little jealous, Finn thought.

'What I wouldn't give sometimes to start over at Wish-cliffe. I think there are spiders' webs in some of the corners that are older than me.'

'You don't mean that.' For Finn, Wishcliffe House had always been the perfect beacon of cosiness and welcoming warmth. With its roaring fire in the winter, apple cider fresh from the orchard and warm biscuits just out of the oven, it was the only place Finn had wanted to spend his school holidays after his mother was gone. Even when Clifford House had been filled with furniture, it had never been welcoming to him without her there. 'Besides, I refuse to believe that Mrs Heath would suffer a spider to live on her watch.'

'True.' Toby gave a half smile at the reminder of his terrifyingly efficient housekeeper. 'Still, do you know there's not a single piece of furniture or deco-ration in that place that Autumn and I picked out our-selves? It's all heirlooms. Whereas here…' He trailed off, perhaps realising that he was treading on uncom-fortable ground.

'Here, my father sold all our family heirlooms, just so they'd never be mine,' Finn said. 'But the joke's on him, because I'm going to buy them all back.'

Toby blinked. 'What? All of them? Isn't that a lit-tle…ambitious?'

Finn had a strong suspicion that 'ambitious' wasn't his friend's first choice of word to finish that sentence. 'Fine. Maybe not all of them. But the important ones I want to track down and buy back. As for the rest of the house, I plan to find pieces as close as possible to the ones that were here before. I'm going to put this place

back the way it was before my father lost his mind.'
And then he would bring the old man back to Clifford
House and show him that he'd lost. That Finn had got
everything he'd tried to deny him and there wasn't a
damn thing he could do about it.

Rubbing a hand over his forehead, Toby gave Finn a
concerned look. 'You don't think that just buying back
the house was enough? I mean, that's what you were
always focused on. What you've been working for all
these years. Can't you, I don't know, just enjoy it?'

It hadn't been enough for Lord Clifford to make
his only son's life miserable. He'd had to take away
everything that was his by rights. To badmouth him
to the whole of society. And to do it just as Finn had
been poised to graduate, to step out into the world of
work and make a life for himself. While the parents
and families of his fellow students had been setting
up opportunities for them, introducing them to people
they needed to know, or at least helping them with job
applications and housing them in the meantime, Lord
Clifford had been systematically undermining Finn's
attempts to make his way in the world.

Every interview Finn had attended after Oxford
had been met by a knowing look from someone on the
other side of the desk—someone who knew his father
or had heard the rumours. Finn Clifford was unreli-
able, a degenerate, a failure. It was a large part of why
Finn had persuaded Toby that they should set up their
own business—and then let Toby be the public face of
the company, at least to start with.

His father had tried to ruin his whole life.

So, no. It wasn't enough just to have the house back, even though that alone was a huge measure of his success. He had to *show* his father how utterly he'd undone everything Lord Clifford had strived to achieve. Turn back the clock to before his mother had left, to when Clifford House had actually felt like home.

Finn shook his head. 'It's not enough, Toby. You know it isn't. You know what my father did. What he is. It's not enough to have the house. I've got to beat him *completely,* or he'll always feel like he's won.'

'Right.' Toby sighed. 'Okay, well, if we're doing this, we're going to need help.'

'We?'

Toby shrugged. 'You're my best friend. You might sound kind of obsessive crazy right now, but if you didn't turn your back on me when I accidentally got married to a woman I didn't know in Vegas, I'm not abandoning you now.'

'And look how well that Vegas thing worked out for you and Autumn,' Finn pointed out. Not only were they still married, but they were planning a spring ceremony and party to celebrate it with all their friends in Wishcliffe. 'Maybe this will be more successful than you think.'

'Maybe.' Toby didn't sound convinced. 'But you're still going to need more help than me—I don't know the first thing about antiques.' Enlightenment hit him, and Finn watched as Toby caught up to where Finn had been since the moment he'd walked into his new old property and realised what his next steps needed to be. 'Victoria! She's the antiques expert. And honestly, I've been a bit worried about her lately. I know she says she likes working at the shop, but she's used to running a whole *estate*. She's got to be bored. And I don't want her to just give up on life the way my mother did when Dad died. This could be the perfect project to get her engaged again!'

'She said no,' Finn said, and watched as Toby's excitement deflated.

'You already spoke to her?'

Finn nodded. 'This morning. She's not interested.'

Toby's face darkened. 'Because she's not interested in *anything* any more. Autumn keeps trying to get her involved with the planning for our wedding celebration, and I've been asking her about playing a part in some of the new projects up on the estate, but she keeps making excuses not to get involved.'

Finn suspected that probably had more to do with Victoria wanting to draw a line between the life she'd lost and the one she was living, but he could see how worried Toby was about her, so he didn't say so.

'What do you think I should do, then?'

'Keep at her,' Toby said. 'Don't let her just give up on everything that used to matter to her. Okay? Keep asking until she says yes.'

Finn had always believed that when a lady said no he should accept that and walk away. But in this case he could almost see Toby's point. Victoria was pulling away from the people who loved her right when she needed them most. And the life she was building for herself, alone…was it one she really wanted? Or the only thing she thought was open to her?

If Victoria had turned him down not because she didn't want to help but because she thought that was what she should do as a widowed woman, then he at least had to give her a nudge, didn't he?

Nothing at all to do with the fact that just the idea of spending more time with her made him smile.

'I'll see what I can do,' Finn said. 'First, do you have a number for Joanne Soames?'

CHAPTER TWO

VICTORIA DIDN'T BOTHER with the front door. She might not know Clifford House the way she knew Wishcliffe, but she knew Finn wouldn't be hanging around in the oversized entrance hall. So she skirted the edge of the driveway and slammed open the back door to the kitchen instead.

Finn, sitting in a camping chair, put down his coffee cup on the blue plastic picnic table beside him. 'Hello, Victoria. This is a—'

'You called my boss.' The fury that had started to rise in her the moment Joanne had told her was reaching fever-pitch. 'I told you no, and you ignored me. You went over my head and called my boss and sweet talked her instead.'

'Well, I knew sweet talk never works on you.' Finn stood and headed to the mostly bare kitchen counter. 'Coffee?'

'You couldn't accept that *I* have the final say in my life?' Victoria asked, before adding, 'And yes to coffee.' It had been a long day, after all. Mostly because of the man holding the jar of instant coffee.

He might have left the antiques shop that morning without a fuss, but his request had stayed in her head long past lunchtime. And when Joanne had arrived to help close up at the end of the day and announced that she'd had a very interesting phone call, Victoria had known she wasn't done with Finn just yet.

'You absolutely do have the final say in your life.' Finn handed her the coffee and motioned to the second camping chair, which was a total mismatch for the first in colour and style. 'I just wanted to make sure you made that decision for yourself, and not for other people.'

'Other people like, say, you?' Victoria stayed standing when he sat down again, taking advantage of being taller than him for once as she looked down at him.

He chuckled at that, which wasn't what she'd been aiming for. He should be feeling guilty for trying to manipulate her, not amused.

'You said you couldn't help because you had to work at the shop for Joanne. So I spoke to Joanne.' Finn shrugged. 'If you don't want to help me because you genuinely don't want to help me, that's fine. I'm sure I can find someone else who will. But if you're saying no because you think you shouldn't for some reason—because of your obligations to Joanne, or because, well, I don't know, some other stupid reason like what you think a widow's life has to look like—then I have to at least give you all the information, and an opportunity to change your mind.'

He looked up at her with a smile so persuasive that

it should have been illegal, and Victoria gave up and dropped into the chair beside him.

What you think a widow's life has to look like.

Was that what she was doing?

She'd been determined not to, but now she looked at the life she was building she had to admit she'd gone for safe over fun, for quiet over passion. Because fun and passion were what she'd had with Barnaby, and Barnaby was gone.

'Joanne said you offered to pay for my time while I was working for you, so she could hire someone else to help in the shop if she needed to, when I was away.' Joanne had also told her to think about why she was saying no.

'Be honest with yourself. Working here at my little shop was only ever going to be your first step back to a new career, wasn't it?'

Because that was what she'd told everyone when she'd taken the job. That it was her first step. She just hadn't actually gone as far as to imagine taking any future steps at all.

'It's only fair, after all,' Finn said. 'If you're working for me, I pay for your services. Just like I would anyone else. I wasn't asking for a favour.'

'Right.' But what *was* he asking for, exactly? 'You said you wanted to buy back some heirlooms, find some antiques for this place. How many are we talking about?'

Finn's smile turned wry as he got to his feet. 'Let me give you the tour.' He held out a hand and pulled her out of her own chair. 'Starting here in the kitchen, where we need, well, everything, as you can see.'

'Like a kitchen table and chairs, that sort of thing?' That should be easy enough to source, at least.

'Exactly. Just like there used to be in here.' He led her out into the hallway and through to what must be a beautiful drawing room—when it wasn't cold and empty. 'And in here they had matching Queen Anne chairs, plus an upholstered chaise longue in a duck egg Chinese design, as far as I can tell from the photos. I'm not sure how easy they'll be to come by. And through here—'

'Wait!' Victoria called out, stopping him before he could whirlwind her into the next empty, soulless room. 'You want to recreate this place exactly as it was when your parents lived here?'

He stared at her blankly. 'Well, yes. Of course. Isn't that what I told you this morning?'

'I thought…well, I suppose I thought you wanted help finding antiques that would suit the place.' She stared around at the white walls and the curtainless windows. Surely it couldn't be healthy, recreating the home she knew he'd hated growing up in.

The summer she'd met Finn, when he was sixteen and she was eighteen, he'd spent more time at Wishcliffe House than his own—and, according to Barnaby, it had been that way since Toby and he were kids. Ever since Finn's mother had left, and his father started drinking.

'I just don't understand why,' she said helplessly.

'Because I need my father to know that I won in the

end. And this is how I'm going to do it.' Finn placed a hand on the doorframe. 'I'm going to show him that everything he tried to take away from me I won back in the end.'

Yeah, this definitely wasn't healthy. 'You don't think that, say, living a full and meaningful life of your own might do that better? People matter more than things, Finn.'

'Not to my father, they don't,' he said wryly. 'I could be President of the Universe, happily married with a whole platoon of kids, and I'd still be his useless, degenerate son to him. This place—our heritage—is the only thing that's ever meant a damn to him. So that's what I have to use.'

'Why?' she asked again, uncertain whether she meant *Why do it?* or *Why does he hate you so much?*

She wasn't entirely sure which one he answered either, when he said, 'If I figure it out I'll let you know. So, will you help me?'

This time Victoria didn't glance around at the empty spaces, the rooms waiting to be filled, the blank walls crying out for pictures. Instead, she looked at Finn—really looked at him, for the first time since he'd walked into Joanne's antique shop that morning.

What she saw there reminded her of her own mirror, not so very long ago. The desperate search for something to make sense of the world.

He was going about it the wrong way, of course. If she'd learned anything in the last thirty-three years it was that acquiring more stuff never led to happiness—

acquiring more people, more love, was the only way she'd ever found to do that.

But if this was what he believed he needed…she could help him. And she could be a friend when he realised that it wasn't enough. Because Finn really looked like he needed a friend right then.

She moistened her lips, weighing her words in her head before she spoke. 'I'll help you. But I'll do it my way, on my terms.'

Finn smiled, slow and warm. 'Whatever you need, Victoria.'

She was going to help him. Which meant he might actually be able to pull this whole scheme off, after all. Relief mixed with joy inside him. 'So, where do we start?'

Victoria looked as surprised as he was that she'd said yes. 'Uh… I guess we finish the tour of the house?'

'The rooms all look pretty much like this one,' Finn admitted. 'Soulless and white. But I guess you need to get an idea of the scale of the problem, so…come on.'

It felt so strange, touring the empty rooms of his childhood home with his teenage crush at his side. Victoria paid attention to everything, asking questions about his memories of what each room had been like and taking notes in a small book she pulled from her handbag.

'You said you have photos?' she asked as they reached the bedrooms.

Finn nodded. 'Not of every room, but most. It

should get us close enough. I've got a designer working on finding matches for the wallpaper, curtains and the like.'

'Right.' She still sounded perturbed at his plan. Finn could understand that. It wasn't as if he was under the impression that this was a totally *normal* thing to do.

But it was what he needed—what his father needed to see for him to understand. To know that he hadn't beaten Finn, hadn't destroyed him, despite all his best efforts.

Once he'd done this, Finn would be free of his father, his past, for ever. *Then* he could move on with his life. But not before.

'Come on.' He led her into the next room, a smaller corner space with large windows on two sides. Even though it, like all the other rooms, was painted plain white, in his memory it was a sunny yellow, with a rocking chair in the bay window where his mother used to sit and sing to him. 'This was my nursery.'

'It's a lovely room.' The words sounded strained, and he glanced over to find her face tense and drawn.

Of course. He'd been so caught up in his own past he'd forgotten for a moment about hers.

She'd lost her child. Her son.

In Finn's memory, Harry had been a vibrant child—always in motion, always smiling and laughing. Losing her husband must have been heart-breaking. But losing her child…

Finn didn't know how Victoria still got out of bed every morning.

'Let's head back down to the kitchen.' He guided

her out of the room and towards the stairs, and she let him. 'It's warmer there, for a start—the central heating is something else that's on my list to get someone out here to look at.' But the kitchen had the old Aga in it, always lit and always warm, just like he remembered from his childhood.

There were *some* good memories associated with this place, he'd come to realise since moving back. They just tended to get lost in the weight of all the bad ones.

'So, how is this going to work?' Finn asked as he put the kettle on for another round of hot drinks.

'As my employer, I was sort of expecting you to tell me that.' Victoria, settled back into one of the camping chairs, looked more herself again, he was relieved to see.

'Yeah, but out of the two of us, you're the only one who knows what they're doing.'

She laughed at that, and he tried not to grin with pride at having achieved it, the way he would have done at sixteen, trying to impress the girl he had a crush on.

Not much had changed in the last fifteen years, he had to admit.

'Well, I think we need to focus in on what you *really* want to achieve here.' She took her mug from him, and Finn sat down beside her to listen. 'I mean, this place is enormous, Finn. If you really wanted to refurnish it exactly as it was when you were growing up, it could take years. Longer, if you wanted exact matches for all of the pieces. The antiques market is buoyant, but there are still some pieces that don't come up—or not for the price you'd be willing to pay.'

'I'll pay anything,' he replied automatically. Buying Clifford House might have dented his savings, but it hadn't depleted them. The business was doing well, and he'd been working towards this for years. He wasn't worried about the money.

'You say that now,' Victoria said wryly. 'Wait until the first time I tell you you're going to have to pay the equivalent of two month's rent for a dining room chair—and you need six of them.'

Finn shook his head. 'I don't care. I'll pay it.'

'You shouldn't.' She gave him an assessing look. 'Finn, the point about antiques isn't just owning them for the sake of it, or because they're old and expensive. You're buying a piece of heritage. A place in history.' Her eyes lit up as she spoke and Finn knew this really mattered to her, so he listened a little harder—and tried not to get distracted by how beautiful she looked when she cared about something. 'Plus a lot of the pieces your father sold won't be up for sale again—at any price, possibly—even if I could track them all down. I think a couple of the paintings went to museums, for instance, if I'm remembering right.'

'Okay, so how would *you* recommend we go about this?' he asked. 'You know what I'm trying to achieve here, and why. How do I do it?'

She looked thoughtful for a moment, staring down at the open notebook on her lap, where she'd been jotting notes throughout their tour. 'I think you need to choose the pieces that really matter—a handful of the real heirlooms, the ones you want back. I'll work on tracking those down and see how many of them we can buy back.'

'Sounds good so far.' He'd never really imagined—outside of daydreams—that he'd be able to get *everything* back. But there were pieces he knew beyond doubt he had to have to complete his plan. The mantel clock given to his ancestor by a member of a royal family—or possibly *the* royal family. The writing desk his mother had brought with her when she'd married his father. A painting of his grandmother. That sort of thing. 'Then what?'

'For the rest of the rooms…let's choose the ones that will have the most impact and start there, trying to replace the furnishings with as close a match as we can get. But for things like the third guest bedroom… Finn, you might just have to accept that we'll find something lovely to suit the space, but it might not be exactly the same.'

He nodded. 'I can do that. I mean, there are some rooms that I don't even have reference photos for—we were always going to have to guess there. And as long as every room is furnished in a similar style, the impact should be the same.'

'Exactly!' Victoria beamed at him, the light in her eyes a full-on blaze now. 'In that case… I think we can do this. Do you want to give me the photos and other reference material now, and I can get started while I'm working at the shop tomorrow? From what you've said, I've already got a few ideas on places we can try, people to speak to, that sort of thing.'

'I'll get them now.' She looked so alive, so engaged by the challenge. Almost like she had before she'd lost everything. Toby had been right; she needed this, even if she hadn't known it.

And Finn couldn't help but feel happy that he'd been the one to give it to her.

'Thank you, Victoria. For helping me with this.'

Her smile warmed places inside him he'd forgotten even existed. 'We'll see if you're still thanking me when I've spent all your money on antique china,' she said.

Finn laughed, and went to fetch the file.

Going through Finn's research at the shop the next day, Victoria realised she might have underestimated the amount of work that was going to be involved in this project.

Oh, she'd known it would be a big job, no doubt about that. But some of the pieces Lord Clifford had sold off were unique, and plenty of the others were incredibly rare. The specific items Finn wanted weren't things she was likely to stumble over at an antiques market or dusty old curios shop in some little town.

She was separating the items in his file into three stacks based on the likelihood of being able to buy them back, buy something similar or find something from vaguely the same period when the Bakelite rotary dial phone beside the till rang.

'Wishcliffe Antiques,' she said, absently filing Finn's mother's china set under 'buy something similar'. 'How can I help you?'

'You already are.' Finn's voice was warm and friendly in her ear, and she smiled despite herself. 'Just calling to see how you're getting on with the files. If there's anything else you need, that sort of thing.'

Victoria surveyed the towering piles of paper. 'I think I've got plenty to be going on with for now, thanks. But if you want to come over later this evening we can discuss our next moves?'

'Sounds good,' Finn said. 'Shall I bring anything?'

'Coffee is always appreciated. See you later.'

She hung up and returned her attention to the files—only for a breeze from the door to send half of them skittering across the floor.

'Sorry! Sorry,' Joanne said as she dropped to her knees to help collect them up again, almost spilling the two takeaway coffees she was carrying over all of them.

Victoria swept in and took the travel mugs from her and placed them safely on the desk. 'Don't worry, I've got a system. But thank you for the coffee.'

Joanne stepped back, hands on her hips, and eyed Victoria's carefully organised stacks as she reassembled them. 'You know, when Finn Clifford called and asked to borrow you for a project, I kind of assumed that was just an excuse for him to get you alone and ask you out.'

Finn? Ask her out? A laugh exploded from Victoria's mouth at the very idea. 'No, this is an actual work project.'

'Well, I can see that now.' Joanne took her coffee

and perched safely out of the way on a vintage school desk. 'What's he got you doing?'

'Buying back or replacing most of the contents of Clifford House.'

Joanna gave a low whistle. '*That* is a project. Shame.'

'Why's it a shame?' Victoria asked, peering at her boss over the top of a photo of the main hallway during some sort of party.

'Because if he *was* looking for an excuse to ask you out, you have to admit he's a bit of a hottie.'

Victoria laughed again at that, even if it didn't feel quite so amusing. 'I've known Finn since he was sixteen. He's like a little brother to me. Well, maybe not brother. Brother's best friend, I guess.'

Because while Toby had always been the sibling she'd never had and always wanted, from the moment they'd met Finn was more aloof, apart, in some ways. For all that he'd been around Wishcliffe House as much as the Blythe brothers, he'd always been on the edges of the action. Victoria supposed that was why they'd bonded at first—both outsiders to this strange family, both trying to find their place.

Finn had been the one to explain the vagaries of Wishcliffe to her—all the little oddities that seemed normal to Barnaby and Toby because they'd grown up with them, but made no sense at all to her that first summer. The one she'd exchanged amused looks with when any of the Blythes did something particularly Blythe-like.

'Brother's best friend is *definitely* not a brother.'

Joanne gave her an assessing look. 'You're absolutely sure he's not working up to asking you out?'

Victoria shook her head with a wry half smile. 'I think I'm sort of past all that now, don't you?'

That caused Joanne to hoot with amusement. 'You're what—thirty-three? Trust me, there's plenty of time left for *all* of that.'

'But I already *had* that,' Victoria said. 'Even if Finn was interested—which, trust me, he isn't, he's totally focused on this project.' And getting petty revenge on his father. 'But, even if he was, I'm not. I was lucky enough to find true love and enjoy it for almost fourteen years. I'm not going to be bitter about losing it, but I'm not looking for a replacement either. Maybe one day, but not now.' And maybe never.

How could she look for love again, when that would be a betrayal of everything she'd had with Barnaby? How could she hunt down another fairy-tale ending, live *two* happy lives in one lifetime, when Harry didn't even get one?

'You know, life doesn't end with loss, Victoria.' Joanne's eyebrows had dipped in the middle into a serious frown. 'Look at me—I didn't even move here to Wishcliffe until after my husband died, and now I have a whole new career with the shop, a new social circle—'

'Yes, but you also moved here to get away from people setting you up on blind dates,' Victoria reminded her.

Joanne threw up her hands in defeat—almost sending coffee flying over the stock behind her. 'Okay,

okay. I take your point. Just…don't give up on happiness, okay? Even if that happiness doesn't look the same way you always thought it would.'

Victoria smiled. 'I won't, I promise. Even this—' she waved her coffee cup at the piles of paper '—has got me excited again. I didn't think I wanted to get involved, but it's nice to have the challenge.'

And when it was over, she could go back to the quiet, comfortable cocoon she'd built for herself, until she was ready to come out into whatever her new world looked like. When she was ready.

Eventually.

The phone rang again, and Victoria answered it absently.

'Wishcliffe Antiques—'

'I don't know where you live,' Finn interrupted her. 'I was all set to come up to Wishcliffe House, but you're not there any more, are you?'

Victoria thought of her tiny cottage by the beach, so far removed from her former home in style—if not actual distance—that it was almost laughable. And then she thought of Finn being there, in her safe space, her old world colliding with her new. Even Toby and Autumn hadn't been to the cottage except to drop off flowers and cake the day she'd moved in.

But this was work. And Finn's project *was* part of her new life, really.

She took a breath. 'Have you got a pen? I'll give you directions.'

CHAPTER THREE

WISHCLIFFE VILLAGE WASN'T big, but somehow Victoria had managed to find a cottage that lay down roads Finn hadn't even known existed. He followed her directions—scribbled on a Post-it note stuck to his steering wheel—out of the main village and down country paths only just wide enough for his low-slung sports car to pass through, the bare branches of overhanging trees scraping the expensive paintwork as he drove, until eventually he saw something he recognised.

The sea.

Victoria's directions had taken him around the headland and to a tiny cove outside the village, and as he grew closer a small, squat white fisherman's cottage came into view. He parked just outside the gate, next to the hedgerow and the sea holly and grasses struggling to grow beside the white stone wall.

The cottage itself sat right on the edge of the beach, protected from the sea winds only by the curve of the cliffs and the stone wall around the property. Finn knocked on the bright blue door and, when there was no answer, wrapped his coat tighter around him and went to investigate.

It was only late afternoon, but already the sun was low over the sea, darkness beginning to encroach on the view. Still, as he reached the other side of the cottage he saw a figure down on the sand, her sunshine-yellow waterproof jacket a beacon in the twilight.

Victoria.

Finn picked his way through grasses and over rocks to the sand, and between the seaweed and shells that had washed up with the last tide, until he reached her.

'Kind of cold for a beach day, isn't it?' He dropped to sit on the sand beside her.

Victoria started at his voice, looking at him with surprise. 'What time is it? Sorry, I meant to head back in before you got here.'

'What were you doing out here?' Finn asked. 'Must have been pretty engrossing to lose all track of time.'

She glanced away. 'I was just…well, I was talking to the sea.'

And she was concerned about his state of mind? 'Did it talk back?'

That earned him an irritated look. 'It's not… When Harry was four or five, whenever he was scared or worried about something I used to tell him to give his worries to the sea. To talk it all out, and let the waves take it away.'

'I like that.' Finn stared out at the waves, white-tipped as they crashed up to the beach. 'I bet it worked too. Just saying things out loud makes them less scary sometimes, right?'

'That's the theory,' Victoria replied. 'Plus, if he did it when I was there, I got to find out what was worrying him too without him having to tell me direct.'

'Cunning.'

Victoria shrugged. 'Parent. Or, well. I was.'

It had been over a year, and she'd obviously trained herself to be able to talk about Harry and Barnaby without losing it, but still Finn could see the tension in the lines of her body, the way she hugged her knees a little closer to her chest.

'So what worries were you sharing with the sea?' he asked. 'Maybe I can help.'

'I wasn't, exactly. Well, I started to. But in the end...' She sighed. 'I guess I was just talking to Barnaby. Again.'

'That makes sense,' Finn said, even though he wasn't totally sure it did.

'It's hard to imagine that he isn't still out there in the world somewhere,' Victoria admitted. 'So when I need to talk to him I come here, and make believe he can hear me.'

'Maybe he can,' Finn murmured. 'I used to do the same, after my mother died. I'd go out to her garden—even though it was all overgrown since she'd left—and talk to her. Until my father caught me one time and... well.' He shrugged.

He hadn't dared go back out to the little walled garden his mother had planted after the thrashing his father had given him for mentioning her name within the grounds of Clifford House. In fact, he hadn't even been back there since he'd moved in.

He wasn't sure he wanted to. Not yet.

'Can I ask what you were talking to Barnaby about today?' he asked.

Victoria shifted, stretching her legs out across the sand as she leant back on her hands. 'I was telling him about this project of yours. I suppose, every other time in my adult life that I've taken on something like this—a challenge—I'd talk it through with him first. Only this time, I had to decide for myself.'

'And you still want to do it?' Finn asked anxiously.

'I do,' Victoria replied. 'But I did have one question I wanted to ask, before we get started.'

'Anything.' He had all his answers prepared—why he was doing this, why it mattered to him, how much he was willing to spend, how far he would go.

But he wasn't ready for the bluntness of her question, all the same.

'Why did you stay away from Wishcliffe, after Barnaby and Harry died?'

'I didn't.' He blinked. 'I came to see you, remember? A month after the funerals.'

'To talk about Toby,' Victoria pointed out. 'You wanted to know how me staying at Wishcliffe another year would affect your business together.'

'That's not…not entirely true.' He never had been any good at lying to her, that was the problem. Even when he'd been sixteen, and he and Toby had got away with the most outrageous lies about their antics when old Viscount Wishcliffe had asked, once he was gone it had only ever taken one raised eyebrow from Victoria and he'd been spilling all the real details to her.

'Isn't it?'

'No! I mean, yes, I was worried about Toby—as my friend, not my business partner. But I was worried about you too.' She'd looked so small, so frail, and all he'd wanted to do was take her in his arms and keep her safe. But that wasn't his place. 'I wasn't avoiding you.'

An outright lie. Because that first visit after Barnaby's death, he'd known. Known that he couldn't take the guilt of looking at her and wanting her and knowing that she was Barnaby's—and Barnaby was gone.

When she'd been married, she was safe. He could look at her from afar and adore her, but never dream of doing anything about it. But that was just another thing that Barnaby's death had changed. Seeing her again, Finn hadn't fully trusted himself not to let on about how he felt, even accidentally. And he couldn't bear the idea of the horror in her eyes if she found out.

And so he'd stayed away.

'Yes, you were.' She sighed. 'It's fine. A lot of people did. I mean, after the first flurry of visits and cards and flowers, the sympathy sort of wore off, and then people didn't know what to say, I guess. I was just a sad young widow, and nobody likes to see that. It reminds them of the unfairness of the universe.'

'I remember that.' The memory came back suddenly, like a dream he'd half-forgotten on waking. 'When my mother left, and again when she died… it was the same. Well, sort of.' She'd been gone for over a year before her death, and his father hadn't allowed anyone to talk about her. But he remembered all his teachers, his friends, other family, worrying about him, making a big fuss over him for a week or two. And then it was as if the moment was over, and he was expected to be back to his normal self again.

As if he hadn't just lost his anchor in the world.

'I'm sorry,' he said. 'I should have visited, should have done more. I guess… I didn't think that there was anything I could do to help, and I was focused on Toby…'

'Of course you were. He's your best friend.' She shook her head. 'I shouldn't have said anything.'

'No.' He reached across and touched her cheek, turning it so she had to look at him. 'You're right. *You* are my friend too, and I should have been there for you, and I wasn't. I'm so sorry.'

Had she ever seen Finn look so serious? If she had, Victoria couldn't remember it. Maybe at the funerals, although she'd mostly blocked out all her memories of that day.

Swallowing, she looked away, and Finn's fingers fell from her face. 'You're here now.'

'Making you work for me.' Finn gave a hollow laugh. 'I don't think this counts as a sparkling example of friendship.'

'I don't know.'

Out at sea, the last of the daylight had disappeared, leaving only the pale moonlight shining on the water. She'd always thought the beach was magical at night. A place for secrets and mysteries.

She wasn't quite sure which Finn was yet.

'I think maybe I needed this project,' she admitted, her own secret to share. 'Joanne keeps telling me that there's still life after loss, but I think I'd been trying to avoid finding it. Hunting down antiques will get me out there, at least.'

'Toby said something similar,' Finn said mildly.

Victoria shot him a glare. 'I thought you said Toby didn't put you up to this?'

'He didn't,' Finn replied. 'But he was the one who insisted I didn't give up. He's the reason I called Joanne.'

'Humph. Well, I'm not thanking *him.*'

Finn laughed. 'You two really are just like brother and sister sometimes, aren't you?'

'He's the only family I've got left, really,' Victoria admitted. 'That's why I stayed so close to Wishcliffe. My mum died not long after I got married, remember? And my dad…well, he doesn't count. So the Blythes were my family. And now—'

'And now Toby's the only one left,' Finn finished for her. 'You know he feels the same, don't you?'

Victoria gave a stiff nod. 'I know. But he's got Autumn now, and the wedding to plan and, well. There's not much space for me. I need to find my own place.'

'Speaking of which, how about you show me this cottage of yours?' Finn got to his feet, brushing the sand from his jeans, then held a hand out to pull her up too. 'It looks a little smaller than your last place.'

Victoria laughed. 'Since my last place was a twelve-bedroomed manor house, that's hardly surprising.'

'I don't know.' Finn shrugged. 'I figured you might have upgraded to a palace or something.'

They joked about her prospective housing options all the way back up the beach, past the little wind-battered gate with the peeling paint and in through the cheerful blue door that had sold the place to Victoria the first moment she'd seen it.

It was only once they were inside that Victoria realised how cold she'd got on the beach. January on the British coast wasn't ever the most hospitable weather, and she'd forgotten her gloves. But her thoughts had distracted her from the falling temperature.

'Do you want to light the fire?' She motioned towards the wood burning stove in the tiny lounge area. 'I think my hands are too numb.'

'Of course.'

As Finn set to work building the fire, Victoria stripped off her coat and scarf and opened the fridge to see what—if anything—she had to offer her guest. Not much, it turned out.

It wasn't that Victoria wasn't capable of cooking, it was just that, having had a live-in cook the whole time she'd lived at Wishcliffe House, she'd never really had much cause or opportunity. And since it was always just her at the cottage, she hadn't much felt like cooking cordon bleu meals for one. So all she had in were her staples. She hoped Finn wasn't expecting anything fancier.

'I can offer you hot chocolate and cheese on toast,' she said finally, as Finn returned to the kitchen counter. Behind him, she could see the wood burning stove blazing merrily.

'Sounds perfect,' he said.

'Sorry, I meant to go to the shops after work to get some real food, or at least a bottle of wine, but I guess I forgot.' Or, rather, she'd been preoccupied thinking about everything Joanne had said, and she'd wanted to get to the beach and talk it out with the waves.

'I said it was perfect,' Finn reminded her. 'I'm not much of a drinker anyway.'

He jumped up to perch on one of the kitchen stools at the breakfast bar that served in lieu of an actual dining table, and started rearranging the magnets on her fridge beside it. Used to Finn's inability not to fidget, Victoria rolled her eyes and set about preparing supper for them.

When she turned back, though, she was surprised to find that her fridge poetry magnets didn't spell out any dirty limericks—presumably because Finn was too busy staring at the photo magnets she'd had printed when she'd moved in.

'I don't think I've ever seen this one before,' he said.

Victoria leaned across the bar to see which one he was looking at and laughed. 'I think that must have been taken the first summer I came to Wishcliffe.'

In the photo, Barnaby had his arms around her waist and they were leaning against one of the old apple trees in the Wishcliffe orchard. It would have been a beautiful, touching photo—if not for Toby and Finn hanging out of the nearby branches like monkeys, ready to pelt them with fruit.

'I remember.' Finn placed the magnet back on the fridge, his smile not quite reaching his eyes. 'That was a great summer.'

'It was.'

She wondered if he was remembering, like she was, how easy life had seemed back then. How the whole world seemed full of possibilities. As if they could do anything they wanted, and nothing could stop them, because they were together.

The sharp, piercing sound of the smoke alarm broke into her reverie and she spun, swearing, to rescue the burned cheese on toast from the grill, while Finn whipped a wet tea towel in the vague direction of the sensor.

'Sorry,' he said as the sound finally abated. 'I shouldn't have distracted you.'

Victoria tipped the toast in the bin and started again. 'Reminds me of trying to bake a birthday cake for Barnaby that time, when you and Toby insisted on helping, despite your obvious raging hangovers.'

'We helped!' Finn protested. 'Well, apart from that bit where Toby had to go and be sick. But I think the decorations really made it.'

'You spelt out "You're really old" with chocolate buttons on it while I was doing the washing-up.'

'Harsh but true,' Finn said with a solemn nod. 'The man needed to be told.'

Victoria rolled her eyes, then took the damp tea towel from him. 'Why don't you go wait in the lounge, and I'll bring this through when it's ready, okay?'

'Okay.' He hopped down and headed back towards

the sofa. Victoria took a moment to watch him go, reconciling the man in front of her with the teenager of her memories.

Finn might have been gone from her life for a while but, now he was back, she was surprised how easy it was to fall into the old patterns of teasing and joking—as well as those few deeper, more meaningful moments in between.

She smiled to herself as she set about grating more cheese.

If nothing else, it seemed like this revenge project of his might at least have brought her friend back to her. And she couldn't be sorry about that.

Considering he was only really used to spending time with her in the vast spaces of Wishcliffe House, Finn was surprised how well the cosy cottage by the sea suited Victoria. It was tiny—he couldn't imagine there was more than one bedroom—but he could see instantly why she'd chosen it. It felt cocooning, safe, in a way he imagined she hadn't much lately.

And she could step outside and talk to Barnaby, Harry and the waves whenever she wanted.

Loitering in the lounge, he picked up another photo—this one a proper framed print. A family portrait—Victoria, Barnaby and Harry all together on the beach, grinning at each other with smiles that screamed of love and contentment.

Finn had never really thought much about True Love outside of fairy tales and movies, until the summer Barnaby had brought Victoria home to Wishcliffe.

Anyone who'd seen them together couldn't help but know that they were in the presence of the real thing. He'd never doubted, after that, the idea that true love was real.

But he also knew it was rare. Precious. And not for everybody. Not for him, chances were, or he'd have found it already.

His parents certainly hadn't found it, or many of the people he'd met out on the road, building the business. Seemed to him that almost everybody was either unhappy in their marriage, cheating on their spouse, divorcing—or all three.

Toby and Autumn, Finn suspected, might be another exception, despite their inauspicious start. Even the first morning he'd found them together he'd seen the spark of it. And that only seemed to have grown over the winter.

Now they were planning their second wedding— since none of their friends or family had got to attend their first impulsive Vegas one—and soon, Finn was sure, they'd be a family of three or four, or more. Settling down as the next generation at Wishcliffe House.

While Victoria hid down here in her cosy cottage.

He'd wondered over the years why Victoria and Barnaby had never had more children. But then he'd seen her red eyes and haunted face on a visit and Toby had obliquely warned him that it wasn't a topic for discussion, and they'd taken Harry out to kick a ball about for a while instead.

Later, he'd learned about the miscarriages—from Victoria herself in the end, one quiet summer evening when they'd been talking on the terrace. How there'd been two before they had Harry, and another two since. How the doctors thought it was best not to try any longer.

More losses she'd had to bear, but at least she'd had Barnaby at her side for those, and Harry in her arms.

Now it was just her.

'Cheese on toast.' Victoria placed a large plate in the centre of the small coffee table.

Finn's mouth started salivating at the scent. 'Did you make it the way you always used to? With the… whatever it was under the cheese?'

'Mango chutney,' Victoria said. 'And yes. Now, come grab your hot chocolate.'

They settled down together on the one small sofa, opposite the fire, and tucked into the cheese on toast— which was every bit as good as Finn remembered from drunken evenings at Wishcliffe, after he and Toby had staggered home from the pub and persuaded Victoria to make it for them.

While they ate, she filled him in on the progress she'd made, organising their task ahead.

'Once we've finished eating, I need you to look through the files,' she said around a mouthful of toast crumbs. 'Let me know if you agree with how I categorised everything.'

He cleared the plates and cups away, washing them up in the single sink under the window, while she spread out the photos and papers he'd given her on the coffee table. When he'd handed the files over, they'd been a mishmash of everything he'd been able to collect about Clifford House—bills of sale for various antiques, photos and press clippings from events held there, magazine spreads filled with descriptions of the house, accompanied with photos of his parents sitting stiffly beside each other, insurance documents detailing the contents of various rooms.

Now, every piece of paper had a coloured flag attached, and Finn could see Victoria's precise sloping writing on each note.

'This pile here is pieces that seemed like the cornerstone ones—the antiques we should try to track down and buy back if possible,' Victoria explained. That pile, Finn noticed, was significantly smaller than the other two. 'The second pile is items I think we can probably buy similar antiques to—same period or general feel, at least.'

'And the third pile?' The largest one, of course.

Victoria sighed. 'Those are the ones where you might want to consider looking for something different. Either they're going to be impossible to match, or they're not worth the money you'd have to pay to get them. They won't add much to the aesthetic, and I don't think they're a good place to focus our energy.'

Finn nodded slowly. 'That makes sense, I suppose.' Even if something inside him rankled at letting any of his heritage go without a fight. 'So you want me to check there's nothing in piles two or three that needs to be in the first pile.'

'Or vice versa,' she replied, although she didn't sound too optimistic about that likelihood.

She'd done a great job, Finn thought, as he started

going through the papers. From the mess he'd given her, she'd developed detailed lists with notes on provenance and estimated costs—one or two of which did make him wince, after all—and whittled down the whole thing until it felt almost achievable.

There was only one item he pulled out of the second pile and added back to the first.

'Really?' Victoria asked as she stared at the photo of a mantel clock that was probably less than two hundred years old. 'Why that? As far as I could tell, it didn't have any distinctive features to link it to Clifford House.' Most of the items in the first pile, Finn had noticed, were items with an obvious and marked connection to the house itself—like the china platter and matching soup tureen with the painting of the house's facade in blue on the white porcelain.

'My great-grandfather was given that clock by some minor royal or another,' he said. 'Granddad used to go on and on about it. My father would definitely notice if we didn't get that one back.'

Victoria placed the photo of the clock onto the first pile. 'I can't believe your father wouldn't have kept at least *some* of these things when he moved out of Clifford House. Is it possible I'm going to end up trying to buy them back from him?'

Finn shook his head. 'Not a chance.' When her brow furrowed in confusion, he explained. 'If he still owned them, they'd come to me when he died. He can't risk that.'

'Couldn't he just change his will?' Victoria asked.

'Apparently not. One of my cannier ancestors legally tied the Lord's possessions to the title, so they have to be passed down to me along with that. When I become Lord Clifford, I get everything that my father owns. Which is why, of course, he's sold as much of it as he possibly can and is now working his way through the proceeds in the bars and casinos of the world. To keep it all out of my hands.' Victoria looked like she might ask him to talk about his feelings for his father any second, which Finn had no desire to do, so he changed the subject quickly. 'Anyway, now you've got all this lot sorted, what's our first move? Go after the items in pile one?'

'Actually, no.' From her expression, Finn suspected he hadn't got away with avoiding that conversation for ever, but for now she was letting him off the hook. 'Those are going to take some time—I need to track down who your father sold them to, whether they've been sold on since, and then start negotiations to see if we can get them back. I'll be working on all of that, of course. But in the meantime I'm taking you to one of my favourite places in the world to make a start on piles two and three.'

'Oh? Where's that?' As if he wouldn't go anywhere she wanted when the excitement in her voice at the idea was so palpable.

'Portobello Road Market, London.'

CHAPTER FOUR

THE FOLLOWING SATURDAY morning Victoria caught an early train up to London, coffee and croissant from the stand at the station in her hand, and tried not to think about how this was the first time she'd visited the city since Barnaby and Harry died.

It hadn't been intentional, the way her world had shrunk to Wishcliffe House and the village over the last year and a bit. There'd just been so much to do, especially while Toby was still away. It had been easier to stay close to home—even if it meant living with the memories every day.

By the time she'd been ready to move out to her little cottage on the edge of the village, she'd not left Wishcliffe in a year. And unpacking her new home, starting her new job, it had all kept her busy enough that she hadn't even really noticed how tied to Wishcliffe she'd become.

A day in London would do her good—especially a day pottering around Portobello Road. And a day with Finn…well, that would probably do their friendship some good too. Spending the evening with him at her cottage had reminded her how much she en-joyed his company—his dry wit, his way of seeing past the words she was actually saying but not pressing deeper when she obviously didn't want to talk about something.

He'd been almost as close to Barnaby as Toby had. He had been Harry's godfather, for heaven's sake. He knew exactly what she'd lost and he felt that pain too, in his own way.

With him, she didn't have to pretend that everything was okay now, and that made her feel more relaxed than she'd have imagined it could.

While the train snaked its way through the English countryside and into the city, Victoria studied the list she'd made, with Finn's help, to guide their search that day. By the time her carriage halted at the platform at Victoria Station, she had a good feel for her priori-ties—and she was itching to get started.

She took the Circle Line clockwise to Notting Hill Gate, where she found Finn waiting for her, as ar-ranged. He, Victoria noted, did not look like he'd been up since stupid o'clock that morning to get there be-fore all the good stuff was sold. Instead, he looked well-rested and relaxed in his jeans and a cream wool jumper over a navy shirt.

She'd feel resentful, but he handed her a cup of cof-fee and she decided to forgive him after the first sip, as rich, earthy notes overtook her senses.

'This tastes amazing.' She checked the cup for a logo, but it was blank. 'Where did you get it?'

'There's a little pop-up stand by my flat, only there

on a Saturday,' he explained. 'I always get a coffee there to start my weekend if I'm in town. I've never tasted coffee like it anywhere else.'

'I forgot how close your flat is to Notting Hill,' Victoria admitted. 'This is hardly a special day out for you. You must come here all the time.'

'Actually, I haven't been in years.' Finn motioned towards the street and they started walking in the direction of the market. 'I guess it's that thing where, when you can visit something any time you like, you never have the urgency to make you actually go.'

'I suppose.' But Victoria knew that if she lived near the famous Portobello Road Market, nothing would tear her away every Saturday.

The start of the market was only a short walk from the Tube. Victoria finished her coffee just as the first stalls came into view, and she popped the cup into the nearest recycling bin before fishing her list out of her bag as they reached the market itself.

'There's a plan, I take it?' Finn eyed the list, and she smiled to see the slight apprehension in his gaze.

Some women liked shoe shopping. Some could shop for clothes for days. Or books, or power tools, or make-up.

Victoria had no interest in most of those. But when it came to shopping for antiques, she had real dedication. She had to, to get the best pieces. And that was why Finn had hired her, wasn't it?

'Of course there's a plan.' There were hundreds of stalls lining Portobello Road on a Saturday morning, not to mention all the permanent shops and the antique arcades snaking off the Main Street. Going in without a plan would be foolish.

'So, where do we start?' Finn asked.

Victoria stood for a moment, letting the vibrancy of the market sweep over her. The bright colours of the cloths on the market stall tables, laden with glinting treasures that just waited to be discovered. The vintage signs hanging from higher bars, their faded paints still bright against the grey of the January sky. Silver tea services hung from hooks on rails above the stalls, the flags and signs of the shops and arcades high on the buildings, and the clash of colours of vintage clothing hanging on rails.

And then there were the sounds and the scents. The rising chatter and calls of the shoppers and the sellers, frozen breaths puffing out with every offer, every sale. The scent of brass polish, musty books, mingled with fresh coffee and cooking meat from the food stalls further down.

I just wish I could have brought Harry to see this.

He'd always been too young, or uninterested, or there'd been too much else to do on the estate. Somehow, it had just never been the right time—and now there was no time left.

She let the loss settle for a moment, the way she'd learned to deal with all these reminders, then let it float away again. Acknowledged, examined—but not letting it take over her day. That was the only way she'd found that helped her deal with the waves of grief that still hit her most days.

But she was here, at the world-famous Portobello

Road, one of her favourite places in the world. And she wasn't going to waste the day thinking of what might have been.

She put her list back in her bag.

'You know what? Let's just get a feel for the place first, yeah?'

Finn's face brightened at her words. 'Sounds good to me! And maybe grab another coffee and a bite to eat?'

'Definitely that,' Victoria said with a laugh.

'Well, then.' Finn held out an arm to her, and she slipped her hand into the crook of his elbow as if it were the most natural thing in the world. 'Let's shop.'

He felt like he was watching Victoria come to life again.

After all the tragedy and pain of the last year, and all the struggle and hard work at Wishcliffe even before that, as Finn followed Victoria from stall to stall along Portobello Road it was as if he were seeing her step back in time. Not because of the age of the objects she was studying, but because she seemed to give up her cares and worries with every step. Her shoulders lowered, her walk became freer, her arms swinging carelessly at her sides.

And she *smiled*.

Not the careful, contained smile he'd seen since they'd reconnected over his antiques project. And definitely not the sad, unsteady smile he'd seen right after the accident. Not even the stressed but happy smile he'd seen so often before that, when the dark circles had almost overshadowed her sparkling eyes.

This smile was the one he'd fallen for when he was sixteen. The one that lit up the air around her with sheer infectious joy.

He wasn't the only one who'd noticed it either. The traders and shoppers at Portobello Road Market might not know what it meant to Finn to see that smile again, but they were affected by it all the same. They smiled back, despite themselves. They offered discounts Finn was almost certain they wouldn't have offered to most. The pimply teenager who served them their coffees and containers of curry and rice even threw in extra onion bhajis without being asked.

Victoria's smile infected the whole market, and it lightened Finn's heart to see it.

'So, where next?' Finn wiped mango chutney from his fingers and took her carton from her to dispose of. 'Is it time to look at the list again?'

Victoria nodded and, taking the piece of paper from her bag, unfolded it and smoothed it out over her knee. 'I got a good idea of what sort of things we can cross off here today just wandering around.'

'Not to mention the hand mirror and the brush set you convinced that poor bloke on the silver stall to put aside for you for later,' Finn added. He'd definitely got the feeling the man wouldn't have done it for anybody but Victoria.

'Yes—we mustn't forget to go back and pick those up.' Victoria frowned down at her list. 'Actually, there was one particular shop I wanted to show you that we haven't visited yet. I think we might have a good chance of replacing some of the family china there.' She looked up with a hopeful smile that made him wonder if there was something special about this shop. A reason she'd saved it until now.

'Then let's go,' he said.

He let Victoria lead the way, as he had all day. He'd half expected her to make a beeline for one of the brightly coloured shops on the main street, but instead she weaved through the crowd and the stalls for a non-descript entrance crammed between two larger shops. There was no sign above the arched entryway, and no indication that there were any antiques for sale there at all.

Frowning, Finn followed as Victoria confidently picked her way down the narrow alleyway, stepping over wicker baskets and dodging tattered pennants hanging overhead.

'Georgie?' she called out, and he saw that she'd stepped out of the alleyway into—

Into a wonderland.

Whether the shop existed outside of the usual dimensions of space and time or was somehow tucked away along the back of the other shops on Portobello Road, Finn wasn't entirely sure—although he hoped it was the latter. Either way, it ran only a few metres deep but what seemed like half a mile long. Every inch of the space was taken up with towering shelves, displays, chairs and tables—all save the narrow walkways between them. And it wasn't only the ground that was filled; overhead hung racks heavy with gleaming pots

and pans, vintage model aircraft paused in flight between the antiques and shelves stacked with books and
knick-knacks all the way to the rafters.

It was as if the entirety of the street outside had been
crammed inside the confines of one dark and narrow
shop.

'Victoria Capon—no, Victoria Blythe now, isn't
it? I never remember that.' A tall, grey-haired man in
glasses eased his slender frame between two book-
cases and emerged into the small entrance area where
they stood. 'As I live and breathe, it is you! To what
do I owe this pleasure, Your Ladyship?' He sketched
a small bow then caught the porcelain pig he knocked
off the nearest sideboard without missing a beat.

'Hello, Georgie.' She reached over to hug the older
man, moving carefully to avoid dislodging any other
treasures, Finn noticed. 'I'm sorry it's been a while.
Things have been—'

'I heard.' Georgie's long face was solemn. 'I was
so very sorry, my dear.'

Victoria's smile wavered, and Finn reached out to
squeeze her hand.

'But you're here on a mission today, I can tell!'
Georgie swept her up with an arm around her shoulder, his movements almost birdlike in their jerkiness
as he nudged her deeper into the labyrinth of his shop.
Finn followed behind, feeling more out of place than
he'd felt anywhere since he'd left Clifford House at
eighteen.

'I'm helping my friend refurnish his family home,'

Victoria explained. 'Here's some of the items we're looking for...'

Georgie snatched the list from her hand as soon as it was out of her bag, his lips moving along with his eyes as he scanned through it, mumbling to himself.

'Hmm, I see, and yes—ah!—of course.' He looked up, eyes bright. 'You'll want the china department, then?'

He spun on his heel and set out into the maze of shelves.

'Are there actual *departments* to this place?' Finn kept his voice low as they followed. 'I thought every new delivery was just dumped on top of the last.'

'That's because you're not looking closely enough, young man!' Georgie's voice floated back around shelves and boxes, and Finn gave Victoria an incredulous look.

She shrugged. 'Georgie knows where every single item of his stock is at all times. And his hearing is *excellent.*'

Finn decided to keep the rest of his observations to himself, until they were back outside.

True to his word, Georgie took them straight to an aisle filled with china—some on display on Welsh dressers, others stacked up on shelves and in boxes.

'You should find something to suit your purposes here,' he said, waving a hand expressively and narrowly missing a willow pattern teapot that sat precariously close to the edge of a shelf. 'I suggest you try the dresser at the end—the turquoise one. Now, if you'll excuse me, I believe I have another customer.'

He disappeared off into the stacks at least a few seconds before the bell on the front desk rang. 'How did he know?' Finn wondered aloud.

'Excellent hearing, my boy!' Georgie's voice floated back.

Finn shook his head, decided to chalk it all up to some sort of Harry Potter nonsense, and moved on.

He found Victoria already crouched down beside the turquoise dresser, her head inside the giant piece of furniture. 'Found what you're looking for in there?'

'Almost,' her voice came back, muffled. 'Hang on…'

Finally she emerged triumphant, holding up a large dinner plate with a hunting scene painted on it. 'Does this look like the Clifford family china?'

Finn studied it. Unnecessary cruelty, aristocratic pursuits and a sense of self-importance? Check. 'Almost exactly.'

'It's the same artist.' Victoria handed the plate to him to hold, then dived back inside. 'Slightly different imagery, but the same feel. I think it should pass muster.' She pulled out a stack of side plates, looked at the pictures and shuddered.

'I guess the family china at Wishcliffe is rather less bloodthirsty?' He had to admit, despite the many meals he'd eaten at that dining table, he wasn't sure he could describe the plates if his life depended on it.

'Just a bit.' Victoria reached up and pulled another plate from the shelf of the next dresser along. 'It's more like this—farming labourers and harvest-themed.'

What was wrong with plain white china, that was

what Finn would like to know. Or, at a push, recyclable paper plates. Most of the time he ended up eating takeaway from a carton, anyway.

'Do you miss it?' he asked as she replaced the china.

'The Wishcliffe dinner plates?' Victoria frowned. 'Not particularly.'

'I meant all of it. You know, the grandeur of Wishcliffe, all the family heirlooms, passed down through the generations, that sort of thing.' Her cottage, while lovely, was rather a step down from what she'd been used to, the last ten years or so.

Victoria considered his question properly this time, if the contemplative look on her face was anything to go by. 'Not really. I mean, there are spots around the house that I miss—the orchard, for instance, or my little study on the top floor. The way the sun came into the library in the late afternoon, that sort of thing. But the actual antiques? To be honest, most of them weren't really my style.'

Finn gazed pointedly around the Aladdin's cave of treasures she'd brought him to, while remembering every adoring look she'd given an antique on their stroll through the market.

'Oh, I love antiques,' she clarified. 'I just meant that if I was furnishing a place from scratch, those wouldn't be the pieces I'd choose. Not because they're not beautiful, but because half the fun is finding the pieces that really speak to you.' She shrugged. 'Barnaby always loved them, though, because they were part of his family. That makes a difference too, I think.'

Finn thought about her tiny cottage with its sparse

furnishings, and wondered if she was still trying to find those pieces that were hers, now she was out in the world alone. 'Is there anything here that speaks to you?'

Victoria grinned. 'Oh, masses. Like…' She reached behind her to yet another sideboard and pulled up a cream coffee cup with tiny green stars on it, and a matching saucer in the same green. As she tilted the cup, he saw the inside was green too. 'These. They're from the nineteen-fifties or early sixties, by Susie Cooper. Georgie doesn't have a whole set here, I don't think. But there's a few different colours for the saucers and cups, all with the same green star design.'

'Of course you picked a coffee cup,' Finn said. The woman was a fiend for her caffeine. 'They're pretty.'

She studied the cup again before replacing it on the sideboard. 'I like them. But they never fitted with the aesthetic at Wishcliffe and, besides, it wasn't like we didn't have enough china as it was. Come on. We need to go pay for this lot and ask Georgie to pack and ship it to Clifford House. Because there's no way I'm carrying it on the train.'

It was already dark by the time she made it back to Victoria Station that evening. Finn had insisted on seeing her to her train, even though she'd pointed out that she wasn't exactly carrying priceless antiques with her—they'd arranged for all their purchases either to be sent on or taken them back to Finn's London flat in a taxi to be couriered later. Still, she was glad of the company when it emerged that her train was delayed for an hour, and they'd had time to grab a quick dinner at a restaurant around the corner.

Finally, though, it was time to head back to Wishcliffe.

'I had a nice day today,' Finn said as they walked towards her platform. 'Turns out this revenge malarky is a lot more fun than I'd thought it would be.'

She couldn't help but laugh at that. 'Well, as long as it's not boring you already.'

'I could never be bored, hanging out with you.'

Probably he was just saying it to make her feel good, but it sent a warm rush through her all the same.

'I had a great day too,' she admitted. 'I wasn't sure about this revenge plot of yours but… I think I'm coming round.'

'Now you know that it means spending someone else's money on antiques you can't afford?'

'Basically, yeah.' Victoria checked her ticket again. 'This is my carriage. I guess I'll see you in a few weeks? For Derbyshire?' Over dinner they'd plotted out their next moves, including a trip to one of her favourite antique emporiums in the Peak District. If Finn had thought that Georgie's was stuffed with antiques, The Mill was going to blow him away.

Finn nodded. 'I'll check it out and book us somewhere to stay for the night.'

'That would be great, thanks.' She stepped up onto the train, pausing when he reached out and grabbed her arm.

'Hang on. I just…' He reached into the leather satchel he carried and pulled out something wrapped in tissue paper. 'For you. Well, for your coffee. The amount of it you drink, you deserve a decent cup.'

Victoria tore back just enough of the carefully wrapped paper to see the green stars of the Susie Cooper cup and saucer she'd admired winking back at her.

'You bought it for me? Why? And, more to the point, when?' They'd been together all day. When could he have doubled back to get it?

Finn chuckled. 'I had an ally. Remember when Georgie sent you off to try and find that missing dinner plate, only to discover it under the desk after all?'

Of course. Georgie was an old softie at heart. 'Well, thank you. I love it. But you shouldn't have.'

'Yes, I should,' Finn replied. 'Think of it as a very small thank you for everything you're doing.'

'Hmm. Maybe I should get Joanne to put up my fee then…' She tapped a finger against her jaw as if really considering it, and Finn barked a laugh. 'Really, thank you.'

'You're welcome.' Down the platform, the conductor blew his whistle. 'Time to go.'

She tucked her treasure safely in her bag, then reached out of the train door to hug Finn goodbye.

'See you soon.' And as she'd done a hundred times since she'd met him, she placed a quick kiss on his cheek as he did the same for her.

But maybe the height of the train made a difference, or the other passengers made the carriage shift. Because she missed.

Not completely. Just enough for her mouth to graze the edge of his, before they both pulled back.

Just close enough to send a surge of something long forgotten racing through her. A heat, an excitement, a possibility that she'd thought only existed in the past for her.

An attraction.

She stumbled back, hoping she wasn't blushing, and waved through the glass as the doors closed and the train jerked into motion. Gazed backwards as Finn stood stock-still on the platform, watching her go.

Then she went to find her seat and resolutely did not think about what that flash of feeling could mean.

She just hoped Finn would have forgotten the awkward moment by the time they travelled to Derbyshire together next month.

CHAPTER FIVE

'YOU'VE BEEN SUMMONED for dinner too then, I take it?'
Finn said when his knock on the front door of Wish-
cliffe House was answered by Victoria rather than
Toby or Autumn.

'I have.' She stepped back to let him inside. 'Although they didn't tell me you were coming.'

'Last minute addition. I told them I'd be at Clifford
House tonight, since we're heading up to Derbyshire
tomorrow anyway, so they invited me for dinner.' Finn
shucked off his heavy winter coat and hung it over a
leather wingback chair in front of the roaring fire that
filled the fireplace in the centre of the entrance hall.
'Where are the Viscount and his lady, anyway?'

It was still weird to think of Toby as Viscount Wishcliffe when for so long it had been his father, and then
Barnaby. Toby was never supposed to inherit, but now
he'd settled into the role it seemed to suit him.

'In the study, I think. Ah—I wouldn't go in there if
I were you,' Victoria added as he moved towards the
corridor that led to the Viscount's study. Her amused
tone indicated exactly what he was likely to discover if

he opened the door and, really, Finn had seen enough of his best friend's bare behind in the showers after PE at school to ever need to see it again as an adult.

Finn paused, raising his eyebrows. 'Really? When they have *guests*?'

'I don't think we count as guests,' Victoria replied. 'We're family.'

The warmth he felt at being considered family easily outweighed the minor annoyance of Toby and Autumn being too *busy* to meet them—and even balanced out the frustration that his best friend was now in the kind of blissful relationship that resulted in regular, just-can't-wait-to-have-you sex in inappropriate places.

Finn had never really wanted or hoped for that kind of relationship—and certainly not marriage. From what he'd seen, the men in his family weren't genetically predisposed to success in love or matrimony, and from what he knew of himself, he couldn't imagine that *he'd* be the one to break that curse.

His parents' marriage had made everyone around them miserable, themselves most of all, until his mother had walked out and left young Finn with a man who despised him, for the love of a Spaniard who got her killed by driving too fast on the coastal roads over in his home country. From what little he remembered, his grandparents' marriage had only been more successful in the sense that they'd stayed married and living, nominally, in the same house. His grandfather had spent most of his time in London, and Finn was almost certain he'd never actually seen the two of them in the same room at the same time.

No, he'd come to terms with the idea of remaining a sole agent a long time ago. If nothing else, it wouldn't be fair to drag anyone else into the seething resentment and betrayal that was his family life. While he was focused on gaining his revenge on his father, there wasn't any space for any softer feelings, really.

Mostly, his need for human touch and affection could be fulfilled by short-lived romances with women who knew exactly what he was—and wasn't—offering and didn't want any more from him anyway.

But he still missed…something sometimes. Companionship, perhaps. Having someone to laugh with, share secrets with. For so long he'd been focused on building the business, making enough money to put his plans into action. And since his revenge project had really taken off, starting nine months ago with the long and tedious negotiations that had allowed him to buy back Clifford House, he hadn't even had time or focus for finding one of those short-term romances he was so good at.

Maybe he was just missing sex. The fact that Toby had managed to get married, fall in love and live happily ever after in the time since Finn last had another person in his bed at night was horrifying—and unexpected. If asked to place bets on which of the two of them was more likely to have a one-night stand in Vegas, Finn knew he'd be the odds-on favourite.

Instead, he'd been back in his hotel room running numbers with his accountant via a video call. And the closest he'd got to a woman recently was the soft press of Victoria's lips against the corner of his mouth at the station, before the train had whisked her away. He knew that she'd meant nothing at all by it—in fact, from the way she'd blushed after, he imagined she was horrified at missing his cheek. But that hadn't stopped him replaying the moment over and over in his mind during the two weeks since. Imagining what might have happened next if she *had* meant it. If he'd tugged her off that train and into his arms and—

Victoria was watching him, he realised belatedly, looking as though she were trying to read his mind. He'd never been so thankful that telepathy didn't exist.

Forcing a smile, Finn threw himself into the nearest chair and motioned for Victoria to take the seat opposite him. Time to get his thoughts back on the things that mattered—buying back everything his father had sold and rubbing his nose in it.

'Since we've got some time, apparently, why don't you fill me in on where we are with the family heirlooms you've been tracing?'

Victoria's face lit up as she pulled her ever-present file out of her bag and flipped through it to find the right section. 'Actually, things are going really well!'

Finn sat back and let her words wash over him, as she talked about the dealers she'd spoken to, the leads she'd followed and the progress she'd made. The excitement on her face, the way she spoke with her hands, her words coming together faster and faster as she reached her biggest triumphs—they all confirmed what Finn already knew.

Firstly, that he'd been right to bring her on board—

not just for her obvious expertise and successes, but because she needed it as much as he needed her.

And secondly, that no woman in the world was as beautiful as Victoria Blythe talking about something that mattered to her.

Eventually, though, Toby and Autumn emerged from the study—looking more than a little ruffled—and it was time for dinner. The four of them took their seats at one end of the giant dining table and chatted like old friends through starters and mains and a bottle of wine.

It was only once they reached the desserts that Finn spotted the slight undercurrent between the newlyweds. A hum of excited apprehension, he decided, as he honed in on it. The feeling that there was something more to come than an apple crumble with cream.

And then he realised that while four glasses of wine had been poured, only three were now empty.

Toby and Autumn exchanged another secret glance, and Finn knew exactly what was coming next. Which was why he was already watching Victoria when Toby spoke.

'Actually, we did have another reason for asking the two of you to join us tonight. We've got some news. We're, uh, expecting a baby!'

The night air was cool and fresh in the apple orchard, the February wind tempered by the trees around her. Victoria sucked in deep breaths and tried to calm her hammering heart as she leant against the low stone wall that surrounded the orchard.

She thought she'd done okay. She'd realised, seconds before Toby had spoken, exactly what he was going to say, and she'd schooled her expression into one of untempered joy and happiness. Which *was* what she felt for her friends, so it wasn't that hard.

It just wasn't what she felt for herself.

Still, this was their big exciting news and she wasn't going to be the one to ruin it by making the moment all about her. So she'd smiled and congratulated them and hugged them both. She'd peppered Autumn with questions about how she was feeling and when her due date was and her upcoming twelve-week scan, all through dessert. She'd grinned and told them she was looking forward to being Auntie Victoria and spoiling their child rotten, laughing when Finn had decided they should team up and get the kid hyped up on sugar and excitement before going home for the night and leaving Toby and Autumn to deal with the consequences.

'Just like we used to do with Harry,' Toby had laughed, and Victoria's heart had almost broken.

But she'd kept smiling. She'd moved them all past the awkward moment with talk about embarrassing family names they might choose and which room they were planning to use for the nursery and if they wanted to redecorate.

She'd kept talking and talking and smiling and smiling until the coffees were finished and she'd been able to excuse herself for a moment.

Then she'd run to the orchard for some fresh air and the space to just *feel*.

'Are you okay?' Finn's voice cut through the dark air around her, warm and concerned.

'I'm fine,' she lied. 'Just needed some air after all that wine.' She'd drunk barely more than a glass, but hopefully Finn wouldn't have noticed that.

'Right.' Yeah, he'd noticed. Seemed like Finn noticed everything.

He leaned against the wall beside her, close enough that she could feel the warmth of him through their clothes.

'I'm not saying… I mean, I get it if you don't want to talk to me about it,' he said after a moment. 'But honestly? Of course you're not going to be okay after that news. So, if you *do* want to talk, well. I'm here.'

Victoria looked down at the damp grass at her feet, black in the moonlight, to hide her smile. Finn wasn't exactly the obvious choice for a heart-to-heart, but she was surprised to find she felt more comfortable with him beside her than she had alone.

'I am genuinely happy for them,' she said.

'Of course you are. It's great news and you're a nice person.' Finn tilted his head to look at her, and she couldn't help but meet his understanding gaze. 'That doesn't mean you can't *also* feel sad, or mad, or lost, or whatever else you're feeling right now. People can feel more than one thing at once. Or so I've heard.'

Victoria let out a sigh. 'I think I have too many feelings to articulate them all. Or even keep them straight in my head.' Yes, she was happy for her friends. But that didn't stop the terrible yawning gulf of loss inside her at the idea that another baby would grow up at Wishcliffe in Harry's place. Or the fury that raged in her heart that he'd had that life taken from him. Or the pain because she was still there to see it all, without her husband and son.

Finn slipped his hand into hers and squeezed. Without thinking, Victoria let her head rest against his shoulder, feeling his warmth and his concern flowing through her where they were joined.

'The way I see it, you're allowed as many feelings as you need,' he said softly. 'And you can have them all at the same time, even if they seem totally contradictory.'

'I guess so.'

'And I'd imagine Toby is feeling some of them right now too. Because, as happy as he is with Autumn and a baby on the way...you know he hasn't forgotten about Barnaby and Harry.' He paused. 'And neither have I. We never will.'

'So what do we do?' she asked, hoping he'd have the answers that were still evading her. 'When our feelings are at such opposite ends of the spectrum that it feels like they're tearing us apart?'

A longer pause this time. Finn huffed a breath against the top of her head, resting his lips against her hair in an almost kiss.

'I guess we just keep feeling them. And we trust each other to help keep us together.'

Trust each other.

Suddenly, one of those other feelings that was swirling around inside her tonight started to make sense. A feeling that she wasn't alone any more. For the whole first year after the accident, while Toby was away tying up his business loose ends and Finn was off keeping his best friend on an even keel, she'd felt alone. Not just lonely, but utterly alone in her loss. In her feelings.

Even at Wishcliffe House, surrounded by all the people who made their living from the estate—friends, colleagues, everybody—she'd still felt alone. Because none of them understood.

But now Toby and Finn were back. Toby had lost a brother, a nephew. And Finn had lost the family he'd chosen over his own, years before. It wasn't the same, but it didn't need to be. The grief was still there, deep and empty, and she wasn't alone in it.

That whole year, she'd been afraid that if she let the grief out, it would swallow her whole.

Oh, she'd done all the exercises her therapist recommended, practised feeling the emotions and letting them pass, journalled her moods and everything else. But none of it had been more than a mask for that huge hole at her centre.

But now she had company in it, that hole didn't feel quite so vast, or so empty.

'Thank you,' she murmured.

'For what?' Finn asked, his words warm against her hair.

'For finding me.' She didn't add that she didn't just mean tonight. She meant all of it—the project, London, taking her out of herself and into the world again.

She suspected Finn knew, all the same.

'We should get back inside.' She pulled away, just enough to look up at him. 'I'm feeling better, I promise.'

Finn nodded, but she could still see the concern in his eyes. The same concern she'd felt even before Toby had made his announcement. She'd almost forgotten, in the tumult of her emotions after. But Finn had been watching her in that moment. Worrying about her.

Victoria wasn't sure what she'd done to deserve a friend like Finn Clifford, but she was damn glad to have him.

Then he smiled, warm and wide, and pressed a kiss to her forehead. A brotherly kiss. A friendly kiss. Not even as close to a real kiss as her miss on the train platform had been.

The heat surged through her at his touch, all the same. And Victoria realised, almost too late, that there were some other feelings she hadn't dealt with or even acknowledged yet.

Lust. Want. For Finn, a man she'd known since he was a gangly teenager and had never considered as anything but a friend.

And with it came the counterpoint emotions of guilt and betrayal, rising up in her throat like acid. Because how could she feel that when the love of her life was dead?

Unaware of her inner turmoil, Finn had already turned back towards the house. 'Come on. We've got an early start tomorrow if we want to make Derbyshire in time for some serious antique hunting.'

Well, if four hours trapped in a car together didn't help her make sense of her feelings, Victoria couldn't imagine what would.

They set out early the next morning, February mist curling around the trees and gateposts as they left

Wishcliffe village and headed north. Victoria was quiet, clutching her travel coffee mug close and staring out of the window as Finn pulled the car onto the main road. He left her to her thoughts, assuming that last night's news was still occupying her.

For himself, it wasn't Toby and Autumn's happy news that kept his brain busy. Instead, it was the way that Victoria had looked up at him, something behind her eyes that he wasn't used to seeing. Those warring emotions she'd spoken of seemed almost visible in her conflicted gaze—only he had the strangest feeling she hadn't been thinking of the new baby, but him. It was the same look he'd seen behind the blushes as her train had pulled away from the platform in London.

What was it that was causing her to fight with herself so?

He hoped he'd find out over the next day or two together. But for the time being he put on the radio and let her think—only turning it down a little as they passed London and she fell asleep, her cheek resting on her coat, against the window.

They made good time, stopping only to refuel—the car and themselves—and pick up more coffees, and arrived in the pretty village of Castleton, where he'd booked their room for the night, just after lunch.

'Are you hungry?' Finn asked, eyeing the local pub they'd be staying at. It looked busy enough, bustling with a few tourists despite the February gloom, and a sign in the window said *No Vacancies*, always a good indication of a popular place to stay. The website had looked nice, but it was always hard to tell until he saw a place in person. He hoped Victoria would like it.

But Victoria shook her head. 'That full English breakfast at the services will keep me going until dinner. Besides, I want to get to The Mill.'

'Might as well keep going then.' He pulled back out onto the road. 'You'll have to direct me.'

The Mill was, naturally enough, an old cotton mill that had been converted into an antiques emporium. Set beside a burbling river, the huge brick building was an imposing reminder of an older, more industrial age. The many white-framed and barred windows on its flat frontage looked out over the Derbyshire countryside like watching eyes.

Victoria had shown him the website but it hadn't quite prepared Finn for the size of the place.

'This whole place is filled with antiques?'

She nodded eagerly. 'Isn't it great?'

'Should have brought more coffee,' he muttered as he followed her towards the entrance.

Inside, Victoria was greeted like an old friend by the owner, much as she had been in London. At least here, there was enough space to spread out and Finn didn't feel as if he was about to be brained by a priceless antique at any moment.

There was a more obviously coherent layout too. He wandered a little way to explore, reassured by signs that read things like *Silver*, *Vintage Toys* and *1960s Furniture*. Still, he didn't wander *too* far. He had a feeling that if he lost Victoria in a place like this, he might never find her again.

'Right. Henrietta's given me a good feel for what we can find here, so let's get started.' Victoria thrust a piece of paper into his hands. He stared at it for a long moment before realising it was a map of the mill. A large multi-floor map with labels so small he had to squint to read them. 'Just in case. If you get lost, we'll meet by the vintage book section on the first floor, okay?'

'How many floors does this place have?' He turned the map over to find the other side just as full.

'Only five. Plus the outbuildings. Come on!' She bounded off, full of excitement again.

Thinking longingly of the nice cosy pub they'd seen in Castleton, Finn followed.

CHAPTER SIX

VICTORIA COULD HAVE stayed at The Mill all day. But after three hours exploring all the treasures Henrietta's emporium had to offer, even she was starting to flag—and Finn looked like he was considering flinging himself out of one of the metal-framed windows to escape.

She thought about taking one last look at the silverware room, just in case, but changed her mind when she saw the resigned look on Finn's face.

'You've been very patient.' She patted him on the arm. 'I'm sure Henrietta will have a lolly at the till for you or something, like she does for the little kids whose parents drag them here on the weekends.'

'Ha-ha,' he said without a hint of laughter. 'You know, when I hired you to do this project for me, I didn't imagine having to be so, well, involved in the actual shopping part.'

Victoria shrugged. 'Antiques like you're buying are all unique, and choosing the right one for a space is a matter of taste. I can tell you what fits the right look or era or designer for what was there before. But only you can choose which ones you actually *like*.'

'I don't have to like any of them. As long as they look the part.'

Victoria paused in adding the latest item they were buying to her list for Henrietta to ship down to Clifford House.

'What are you going to do with it, once you've proven your point to your father?'

'That particular sideboard?' He gestured to the heavy wooden furniture between them. 'Probably leave it in the hallway, or wherever it ends up. Come on, we should get going.'

She frowned. He was trying to put her off. And suddenly she was wondering why she hadn't asked these questions weeks ago.

She put her clipboard and list down on the sideboard. 'What are you going to do with Clifford House, Finn? Are you going to live there, take on the estate? Will you sell all the antiques we buy and refurnish it again? Or are you going to sell the house, antiques and all, and move on with your life?'

Across the way, Finn dropped the silver sugar bowl he'd been fiddling with and it clanked across the polished surface of the sideboard. Victoria reached out and righted it while she waited for her answer.

'I guess… I hadn't really thought that far,' Finn admitted. 'I've been so focused on getting this done, I didn't think past showing it all to my father, and winning.'

She shook her head. His obsession with beating his father at his own game could only lead to misery, she was sure of it. But it seemed like something he had to do to move on with his life, and she could understand that. It just couldn't be the end of everything he was hoping to achieve.

'Finn, beating your father isn't winning. If you spend all your money doing up Clifford House like the childhood home you remember, but then don't move on with your life, you won't have won anything at all. You might "beat" him, but you won't *win*.'

'Maybe just beating him is enough.' Finn's smile was crooked, and it hurt her heart to see it.

Victoria sighed. 'We're not going to agree on this. Come on.' She still had weeks left of working with him on Clifford House to get him to see her point.

As someone who'd had her whole life ripped away from her, she knew how that could leave a person adrift. She sensed that Finn would feel something of that when his big life's goal was achieved—and probably didn't leave him feeling as fulfilled as he'd expected. Then he'd understand what she was trying to tell him.

When she reached the till with her final tally for Henrietta, she was surprised to see one more item placed on the desk, to be added to the order.

A burgundy and white saucer and coffee cup, with tiny green stars on the outside.

'Where did you find that?' she asked Finn.

He shrugged. 'In the nineteen-sixties ceramics section, of course. I figure this way, when we're working late at the cottage together, we can *both* have stylish coffees.'

Victoria rolled her eyes as Henrietta wrapped the

cup, a knowing smile on her face. 'What I want right now is dinner.' On cue, her stomach rumbled, making Finn chuckle.

'Leave the rest of this to me,' Henrietta said. 'You guys get going and enjoy your time here in Derbyshire.'

Outside, night had fallen fast—or at least evening, which started at around early dinnertime in February. Victoria pulled her coat around her as they walked out to the car and hoped that the pub where Finn had booked rooms for them for the night had a roaring fire.

Finn frowned at his phone as he slid into the driver's seat.

'What's up?' she asked when he didn't start the engine.

'Apparently The Mill has reception-blockers in the wall or something. I've just got a full twenty-five emails through, a few texts and…four missed calls from the pub we're staying at tonight.'

Oh. That didn't sound good.

He stabbed at the screen then held the phone up to his ear. Even though it wasn't on speakerphone, Victoria could still clearly hear the receptionist saying, '…been trying to contact you to confirm your reservation for tonight, as our policies clearly state that if you haven't checked in by phone or in person by four p.m. we cannot hold your room any longer.'

Victoria's gaze flicked to the clock on the dashboard. Five forty-five. Oh, that wasn't good.

Not good at all.

In the event, Finn supposed he should be glad they'd only given away *one* of the two rooms he'd booked for the night. But since that meant sharing the remaining room with Victoria…

He was seriously considering spending the night in his car.

The worst thing was it was his own stupid fault.

If he'd looked at his phone at all that afternoon he'd have seen he had no reception. He could have popped outside to check his messages. He couldn't remember another day when he'd gone all afternoon without at least *glancing* at his phone.

But he'd been too caught up in watching Victoria wandering around The Mill, too engrossed in the light in her eyes, the way she'd flitted from object to object and told him everything that mattered about each one, without even reading the labels most of the time.

It was just so hard to concentrate on anything else when she was in the room.

'I am really sorry about this,' he said for what was probably the fifth time as they sat down at a table in the bar area of the pub.

Victoria's smile didn't quite reach her eyes. 'It's okay.'

'I could just drive us straight home tonight if you wanted,' he offered. 'Or find somewhere nice between here and there to stay?'

She placed her hand over his on the table between them. 'Finn, it's fine. We've had a long day, we have a room at a nice pub with a great-looking menu—ooh, pie of the day, I wonder what type it is?—and a nice roaring fire. We're adults, and friends. I think we can share a room for one night without it being a big deal, don't you?'

'Of course we can.' He tried to smile, to relax his shoulders. But in his mind's eye all he could see was the single large double bed in the one room they had to share.

If only there was a sofa, at least…

Victoria held out a menu to him. 'Come on. I'm starving. What are you having?'

The pie of the day turned out to be chicken, ham and leek and served with chips, so they both ordered that. They kept the conversation light—away from issues like the future of Clifford House or his revenge project, or even Toby and Autumn's baby. In fact, it wasn't until Victoria ordered a third glass of wine with their desserts that he realised she was stalling.

'I could always sleep in the car, you know,' he said.

She jumped at his words, spilling a little wine over her hand. 'What? No. It's fine.'

'I'd just hate for you to have to get drunk to spend the night in the same room as me.' For himself, he'd been nursing his second pint for over an hour. He wasn't a big drinker—a legacy of growing up with a father who liked to share his hatred for the world after a few drinks of an evening—and he knew that Victoria wasn't usually either. Her vice was caffeine, not alcohol. She hadn't even had a second glass after Toby's announcement the night before.

Which meant she had to be really nervous about tonight. He didn't like the idea of her being nervous around him, ever.

'I'm not getting drunk, Finn,' she said with perfect articulation. 'If I was, you should be worried, because I have it on good authority that I snore when I'm drunk.'

Barnaby's authority. The only man who she'd shared a bed with in over a decade, he was certain.

Of course she was nervous. And he was an arse for not seeing why sooner.

He fumbled for the words to apologise, but before he could find them she'd already moved the conversation on.

'So, Clifford, any women in your life to warn me about *your* snoring right now?' She leered across the table in a way that should be sleazy but was actually faintly hilarious. 'Or who might complain about me sharing your bed tonight?'

'No women,' he said shortly. 'I'm…not interested in romance right now. Got bigger things to focus on. Like the business.'

She snorted in a way he was almost sure she wouldn't have done after only one glass of wine. 'You mean your revenge project. That's the only thing you're thinking about these days, huh?'

It wasn't, not by a long chalk. Because what he mostly found himself thinking about these days, whenever his mind wandered, was *her*.

'I have plenty to think about,' he answered shortly.

Victoria leaned closer across the table, moving her glass of wine safely to one side. Her hair fell in a dark curtain either side of her pale face, and her eyes shone as she met his gaze. 'You should be thinking about romance, you know. About love.'

He blinked. 'Why on earth would I want to do that?'

'Because it's what's next. Oh, it doesn't have to *actually* be love and marriage and all that if you really don't want to. But you need to fall in love with *something.* Anything. Find something to be passionate about. You get your revenge, you can say goodbye to that whole part of your life, Finn.' Her eyes were dark, her words intense, and he knew she'd been thinking about this since their conversation at The Mill. 'You get to live happily ever after, if you want to. You just need to go out and find it.'

'And is that what you're doing?'

She shrank back. 'I *had* my happy ever after, Finn. I'm not looking for another one.'

'Well, maybe I'm not either.' Finn hoped that might be the end of the conversation.

'But *why* not?' Apparently not.

He sighed. 'Look. If you're asking if there's any great heartbreak in my life, there isn't. I haven't been burned by a scandalous woman, or scarred by a horrible break-up. I'm just not in a place where romance is really on my radar.' That sounded simple enough, right? Nothing to argue with there.

Unless your name was Victoria Blythe. 'I just worry about you. Toby's all settled now and—'

'And you think I should be too.' He shook his head. 'There's more to life than just sex and relationships, you know.'

'I *do* know,' she replied pertly. 'Or else I'm in for a long and boring existence. But for you... Finn, I worry about you being alone. You've been so focused on this revenge project of yours, I don't think you've even thought about what happens next. But when it's over…what are you going to fill that hole with?'

When it's over. God, was it possible that it could be, and soon?

Ever since the day in his third year at Oxford, when the news had reached him—via a less than friendly classmate—that his father had sold Clifford House out from under him, Finn had been thinking of ways to get it back. Everything he'd done in his professional and personal life since the age of twenty-one had been focused on this.

He'd never thought past that moment.

But even if he tried now, it was hard to envisage it. Hard to imagine a world where he wasn't consumed by the need to prove to his father that he couldn't beat him. That he was stronger than his father had ever imagined he could be.

Lord Clifford had believed that his son was a no-good degenerate, and had sold almost everything he owned to keep it out of Finn's hands. Now Finn was proving him wrong.

But *after?*

Finn shook his head.

'I'll worry about that when it happens.' He reached for his pint. 'Besides, it's not like I *never* date.'

'Not seriously, according to Toby.'

'Well, no. I'm not looking for anything long-term, so I don't want to lead anyone on.'

'But why not long-term?' Victoria pressed. 'Is it because of your parents? What happened between them? Because you have to know that isn't your fault.'

Not according to my father.

It seemed that three glasses of wine turned Victoria into a psychiatrist. And he could already tell she wasn't going to let this go.

Not unless he told her the truth.

Finn contemplated the pint glass in his hand, drained the last of the contents then placed it back down on the table. Yeah, this was probably a big mistake.

But he was going to do it anyway.

'Honestly? I don't look for anything serious because the only woman I've truly wanted for the last fifteen years was you.'

Victoria blinked. And then she blinked again.

'What?'

Maybe she'd already fallen asleep and this was some really weird dream. Otherwise…

Finn chuckled, low and self-deprecating. 'Don't worry. This isn't some epic tragedy of broken dreams or anything. It's just… I had the biggest crush on you, the summer we met.'

'Fifteen years ago.' When she hadn't thought of Finn as anything more than a hanger-on to Barnaby's little brother. Of course, he'd grown up a lot since then… 'Are you really telling me that one crush when you were sixteen has ruined you for love?'

That earned a proper laugh. 'No. I just… I saw

what was possible, and I didn't want to settle for anything less.'

'You mean the relationship I had with Barnaby?' Because that she could understand. Her marriage had been a true love fairy tale and she could totally get Finn wanting to wait for something that good.

His gaze slid away from hers. 'Something like that.'

He was lying. He meant *her*. God, he'd had a crush on her the whole time she'd known him and she'd never even realised.

Or had she? There had been moments…times when it was the two of them standing on the outskirts of the family, outsiders together, when she'd wondered why a teenage, then twenty-something, boy would choose to hang out with her instead of doing anything else. She'd put it down to his reluctance to go home, but maybe it had been more than that.

Then there was that almost kiss at the station. The way it had raced through her body, heating her blood… Could it have done that if he hadn't been feeling the same?

And last night. When he'd known, more than Toby even, how she'd be feeling. He'd known where to find her too. And he'd given her exactly what she needed—comfort and understanding.

Suddenly, she saw Finn in a whole new light.

'You know, I feel like the right time to share this information was probably *not* just before we have to share a bed together for the night,' she said.

Finn winced. 'Yeah, sorry about that. I just figured

you weren't going to give up until you got to the truth, and this saved some time.'

'That's fair.'

He met her gaze again at last, and it felt as if the barrier behind his eyes was…not gone, but perhaps a little thinner. Enough that she could almost see through to the other side. To the heart of him.

If she wanted to.

'You know you asked me why I didn't visit again, after the funerals?' Finn said.

'Apart from to talk about Toby that one time, yeah.' He'd been so awkward that day. So un-Finn-like. She'd assumed it was the proximity to death and loss that had set him off-kilter.

'This was why.'

She frowned. 'Because of an ancient crush?'

'Because…when you were married to Barnaby, it was sort of okay. I mean, I was never going to do anything about how I felt, obviously, because you were with Barnaby and you loved him and you were both so happy together. It was…safe.'

Oh, now this was starting to make sense. He'd fixated on her because she was *safe*. Not because she was *her*. He knew he never stood a chance, so never had to do anything about it, but his crush had enabled him to keep other women at a distance for years, because of her. God, the human psyche was complicated. She wasn't sure her psychology A Level was up to this level of denial.

'But after Barnaby was gone…' Finn trailed off, and Victoria put aside her psychoanalysis to meet his gaze.

Her heart caught at the torment behind his eyes. 'It just felt so wrong. I felt guilty that I was there to look at you when he wasn't. He was like a big brother to me too, you know. And I just… I'm sorry. I couldn't deal.'

Victoria took his hand across the table. 'You came back, though. You gave me this opportunity, helped me get out of Wishcliffe and look for my future. You're a good friend, Finn.'

His smile wasn't completely convinced. 'A good friend probably wouldn't have been lusting after his friend's wife in the first place.'

'True.' But since he'd never let on, she suspected Barnaby would have forgiven him. She suspected it was far less to do with her than what she represented for Finn, anyway.

And when it came to lusting, she wasn't entirely innocent either.

She dropped his hand as the memory of the night before came back, warming her from the inside out. Just standing close to him had been enough to set her mind to wandering.

How on earth was she going to spend a night in a bed with him, after everything he'd told her?

CHAPTER SEVEN

FINN STARED AT the large double bed and wondered if there was a mattress in the world big enough for this. What had he been thinking, confessing his ancient crush to Victoria *tonight*?

Well, he knew the answer to that. He hadn't been thinking at all. He'd been watching her in the firelight, amused and touched by the effort she was putting in to figuring him out. And of course she hadn't stood a chance without the fundamental fact that her mere existence had ruined him for other women.

He rather suspected that she'd drawn her own conclusions about his lack of a love life, and they weren't necessarily the same as his. But all the same, the truth was out there now.

And they still had to share a bed together tonight.

'Mind if I use the bathroom first?' Victoria asked, and he nodded his agreement.

He needed a moment alone to think this through.

As the bathroom door locked behind her, Finn sank down to sit on the end of the bed. The room itself was nice enough: pale walls with thick curtains in a deep, warm red, local landscapes on the wall. In the bay window there were two small cocktail chairs—nice to look at, perfectly fine for occasional sitting, he was sure, but no good for sleeping. And there was barely enough floor space either side of the bed for him to stretch out and sleep on the carpet.

No, it would have to be the bed. They were both adults. This would be fine.

Maybe it would even be easier, now it was all out in the open. If he hadn't told her, he'd have spent all night terrified he'd do something in his sleep that would give him away. Now, he didn't need to worry about that. It was a big bed, and he was a grown man. He'd keep to his side, keep his hands to himself and it would be morning before he knew it.

The bathroom door clicked open again and Victoria appeared, dressed in a warm pair of pyjamas with ice-skating penguins on. 'All yours.' Obviously seeing his smirk at the pyjamas, she looked down at herself and rolled her eyes. 'What? They're warm. And I wasn't really expecting anyone else to see them.'

'They're adorable.' And, weirdly, no less tempting than some lacy and silk confection would have been.

'Harry bought them for me, his last Christmas,' Victoria said.

'I love them.' Grabbing his wash bag from his case, along with his own choice in nightwear—black, comfortable and otherwise nondescript—he headed for the bathroom. 'You pick a side. I won't be long.'

How many months had it been since he'd shared a bed with someone for a whole night? He tried counting back in his mind as he cleaned his teeth, but once it got over a year and a half it was just depressing him, so he stopped.

Finn met his reflection's gaze in the mirror. 'It's just a bed. Just one night. It's going to be fine.'

When he stepped back into the bedroom he found Victoria already snuggled up on the left side of the bed, her phone charging beside her and only the bedside lamps still on. Cautiously, taking care not to touch her even a little bit, he slipped under the covers on the other side of the bed.

'Goodnight, Victoria.'

''Night.' The word was slurred, as if she was already half asleep. Obviously that last glass of wine was going to knock her out for the night.

Lying flat on his back, Finn allowed himself a small smile. It really was going to be okay.

At least he thought so until ten minutes later, when Victoria gave a very small, cute snore and rolled over. Right into his waiting arms.

Hell.

He was going to hell, and that was all there was to it.

But as she snuggled against his neck Finn had to admit—it might be worth it.

Two weeks later, Victoria still came into consciousness most mornings with the memory of sleeping in Finn's arms fresh in her mind. When she'd awoken and discovered they'd become tangled in the night, she'd slipped out as sneakily as she could and escaped to the bathroom before he woke up and realised what had happened. Which at least meant the morning after hadn't been nearly as awkward as it could have been, her penguin pyjamas notwithstanding.

That should have been the end of it. A funny tale to tell at dinner parties in the future, maybe.

But no. Because she couldn't stop dreaming about how good it had felt to sleep in his arms.

Just sleep! It wasn't as if she even remembered anything except that blissful moment on waking, before she'd realised what it meant.

She'd assumed, the first time she woke up with the memory, that she was thinking about Barnaby. A new way to miss him, to add to all the others she experienced on a daily basis. But no. Her half-asleep mind was very clear on that. Had been even back in that room above the pub in Derbyshire. She might have forgotten, just for a moment, what it meant and why it was bad. But at no point had she thought the arms around her belonged to anybody but Finn Clifford.

It was just as well he'd been busy in London with his actual job for the last two weeks, while she'd been conducting research and investigations from the shop in Wishcliffe, with Joanne weighing in with a new line of enquiry from time to time. Her only contact with Finn had been the occasional email or phone call to check on progress.

Even those, though, made her remember that night. Those arms.

'Is that another email from Finn?' Joanne had asked

the day before as Victoria had sat at the computer—
hidden away in the back office.

'How did you know?'

Joanne had cackled at that. 'You're blushing.
Again.'

So, yes. Two weeks apart had been great—but it
didn't seem to have done any real good.

And now she was meeting him at the Eurostar ter-
minal in St Pancras Station in London, ready to head
across the Channel to follow her latest lead on one
of the more distinctive Clifford House heirlooms—a
painting of Finn's grandmother by a minorly famous
artist that had come up for sale at the Drouot auction
house in Paris.

'I promise I definitely booked a suite with two bedrooms this time,' Finn said as he greeted her with a
kiss on the cheek. 'And I called to double check.'

Victoria forced a smile and hoped she wasn't blushing at the memory he evoked. 'Good to know.'

They made their way through passport control,
picking up coffees while they waited to board. Once
settled in their seats on the train, Victoria busied herself studying the auction catalogue on her tablet, while
Finn opened his laptop and got on with his own work.

But she couldn't stop her attention from wandering
away from her screen and back to his face. His familiar, comforting face—that somehow didn't feel comforting or familiar any more. She scanned his dark
brows over bright eyes, the sharp lines of his jaw, the
softness of his mouth…

No. Not safe and comforting. If anything, being around Finn these days felt almost dangerous.

Not because of anything he was doing, of course. But because of the feelings that rose up inside her as she watched him.

What was it that had changed? Was it sleeping in his embrace? Or his confession of a long-running crush? Knowing that someone wanted you was a powerful thing. Was it simply that information that was causing the spiral of heat and want inside her? The unbearable need to push his dark hair away from his forehead and kiss him until he forgot all about his damn emails.

She looked away sharply, staring back down at her own screen again. Paris. Antiques. The auction. That was what she was supposed to be thinking about.

Not Finn's arms or lips. Or his smile as he'd told her that, ever since he was sixteen, she was the only woman he'd been thinking of.

She almost scoffed aloud at that. She might not have kept up on *all* the details of Finn's love life over the last fifteen years, but she knew enough from Toby to be sure he hadn't been anything close to celibate.

And still… He'd been thinking of her. And now she was thinking of him.

When Barnaby had been alive it had been almost inconceivable for her to look at another man in that kind of way. Film stars, sure. But actual real life breathing men she knew? No. It just hadn't occurred to her. Barnaby had been more than enough for her.

She'd thought that all her sex drive, her ability to be attracted or aroused by men even, had died with her husband. But now, almost a year and a half after his death, she was faced with the fact that she'd been wrong about that. Very wrong.

Because watching Finn read his emails was somehow the sexiest thing she'd seen all month.

If she was honest with herself, she knew those feelings had started before his confession too. That night in the orchard, for instance. She'd known then. Even when he'd come to her cottage, there'd been an inkling of something, unacknowledged until now.

And when she'd seen him at Clifford House, surrounded by empty rooms and bad memories...she'd wanted to save him. Wanted him to save her, maybe, too. Wasn't that why they were both here?

'If you frown any harder at that tablet, the screen's going to shatter through pure fear,' Finn observed from across the way. He closed his laptop, folding his hands on the top of it and studying her with honest concern. 'What's up?'

You. The way you keep looking at me. The things I keep thinking when you look at me that way. The fact I can't stop remembering how it felt to lie in your arms...

'I need more coffee,' she said, pushing her thoughts away.

Finn grinned and got to his feet. 'Of course you do. I'll go see what I can find.'

Victoria watched him make his way down the carriage to the buffet bar, then realised she was staring at his very attractive arse in his suit trousers and sank down into her seat with a groan.

* * *

Finn loved Paris. But most of all he loved watching Victoria *love* Paris.

'You've really never been here before?' he asked as she leaned over the balcony of their suite, taking in the view of the Place de la Concorde. The view, he had to admit, was fabulous. But he'd been far happier to see the two bedrooms, as promised, when they'd arrived at the suite. He wasn't sure his self-control could take another night in bed with Victoria without exploding with the need to touch her.

'Half a day on a school trip, twenty years ago. Doesn't count.' She waved a hand, dismissing the whole experience.

'It really doesn't. So, what do you want to see first?'

She spun around, eyes wide. 'We don't have to work? I mean, I know the auction's not until tomorrow, but there are some great antique shops we could visit. Or, if you've got other work to get on with, I could go and find something to do…'

As if he was going to let her experience Paris without him.

'Nope. This afternoon we're just tourists, okay? Grab the guidebook and your comfortable shoes and we'll see what delights we can discover.'

Her wide smile was reward enough. The excited kiss she pressed to his cheek as she ran off to get her things together left a lingering warmth that made him wish, not for the first time, that things were different and they *didn't* need two rooms in their suite.

Paris in February wasn't warm, but they were lucky

to have a dry and bright day that made the wide avenues and white stone of the city shine. Map in hand, Victoria led the way, starting with—of course—a coffee from a little bistro off the Place de la Concorde.

'I want to visit the Eiffel Tower,' she said, placing a polished fingernail on the map. 'And we need to at least walk *past* the Louvre, even if we don't have time to go in today.' There was a wistfulness in her voice that made Finn want to promise that he'd bring her here again one day and they'd spend as many hours as she wanted exploring that famous museum. But it wasn't his place, so he held his tongue.

'The Musée d'Orsay would be great too, and I'd like to see Notre-Dame, but actually…' She trailed off.

'What?' he asked, intrigued.

'I'd really like to go to the Pompidou Centre.'

Finn laughed. 'Modern art? You?'

'I can't like old things *and* new things?' Victoria shrugged. 'I'm an art-lover, first and foremost. I love *all* types of art.'

'Then the Pompidou Centre it is.' Finn drained his coffee then reached across to close her map. She'd found one of those pop-up ones at the station, delighted by the simple way it unfolded and refolded after use.

Victoria eyed him with obvious suspicion. 'Why do I feel like you gave in remarkably easily on that?'

He grinned. 'Because you don't know that my favourite crêperie in Paris is right around the corner from the Pompidou Centre.'

Laughing, she followed him out of the café and they began their exploration of the city of love.

Finn had never been a massive fan of modern and contemporary art, but he had to admit that the displays in the Pompidou Centre caught his imagination. Or maybe it was just the engaging way Victoria spoke about them. She had something interesting to say about every piece they saw—even ones that appeared to be nothing more than an oversized canvas painted blue.

Once or twice, Finn even caught himself imagining a piece—or something similar—hanging on one of the empty walls of Clifford House. Something new, something different.

He shook the thoughts away though, and dragged Victoria out of the gift shop and around the corner for crêpes.

Fortified by more coffee and the thin, delicate pancakes the French excelled in, they headed back out to view more tourist spots on their way back to the hotel. Since Victoria refused to take the subway—'I'll miss vital Paris views underground! Come on, we can walk it!'—Finn estimated they'd walked many miles by the time they returned to their suite.

From the way Victoria collapsed on the sofa, she agreed. 'We don't have to move ever again, do we?'

Finn took the chair opposite her, his aching feet grateful. 'Depends on if you want dinner tonight or not.'

'I am a little hungry,' she admitted, sitting up straighter. 'Those crêpes were delicious, but not exactly filling.'

'I've got a table booked in an hour,' Finn told her. 'If you want to change. You don't need to, though.' As always, she looked beautiful. Rumpled and exhausted, but beautiful.

'Where?'

'Across town. Don't worry. We'll take a taxi.'

'Oh, well, in that case…' She levered herself off the sofa and headed for her bedroom with en-suite bathroom. 'I'll go take a shower.'

And now all he was going to be able to think about was Victoria, naked and wet, just the other side of that wall. Great.

'I'll just…wait here.' He slid a little farther down in his chair and closed his eyes. Just for a moment.

'Finn? Are you ready? Oh!'

He started awake at the sound of Victoria's voice, blinking in the sudden brightness of the room as she switched on the light. Hell, had he fallen asleep? He couldn't remember the last time he'd taken a nap in the daytime, but Victoria's exploration of the city had clearly tired him out.

'Sorry! I'll just change my shirt.' He rubbed at his eyes, trying to wake up, then looked up at her—and stopped.

She'd changed into a dress—nothing too fancy, just a deep red cocktail dress that clung to her curves before relaxing into a soft, swirling skirt that stopped just above her knees. Her hair was pinned up on the back of her head, leaving her long, pale neck bare down to the neckline of the dress, which dipped just a little lower between her breasts. In her heels, she might be almost as tall as him, if he were standing.

Which he wasn't. Because he was too busy staring.

'Finn?' She pursed her lips—her luscious, red and glossy lips—with obvious concern. 'Are you okay?'

He swallowed and forced himself to loosen his too-tight grip on the arms of the chair. 'Fine. I'll just… Shirt. Yes.'

Stumbling to his feet, he headed for his room with only one thought in his head.

How was he supposed to keep thinking of Victoria as nothing more than a friend and childhood crush when she looked like that?

CHAPTER EIGHT

THERE WAS SOMETHING in Finn's eyes tonight that she'd never seen before. Or never noticed, at least.

It was there when he emerged from his room, hastily changed into a fresh shirt and his hair damp where he'd smoothed it down. It was there in the taxi, as they sped through Paris at night. She'd taken the opportunity to observe the city lights, but whenever she glanced back he was watching her.

And it was still there now, as he sat across the table from her in the restaurant, candles flickering in their holders between them.

She couldn't put her finger on exactly *what* it was, but it felt...it felt like the candlelight. Too hot to touch but illuminating all the same.

'How's your meal?' Finn asked, but the words were meaningless. His eyes said so much more.

'Delicious,' Victoria replied. She wondered what her eyes were saying, underneath.

The tug she'd felt between them, growing over the last weeks they'd spent together, felt more like a tether tonight. Handcuffs, even. Tying them so closely that she couldn't imagine walking away from this man.

But she had to. Didn't she?

Finn might think his crush was what kept him from seeking true love, but she knew it was far more than that. From what she knew of his parents' relationship, and his unhealthy thirst for revenge, she suspected that he was simply afraid of love—afraid to give it, or afraid he wasn't capable of receiving it.

She hoped that, once he'd put his past with his father behind him, he'd be able to move on and find happiness the way she had. But it wouldn't be with her. She'd already had her shot at a happy ending and, besides, from what he'd said in Derbyshire she knew that the guilt would weigh on him as much as it would on her.

She wouldn't betray her husband's memory, and he wouldn't betray the man who'd been a big brother to him.

But she couldn't help but think… Would Barnaby really want her to be alone for ever?

She was only thirty-three. If she was lucky, she had many, many years to live ahead of her. And while she wasn't looking for another fairy-tale ending, the idea of living them without *any* company left her cold.

A chill that was swept away every time she met Finn's gaze.

They lingered over desserts and coffee, talking about everything and nothing. Victoria purposely stayed away from the sort of conversation they'd shared in Derbyshire—the heart-to-heart that had brought down that wall between them right before they had to sleep in the same bed. Instead, they talked about the things they'd seen that day, and made plans to visit Notre-Dame after the auction in the morning, before they had to catch their train home.

'I've kept the suite until it's time for our train,' Finn told her. 'So we can explore to our hearts' content, and still have time to freshen up and change before we travel.'

'You've thought of everything.' Victoria lifted her gaze away from their shared bubble and took in the emptying restaurant. 'It's late. We should get back.'

'I'll get the bill and ask them to call us a cab.'

She'd walked for miles already that afternoon, and it really *was* getting late. She had an early start and a big day ahead. A taxi was the sensible thing to do.

And yet…

'Is it too far to walk?' she asked.

Finn, who'd turned to attract the attention of a waiter, paused. 'You haven't walked enough already today?'

How could she explain that she just wasn't ready for this night to end, without giving away the thoughts that she really *wasn't* ready for yet?

'I thought the night air might do me good, after all that delicious food.'

Not her best ever excuse, but he seemed to buy it. When the waiter came, he asked only for *'l'addition, s'il vous plait'*, and soon he was settling her coat around her shoulders as they stepped out into the chilly night air.

'You're okay to walk in those?' He nodded towards her high heels, and Victoria laughed.

'Oh, yes. I've run miles in these things before.' She set off ahead of him to prove the point and he hurried a little to catch up, taking her arm. 'Every time we threw any sort of a party at Wishcliffe, I was always chasing around in stupid shoes trying to make sure everything ran smoothly. Got more steps in at those parties than when we'd go out hiking.'

The memory didn't sting as much as usual, something she put down to the wine. Maybe, now Toby was Viscount, Wishcliffe would be filled with the noise of parties again. They'd already done a great job with the Fire Festival back in the autumn, even if the usual Christmas celebrations had been a bit rushed as Toby had been over in Vegas getting his wife back right beforehand.

But she had a feeling there'd be a lot more parties on the horizon, starting with Toby and Autumn's second wedding. And she'd get to sit down in a corner somewhere and enjoy them, rather than having to run the whole thing.

That could be nice.

She could almost feel the hope that had started filling her again rise up, like the first snowdrops after the winter. Paris was preparing to burst into springtime, and so was she. Walking through the darkened streets arm in arm with a handsome man, seeing the Eiffel Tower lit up in the distance, the city lights gleaming just for them.

It felt…romantic. In a way that Victoria was almost done denying.

Barnaby wouldn't expect me to be alone for ever.

Maybe she couldn't—wouldn't—find another fairy-tale ending. But that wasn't the same as finding a friend she was attracted to and sharing some moments with them.

She and Barnaby had never visited Paris together. Maybe that was what made it easier. Every memory she found here was a new one, not overlain with the ghosts of her past. Here, it was just her and Finn, enjoying the city together.

'Thank you for tonight. For today. This whole trip, really.' Victoria looked up at him as they approached their hotel. 'It's been…amazing.'

'For me too.' Finn's voice sounded strangely rusty. 'Victoria—'

'Bonsoir, monsieur et madame.' A man in the livery of the hotel held the heavy front door open for them, interrupting whatever Finn had been about to say.

She was glad, in a way. She wasn't sure she was ready to hear it.

But she was ready for *something.* Anticipation thrummed in her veins as they caught the elevator up to their suite, along with an elderly couple on the floor above. And as they exited, heading for their rooms, she felt her heartbeat kick up a gear.

Something was going to happen tonight.

The lights in their rooms switched on as Finn slipped his key card into the slot. Victoria kicked off her shoes and bounced on the balls of her feet a little as she stared out at the vision of the Place de la Concorde at night laid out beyond their windows.

She was going to *make* something happen.

'Victoria?'

She spun around at the sound of Finn's voice, and found him watching her with a small frown line between his brows.

And suddenly she knew exactly what she wanted to do.

He was standing right in front of her bedroom door, which made things a lot easier. Smiling at the puzzled look on his face, Victoria stepped closer, reaching up to smooth his brow with her fingers.

Then, with one hand cupping his cheek, she stretched up on tiptoes and kissed him.

Finn froze for a moment, then his hands were on her back, holding her close as she sank into the kiss, letting it overwhelm every one of her senses. He was everywhere around her, his scent, his heat, the touch of him and the taste. The sound as he moaned her name into her mouth...

She pulled away, her face hot. This was too much. She'd thought she was ready, but not for this...this all-encompassing *feeling*.

'Victoria,' he said, as if it was the only word left to him.

She shook her head to cut him off, then braved a wobbly smile. 'Goodnight, Finn.'

The bedroom door shut tight behind her, but she still heard his whispered reply follow her in.

'Goodnight, sweetheart.'

The following morning, as Finn trailed behind Victoria at the famous Drouot Auction House, he was still thinking about that kiss. Victoria, meanwhile, seemed to have decided to ignore it completely.

'What do you think of this?' She motioned towards a carved wooden-framed mirror. 'For the Green Bedroom, maybe?'

Finn thought it was a mirror, and that he looked exhausted in it because he'd been awake all night trying to figure out what that kiss meant. But that probably wasn't what she wanted to hear.

'I thought you had a plan for the pieces we're bidding on today?' he said instead.

Victoria shrugged, a secret smile still lingering around her lips as he studied her reflection. 'I do. But it never hurts to allow for a little…spontaneity.'

She'd moved on to the next item before he could ask if that spontaneity extended to unexpected kisses.

The auction house allowed prospective buyers only a short time to peruse all the items up for sale before they closed to prepare for the auctions themselves. Since the auction was taking place over multiple rooms across two floors, Victoria assured him that strategy was essential.

He hoped she was up to being strategic for the both of them, because his mind was *not* on the game today. He barely even registered that the next item Victoria showed him was the one they were in Paris for in the first place—the oil painting of his own grandmother.

'Here it is,' she said, checking the details again in her catalogue. 'It's up early on in this room, so this is where we'll need to grab a seat as soon as the house reopens. What do you think?'

Finn surveyed the painting dispassionately. Truth be told, he barely remembered his grandmother, except as a glowering old woman who seemed unhappy with the world around her. He wouldn't have remembered the painting either, if it wasn't for the magazine shoot that showed it above the fireplace in the entrance hall.

'It's more flattering than any of the photos I've seen of her,' he said in the end. 'But I still can't imagine why anyone else would want it.'

Victoria shrugged. 'There's a small but growing following for the artist's work. It might not make much, but there'll definitely be other people here after it.'

They didn't want it as badly as he did, though, Finn knew. They'd care about things like the investment opportunity or resale value. He just cared about his father seeing it when he walked into Clifford House again as his guest.

He reckoned that was probably worth more to him than anyone else would be willing to pay.

'Come on.' Victoria was already moving into the next room. 'We haven't got long.'

The painting slipped from his mind almost as soon as it disappeared from sight, as he focused again on Victoria's slender form as she made her way through the rooms of the auction house. She was perfectly assured, completely at home here. While he felt as if he was floundering in quicksand, trying to make sense of it all.

What had she meant by that kiss? Had it simply been a wine-fuelled moment she was trying to forget, while he was tortured by the memory of holding her in his arms, knowing that it might never happen again?

He had to talk to her about it. And soon.

They had two hours after their preview of the pieces before the auction itself started. Finn steered Victoria towards a street café he'd spotted on their way in, hoping for lunch—and some conversation.

Technically, he got both. Over *croque monsieurs* and *frites*, served with strong coffees, of course, Victoria talked endlessly about the auction house, the pieces up for sale, the violinist playing in the street behind them, their plans for the afternoon ahead, what time their train back left tomorrow—everything except the one thing Finn really wanted to talk about.

That kiss.

Finally, he had to break into her endless monologue. 'Victoria… I wanted to ask you—'

She jumped to her feet. 'Look at the time! We'd better get back fast if we want to get a good seat in the auction room we need. Come on!'

And just like that, his chance was gone.

Back at the auction house, they bustled their way through the crowd—Victoria leading with her elbows, he suspected—and got seats she deemed acceptable in the room she wanted. By the time they were settled the room was full and latecomers were plastered against the walls trying to squeeze in.

'Don't worry,' Victoria said, smoothing her skirt as she sat. 'Most of them aren't here for your painting. There's another lot a bit later that's stirred a great deal of interest, apparently.'

How she knew that, he had no idea.

He'd just about resigned himself to the fact that talking about the kiss would have to wait until they were back at the hotel when Victoria turned to him and said, 'Sorry. You wanted to ask me something? Back at the restaurant?'

At the front of the room the auctioneer was taking his position behind the desk.

'Oh, it'll keep, don't worry.'

'No really.' Victoria frowned at him with obvious concern. 'I know I can get a little, well, hyped up on auction days. But that doesn't mean I'm not listening. What's up?'

Surely she *had* to know what he wanted to talk about? Didn't she? Unless last night's kiss meant so little to her that she'd already dismissed it from her memory completely. Or perhaps she assumed he'd never be so uncouth as to bring it up, when she'd obviously rather he forget it.

But which was it? He had to know.

The auctioneer was speaking, now. Finn's French was passable, but nowhere near as good as Victoria's, so he knew he'd have to leave all this to her. But she wasn't listening to the auctioneer. She was looking at him.

'Later,' he said.

'Is it…about last night?'

His heart jumped. 'You mean the fact that you kissed me? Yeah, kind of.'

Somewhere behind them, someone hissed for them

to be quiet. Finn ignored them. Didn't they know that this was *important?*

'I'm sorry. Should I not have done?' Victoria's eyes were wide and soft as she looked up at him, but Finn was almost certain he saw a hint of mischief behind them.

The auctioneer was announcing the first lot—not one they were interested in, thankfully.

'You definitely should.' Finn kept his voice to a low murmur, as around them the bidding started.

'Then you think I should do it again?' Victoria asked.

Around them, paddles were flying into the air as bids were cast. The auctioneer's rapid-fire counting was beyond Finn's translation even if he'd been speaking English, he was sure. The whole thing seemed like utter chaos.

Except for the small bubble in the centre, where he sat with Victoria, her words echoing around his head. *Do it again. Do it again. Again. Again...*

Oh, how he wanted her to do it again.

The auctioneer's gavel crashed into the table, making Finn jump, although he tried to hide it.

'Your painting is next,' Victoria said mildly, as she shifted in her seat to face the auctioneer again instead of Finn. 'We should pay attention.'

Behind them, someone grumbled something in French that sounded like agreement with her.

But Finn didn't agree. He knew that the painting was important—the whole reason they'd come to Paris, in fact—but suddenly it had paled into insignificance beside the conversation he was having with Victoria.

'Do you *want* to do it again?' He thought he knew the answer, but he needed to hear it from her own lips to be certain.

'He's starting, Finn,' she murmured back.

'I don't care.'

'You will if I lose this painting.' She raised her paddle as the bidding got underway. Glancing up, Finn saw the auctioneer pointing to her as his fast rattle counting continued.

'I care more about this,' Finn whispered sharply. 'More about us. You and me.'

And, to his surprise, he realised that he meant it.

Victoria looked away from the auctioneer in shock. 'Really?'

'Really.' There was grim determination on Finn's face, as if he'd transferred all his passion for revenge over to her. The single-mindedness in his gaze sent something warm spiralling around her middle.

Up front, the auctioneer called on her and she forced herself to focus, bidding again on the painting of Finn's grandmother, and mentally clocking that they were already fast approaching her highest bid level. Finn hadn't set many limits, but she refused to bankrupt him in the name of revenge. Everything she bought for Clifford House had to be able to hold its worth. That way, when it was over, he could sell them again and not be too much out of pocket—the price of a trip to Paris notwithstanding.

'Victoria.' His voice slipped under her defences, warm and low, like a lazy sunny afternoon.

'After.' Another bid. There was another person bidding via telephone and they seemed determined to take the piece. Victoria gritted her teeth and raised her paddle again. Just a little higher...

'Now,' Finn demanded. 'Do you want to kiss me again?'

The person holding the telephone shook their head, and victory surged through her. The auctioneer called it once, twice, then banged the gavel.

The painting was Finn's.

She turned to him, beaming, and took his face between her hands and kissed him—hard. 'Does that answer your question?' He blinked, apparently unable to form words. 'Come on. There's paperwork to do. And then I think we need to continue this conversation somewhere a little more private, don't you?'

The paperwork—confirming the sale, arranging payment and insurance, not to mention organising to have the piece shipped to Clifford House—took a frustratingly long time. Victoria was aware of Finn fidgeting, shifting from foot to foot and fiddling with the leaflets on the desk the whole time.

She tried to ignore him and focus on the task at hand, but inside she felt just the same.

Do you want to kiss me again?' he'd asked her, and that had been easy to answer. *Of course* she did. How could she not want to experience again the heady passion that had flooded her senses when his lips met hers the night before?

Whether she *should* was a whole different matter. And even now she *had,* the question of what happened next remained, floating in the air between them like a shouted bid.

Finally the paperwork was finished and, by unspoken agreement, they got a taxi straight back to the hotel. There were no other pieces she'd seen at the auction that mattered more than the conversation they needed to have, anyway. The painting was what they'd really come to Paris for, and she'd already won that for him.

Now they could focus on something other than revenge for a while.

'I care more about this,' he'd said in the heat of the auction. For a split second he'd cared more about kissing her than about his revenge plan, and Victoria had to admit that felt pretty damn good. Not just for her ego—although it didn't hurt. But because it was the first sign he'd given her that he could think beyond hurting his father to something he actually wanted for himself.

Not that she expected or wanted to be his what came next. Not in the forever way.

The taxi pulled up outside the hotel. Finn paid the driver and they made their way to their suite in silence. They'd had too much of this conversation in public already.

But once they were in the suite Victoria found herself stumbling for the right words to say. The usual euphoria of winning an auction for a piece she really wanted had faded with the paperwork, and even the buzz from kissing Finn again was waning.

All she had left now was reality, and that was far less fun.

She'd had enough of reality, the last year or so. Paris… Paris hadn't felt like reality, so far. It had felt like a dream. A chance to escape everything that came before.

She didn't want that to end.

So maybe…maybe she didn't need words at all.

'So I…' Finn's face was so serious as he shut the door behind them. That didn't fit the fantasy either. 'I guess we need to talk.'

Victoria stepped closer, nodding. 'We probably should.'

'We definitely should,' Finn replied, but his gaze was locked to hers now as she took another step. Nearer, so near she was almost touching him.

'Or…' Victoria murmured. One more step…

'Or?' Finn echoed.

She reached out and ran her hand up his arm, all the way to his cheek, stretching up on her tiptoes until her lips were mere millimetres away from his.

'Or we could skip the talking altogether.'

CHAPTER NINE

FINN'S BODY AND brain were screaming at him, pulling him in two different ways at once. His body, understandably, wanted to sink into everything she was offering now and ask questions later. It wanted to lift her into his waiting arms and carry her to bed. It wanted to kiss every inch of her perfect skin, to discover her anew.

His brain, however, had other ideas. Annoying, sensible objections to his body's preferred course of action.

'Wait.' His brain forced the word out over his body's objections.

Victoria pulled back, just a little, and he felt the hesitation building in her. He reached out to place his hands on her waist, keeping her close but not touching, near enough that the heat between them couldn't escape entirely.

'I can't tell you how much I want this,' he said with feeling. 'Really, the words don't exist. But…'

'Why does there always have to be a but?' Victoria muttered. *That's what I'd like to know,* his body added mutinously.

'But I need to know that you really want it to happen,' his brain pressed on, regardless. 'And that you won't regret it afterwards.'

'I won't if you're doing it right,' Victoria said with a smile that heated his blood, and leaned in for another kiss.

He kissed her back, his arms tightening around her as he held her tight against him. After all, even his sensible brain wasn't a bloody saint.

'Bed now?' Victoria asked against his lips, her voice hopeful.

'Just…just promise me we'll still be friends afterwards.' That was all he could really hope for here, he knew that. But even having Victoria in his bed wasn't worth losing the friendship they'd built over the last fifteen years and strengthened while working together the last few weeks.

Victoria stilled in his arms, the heat in her eyes suddenly fading to a more familiar seriousness. 'I promise, Finn.'

He held her gaze, needing to be certain. And then he gave in to his body and swept her up in his arms, holding her tight as he kissed her long and deep.

He'd worry about everything else tomorrow. Tonight, he had her in his bed, and tomorrow they'd still be friends. That was all he needed to know for now.

The bedroom door swung shut behind them as he laid her down on his bed, still fully clothed. For a long moment, all he could do was stare at her, drink in the image of her there, waiting for him. Committing every detail to memory.

Then she wiggled against the sheets, propping herself up on her elbows, and said, 'Well? Aren't you going to join me?'

His mind had taken a back seat now, and his body was fully in charge. Love and relationships might be beyond him, but *this* he knew how to do.

Kneeling on the edge of the bed, he kissed her once more on the lips before beginning his journey down her body. As his mouth brushed against her cheek, her neck, her collarbone, all his fears about tonight melted away. Because this was where he was meant to be. With her.

He might never have imagined actually being close enough to touch her, kiss her, before Paris, but still his body seemed to sense exactly what she wanted. Needed. As he unzipped her dress and pushed it down off her shoulders, following the fabric with more kisses, she made tiny noises in the back of her throat that told him he was 'doing it right', as she'd put it.

Finn's body was throbbing with need, but he didn't want to rush any of it. If he only got one night with Victoria, he was going to enjoy every second. So he drank in the sensation of her skin against his mouth, memorised the small moan that tore from her throat as he wrapped his lips around her nipple for the first time, and the way it stiffened under his tongue. He was sure there was no way he'd ever forget the silken feel of her skin against his as she stripped off his shirt and yanked him down to kiss her again. And as he worked his way lower, tugging her dress down over her hips and moving his mouth between her thighs, he knew he'd never forget the way she tasted. The way she writhed against him as he plundered her with his mouth, bringing her all the way to the edge before looking up to meet her eyes.

'Finn.' His name was half entreaty, half prayer on her lips, and it sent a wave of heat flooding through him. Hands on her thighs, he spread her wider and brought his tongue back to her core, pressing deep until she shook with pleasure.

He stayed where he was until she'd recovered herself, when she reached down and touched his shoulder. 'Up here, now,' she murmured, her voice hoarse. 'I want you inside me.'

Finn wasn't slow to obey. After all, this was his one night.

And he intended to make the most of every moment of it.

Victoria awoke the next morning to the weak spring sunshine through the window of Finn's bedroom. Blinking in the pale light, she took stock of herself, and her situation.

Body—feeling excellent.

Finn—still fast asleep beside her.

Mind—in need of coffee if she had any hope of properly processing everything about last night.

Easing herself out from under the sheets without disturbing an obviously exhausted Finn, she padded through to the main room of the suite, swiping a fluffy bathrobe as she went. The coffee machine was all set up to go, of course, so it was the work of moments to make herself a strong black coffee and carry it out onto the tiny balcony attached to their rooms.

Down below, Paris was already wide awake. Victoria shivered a little in the morning air as she watched Parisians and tourists alike go about their day, oblivious to her observation. As if the world was exactly the same as it had been when she and Finn had walked across the Place de la Concorde on their arrival. When, in truth, everything had changed.

I slept with Finn Clifford.

Nope, not enough coffee in her system to deal with that yet.

She drained her cup, then headed back inside. Since there was still no sign of movement from Finn's room, she headed to hers for a quick shower, then dressed in jeans and a jumper that would be comfortable for the Eurostar home. When she emerged, Finn's room was still dark, so she poured another coffee and, better protected against the chill, headed back out to the balcony.

With the first sip of her second cup, her thoughts started to gather—as they always did. Barnaby had often joked that anything he said to her before her second cup of the day simply didn't go in, and he hadn't been entirely wrong.

Barnaby. I slept with a man who isn't Barnaby.

And there it was. The thought she'd been avoiding all morning. Longer, even. The thought she'd refused to hear even as Finn was asking her to wait, to be sure, to promise they'd still be friends.

Hands wrapped around the warmth of her coffee cup, Victoria let the guilt rise up in her, and then ebb away again slowly.

It had been over a year. She was only in her early thirties. It was ridiculous to think that she would want to go through the rest of her life without having sex ever again. She'd already accepted that Barnaby wouldn't want that for her either.

So the guilt was there, but it wasn't overpowering, the way it might have been before now. Working with Finn had opened the world up to her again, in ways she hadn't expected. She'd moved out of the safe cocoon of Wishcliffe and her cottage. She'd found a place in the wider world once more.

And a place in Finn's bed, for last night at least. The residual guilt that remained centred, she was pretty sure, on the fact that it was *Finn* she'd slept with. A man who'd loved her husband like a brother. Who'd had a crush on her when Barnaby was still alive.

But even that she couldn't make stick. She'd never once thought of Finn that way when she was married, and Finn had never let on about his feelings for her either. They hadn't done anything wrong.

So. If she wasn't feeling guilty, what *was* she feeling?

Victoria stretched her legs out in front of her and smiled, feeling like a lazy cat in the sunshine.

She was feeling *good*. As if her body had remembered all the things it was capable of. As if she'd woken up after a really long slumber.

As if she wanted to do it again.

She glanced back over her shoulder into the suite, but there was still no sign of Finn. That was good. That meant she had time to decide what happened next before he got there.

Except…except what happened next was up to him too.

She sighed. Apparently they needed to have that talk after all. At least it had to be easier having it the morning after rather than last night, when all either of them was really thinking about was tearing each other's clothes off.

Sinking a little deeper into her chair, she let herself relive the memories. The feel of his body, bare against hers. His hands, exploring her skin. His lips, following those talented fingers until she was screaming for him. How he felt, moving inside her, so close he was almost a part of her, dragging her closer and closer to the edge until—

'Good morning.'

She started at the low rumble of Finn's voice as he appeared in the doorway. He hesitated there, apparently uncertain even after the promise she'd made. She supposed she *had* slipped out of his bed without waking him. He had reason to feel apprehensive about his reception.

She smiled and held up her cup. 'I needed coffee.'

The tension in his shoulders lessened a little and he returned her smile as he dropped into the chair opposite her. 'Of course you did. But you're…okay?' She heard the question he wasn't asking. *Are* we *okay*?

'Very okay,' she assured him.

The last of the tense lines of his shoulders faded away. 'Good. But we probably do still need to, well…'

'Talk,' she finished for him. 'I know. Just let me grab us some more coffee first.'

Making the coffee didn't take nearly long enough for her to figure out exactly what she wanted to say to him, but at least it allowed her to regroup a little. Thinking serious thoughts was hard when Finn was just *sitting* there, his shirt buttoned up wrong and his hair delightfully ruffled. When she could just drag him back to bed…

But no. He was right. Talk first.

'You asked me to promise yesterday that we'd still be friends this morning.' She handed him his coffee, then took her seat again.

'And are we?' His eyes over his coffee cup were troubled, and she tried to soothe them with a smile.

'Always, Finn. You're part of my family—the Wishcliffe family. I'd never let us do anything that would ruin that for either of us.' But for him most of all, she realised. Given what a disaster his blood family were, Wishcliffe and Toby were all he had. She could never let this become something that made him feel as if he wasn't welcome there.

'That's…good. Okay, good.' Finn, of course, was still on his first cup of coffee. She reckoned detailed emotional insight was probably a good few sips away. Which meant she had to go first with what happened next.

'Last night was…it was wonderful. I don't regret a moment of it.'

'But you don't want it to happen again?' Finn guessed.

Victoria hesitated, surprised by his assumption. *Did she want it to happen again?* Her body was screaming, *Hell, yes!* And, to be honest, her brain wasn't far behind. They'd stumbled into a good thing here; why would they give it up?

Only her heart gave her any pause at all.

'Do *you* want it to happen again?' she asked, while she tried to untangle her heartstrings into a way she could explain to him.

His smile was almost sad. 'Victoria, if I could have last night every night for the rest of my life, I would. But if last night was a one-off, I'd still just be happy to have had one night with you.'

She swallowed an unexpected lump in her throat at his words. *Every night.* That sounded awfully close to the sort of emotions she wasn't thinking about.

No. Finn didn't mean *that.* He just felt, like she did, that the kind of sexual connection they'd discovered between them wasn't something to be ignored. That was all.

But she had to be sure. Which meant putting all her cards on the table. Sealed bids, best offer only.

'The thing is… I like you, Finn. You're my friend, my employer for now, and much more than that. My confidant, maybe. And God knows I want you too. I don't want to give up the kind of incredible night we had last night without a fight. But… I need to be honest about what I can offer you, and what this can be.'

Finn's gaze turned wary. 'Okay. I'm listening.'

'I've done true love and fairy-tale endings. Barnaby was the love of my life, and I'm not looking for anyone to replace him.' He flinched at that, but Victoria knew there was no point not being blunt about these things. If he didn't want what she could offer him, then she'd live. But if she let him believe she could give more, and then broke his heart...she'd never forgive herself.

'I'd never look to take Barnaby's place,' he said softly.

'I know.' And that was why he was such a perfect choice, really. He wouldn't expect more than she could give because he understood why she couldn't give it. 'All I'm saying is... I'd like to enjoy whatever this is between us, while it's there. But I can't go into it if you think there's a chance of it ending up with a white dress and a church. I'm not looking for love, Finn. But companionship, friendship and great sex... I would very much like to share that with you.'

How long had she been out here drinking coffee and thinking about this? Finn had barely been able to remember which city he was in when he'd woken up, all mental and physical powers drained by their incredible night—and afternoon—together. But then, he'd always known that Victoria was better than him at many things, and it seemed that the ability to think in complete sentences after mind-blowing sex and very little sleep was just another one of them.

Taking a sip of his coffee, he tried to work his way through what she was saying. Offering, even.

Companionship, friendship and great sex.

Hell, were there really people in the world who wanted more?

Finn had never expected love to walk into his life, not really. And he'd known, even before their first kiss, that Victoria certainly couldn't offer it to him. He was no Barnaby replacement. They'd been clear on that from the start.

But if he were ever going to love anyone, give his heart utterly and completely, it would be to Victoria. Knowing she wouldn't accept it made it easier, in a way. He didn't have to worry about the happy ever afters, or even marriage.

I can't go into it if you think there's a chance of it ending up with a white dress and a church.

Well, good. Because he didn't want that either. Marriage in his family *always* ended badly, and he had no reason to think he'd be any different.

In a way, this was like any of a hundred business deals he'd made over the years—which was appropriate, given that he and Victoria had reconnected over work in the first place. Setting the parameters so that neither of them got blindsided later on. No different than him getting her to promise they'd still be friends this morning—and she'd kept that one.

Victoria was asking him to promise that he'd never expect love and marriage from her. And in return she was offering everything he'd ever wanted. Her time, her affection and friendship, and her in his bed. Or him in hers, he wasn't that fussy.

And if there was a part of him that worried that it wouldn't be enough, that ultimately he'd want every-

thing she *couldn't* give, as well as what she could…
he pushed it down deep inside himself and ignored it.

He *didn't* want it. And even if he did…if this was
all of Victoria he could ever have, it was still more
than he'd dreamed of. Still more than he thought he
deserved.

Companionship, friendship and great sex with
Victoria was worth more than *any* number of happy
ever afters with anyone else.

So Finn smiled, feeling the truth of it on his lips.
'I'm not looking for love either. But the rest of it sounds
pretty great.'

Something flared behind Victoria's eyes, and ig-
nited an answering heat inside him—one not sated
by last night's activities. One he wasn't sure ever could
be.

Victoria put down her coffee cup, and Finn knew
exactly what came next. The deal was agreed, now it
was time to seal it.

And thankfully this deal didn't involve boring
paperwork.

'Starting now?' she suggested. 'Or did you want
to visit Notre-Dame or the Musée d'Orsay this morning…?'

'Those antiques have waited this long, I think they
can wait a little longer.' Finn took her hand and turned
it over, kissing her wrist and grinning as it made her
shiver. 'I'm not sure you can.'

As he led her back to the bedroom, Finn gave thanks
for late hotel checkouts.

CHAPTER TEN

TWO WEEKS LATER, Finn sat against the bar in the King's Arms in Wishcliffe and decided that life was pretty damn good.

Across the pub, Victoria was deep in conversation with Lena, the manager, probably telling her all about her latest triumph in tracking down the last essential piece for the Clifford House revenge renovation—a mantel clock that had been presented to one of his ancestors by a prince. Not necessarily a British prince, but still—royalty was royalty. And his father would hate him owning it, which was the most important thing.

It was coming up for auction in London in a week's time, and Finn was already planning how to make the trip special for Victoria. They could stay at his flat, he supposed, but maybe she'd like something fancier. Maybe they could recreate their trip to Paris—only with a suite with *one* bedroom this time.

That was the other thing making life great, of course—his relationship with Victoria. Since Paris, he'd barely gone back to London for longer than a day, returning to her cottage by the sea as often as he could. They spent their days working on buying back the contents of Clifford House, their evenings laughing and chatting about everything and nothing, and their nights…

Well. Finn couldn't think of a more blissful way to spend a night than in bed with Victoria.

They hadn't gone public with their relationship as yet, especially not with Toby and Autumn. Which Finn understood completely. Of course Victoria didn't want to upset her late husband's brother with news of a new romance that wasn't actually going anywhere. Besides, in their loved-up bubble at Wishcliffe House, Finn was pretty sure that Toby and his new wife wouldn't understand, anyway.

It had seemed simple enough when they'd agreed the terms of their relationship that morning in Paris, but when it came to explaining it to others… Finn chose not to. He and Victoria were enjoying each other's company, and why did it have to be anything more complicated than that, anyway?

He'd mostly decided to just stop thinking about it and enjoy life instead. Some days it seemed as if he'd done nothing since the day he'd left university but *think* and plan and scheme. Now, finally, his plans were coming to fruition and he could just enjoy them.

'It's good to see her happy again.'

The voice beside him startled Finn, though he tried not to let it show. He'd been so engrossed in watching Victoria, he hadn't even noticed her boss coming to stand beside him.

'It is,' he agreed. 'Very good.'

Joanne had moved to Wishcliffe village long after he'd left, so he only knew her through the stories Victoria had told him, and a few limited interactions when he'd visited the shop. Plus, of course, the phone call that had led to Victoria working for him in the first place. He really should thank her for that. Maybe flowers. Or an antique vase for putting them in...

'When you asked about her working for you, I wasn't sure it was the right thing,' Joanne said thoughtfully. '*Not* that you gave me much chance to refuse.'

'I'm used to getting what I want,' Finn said. 'Plus her brother-in-law insisted it was a good idea.'

'It was, much to my surprise.' She looked up at Finn and he tried not to flinch under her scrutiny. 'For her, at least.'

'And for me,' Finn insisted. 'My project is almost finished, and I know I'd never have managed it without Victoria. Besides which, it has been good to rebuild our friendship again.'

'Friendship,' Joanne scoffed. 'Is that what the kids are calling it these days?'

How much, exactly, had Victoria told her boss? Finn wasn't sure he wanted to know.

'We're friends,' he said flatly. 'Old friends.'

'Right. Like I couldn't see the difference when the two of you came back from Paris.' Joanne shook her head. 'I might be out of practice at that kind of thing myself, but I know it when I see it.'

'What kind of thing?' Oh, why had he asked that?

He *really* did not want to be having this conversation, and he'd just given her licence to continue it.

'A good old-fashioned fling.' She gave him an amused look. 'What, did you think your generation invented sex? We used to have them too, you know. And it's just what she needs. A hot, fun fling to get the awkwardness out of her system. Then, when you're done, I think she'll be ready to move on for real. Find love again.'

Joanne nodded with satisfaction, but Finn felt his heart start to plummet in his chest.

When you're done. Move on. Find love.

Those were all the things he hadn't been thinking about, while he'd been busy enjoying life.

Victoria had been very clear about what she could offer him, on that balcony in Paris. And he'd accepted her terms eagerly, not least because they matched his own expectations. He knew that love and happy ever afters weren't for him—he was too blackened and embittered by revenge, by his family, by every relationship anyone who shared his blood had ever wrecked and ruined.

But while he knew Victoria was capable of so much more, he hadn't thought about her wanting it. She'd been so definite that she'd had her happy ending and she wasn't looking for another one. What if she just didn't want that *with him?*

He wouldn't blame her. Nobody could seriously look at his lineage—or even his own past—and pick him out as Prince Charming. But while he was happy living in this not-quite-a-relationship when it was all either of them could give, he hadn't honestly thought about what happened next.

What if this was just a stopgap for her? The idea of Victoria moving on with anyone else made him want to vomit. He wanted her to be happy, of course he did. But that didn't stop the urge to burn the world down if she left him to be happy with someone else.

To find another fairy-tale he couldn't give her.

'Uh-oh,' Joanne said beside him in a sing-song voice. 'Somebody's gone and fallen in love, haven't they?'

Finn flinched. 'I don't know what you're talking about.'

'Yes, you do.' She twisted to face him, forcing his gaze away from Victoria and onto her. 'You've gone and fallen in love with her. I can see it in every look you send her way.' Joanne settled back on her heels, smiling up at him. 'Well, this is going to get very interesting.'

Not the word Finn would have chosen.

'If you'll excuse me.' Without waiting for her permission, he stalked across the pub away from Joanne, towards Victoria. He'd take her home—no, not home. His home was Clifford House, and that was still just boxes of antiques and bare walls, despite their best efforts.

He'd take her back to the cottage and he'd make love to her, and he'd cling on to everything they had, even if it wasn't *everything*.

Because it was all he could have, and it would have to be enough. He'd promised them both that.

Victoria woke alone the next morning and smiled at the empty space beside her in the cottage's small double bed. Given the way that Finn slept, curled tight around her, the size of the bed had never really been a problem, but she sometimes thought of the giant bed in that Paris hotel and wondered how having a little more space would feel. Not for sleeping, exactly, but for everything that came before…

Where *was* Finn? She'd assumed he'd got up to fetch her coffee, as he often did in the mornings, but she couldn't hear him pottering around the cottage. And given the diminutive dimensions of the place, it was hard not to hear everything that went on inside its walls.

She lay very still and listened. Nothing.

And definitely no coffee.

Bemused, she got up and dragged on some warm clothes before heading out to the kitchen. The coffee maker was on, which she took as a good sign. As she waited for her first caffeine shot of the day to bubble into her mug, she stared out of the kitchen window at the beach and the waves beyond.

And then she saw it. A head bobbing in the water.

Fear and panic raced through her as she left the coffee behind and, shoving her feet into the boots by the door, raced out the back towards the beach. By the time her boots hit the sand she was running—only slowing when she saw Finn stand up in the shallows, water streaming off his wetsuit. The wetsuit she *knew* he'd brought down to the cottage because he planned to go swimming this morning. He'd told her that and still she'd panicked.

Because as much as she loved the sea, had grown

up with it, she'd never consider it safe again. Not after Barnaby and Harry.

The cove here was sheltered, shallow, and not prone to troublesome currents. Finn was a strong swimmer—he'd grown up in these waters along with Toby and Barnaby. There really was nothing to worry about.

She walked more steadily down to the water's edge and she knew the moment that Finn sensed her presence because he spun around to face her, his smile wide. When had he become so attuned to her movements?

'Coming in?' he asked, raising his eyebrows. 'The water's lovely.' A blatant lie in March.

'Bed was lovely too,' she replied. 'But it got a little lonely.'

'You mean there was no one to fetch your coffee.'

'That too.'

He waded out of the waves towards her, and she couldn't help but admire the way the wetsuit clung to every inch of his toned physique. 'You came out to find me instead of coffee? I'm touched.'

'I'm going to get some now, though.' Victoria smiled, not wanting to let on to the moment of panic that had sent her running out there. 'Are you going back in? Or coming with me?'

He stepped closer, still dripping, and she knew before he even grabbed her that she wasn't getting back inside dry. As he hauled her up against his wet self she felt the water seeping through her clothes and couldn't even bring herself to care. Not when he was kissing her, deep and long, as if they'd been separated for months not minutes.

'I think we'd both better go in and get out of these wet clothes. Don't you?' His smile was pure mischief but his eyes were warm with lust and…

And something else.

Something unexpected.

Something she wasn't ready to see. Something she might not ever be ready to see.

And the worst part was, the sight of it still filled her with a terrible joy.

Swallowing, she shoved the feeling down deep inside. It was just the panic of waking alone, of seeing him floating in the sea. Memories messing with her brain, that was all.

'You're right. We'd better get inside.' She forced a smile. 'And naked.'

'I will never argue with that plan. Come on!'

He grabbed her hand and together they raced back towards the cottage, and bed. And while he was still touching her, kissing her, she could ignore all the other feelings that the morning had brought. She just had to focus on where their bodies touched, on the laughter in his voice as he pressed tickly kisses to her side, the heat as he slid home inside her. The rising, rising tightness low in her belly that crested like a tsunami as she fell apart around him.

If she could just focus on the touch between them and forget everything else, things would be fine.

It worked, for a while. But eventually—after a rest,

several coffees and breakfast—Finn had to leave, heading back to London for meetings for a few days.

She kissed him goodbye at the door, lingering to wave as his car took the corner and disappeared behind the scratchy seaside hedgerow. Then she let the door clatter shut behind her, poured herself another cup of coffee in her starry cup and sat at the kitchen counter staring at nothing as the thoughts she'd kept at bay all morning flooded back in.

She knew what she'd seen in Finn's eyes on the beach, even if she wasn't ready to admit it to herself— and even if he wouldn't acknowledge it either, or didn't even realise himself.

But, more than that, she knew what had been in her heart that morning when she'd raced out onto the beach to find him.

She hadn't looked at those rolling waves and thought of Barnaby or Harry. She'd looked at the sea and thought of Finn. Searched for Finn.

Her heart had clenched for Finn, the same way it had for her husband and her son.

The guilt swamped her, wave after wave of it, until she was battered down and smoothed over by it, until it felt as if there was nothing else left inside her beyond it.

Because she loved Finn. And that was the biggest betrayal Victoria could imagine.

Finn shifted his weight from foot to foot as he waited outside the London auction house. One week. A whole week since he'd seen Victoria—or even spoken to her properly, as things had been so busy for both of them—and now she was late. He'd hoped they'd have some time together before the auction—to grab lunch at least, or even take a quick trip back to his flat so he could say a *proper* hello. But then she'd messaged to say that she'd been held up at Wishcliffe, and then her train was delayed, and now it seemed to be taking her forever to get across London and the auction would be starting soon.

Up for bids today was the famous Clifford clock, the prize piece he needed to sit on the mantel at the centre of his entrance hall to make maximum impact on his father when he saw it. Finn knew Victoria wouldn't miss this on purpose.

And yet he couldn't help the small niggle at the back of his mind that wondered why she hadn't come up to town last night and stayed with him, or taken him up on his offer to drive back to Wishcliffe yesterday afternoon, so they could travel to London together this morning. All her reasons had seemed perfectly logical at the time, but now they felt more like excuses. Like maybe she was avoiding him.

Unbidden, Joanne's words from the pub, their last night together, came back to him—and he shook them away angrily. He wasn't that stupid. This wasn't love. He hadn't asked Victoria for anything more than she had freely offered him, so she had no reason to pull away.

Unless she's done with me. Unless she's ready to move on to her next happy ending.

The thoughts didn't make it any easier to stop fidgeting.

Finally, he saw Victoria's dark hair bobbing through the crowd on the street, and she approached him with a smile that didn't quite reach her eyes.

'You're here!' He reached out to fold her into his arms, dismayed when she stiffened at his touch.

'Sorry I'm so late,' she said, disentangling herself from him. 'Come on, we'd better get inside.'

They found seats in the room where their auction was taking place easily enough, although most other seats filled up around them as the start time drew closer.

'I missed you this week,' Finn said, hating how needy he sounded.

She flashed him a faint smile. 'Well, I'm here now.'

But she wasn't, not really. Not with him. She was a million miles away—avoiding him.

Finn knew that look, that disconnect. It was the same expression he remembered from his mother's face, in the days before she'd left. It was the look his grandmother always had whenever his grandfather was in the building.

And it was the way his father had looked at him his whole life, almost, ever since his mother had left.

At least Victoria didn't have the disgust and disappointment to go with the distance. Not yet, anyway.

'We need to talk,' he said sharply. He couldn't play the besotted fool any longer. If she was done with him, he needed to know about it. He was a grown man. He could handle it. But he needed to *know*.

'Later,' she murmured as the auctioneer at the front of the room indicated a very familiar-looking clock.

That was what he was here for, where his focus should be. On buying back that piece of his history, the thing that would rub salt into the raw wound he'd given his father by purchasing Clifford House.

And instead he was obsessing about Victoria. Even his sixteen-year-old self would be embarrassed by this.

'Not later,' he ground out. 'Now.'

Bidding started and Victoria didn't even look away from the auctioneer as she replied. 'Later. I need to concentrate on this.'

'I don't care about the damn clock, Victoria.'

'Yes, you do.' She raised her paddle and earned a nod from the auctioneer.

'Not any more.' The admission hurt, but the truth of it was clear in his voice, even to his own ears.

Somehow, over the last couple of months, she'd come to matter to him so much more than a clock. More than any family heirloom.

More than beating his father at his own game and reclaiming his birth right, even.

For his whole adult life, the only thing that had mattered to him was his revenge. And now the one thing he cared about most was…

Damn. He *had* fallen in love with her.

God, he was such an idiot. And he definitely couldn't let her know.

She bid again on the stupid clock, ignoring him completely.

'Victoria, I'm trying to tell you something important here.'

'Well, don't.' Her words were clipped, her focus on the auctioneer absolute. 'I have to do this, Finn.'

'And I have to talk to you. I have to know what's going on. What's wrong.' How could he fix it if she wouldn't even talk about it?

He knew that she'd never love him, not the way she'd loved Barnaby—and not the way he loved her. But he could live with that. He could live with almost anything if she'd just look at him again the way she had that morning on the beach, before he'd left for London.

What could have gone so wrong in just a week?

One more bid on the clock, and the auctioneer called for any more. If there weren't then the clock was his. One step closer to his revenge.

And he just couldn't care at all.

'Victoria. Please.'

She turned to him at last, but the distance behind her eyes cut deep. 'Finn, just let me do my job, okay?'

'Last chance to bid on this incredible piece!' the auctioneer called. Finn tuned him out.

'As your boss, I'm telling you this is more important than the job,' he said.

Victoria shook her head sadly. 'You're not talking as my boss right now.'

'A no from the lady in the front,' the auctioneer said. 'So, sold to the gentleman in the green jacket!'

'What? No!' Victoria objected, but it was too late. The auctioneer was already moving on to the next item for sale. 'I need to—'

'We lost it, Victoria,' Finn murmured. 'Let it go.'

She shot him a glare. 'Fine. Then there's no need for me to be here any longer.'

Victoria pushed her way out of their row of seats and towards the door, Finn hurrying to follow. But where she was slender enough to slip through gaps between people without too much disruption, his own wider, bulkier frame caused more trouble—and complaints.

By the time he made it out of the room, she was nowhere to be seen. He raced out to the street, only to be confronted with a sea of people—and no sign of the only one he wanted.

He'd lost the clock, and an important piece of his revenge. But he knew that wasn't why his heart was aching.

He'd lost *her* and he had no idea why, or how to get her back.

CHAPTER ELEVEN

VICTORIA DIDN'T HAVE words to express how much she was dreading today.

Hiding out in the bathroom at Wishcliffe House, she sat on the edge of the tub and counted the reasons.

One. It was Toby and Autumn's wedding day—well, second wedding day really, but since nobody had been invited to the first one, it was the only one that counted. And of course it was being held here at Wishcliffe, in the charming little chapel on the boundary between the estate and the village, just like Victoria and Barnaby's had been, with a party back at the house afterwards. As happy as she was for the couple, reliving her own wedding day only eighteen months after being widowed was…hard.

Two. Autumn had really embraced the spring pastels for her wedding theme, and Victoria was stuck wearing a pale green dress that made her look sicker than she felt.

Three. Finn was going to be there. In fact, Finn was best man, which made it inevitable that she'd be sat near him and probably have to dance with him, even if he was angry enough with her after London to try to avoid her.

London. God, she'd relived that day in her head so many times over the days since. How she'd managed to screw it up so badly was still a mystery to her, though.

She'd been scared, that was all. Scared to see him again, knowing that she loved him. Guilty as all hell too—*that* hadn't faded since her revelation. And confused. Mostly confused. Because what the hell did she do next?

She couldn't just carry on as she had been—the guilt would bury her. And if Finn felt the way she thought he did…well, the guilt would destroy them both, in the end.

Walking away now might hurt his pride, maybe even dent his heart, but it would leave him free to find someone who could love him back without guilt and pain. Holding onto him when she knew that another happy ending wasn't on the cards for her, that she'd already had her one true love, well. That wasn't fair.

So she'd tried to find a way to let him go. She'd intended to focus on the auction, on doing the job he'd hired her for, and *then* address the personal. But Finn, impatient as ever, had tried to do both at once, and they'd ended up doing neither.

Now here she was. On Toby and Autumn's wedding day, hiding in the bathroom attached to her old room.

'Victoria? Are you ready?' The American twang of Autumn's second bridesmaid, her friend Cindy, rang out outside the door. 'Autumn's almost ready to head down.'

'I'll be right there,' Victoria called back. Then she flushed the toilet for good measure, and heard Cindy shut the bedroom door.

She checked her hair and make-up one last time and took a breath. She just needed one more minute.

In one more minute she'd know whether or not she needed to add a number four to her list of things she was dreading about today. And whether the whole situation with Finn had just grown a whole lot more complicated.

Victoria steeled herself, then looked down at the small white and blue stick on the counter and watched as the word *Pregnant* appeared on the display.

For a moment—a brief, brilliant moment—rising hope filled her. A sense of amazement, after so many losses—not just Barnaby and Harry, but the miscarriages that had come before and after her rainbow baby. And the usual fear too, the worry that this might not last. That another much loved and much wanted baby might not survive inside her. But mostly just the joy that a new life would always bring her.

Until reality came crashing down again.

Her heart stuttered as another wave of guilt and self-loathing washed over her. A baby. When she'd already lost one child she loved more than the whole world itself. Would this baby be a miracle, or another heart-breaking loss?

And, either way, how could it be anything but a betrayal?

She closed her eyes for a second, the sheer volume of emotions swirling around her head and her heart threatening to overwhelm her. But she couldn't afford to be overwhelmed. Not today.

Steeling herself, she opened her eyes. The display still read 'pregnant' as she stashed it at the bottom of the bathroom bin and washed her hands. She forced herself to smile as she met her reflection's gaze in the mirror, but it looked fake, even to her own eyes.

Four. She had to tell Finn Clifford she was expecting his child.

Wishcliffe was filled with flowers.

The house, the driveway of the estate, the village itself—and most especially the little chapel that sat between the village and Wishcliffe House—all bloomed with tulips, daffodils, hyacinths and every other spring flower the locals had been able to pull up and tie a ribbon around. It was making Finn's nose itch.

'I hope none of the guests have hay fever,' he muttered as they waited outside the chapel to greet the people arriving for the service.

That earned him an elbow in the ribs from the groom. 'I think they're lovely,' Toby said. 'They're a sign of how happy everyone is that Autumn and I are getting married.'

'Again.' Of course Finn was proud to stand up as Toby's best man, but as they'd actually been married since that chapel in Vegas in September, the whole rigmarole seemed a little overdone to him.

'Properly this time,' Toby said. 'With everyone here to see.' He looked so delighted at the prospect, even Finn had to smile.

Smiles had been hard to come by over the last week. He hadn't heard a word from Victoria, besides a rather terse email about a delivery of a writing bureau to Clifford House. Whatever the problem was, he didn't want to push her any further away, so he'd waited patiently, figuring that when she'd worked through things in her head she'd come to him. Eventually.

Of course it helped that he knew they'd have to see each other today for the wedding. He was cursing the tradition that the bride was always late, though, as he tried not to fidget outside the church. Autumn had wanted her two bridesmaids with her, to walk down the aisle.

The vicar poked his head out through the heavy wooden doors of the chapel. 'It's time, gentlemen.'

Toby was grinning nervously as they made their way down the aisle—which was absurd since they were *already married,* but Finn didn't comment on it. Instead, he decided to be grateful that Toby was doing all the smiling and being polite to guests, because it meant he didn't have to.

By the time they were at the front of the chapel, though, the memories were coming thick and fast, eclipsing the actual events of the day.

This was the chapel where he'd sat and watched Victoria marry Barnaby, the sheer joy and love on both their faces clear for everyone to see. Where he'd stood up as godfather at Harry's christening.

And where he'd endured Barnaby and Harry's funerals.

If those memories were overwhelming him today, how much worse must they be for Victoria?

'Stop scowling,' Toby muttered to him as the organist switched from the gentle background music to something more commanding, transitioning into the familiar notes of the Wedding March.

It was time.

I should have found her before this. Held her. Helped her face this day.

He'd been so focused on what was wrong between the two of them, he hadn't thought until now about how impossibly hard this week must be for her.

The wooden doors began to creak open again and the whole congregation stood and turned. Finn ignored the waiting crowd, focused on that growing gap between the doors.

Then the doors were fully open and all he could see was Victoria, her face pale and a little wan and her shoulders tense.

'God, she's beautiful,' Toby murmured.

'Green's not her colour,' Finn replied, before he realised that Toby was probably talking about his bride, not his sister-in-law.

But Finn couldn't make himself look at Autumn. He couldn't look anywhere but at Victoria.

She looked tired. Worn down. He wanted to step towards her and take her in his arms, but he couldn't—for so many reasons.

Would he ever get to do that again? He didn't know. And he didn't know *why*. The same way he'd never known why his father hated him. It was the not knowing that kept the pain coming, he was sure.

Autumn took the last few steps to the altar and took Toby's arm.

'Ready?' Finn heard his best friend ask softly.

Autumn nodded, then flashed Toby an impish grin. 'Think you'll be able to remember this one?'

'I'm pretty sure today will be one I'll never forget,' Toby replied. 'I can't wait to see what new memories we can make together.'

God, they were sickeningly sweet. Normally Finn would be nauseated by the whole thing. Today...today he just wanted what they had. Something he'd never even let himself imagine he could have before. Something he'd sworn to Victoria he didn't want.

Autumn sniffed. 'Don't make me cry. We've got the whole service to get through.'

'Just blame it on the flowers,' Toby replied. 'That's what Finn is going to do when he gets tearful.'

Finn did roll his eyes at that. And he turned to pay attention to the service as the vicar started to speak. It was his best friend's wedding. He wasn't going to miss that a second time.

He patted the pocket of his jacket to check he still had the rings. But then he let his mind wander—to the woman standing on the other side of the aisle, behind the bride, putting on a brave face on a day full of painful memories. The woman he loved, even though he shouldn't.

The woman he at least had to try and win back. She wouldn't ever love him the way she'd loved Barnaby, and he'd never be able to give her back the life she'd lost. But he could settle for less than the fairy-tale.

Whatever she was willing to give him, he'd take.

But first he had to get her talking to him again.

Victoria was going to be sick.

There was just no way she was going to make it through this ceremony without vomiting in her tastefully arranged spring flower bouquet and ruining Toby and Autumn's big day.

She wasn't sure if the nausea was because now she knew for sure she was pregnant the morning sickness was catching up with her, or because this place was so full of memories she felt whiplash being here again and revisiting all that love and loss.

Or maybe it was just because Finn was standing at the front of the church, sneaking glances at her as if he wanted to drag her out of there and force her to talk to him.

She made it through the ceremony—just—by focusing on the stained-glass window behind the altar and thinking of nothing but fresh air and her breathing. Most of all, she did not look at Finn. Not even a glance. However much she wanted to.

But then the organ started up again and Toby and Autumn were making their way back up the aisle together, and she had basically checked out of the entire freaking wedding. Worse, now Finn was holding out his arm to her, ready to walk her out.

Biting the inside of her cheek, she took it.

Breathe in, hold, breathe out. Smile if you can. But mostly just breathe in, hold, breathe out.

She was going to make it to the door. She was.

The heavily scented air hit her lungs as soon as they stepped outside—sunshine and flowers and pollen and cut grass—and suddenly it was all too much. She wrenched her arm free of Finn's grasp and sprinted around the corner of the chapel, thankful that Autumn had let her wear flats with her long dress.

Out of sight of the crowd of wedding well-wishers, Victoria rested her forehead against the cool stone of the chapel and tried to ride out the latest wave of nausea.

'Victoria?' Finn. Of course he'd followed her. 'Are you okay?'

It took every bit of her strength to turn away from the wall and force a smile. 'Fine. Just...hay fever. Too many flowers.'

'Right.' He didn't look convinced, but at least he wasn't going to contradict her. 'I told Toby they'd be a problem.'

'I'll be right back out in a moment,' Victoria promised, her head swimming. 'I know they'll want to do the photos soon.'

Finn stepped closer, his hands in his pockets, concern in his eyes. 'They will. Victoria—'

'Finn, I can't right now.' If he tried to force a conversation now she was going to throw up on his shoes. 'Whatever you want to talk about...please, it's just going to have to wait.'

'I'm not trying to—Victoria.' He wasn't going away. He was moving closer. This was not the idea. Why couldn't he just leave her alone with her misery and the constant swirl of conflicting emotions? 'I just want to be sure that you're okay. You don't look…well.'

She almost laughed at that. 'I'm fine, Finn.'

Pregnant, but fine.

She needed to tell him, of course she did. Would he be happy or horrified? She honestly didn't know. But, either way, it sure as hell wasn't what they'd agreed to when they'd started this. They'd have to discuss this, decide what happened next together. But not here, and not now. The nausea would fade again in a while— it always had with Harry. She just had to ride it out.

'I don't think you are.' He reached out to place a hand on her shoulder, his touch gentle. Loving.

She pulled away, spinning around to face him. 'I'm fine. I just need a few minutes. Will you please just leave me—'

The spinning had been a bad idea. Because now the bright spring sunshine was in her eyes, making her head hurt, and her stomach hadn't moved quite as fast as the rest of her and felt as if it was about to complete its revolt at any moment.

But most of all because now she could see Finn— the fear and love on his face. And beyond him, towards the edge of the churchyard, two familiar gravestones that she'd been avoiding since this whole thing began.

Barnaby. Harry.

Self-loathing and guilt swirled in her chest while the pregnancy nausea rose, unstoppable this time. She pressed one hand to the stone of the church and held the other out to keep Finn away, bending in the middle as she threw up all over the vicar's carefully planted daffodils.

'Victoria!' Finn grabbed for her and she lurched back out of his reach. Apparently even vomit wasn't enough to drive him away from her.

But she was not having this conversation here, now, like this. Not when she felt so utterly unsettled, so unlike herself. She needed to gather up her defences to tell Finn her news.

So, grabbing her skirts in both hands and praying the dress was still vomit-free, she turned and ran.

The photos, the meal, the toasts…the whole rest of the wedding day passed in a blur for Finn. He didn't even have the mental space to worry about the speech he needed to give about Toby. His whole brain was focused on Victoria.

Victoria, who'd wanted to get away from him so badly she'd been physically sick.

He knew what she'd seen, of course. What had caused such a violent reaction.

Her lover in the same space as the graves of her one true love and their son. It had made his own stomach cramp with guilt when he'd turned and realised.

He knew he shouldn't have followed her, but she'd just looked so…lost. And now he knew for sure how he felt about her, he couldn't just walk away. It was as if there were a thread from his heart to hers and he couldn't do anything but follow it back to her, every time.

Even if she would prefer to snap the thread.

And this metaphor was getting too tortured even for his lovesick brain.

The wedding guests all laughed at something Toby had said in his speech, and Finn tried to smile along as if he'd actually been listening. Autumn stood up beside her husband and took the microphone.

'I can't say enough how thankful I am for how welcome everyone here at Wishcliffe has made me,' she said. Sounded as if they were wrapping up, so Finn felt in his pocket for the notecards he'd made for his own speech. He didn't really need them—he'd had it memorised for weeks, like any important work presentation or similar—but it was always good to have a backup. Toby was probably the only person who'd ever call him a best man, and Finn didn't want to screw it up for him.

'And so it feels right to share our exciting news with you today, while we're all together,' Toby added.

Finn froze, index cards in hand. They were going to announce the pregnancy. His gaze instantly sought out Victoria, remembering that night in the orchard after Autumn and Toby had told them about the baby.

She looked pale but calm. At least until she met his gaze and her skin became tinged with green. As if she might be sick again at any moment.

'In just a few short months, at the end of the summer, we'll become a family of three,' Toby announced, the pride in his voice clear.

As the guests cheered, Finn struggled to look away from Victoria as a memory came rushing back. Of visiting Wishcliffe when Victoria was expecting Harry, and she was unable to keep much more than toast and biscuits down for weeks.

And he knew. He just knew, in that moment, that Victoria was pregnant with his child.

His heart soared for a moment at the very idea, before crashing back down into his stomach as reality hit.

This had to be breaking her heart. They'd never talked about whether she wanted to have more children, but if she did he knew it wasn't like this. Not when her grief for Harry was still so raw and so deep. And not with a man she didn't, couldn't love.

Finn knew that her guilt over being with another man after Barnaby was only assuaged by the fact that he was someone she'd never have a future with, never seek that happy every after with. And this…well, it had to feel perilously close to what she'd been avoiding from the start.

How long had she known? Was this why she'd pulled away in London? Had she even planned to tell him at all? Finn had so many questions he needed answers to, and he knew he'd have to get Victoria alone, and soon, to ask them.

But a small part of him wanted to pretend that he *didn't* know. To let Victoria hide from him a little longer. Because if he didn't know about the pregnancy, then he didn't have to deal with all the emotions it stirred up in him either. Not yet.

Like the terror of being a *father*. How could he possibly do that? Risk repeating his family's inherited mistakes over and over—raising a child who hated him as much as he hated his own father. As much as his father hated him.

'Finn?' Toby nudged him, and Finn realised that the whole room was waiting for him to give his best man's speech. As if his world hadn't just shifted on its axis into a terrifying, unrecognisable place.

But it was Toby's wedding day, and Toby was the best family he had. He wasn't going to screw up now.

So Finn faked a smile and thanked whatever foresight had prompted him to bring cards for this one, and began his well-rehearsed, light and fun but not *too* embarrassing speech to the Viscount of Wishcliffe and his bride.

But his gaze still flicked back to Victoria every minute or so, to ensure she was still there. Because they *were* going to talk, as soon as this was over.

He might be terrified, but that wouldn't stop him doing the right thing.

Victoria would never love him, he knew that. But he'd offer her anything she wanted to make this situation right. Money, marriage, Clifford House itself.

Because, above all else, Finn Clifford knew two things with a sudden, clarifying certainty.

One, he was never going to love anyone else the way he loved Victoria Blythe.

And two, he was *never* going to repeat his father's mistakes.

CHAPTER TWELVE

FINN'S SPEECH WAS funny, charming and touching—everything a best man's speech should be. But Victoria had seen him rehearsing it enough times to know that he wasn't giving it his all. In fact, he wasn't focusing on the speech at all, if the way his gaze kept flicking back to her was any indication.

He knows. He's figured it out.

She could pretty much pinpoint the moment that he'd worked out what was happening too. She'd watched the colour drain from his face as he'd stared at her while Toby announced their happy news. Finn wasn't an idiot. He knew.

Which was why she wasn't at all surprised when, as soon as the applause following his speech had faded away, he excused himself from the top table and headed straight for her.

'Not here,' she said quickly, and he nodded.

By unspoken agreement they headed out of Wishcliffe House and towards the orchard, which had the benefit of being separated from the rest of the gardens by a wall, and the gate Autumn had installed in it was fairly well hidden. They should be able to avoid being overheard by any roaming guests there.

'Were you going to tell me?' Finn asked, the moment the gate swung shut behind them. His jaw was set, as if he was waiting for her to hit him with a 'no'.

Victoria sighed and rested against the wall. Pregnancy was exhausting at the best of times, and this was anything but that. Finn stood beside her, both of them looking ahead into the trees.

'Of course I was,' she assured him. 'I mean, not necessarily in the middle of Toby's wedding, but yes. I was going to tell you. I only found out myself this morning.'

He jerked around to look at her, surprise clear on his face. Victoria frowned. Why was he surprised? Oh, unless he thought that was why she'd run away in London.

Pity she hadn't thought of that sooner. It could have been a neat excuse.

But no. She owed Finn honesty, as much as anything else.

'Do you know…? What do you want to do?' His voice faltered as he asked, as if he were afraid of the answer. She just didn't know which answer would scare him more. 'Or do you need more time to think? I assumed… Well, I thought you'd known for longer.'

'Since London,' she guessed, and he nodded. 'No. I just took the test this morning. But I already know what I want.'

The answer had come to her easily in the end. Her whole future rolled out in front of her, like a movie trailer. There'd never been any question, for her. After so much loss, how could she do anything but embrace the miracle of new life when it was given to her? As scared as she was, as guilty as she was, she couldn't deny the tiny crack in her fear that was letting the joy in.

'You know I'll support you, whatever you decide. I'm here for you.'

Then why did he look as if he was getting ready to run? Victoria knew that kids had never been in Finn's life plan, mostly because he didn't have one, beyond his revenge on his father. But for someone who'd always been so open, so tactile—always moving, always touching, always smiling… Now, he seemed frozen. Paralysed by her news.

Terrified, even.

'I'm keeping the baby, of course,' she said, and watched his shoulders tense just a little more. Another few words and Toby and Autumn would have a new statue in the orchard instead of a best friend. 'I already lost one child, and this…maybe this is my second chance.'

The child growing inside her hadn't asked for any of this, not even to be born into this world, into this family, into Victoria's own losses. The baby didn't deserve any of the guilt that hung over her like a fog.

If she was lucky enough to be given this second shot at motherhood, then Victoria would do everything she could to do it right. To love her child, keep them safe—and make sure they knew all about the family that had come before them. Their place in the world.

Except this wasn't Barnaby's child she was carrying. And that made a difference.

Finn obviously knew that too.

'Do you want to tell people…do you want them to know the baby is mine?' By people, she assumed he meant Toby most of all. While she was sure that *many* people in Wishcliffe—a notorious hotbed of gossip—would have opinions about her pregnancy, she was equally certain that Toby's was the only one he cared about.

She obviously took too long to reply, because Finn went on. 'You could always claim you'd had Barnaby's sperm frozen or something, that you wanted another baby to keep a piece of him alive. Or something.'

Was that what he'd been thinking while he'd been giving his best man's speech, or had it just come to him now?

'Is that what *you* want?'

His Adam's apple bobbed as he swallowed. 'I want to do whatever will make this easiest for you. Whatever you need.'

'I don't want to lie to my child about who their father is.' She should be outraged at the suggestion, Victoria was sure, but somehow she couldn't blame him for making it. After all, she'd spent their whole relationship making it clear that he was never anything more than a stand-in for the man she'd loved and lost.

She'd never told him that he'd become so much more than that to her. And now it was too late.

Finn gave a stiff nod. 'Okay. Then…do you want to get married? You know, the honourable thing? If…

if the child is going to be mine, then they'll inherit Clifford House one day. I wouldn't take that away from them.'

The way his own father had taken it from him. Suddenly, she wondered how much of the tense fight-or-flight vibes Finn was giving off were to do with her and the baby, and how much were to do with Finn's relationship with his own father.

Then the first part of his statement caught up with her. *Married. Again.*

She shuddered, the guilt suddenly overwhelming her again. 'I can't marry you, Finn.'

'No. Of course not.' He sounded as if he'd been crazy to even suggest it. Which he was, but not necessarily for the reasons he thought. She wanted to explain, to tell him how he deserved his own shot at a happy ending, with someone who could love all the things about him that she did—without the guilt and self-loathing that came along with it.

She'd already betrayed Barnaby and Harry's memory by moving on so fast—falling into bed with Finn was one thing, falling in love with him and carrying his baby was a whole different level of betrayal.

'Marrying you, starting a family together like a normal person could…it would feel like I was erasing my past—starting over as if Barnaby and Harry had never existed. I can't do that.'

'I understand.' His voice was low, rough, and she could hear the pain in it. But she also believed he really did understand. Maybe he was the only person that would. 'So, how do you want to do this?'

'I don't know.' Her body was crumpling into the wall behind her, folding in on itself under the weight of all the decisions she needed to make. 'I think…if we're going to be parents together, I don't think we can be anything else.' That would be too much like replacing the family she'd lost, wouldn't it? She couldn't risk falling deeper in love with Finn, with their lives together, and forgetting what she'd had before. 'Beyond that, can you give me some time? I need to think. Figure it out.'

'Of course.'

He started to push away from the wall and she stopped him, one hand on his arm. He stared down at her fingers as she spoke.

'Being a mother again, after what happened to Harry…it's terrifying to me. But that doesn't mean I don't want it.'

'I know.' He swallowed again, then looked at her with a smile that didn't go near his eyes. 'I'll be here for you. Whatever you need. As a friend.'

They were the words she wanted to hear. But she could still see the wall they'd put between them, the fear and shame and stiffness. Her heart ached with the loss of what they'd had.

But this was the right thing. It would be better this way.

Hadn't she already learned that in life you never got everything you wanted? Because when you had it, the universe was always waiting to take it away again.

So she wouldn't ask for everything this time. She'd be content with what she could have.

It would just have to be enough.

'We should get back to the wedding,' she said, and Finn nodded.

'I'll be right there,' he said.

With one last look back at him, slumped against the orchard wall, Victoria made her way back towards the house, the wedding and her future.

Alone, except for the tiny life building inside her.

The front door of Clifford House slammed shut, rattling even the heavy stone walls.

'Finn!' Toby's voice echoed through the empty rooms, making Finn wince as he reached for his mug on the kitchen counter. Looked like his best friend was back from honeymoon then.

The past two weeks had been a weird kind of limbo. Stasis. Waiting for Victoria to decide his future.

But if Toby was here, that meant the waiting was over. She must have told him.

And now Finn had to face the shame of his betrayal of his best friend's dead brother.

'In the kitchen,' he called back, and reached for the new coffee pot to pour a cup for his friend.

'Well. You look even worse than she did.' Toby stood in the doorway and scrutinised him until Finn flinched under his gaze.

'Coffee?' He offered Toby the mug, and he took it. Plain white utilitarian mugs. Nothing like the starburst patterns on the ones he'd bought for Victoria.

He'd been stalking online marketplaces for them ever since. If he and Victoria managed to make it to

Christmas as friends, as well as co-parents, he had a whole box of them ready to wrap up and give her.

But that felt like a big if right now.

'Tell me what's wrong with my sister-in-law,' Toby said bluntly, as he dropped into the second camping chair. The other rooms had actual furniture now, thanks to Victoria, but Finn preferred it in the kitchen. It was the one room the previous owners had remodelled completely, so it held no memories of his family, even if it did have some of Victoria.

'What did she tell you?' Finn wasn't about to stumble into unintentionally blowing any secrets Victoria hadn't chosen to share. And from the exasperation in Toby's voice he got the impression that she'd told him a lot less than Finn had expected.

'Next to nothing,' Toby admitted. 'But she looks wrecked and she won't talk to me or Autumn, and you've spent more time with her lately than anyone so I'm betting that you know what's going on.'

Finn had never been any good at lying to his best friend. In fact, he'd never even bothered trying. Still, he didn't trust himself to speak without the whole sorry tale spilling out, so he settled for a curt nod instead.

Toby placed his mug on the small table between them and leant forward, his elbows on his knees and his eyes deadly serious.

'She's my sister, Finn, or as good as. You have to tell me everything.'

Everything.

Finn met his friend's gaze, swallowed, and started talking. Toby deserved to know.

It took less time than he'd imagined to share the bare bones of what had happened between him and Victoria. The hardest part was watching Toby's glare deepen with every word.

By the time they reached the wedding, and Victoria throwing up outside the church, Toby had already leapt to the right conclusion.

'You knocked her up. You got my sister pregnant and then *left her*?'

'No!' Finn replied vehemently. 'Well, not voluntarily.'

'Not voluntarily?' Toby ground out, looking like it was taking all his willpower not to punch Finn. 'Is that in relation to the pregnancy or the leaving?'

'The leaving. Well, both,' he amended. 'I mean, the pregnancy wasn't intentional. But everything else… I offered to marry her, to give her this place, anything she wanted. I only left because she told me she wanted time to think about what happened next. In fact *she* left *me*.'

Not that any of his excuses made him feel any better about it all. If Toby was right, and Victoria really was in a state about all this, then he should be with her. He should be making things better somehow.

Even if he hadn't got the faintest idea where to start.

'How are you going to fix this?' Toby asked, unknowingly echoing Finn's own thoughts.

'I don't know.'

'Well, you'd better figure it out. Fast.' He eyed Finn with suspicion. 'Assuming you love her?'

Finn looked away. 'Of course I do. Have you *met* her?'

'Well, then.' Lurching from his camping chair, Toby began pacing the length of the kitchen. 'What you need is a grand gesture. Something that shows her how you feel!'

'Like you flying to Vegas to chase Autumn down?' Finn guessed.

Toby nodded enthusiastically. 'Exactly! It needs to be big and meaningful. There must be something the two of you have shared that has a secret meaning for you both. I don't want details, but…there's something, right? Something you can use to show her how you feel?'

Finn thought about Paris, or Derbyshire, or Portobello Road. He thought about the coffee cups with stars on sitting in his cupboard, unwrapped.

Then he shook his head.

Toby slumped back into his camping chair. 'There's nothing? Really? You guys have been together for months, behind my back. How can there be nothing you've shared that means something to you both?'

Finn gave him a wry smile. 'There's a million things. Every moment I spent with her…it was magical. That's not the problem.'

'Then what is?'

'She's already had the grand gestures. The fairy-tale perfect life as lady of the manor. She lost it.'

'I remember,' Toby said drily. 'And now she can have it again.'

Finn shook his head. 'She doesn't want that. She doesn't want to start over with me as if the past never happened. I can't take Barnaby's place, and she doesn't want me to. And I don't know… I don't know how to be there for her, how to love her, when we both feel such guilt just being together.'

That was the heart of it, he realised. He wanted Victoria to be happy, to have a life full of joy again, not loss and guilt. And he only seemed to make those things worse.

'You can't make her guilt go away,' Toby said, his voice heavy, obviously thinking of the brother and nephew he'd lost. Finn knew that he was a poor replacement for them too. 'And no, you can't be Barnaby. But you can figure out how to be the best Finn you can be—the best partner for her in this. The man she needs you to be. And Finn?'

He looked up to find his best friend glaring at him again. 'I know.'

Toby said it anyway. 'You'd better bloody find a way to be that man.'

Finn put down his coffee cup and studied the Clifford House kitchen. Then he stood and walked to the door, looking around the white rooms with their stacks of antique furniture, ready to be put in place for the big reveal. For the revenge that he'd waited so many years for.

This was where it had all started for him. It had made him the man he was.

But that wasn't the man Victoria needed right now.

And suddenly he knew exactly what he needed to do to become that.

Grabbing his keys from the bowl by the front door, he called out to Toby, 'Lock up behind you, will you?'

'Where are you going?' Toby asked from the kitchen doorway.

Finn flashed his friend a tight smile. 'To do something I should have done years ago.'

The waves lapped gently against the sand, growing ever closer to the toes of Victoria's trainers. She'd been out here so long the tide had turned, and the afternoon was turning into evening. The spring breeze was chilly, but she'd wrapped up in her coat to ward it off.

There was nowhere else she wanted to be right now.

The sea had always given her comfort, long before it took away her family. Her love.

But now she felt she was coming full circle, she needed the sound of the waves again, building, breaking and cresting anew, the never-ending cycle of tides familiar and meditative as she watched.

Tearing her eyes from the sea, she looked down instead at the photos in her lap. One was a favourite shot of her with Barnaby and Harry, on the beach, just a few months before the accident that stole them from her.

The other, a blurry black, white and grey shot, showed her baby. With her history of previous miscarriages, plus her obvious concern about the pregnancy overall, her GP had been persuaded to refer her for an early scan. So now she had the photographic proof of the life growing inside her.

She'd gone to the scan alone, like she'd done everything alone for the past two weeks. As she had for a year, before Finn asked her to help him with Clifford House. It was only once she was there, with the gel on her belly and the technician pointing out the blur on the screen that was her baby, that she realised that Finn should be there too.

She'd realised something else too, though. A stinging sharp realisation that she hadn't been able to think all the way through to its conclusion there, half naked on the examination table. So she'd tucked it away until she was back here and could consider it properly.

She was carrying her future inside her. She'd known it, of course, since the moment she saw the positive pregnancy test, maybe even before. But now...

Now it felt real, in a way it hadn't before. Now, the ramifications of that were hammering home inside her head. And, like she'd always done before, she'd come to the sea to talk to the one person who'd always helped her make sense of her head before, and the one child who had filled her whole heart—until now.

She was kind of glad there was no one else on the beach to see her, though. Because the only way she could do this was out loud.

'Barnaby...' Her voice sounded rusty, from long minutes sitting in the cold in silence. 'Barn, I've done something. And I think I might have screwed up, and I need to talk to you about it.'

'Then talk. You know I'll always listen.' That

was what he'd always said, with no judgement, no questions. Just giving her space to work through her thoughts and her problems out loud.

'I'm pregnant,' she said bluntly. 'And the father is Finn Clifford.'

She couldn't even imagine what Barnaby's response to that would be, so she ploughed on regardless.

'We didn't mean for it to happen. But…he came back into my life and he made me feel alive again, for the first time since I lost you. It was fun, and freeing. And I thought that was all it could be. That I was past feeling anything more than that.'

Victoria looked down at the photos in her lap again. At Barnaby's dear, loved face. At Harry, so young and full of life. And at the baby inside her now.

'But I was wrong. Because I fell in love with Finn.' God, it felt good to say it out loud at last. 'I love Finn, and I ran away from him because it felt like a betrayal of you. I pulled away from any suggestion of us being a family together, because it felt like I was forgetting Harry, and you. And I'm still scared about being a mother again, terrified of the idea of moving on alone, without you, but…' She swallowed around the lump in her throat, realising that the salt water on her cheeks had nothing to do with the spray from the sea. 'But I realised today I don't have to do it alone. Do I?'

She'd chosen to be with Finn because she didn't want to be alone for the rest of her life, even if she hadn't expected love to be a part of it. Now it was, could she really throw it away? Keep living in the past, rather than embracing her future?

She owed it to her baby to live the best life possible, to find joy in the world—and love too.

But, more than that, she owed it to herself.

'I'll never forget the love we shared, and I'll never stop loving and missing you. Just like there'll never be a day where I don't think of Harry, don't remember how I love him and miss him too.' She couldn't see the photos any longer, her eyes blurry with tears. 'But I think you'd both want me to keep on living, even if you're not here to see it. I think you'd want me to be happy.'

She deserved to not keep living in the past. She deserved to be happy—and so did Finn.

'He's not you, Barn, but I wouldn't want him to be,' she said. 'Just like this baby won't be Harry. I'm not looking for a replacement for either of you. I'm looking for my future, and it won't look the same as my past. But I think that's okay. I'm not the same person I was then either.'

She pushed herself up to standing, her legs aching from sitting still for too long, the two photos still clutched in her hand.

'I love you both,' she said. 'I always will. But there's room in my future, and my heart, for more love. And I think you'd want me to go after it.'

With a last look out over the waves, Victoria turned and headed for her little cottage, to figure out what happened next.

CHAPTER THIRTEEN

IT WASN'T HARD for Finn to find his father in London. He just headed straight for his club.

It seemed archaic that such institutions still existed in the modern city he loved, but if there was an exclusive, patriarchal and outdated club to be part of, of course Lord Clifford had joined it.

It wasn't hard to get admittance either. Finn was famous enough—well, infamous, really—in the same circles that his father moved in to find someone willing to sign him in as a guest, even if he suspected they were only doing it for the amusement factor of seeing Lord Clifford face his notoriously hated heir in public.

Lord Clifford looked up, saw his son and calmly closed his paper, folding it neatly on his lap. Finn's sponsor looked a little disappointed.

'What the hell are you doing here?' Finn's father's voice was strangely even, unbothered, although his words and his eyes showed his displeasure clearly. His fingers, however, trembled just a little as he reached for his ever-present glass of brandy.

Not making a scene had always been Lord Clifford's guiding principle. That was why he hadn't just tried to disinherit Finn through the courts, breaking the entail on the Clifford line legally, rather than just selling it out from under him. Why he'd let Finn's mother leave, but never granted her a divorce. She'd only become free of him in death.

Appearances were everything. And he'd rather appear an aristocrat with no land—of which there were plenty these days—than a man who couldn't control his wife and son.

Finn took a seat opposite him and studied the man who'd raised him with fresh eyes. He'd always been so overbearing, filling Clifford House with the force of his voice, his anger alone. Now, he seemed…smaller. Shrivelled. As if the bitterness he'd harboured for years was consuming him at last.

Is that how I'd look if I'd never moved on from my revenge plan?

'Well?' Lord Clifford demanded. 'Not got anything to say? Might as well get out.'

Finn smiled a slow, knowing smile. He'd heard a slight shake in his father's voice—nerves rather than anger now. He didn't want Finn to make a scene.

'I came to tell you that you are going to be a grandfather.'

Lord Clifford scoffed. 'Knocked some girl up, have you? Out of wedlock, of course. You're a disgrace. Just like I always expected. At least they won't get their bastard hands on our family legacy.'

'Because you sold it rather than letting it go to me,' Finn said. 'You despised me that much.' Something crossed his father's eyes, an emotion Finn couldn't quite name but it had a lot in common with hatred, he suspected. 'Or was it my mother you hated? For leaving you, forcing you to bring me up alone, when you were clearly so unsuited to the task?'

Anger flashed across his father's face at the very mention of his wife. 'Have you really not figured it out yet, boy?' His voice was a harsh whisper and, despite the other occupants of the room visibly straining to hear, Finn suspected their conversation was still private.

Unless Finn chose to change that.

For now, he kept playing his father's game. 'Figured what out, Father?'

'That I'm not your bloody father.' He spat the words at him, and Finn froze. 'You really thought your mother was faithful before that whore left me? No. I always knew you couldn't be mine. No child of mine would be so...' He eyed Finn up and down. 'Pathetic.'

He's not my father. I am not my father.

'Are you sure? Did you get a DNA test done or did she just tell you?' Suddenly, the truth of his life felt within his grasp. The information that would finally make sense of his childhood.

'Oh, she'd never admit it, of course.' Lord Clifford sat back in his chair, his voice still soft, a sort of manic glee in his smile. As if letting Finn in on his secret was cathartic for him. The ultimate revenge, at last. 'And I wasn't having one of those tests done—the records would get leaked, wouldn't they? But I knew the truth in my bones; I knew it.'

Not for sure, he didn't, Finn realised. There was no proof and Lord Clifford wouldn't have wanted any. That would have led to a scandal. Talk. There'd been enough of that when his mother left, and Finn vividly remembered the rampages his father had gone on, safe from prying eyes in the solitude of Clifford House, whenever there was a news story about her and her new lover.

'But without proof you couldn't disinherit me, right?'

Lord Clifford gave a scratchy chuckle. 'Your mother didn't know that, though. I told her if she tried to contact you after she left, I'd strip you of everything. No title, no money, no house. Nothing.'

'That's why she never came back.' It wasn't a question—he could feel the truth of it. All these years, he'd thought it was because she loved her new life, her new lover, more than her son. But she'd done it for him.

If she hadn't died, maybe he'd have learned sooner—once he became an adult and could seek her out. As it was…his father had hidden this truth from him for so many years.

His father nodded, still smirking. 'I didn't want the talk, of course—it was bad enough after she left, but if they'd known about you, well, the gossips would never have stopped talking. So I kept your shame to myself. But I couldn't have the Clifford family estate and fortune falling into your hands either.'

'So you sold Clifford House and all its contents the moment I was old enough to inherit.' He could feel his father's self-satisfaction at what he'd achieved glowing from him like the fire they sat beside.

Lord Clifford took another gulp of his brandy, settling in his chair, a victor in his own mind.

Finn studied his nails, before adding nonchalantly, 'Of course, you might have missed the part where I bought it back.'

Lord Clifford spluttered on his brandy. 'What?'

He could have raised his voice, made a scene, done all the things his father hated. But Finn didn't need that. He just needed his father to know the truth.

'I bought Clifford House. I tracked down the antiques, the heirlooms, and I bought them all back. Clifford House could be exactly as it was when my mother left, if I wanted. But I don't.'

He'd thought he needed to take his father back to Clifford House, to rub his nose in everything he'd achieved. He'd had thoughts of a gala, a gilded invitation, and an audience for his revenge.

But now he realised he didn't need any of those things. He even kept his voice low enough to frustrate the eavesdroppers as he went on.

'Maybe I'm your biological son, maybe I'm not. I don't think it really matters. I already know I'm not your son in your heart, and there's not a damn thing I could have done differently to change that.' All those years wasted, thinking if he had just been *better* somehow, maybe his father might have loved him. He couldn't get them back, but he could move on.

'What comes after your revenge?' Victoria had asked him. And now he thought he knew.

Letting go.

'Like you'd have done anything differently,' Lord Clifford scoffed. 'This is the way the world works, boy.'

Finn shook his head. 'Not my world. In my world, no possessions—no house, no title, no antiques—matter nearly as much as people do.'

He was still terrified at the prospect of becoming a dad, but he knew for sure that he wouldn't be the same kind of father his own had been. No child deserved that sort of parenting.

Finn pushed his chair back and got to his feet. 'Goodbye, Father.'

And he walked out of the club, past the disappointed eavesdroppers, and went home to find Victoria.

Victoria tucked the photo of Barnaby and Harry back into its frame, then stuck the scan photo to the fridge door with a magnet. She poured herself a cup of coffee in her favourite starry cup and was just staring at her phone, finding the courage to call Finn, when she heard the knock on the door.

Probably Toby again. Or maybe Autumn this time. They'd been checking on her daily since they'd returned from their honeymoon, and she hadn't heard from them today. She was going to have to tell them the truth soon. But she needed to talk to Finn first.

She crossed to the door and opened it, her heart jumping as she found Finn Clifford standing on her doorstep.

'Hi.' His hair was scruffed up, as if he'd been running his hands through it in the car, and his suit was rumpled. But the look in his eye, the fervent way his gaze ran across her, as if checking for changes, told her he'd missed her as much as she'd missed him.

'Can I come in?' he asked.

Nodding, she stepped out of the way to let him in. 'I'm glad you're here.'

He gave her a relieved smile, some of the tension dropping from his shoulders. 'Yeah? Good. I wasn't sure…after everything.'

She'd made him think she didn't want him around, when in fact the exact opposite was true. It had just taken her a while to see it.

Victoria headed for the fridge and took down the scan photo again. 'I was about to call you. I wanted to show you this.'

Finn's fingers trembled slightly as he took the small square of paper from her. 'This is our baby?'

Warmth filled her at the awe in his voice. 'Our baby,' she agreed.

He stared at the scan for a long moment before saying, 'I went to see my father today.'

She reached for her coffee. 'How did that go?' She wasn't one hundred per cent sure she wanted to know. Not if it meant that Finn was still focused on his revenge plan above all else.

'He believes I'm not biologically his,' he said baldly, and Victoria looked up in surprise. She'd heard plenty of rumours about the Clifford family and their animosities, but never that. 'He has no proof, and my mother denied it, but he's sure. That's why he hated me, my whole childhood. Why he took away my birth right and sold it, rather than let it fall into my hands when he died. Because he wanted to hurt me, and my mother, and still keep face. It was all about him—not me. Not really. There was nothing I could have done to change any of it.'

Victoria smiled softly. She'd never really doubted that Finn's father was at fault, but it was nice to see that now *Finn* believed it too. 'Did you tell him about Clifford House? About the antiques.'

His response was a slow nod. 'I told him. But…it doesn't matter any more, not really. I don't need him to come here and see it. I don't need to prove anything to him.'

'Because he's not really your father?'

'No. Because he's not worth it.' Finn took a long, shuddering breath, placed the scan on the kitchen counter, then reached out to take her hands. 'I realised that before—that horrible day at the auction in London, I think—but it was only today that it fully sank in what that means.'

'What does it mean?' She hadn't meant to whisper, but the words came out that way anyway. As if the whole future of the universe hung on his next words.

'It means… I was living in the past. Even though I thought I'd grown up, moved on and found my own life, inside I was still locked up at Clifford House, not understanding why my father hated me, why my mother left and never came back. I couldn't see a future that didn't repeat my parents' mistakes.

'I thought that buying back Clifford House would prove something—that I was worthy, perhaps, or that my father had been wrong about me. But when I got there…it was so empty. So devoid of any of the things I wanted in my life, and all it did was remind me of how wretched my existence had been there. And I kept on trying to fill it anyway, because I just didn't know what else to do. Until you.'

'Me?'

'You. You helped me fill the damn house—even though you thought I was a fool for doing it.'

Victoria winced. 'Ah, you noticed that, did you?'

'You weren't subtle about it, sweetheart.' Finn was still smiling though, so she figured it was okay. 'You showed me that I needed to be thinking about the future, not the past. And for me…for me, you *are* my future. You and our child, however you want me to be a part of that. And I'm hoping—' He broke off, as if he was afraid to say the words.

'What are you hoping, Finn?' Because she really hoped it was the same thing that she was hoping.

'I know I can't be Barnaby for you. I could never replace the love of your life, and I wouldn't try. But I love you, you see—more than I ever imagined I could love anyone. More than I thought I was capable of. So I'm hoping there might be a corner of your heart left for me. That you might want to build that new future together, as a family. Because I want more than just visitation rights and co-parenting. I want to do so much better than my own parents. And I want to do it with you, because you're the best person I know.'

Victoria looked up into his hopeful, helpless, scared

eyes and smiled as the rightness of it all washed through her.

'Okay.'

Finn blinked. 'Okay?'

He was offering her his whole heart, and asking for her future in return, and all she said was *okay*?

Reaching up, Victoria placed her hand against his cheek and smiled again, the soft, sweet smile he loved so much. 'Let me get you a coffee,' she said. 'You're not the only one who had an epiphany today, you know.'

They settled together on the sofa in the lounge, matching starry coffee cups in hand. It felt domestic. It felt like home.

'When I went for the scan... I went alone, because I've got so used to doing things alone over the past year or so. But when I got there I realised... I wanted you with me.'

'You know I'd have been there if you'd asked, right?' Finn said.

She nodded. 'And next time I hope you will. But...' She took a deep breath, and he knew that whatever came next wouldn't be easy for her—but it would be important.

He put down his coffee cup and listened.

'That day in London...that wasn't the start of it. Me pulling away, I mean. It was that last day you were here, and you went for a swim on the beach. Do you remember?'

'Of course I remember.' Before now, it was the last time she'd looked at him like he mattered to her.

'I realised two things that day. First, that you were in love with me.'

He barked a laugh. 'You knew before I did, then.'

She gave him a look that seemed to say *Are you honestly surprised by this?* And when he thought about it, he wasn't really, so he let her carry on.

'Second, I realised that I loved you too. And it terrified me.'

Finn thought his heart might just stop in shock. 'You *loved* me? Then why—?'

'You know why.'

'Barnaby. And Harry.'

She nodded. 'It felt like I was betraying them. Erasing my past to build a future with you.'

'And do you…do you still feel that way?' God, he hoped not. Because if anything could dampen this small flame of hope that was burning inside him, it would be that.

'You said you knew I could never love you as much as I loved Barnaby,' she said, which wasn't an answer at all.

'And I'd never expect you to,' he added quickly. 'What you and Barnaby had, that was once in a lifetime. I'm not going to try to match up to that.'

'That's the point. You don't need to.' Placing her cup of coffee on the table, she smiled at him. 'That's what I realised, you see. It's not that I can't love you as *much* as Barnaby, the same way I'm not worried that I won't love the new baby as much as I loved Harry. I'll *always* love the ones I've lost. But that doesn't mean I can't love you and the new baby just as much, in a new way. Because I'm a new person now too.'

It was so much more than he'd ever hoped for, Finn couldn't find the words to tell her.

She seemed to understand, though, because she took his hand in hers and held it to her heart. 'Grief doesn't mean you lose that part of your heart. I get that now. But just like with having another child, your heart keeps growing, expanding, to make room to love new things, and new people. Like I love you.'

He didn't need words anyway, Finn decided as he swooped in to kiss her, pouring all his love and hope into the kiss.

'So we'll be a family?' He pulled away just enough to speak, resting his forehead against hers.

'A family. Yes.' She gave an apologetic smile. 'I haven't thought it all through yet—the details, I mean. How it will all work—'

'Doesn't matter,' Finn said fiercely. 'As long as I love you and you love me—we can figure out everything else later.'

And then he kissed her again. Because the one thing he knew for sure was, whenever, wherever Victoria was with him, he was home.

EPILOGUE

CLIFFORD HOUSE WAS full.

Full of people, full of music, full of chatter and full of love, spilling out into the gardens and the warm summer evening air.

What it *wasn't* full of was antiques that Victoria was pretty sure Finn had never even liked in the first place. Oh, they'd kept some pieces—the painting of his grandmother, for instance, and the huge dining table that let them invite all their friends and family around for dinner at the same time. But they'd supplemented them with items they really loved—new buys next to antiques, thrift store finds next to upcycled objects. They'd built a home that felt like *them,* and Victoria was thrilled they got to share it with the people they loved tonight, at their housewarming party.

Most of the people at the party she'd known for years, but there was one newcomer—a darkly attractive, brooding sort of man—who was hovering on the outskirts of the festivities. While Victoria had watched, she'd seen a few people try to engage him in conversation, before moving on when their efforts were met with what seemed like a polite but indifferent rebuff.

Everyone in the room knew who he was, though. Hell, everyone in the *town* and probably two towns over knew he was Max Blythe. The illegitimate older brother of the Viscount of Wishcliffe, Toby Blythe. The man who would have been her brother-in-law, if Barnaby had lived.

Ever since Toby had announced that Max would be taking over the manor house at Wells-on-Water, just across from Wishcliffe, the whole area had been abuzz with the gossip. And now he was here…well, Victoria didn't see the gossip dying down any time soon.

As hostess, though, she definitely had a duty to go and say hello. Toby had introduced them at one of his and Autumn's Sunday dinners at Wishcliffe the week before, so at least they'd got that awkward first meeting out of the way already.

She made her way across the ballroom, her ever-growing belly clearing a path. She was sure she hadn't been this big at five months with Harry. Her only consolation was that, at eight months along, Autumn was even bigger. That and the fact that Finn really seemed to like her pregnant…

'Victoria,' Max said as she reached him. 'Thank you for inviting me tonight. You have a lovely home.'

She inclined her head to accept the compliment. 'Thank you for coming. I'm sorry my home is filled with such gossips.'

He chuckled at that, which she liked. At least he didn't seem to be taking his notoriety too seriously.

'Why don't I find someone to introduce you to who probably won't ask you too many invasive questions?' she suggested.

'That would be nice,' Max replied.

Victoria scanned the room until her gaze landed on a familiar blonde across the way. 'Perfect.' Taking Max's arm, she led him towards her target. 'Max, let me introduce Lena Phillips. She's the manager of the King's Arms pub in town.'

Lena turned, her perfectly arched eyebrows raised in surprise. 'Max Blythe. Really.'

'Apparently so,' he said. 'Hello, Lena.'

Victoria looked between them, sure she was missing something here, but completely unsure what.

But, before she could ask, Finn appeared at her side. 'Excuse me, Max, Lena, I just need to borrow my fiancée for a moment.'

'Borrow me?' Victoria objected as he steered her out of the ballroom and towards his study. 'What am I? A phone charger?'

'You are the light of my life, my future and the mother of my child,' Finn pronounced. 'And I need to show you something.'

'It had better be something good,' she grumbled. 'I was just about to figure out what the deal is with Max. I think he and Lena might have history.'

'It *is* good. Look.' He motioned towards the computer screen on his desk, and Victoria cooed at the sight of the most darling carved antique crib.

'Oh, that would be *perfect* in the nursery!'

'I know!' Finn moved behind her, his arms wrapped

around her growing belly, his breath warm against her ear. 'The only catch is, we need to go to Paris to buy it.'

'I have very fond memories of Paris,' Victoria said.

'Mmm, me too.' He kissed her ear. 'It's our place, right?'

Victoria turned in his arms and smiled up at him. 'You're my place. You're my home now.'

And as she kissed him she knew that her future—and her heart—were safe in his arms.

* * * * *

REUNION WITH
THE BROODING
MILLIONAIRE

ELLIE DARKINS

MILLS & BOON

For Charlie, Loobie, Rosie and Harry.

CHAPTER ONE

'WHAT ARE YOU doing here?' Jonathan asked, his heart stuttering as he realised who had just walked into his house. He couldn't be the only one who could hear his voice was so strained that it was starting to crack, but how else was he meant to sound when he was faced with the woman he'd been thinking about but hadn't seen for the last seven years.

Rowan stared at him, looking as shocked to see him as he was to see her. He'd had barely more than glimpses of her since then—anything more direct than a sideways glance would have risked a flood of emotions he'd never trusted himself to examine, for fear of what he might learn.

A few minutes ago, his sister, Liv, had walked into the house—a small manor in the Cotswolds that he'd inherited from his grandparents a few years back, and was getting ready to sell—without a word of explanation as to why her best friend was there. Then she'd walked straight up the stairs, leaving him and Rowan in the hallway, staring at each other.

'Livia invited me,' Rowan said, falteringly, and Jonathan would have given every penny in his bank account to know what she was thinking at that moment. 'I had no idea you'd be here, or I wouldn't have come. I'm sorry, I think I can still make the last train back to London if I hurry.'

He couldn't take his eyes off Rowan, who was staring him down in equal shock. He was distracted by a flashback of the last time that he had seen her and— No. He couldn't. He'd forced himself not to think about that night. It was the only thing that had stopped him from doing something stupid. He wasn't about to change that now.

He checked his watch. 'No, you'll have missed it,' he said with a sigh. 'God forbid Liv would check with me before inviting you.'

That made her look directly at him at last. 'Is it really so terrible that I'm here?'

Jonathan sighed, because of course it wasn't, and it was. It was torture, and it was wonderful. But he couldn't tell Rowan any of that. He couldn't let himself think that. He had to shut down his thoughts before they could lead him in a direction he couldn't afford to follow.

'The roof's leaking,' he blurted, and Rowan widened her eyes. 'None of the rooms on the second floor are habitable. I cleared a room each for Liv and Caleb but there isn't a spare.'

Rowan fixed him with a look. 'I'll share with Liv.'

Jonathan nodded. 'Yes. Right. Of course.' *Why* had he had to bring up sleeping arrangements? He should never, *never* be allowed to think of Rowan and beds together. He'd drive himself insane.

Livia called from the top of the stairs, and Rowan shouted up that she'd be there in a minute. 'Well, Jonathan,' Rowan said in an impressively cool voice that made him hope that she'd forgotten what had happened between them, and that perhaps he could just pretend that he had too.

'It's been such a long time,' he blurted out, and nearly slapped a hand over his mouth to stop himself making it worse. Why had he said that? When he could have turned on his heel, retreated to the library and avoided her until she left. Bringing up the last time he had seen her was the very last thing he should be doing.

'Seven years,' Rowan said, with crossed arms and a raised eyebrow that told him that his luck was out and she remembered exactly the things that he had said back then. 'I have a race at the weekend and Liv is going to be my support crew,' she went on, putting him out of his misery. He could only be thankful for her mercy, because she'd somehow dissolved every defence mechanism that he'd honed over the years just by appearing in front of him. 'She promised me a few days of R&R here first. If I'd known that this was a family thing...'

'Right. Of course,' he replied. 'It is. Caleb's here too. I asked them to come and see if there was anything they wanted to keep before the estate agent comes next week. I...er...' He hesitated, not sure why he was explaining all this. Not entirely sure why she was staying to listen to him. 'I have a lot of work to do,' he added, hating how stuffy that sounded. As if he were a professor of hers, or a grandparent, rather than a man a scant few years older than her who once considered himself her friend. And had... Well, the less he thought about that the better.

'Far be it from me to keep you,' Rowan retorted, and he supposed that he deserved that. He knew that he sounded like a prig, but around Rowan, more than anyone, he couldn't afford to let his guard down. She would be so easy to love. Perhaps if he wasn't quite so aware of that, he could let himself...like her a little more? Could enjoy her being in his life in a peripheral sort of way. But he knew how dangerous that would be. Knew that spending time with her led to wanting her, led to...

He couldn't afford to love her. To love anyone else.

He already loved his family. He loved his job—as head of the business his grandparents and parents had left to him. And the responsibilities that came with them ate up every last shred of energy and reserves that he possessed. There simply wasn't space in his life for him to love anyone or anything else.

When it came to Rowan, he knew that he had to be careful. Because he hadn't guarded himself as well as he should have when they were friends, and it had led exactly where he knew that he couldn't go. Was it lonely, knowing that he was never going to have the thing that he knew he would want, if he allowed himself to be selfish? Of course it was. Some days, it had been so lonely that he hadn't been able to bear it.

But that was a small price to pay. Because he knew that the alternative was hurting the people he loved. He simply couldn't picture a life where he had the time and commitment he would want to give a loving, committed relationship. And so he had decided that that simply couldn't happen for him. He had kept his distance from Rowan and tried to forget her.

His entire adult life had been one carefully considered decision after another—balancing his responsibilities, parsing out his attention where it was needed most. He had protected his family and their business for every minute of the ten years since his parents had decided that they would be happier living in a South American country than facing the consequences of their unorthodox financial arrangements and the enormous bill the HMRC had landed on their doorstep.

No, they had left it to him to try and dig their family company—Kinley, a prestige brand in British fashion for more than a century—out of the financial and legal hole that they had created, not to mention the welfare of his siblings, then at university and boarding school. He'd kept the business afloat, just about. And his siblings? That had fared about as well. Not a great flaming tragedy—yet. But not something that he could look upon with any sense of pride or finality.

It seemed that he had failed, miserably, at the one thing that gave him any chance of protecting his heart. Rowan had been impossible to forget, and that was even before she had turned up on his doorstep. Just like that, all those years of effort had been washed away.

'I guess I'll see you, then,' Rowan said, turning and walking up the stairs without a backward glance.

Jonathan stared after her, praying that she wouldn't turn back and catch him. He shouldn't watch her. Had no right to look at her, and yet he couldn't help himself.

He was going to kill Livia.

CHAPTER TWO

How was Jonathan in the hallway *again*? Rowan asked herself as she came downstairs later that evening.

'Liv's having a shower so I'm going for a walk before dinner,' she threw out there, pointedly not inviting him just so that he would know that she wasn't seeking him out. That was the last thing that she wanted. She would never admit it, but she had been hiding in their room since she had arrived, and the claustrophobia was making it hard to breathe. She just wanted some fresh air, and this far out into the Cotswolds, that basically meant walking or running. She was meant to be resting her legs this week—with a hundred miles to run on Saturday she had to think carefully about every step that she took—but there was no way that she could be cooped up inside the house until then. Maybe she should have followed her first instinct and booked herself on the first train back to London in the morning. She could make her own way back and find an Airbnb for the night before the race.

She walked through to the boot room to find the walking boots that Liv had promised should be in there and tried not to notice Jonathan's footsteps following her. It took every shred of resolve she had not to turn to him. She felt his presence all over her skin, a flush of shame and embarrassment. The worst part of it all was the fact that he still had this effect on her. That seven years after she had last seen him she could still feel his lips against her skin. Feel the way that she had showed him exactly how she felt about him and he couldn't have pushed her away harder if he'd been actively trying to break her heart.

'Rowan, can I have a word?' he said quietly.

'Don't,' she whispered, glancing over her shoulder to make sure that Liv and Caleb weren't about to sneak up on them. The only thing that could make his rejection of her worse would be if other people found out about it, and she could no longer pretend to herself and the whole world that it had never happened. 'It's ancient history,' she added, hoping that she could at least make him believe that she felt that way. She didn't need to pick the scab over that memory any more than she already had.

That was fine. Perfect. There had been a time that she would have teased him about being stuffy and tried to ease some of the atmosphere between him and Livia. When a half-smile from him would sustain her heart for days. She'd always thought that she'd had a way of reading Jonathan, a way of seeing him, that was different from his family. When he'd been pitched into the position of *de facto* parent to Liv, her best friend had seemed to see it as a challenge to re-live her rebellious teenage years. Without complicated family dynamics, her relationship with Jonathan had been simpler. She'd always been able to tease a good mood from him, even when the pressure of his new responsibilities had weighed heavy in the crease of Jonathan's forehead and the new curve of his shoulders as he sat at his desk in the London family home.

She had thought of it as a kindness, at first, to try and cheer him up when Liv was always giving him a hard time. But the reward of each smile grew larger, and she challenged herself to win a grin, a chuckle, a laugh. And by the time she had done all that, she couldn't pretend to herself that she wasn't doing it for herself too. That she didn't get a flush of satisfaction knowing that she could reach him when everyone else received a scowl just for darkening his door. Livia never tired of complaining about what a bear he was with her.

Rowan had thought that what they had was a friendship. That those chats they'd had, over the kettle, or from his office doorway while Liv had cued up a movie or taken a shower, were some of the most genuine, authentic conversations that she'd ever had. And she'd grown to look forward to them. To anticipate the nights that Livia suggested they hang out at her place with a movie rather than go out to a bar or a club. She never told her friend about her conversations with her brother, though. She knew that Livia would laugh at her. Jonathan was someone to ridicule, in her friend's eyes. Not someone to fancy. But God did she fancy him.

He was tall, lithe, sandy-haired. His beard was always as neat as his carefully ironed shirts. She never failed to wonder at that. His whole world had fallen apart, he'd been landed with responsibility for his family and the family business. And instead of drinking overly sweet cocktails and angry-kissing strangers in nightclubs—Livia's chosen coping mechanisms in times of distress—Jonathan had exerted exceptional levels of control over his business, his family and his appearance. Livia hadn't exactly thanked him for it, and in their younger years Rowan had had to bite her tongue and hide her true feelings about Jonathan.

Which meant that she'd never spoken to her best friend about the night when Rowan had decided to lean in to what had felt like a 'moment.'

She and Jonathan had found themselves alone of an evening, while Liv was stuck on a delayed train home, instead of at the movie and pizza night that they'd planned. So Rowan had ended up sharing a pizza and a bottle of wine with Jonathan instead. But they hadn't got round to the movie. Instead, they'd found themselves talking on the sofa. For hours. The windows had grown dark while they chatted, and they'd moved closer and closer, at one point pulling a blanket across both of them when a chill had reached them. Looking back, she hadn't been able to work out how they had moved so close together. She knew that she hadn't done it on purpose. But at some point, her feet had found their way into Jonathan's lap. His arm had fallen over the back of the sofa and started playing with her hair. An hour later that same arm was around her shoulders, and she wasn't sure who leaned in first but their lips were brushing together, first gently and then with an urgency that she had never felt before.

Hands had wandered and Jonathan's mouth had explored her jaw, her throat, her collarbones. Somehow, she had found herself lying back, Jonathan between her thighs, her legs around his waist pulling him closer.

She hadn't had the brain function to properly think about where it had been going, all she'd known was that she'd had no intention of stopping. It was everything that she wanted, everything that she had been waiting for. Jonathan was everything that she'd wanted, she'd realised, as she pushed one hand into his hair and the other under his shirt.

But then he'd pulled away, panting, and where she'd expected to see her own desire reflected in his face there was only shock. Something that was terribly close to horror.

He'd apologised and pulled his clothes back into place and turned his back on her, while she'd sat up on the sofa, asking herself what had gone wrong, what *she'd* done wrong to put that expression on his face.

'I'm sorry, I shouldn't have…' he'd stammered. And then looked at the bottle of wine they'd been sharing and blanched. 'You've been drinking. You don't even know what you're doing. Oh, my God, you're barely more than a kid. I'm sorry, Rowan.'

She'd not waited to hear the specifics of what he was sorry about. She'd pulled her T-shirt down over her breasts, pushed her hair back into a ponytail and got out of there before the tears could start. It had been years since that humiliating night and she had been lulled into a false sense of security, believing that hers and Jonathan's paths simply wouldn't cross again.

She had told herself that Jonathan probably didn't even remember it. Probably didn't even remember *her*. But as soon as she'd seen him standing in the hallway, she realised how wrong she had been. Not only did he remember, he was still visibly cringing at her mistake. Never in her adult life had she felt as mortified as she did in the moment that he'd told her that she didn't know what she was doing. She'd realised as soon as Jonathan kissed her how long she'd been waiting and hoping for that to happen, that she'd not been able to admit it even to herself, because she'd never thought that it would happen. And then it had happened, and as soon as Jonathan's brain had caught up with his libido he'd blamed it on having had too much to drink and all but thrown her out.

She had been under the mistaken impression that she no longer knew how to burn with shame and self-loathing, but her mind was filled with the words that she'd heard over and over again at school: that she was a freak, that no one would ever fancy her. That no one would find a girl who was taller than him sexy. Words that had continued to echo long after she'd left the classroom behind.

She'd thought that the therapy she'd invested in handsomely over the years had undone the damage that a decade of school bullying had created. That had been proved laughably false as her face burned and hands shook, all while Jonathan regarded her with what could only be pity.

Well. That had been when she was just twenty-one, barely out of university. She was older now and she knew better. She knew she could look at Jonathan and feel nothing, except perhaps sympathy for the girl she had been, with her hang-ups and her insecurities about her body, and her secret tears over the teasing she had endured day in, day out at school. Which she'd thought Jonathan was above until he'd hurt her worst of all.

She could feel him standing behind her while she found Liv's walking boots and pulled them on, tugging hard on the laces.

'Rowan?'

She looked up at his earnest tone of voice, and tried to prevent herself melting just a little bit at the sight of his concern.

'I didn't know you would be here this week,' she told him. It seemed like the most important thing, for him to know that she hadn't intentionally crashed this family week. That she hadn't chosen to spend a week in a house with him. If it had been up to her, she wouldn't ever see him again. 'My race at the weekend starts a couple of miles away and Liv asked if I'd like to spend a few days here, and… I wouldn't have come if I'd known.'

'You don't have to avoid me,' he replied, with a coolness that made her shrink away from him. Because somehow she'd rather that Jonathan was avoiding her than indifferent: indifference from someone she'd once felt so *much* for was unbearable.

'I didn't say that I was avoiding you,' she rebutted him, childishly, because it had to be obvious to him that she had, of course, been avoiding him. And the reason why had to be entirely self-evident.

Jonathan pinched the bridge of his nose. Rowan got the feeling that he was finding this very trying, and she couldn't make herself feel sorry for it.

'Okay, we're not avoiding each other. And we're not making an effort to see one another. We're just two people who exist independently in Livia's orbit.'

'That seems like an accurate assessment,' Rowan confirmed. She allowed herself a quick peek across at him, but looked away as soon as she realised he was watching her. 'Honestly, Jonathan, it's fine,' she lied with a resigned sigh. 'We're fine. If you were going to talk about what I think you were going to talk about, there's no need. I haven't thought about it for years before tonight. I just want some fresh air and to stretch my legs.'

Relief was evident in his face, and she tried not to be too hurt by the evidence that he was so keen that they both keep what had happened very much in the past. 'I'll probably get the train home in the morning anyway, so you won't have to worry about seeing me again. I mean, we made it seven years before this, maybe we won't ever see each other again after tonight.'

CHAPTER THREE

ROWAN HAD STOMPED around the grounds of the manor for an hour, trying to get Jonathan's face out of her mind. She was past this. She'd spent so much time and money trying to get him out of her head. Had been on so many dates to try and find someone who would make her forget him.

But nothing had worked. Yes, in time, she'd thought of him less. There were times when she'd met someone funny and cute and kind, and one date had turned into two had turned into three. And then when she'd taken the plunge and thought about sleeping with them, Jonathan's face had got stuck in her head, and somehow no one had quite measured up to the man who had broken her heart.

Which was how she had found herself as the last virgin in London, desperate to move on, but never quite getting there. Now here she was, stuck with him in a picture-perfect house in the countryside. As she'd walked around the gardens, an idea had started forming, one that she couldn't quite convince herself was completely terrible. All this time, she'd clung on to what had happened that night, to the way that Jonathan had rejected her. She'd let that rejection reinforce all the worst things that she'd ever heard or believed about herself. Trying to forget it—forget him—trying to pretend that Jonathan didn't exist, hadn't worked. So perhaps she needed to do something else to get past this.

What if she could have a do-over? A chance to do things on her terms this time: kiss him, have things end without her lying in a heap of shame and self-loathing, call it quits. Maybe then she could have some closure and move on. It had to be worth a shot—after all, nothing else had worked, and she couldn't stay hung up on him for ever.

When she'd finished exploring the gardens, she'd gone back upstairs to the room that she was sharing with Liv, her stomach rumbling, her mind buzzing with her new idea. With perfect timing Caleb had knocked at their bedroom door and asked if they wanted to order pizza.

Rowan had always had a soft spot for Caleb. He'd still been away at boarding school when his parents had done a bunk, and she'd never seen as much of him as she had of Livia and Jonathan. Now, as an adult, he was even more of a mystery. She'd never been exactly sure what his job was, only that it was something frighteningly clever with computers and there was almost certainly something to do with cryptocurrency, and she'd heard him speaking at least three different languages in Zoom calls since they'd arrived.

Liv and Rowan ordered their usual, and then heard a string of message alerts coming from Caleb's room and he looked behind him. 'Can someone go down and ask Jonathan if he wants anything while I deal with that?'

When she glanced across at Liv, her friend was making puppy-dog eyes, which could realistically only mean one thing. 'Will you do it? Please?' Liv and Jonathan's relationship had been strained ever since he'd been expected to take over the parenting role. They barely spoke now, unless Jonathan insisted on it, and Rowan had no desire for them to start arguing. It was probably best for everyone if they stayed out of one another's way this week.

Besides that, it was the perfect excuse to go and talk to him—work out if this ridiculous plan of hers was even going to be possible. There was no point in pinning all her hopes for moving on—on the chance of kissing him again—if he wasn't at all interested. She wasn't going to do this unless she was sure that he wanted to. And she wouldn't be able to find out if she was always hiding upstairs.

'Yeah, I'll go ask him,' she said, hoping that she was making it sound casual. She just had to know whether this idea of hers even stood a chance.

She made her way down the stairs and towards the library, because she knew without even having to think about it that that was where she would find Jonathan. Always in the room with the highest concentration of books. Here at the manor, it was the library, with its floor-to-ceiling bookshelves, sliding ladder and French doors where she could picture him looking moodily out at the gardens.

With just socks on her feet, she barely made a

noise moving through the house, even on the scuffed old flagstones of the entrance hall. She realised how stealthy she had been when she reached the door of the library, to find Jonathan at the ocean-liner-sized desk. Head leaning on one hand, train track creases across his forehead and between his eyebrows.

His gaze was fixed on the laptop screen, and she saw his eyes moving steadily side to side as he concentrated on whatever it was he was reading. She allowed herself a moment to watch him, aware even as she did so that it was both foolish and self-indulgent. Any minute now he was going to look up, or Liv was going to appear behind her, and she would have to explain herself. But it had been so long since she'd let herself look. When they'd first met, she'd been too shy. Averting her eyes, her cheeks on fire any time they had been in the same room, no matter talking to one another. But as their friendship had progressed, she'd grown bolder, meeting his gaze and holding it while they talked. But that confidence to look at him as an equal had been shattered years ago, and now she had to take what she could get. Like spying on him from a doorway while he was working. She cleared her throat, breaking the silence so he'd have no reason to think she'd done anything but just walk up.

For a moment, just as he looked up, she'd been convinced that he'd been about to smile. But it couldn't have been more than a trick of the light, because it was gone by the time she had blinked.

'Yes?' he asked, shattering all her illusions of intimacy.

For a moment she nearly lost her nerve and escaped back upstairs. But she was here for a reason, and she wasn't going to let his rudeness put her off her goal. Now that she'd thought it, kissing him again seemed like the only way she was ever going to leave that disastrous evening behind her. She needed to do this. She *was* going to get over him, and then she *was* going to go the whole of the rest of her life without thinking about him ever again. 'Caleb's ordering pizza,' she said, in a voice that she hoped gave away none of the above. 'Do you want anything?'

'Caleb could have asked me himself,' Jonathan observed, and Rowan felt her heart plummet to somewhere around the floor. Could he really not bear to talk to her even to give her his pizza order? She kept her face smooth, as she had had to learn to do at school, so he couldn't see how much that affected her.

'He asked me to,' she said calmly, refusing to be hurt that he was pushing her away. She'd simply not let him. She knew how Jonathan built walls when he was stressed—which was always—and they'd crumbled for her before.

She couldn't quite believe that she was putting herself through this again, but if she didn't, what did she have to look forward to—a lifetime of comparing every man that she met to him, and never quite being satisfied?

'I wasn't planning on stopping for dinner,' he said, and she could see that he was itching to get back to whatever he was doing on his laptop. He needed to take a break, but nothing would make that less likely to happen than to point it out to him.

'I wasn't asking you to,' she said shortly, not trusting herself to say more.

He sighed and rubbed at his forehead. 'Fine. I can stop for half an hour,' he said, though she hadn't challenged him. 'Just order me whatever you're having.'

He glanced up at her, a touch of pink in his cheeks, and she wondered what he had been thinking. Her smile as she looked down at her phone was involuntary and entirely unwelcome. 'Food will be here in an hour,' she told him, and turned in the direction of the kitchen. She found the larder and the wine rack, poured herself a glass of red wine and sat at the table, seeing off a few emails on her phone while she sipped at it and waited for the pizza.

She was still sitting at the table when the doorbell rang. She walked into the hallway with her eyes fixed on her phone and walked straight into Jonathan as he exited the library.

'Oof, what are you—'

'I was going to get the—'

She stepped away from him, brushing down her clothes and refusing to be embarrassed just because her chest had knocked accidentally against his. She was a grown-up. A professional. She was an accountant, for goodness' sake. A woman who had decided what she wanted and was confident that she could get it. That's what she would tell herself, every day, until she believed it—or until Jonathan proved her right.

Which, seven years of therapy later, would probably be easier.

She hadn't moved, she realised when the bell rang again, and nor had Jonathan. His hand had come to rest on her upper arm, to steady her, she supposed, though they were practically the same height and she wasn't prone to toppling over. But the weight and warmth of his hand on her arm was sparking heat through her whole body. She'd forgotten what it did to her when she was the sole focus of his attention, when he looked her in the eye and it felt like whatever else was happening in the world it didn't matter in that minute. That when their eyes met, it conjured up some dimension where only they existed, and the real world couldn't touch them. This was what had led her into so much trouble before, and she didn't know whether she should be pleased or terrified that that place still existed.

Her cheeks warmed as she waited for him to step back. But he didn't. Was he feeling this too? she wondered. Was he remembering how good it used to feel, when they looked at each other like this? When everything else fell away, and it was just this?

'Was that the door?' Liv asked from above them, where she had appeared at the top of the stairs.

Rowan stepped away from Jonathan with a start and moved quickly to the front door, before the delivery driver decided no one was home and disappeared with their dinner. Before Jonathan had a chance to guess at what she'd been thinking and feeling. 'Food's here,' she called up, her voice shaking slightly.

CHAPTER FOUR

ROWAN WASN'T A kid any more. He didn't know why that should be a surprise, given that she was the same age as Liv, whose birthday he remembered every year. With their parents absent and their grandparents dead, it was yet another thing that was his responsibility.

Somehow the change in Rowan still took him by surprise. She'd been the tallest woman he knew since he'd met her. As a young woman, those long limbs had given her an awkward air, and she'd seemed to want to keep her body as small as possible. But that had fallen away as they had become friends—and he was sure that they had been friends.

Had she seen the way that he had started to look at her, how his gaze had lingered on her hair, her long legs, the way that she smiled when they talked, and she was her most relaxed self?

Until the day it had all gone wrong. He cringed to think of it now, how close he had come to losing control, and all the ways that he could have hurt Rowan and himself if he hadn't come to his senses and put a stop to it when he had.

They had spent the whole evening together, that day. He couldn't even remember now what they'd talked about. He couldn't even remember where Liv was. He was just so pleased to see Rowan on her own, for once. They had spent hours together, laughing, mostly. And it had been the first time since his parents had left that he'd felt truly relaxed. Had been able to stop worrying about the business and Liv and Caleb and what the hell he was going to do about the financial black hole at the middle of it.

The freedom of just *not worrying* for a few hours must have gone to his head. He'd felt positively drunk on it. It had seemed like the most natural thing in the world that they had moved closer and closer together as the night had gone on. That when a strand of Rowan's hair had fallen by his hand on the back of the sofa that he'd picked it up and let it slide through his fingers. When he looked down and realised that he'd used the arm around her shoulders to bring her closer that he'd brush his lips across hers.

The first touch of her lips had been like a match to dry kindling. He'd been utterly consumed by it. He'd acted entirely on instinct, in a way that he hadn't allowed himself for years. And who knows how far he would have let it go if he hadn't caught sight of the empty wine bottle out of the corner of his eye as he was shifting to press Rowan deeper into the sofa cushions.

It had suddenly crashed into him, what a colossal mistake he was making. Because Rowan deserved so much more than he could give her. So much better than to make a decision like this when she was tipsy and not in possession of all of the facts. Because he knew without a doubt that he didn't have room in his life for a relationship. Not for the sort of relationship that he knew he would want with Rowan. The type where he would want to love her and cherish her and protect her. Every minute of his life was spent worrying about the people he loved. The business he needed to keep afloat. He couldn't spare a minute to loving anyone else without something—someone—else suffering.

She deserved someone who could take care of her. Not someone who would take advantage of her after a bottle of wine and not have any time for her in the morning.

And because he was an idiot who never missed an opportunity to make things worse, he'd said something about her not knowing what she was doing, something about how young she was, and she'd disappeared from his life since that day. He thought that he'd never see her again.

She looked so different now to the last time that he had seen her, and it was harder than ever to ignore how he felt about her.

She held herself differently: her shoulders pushed back, her spine straight, hands confidently on her hips. She was taking up space, unapologetically, and observing him impassively. He hardly recognised the woman who had once felt like one of his closest friends. She was undeniably beautiful. He had always thought so, objectively speaking. But there was something mesmerising about her now. How was he meant to sit across from her and eat pizza without talking to her, explaining himself? Without doing something incredibly stupid, like falling for her?

He scrubbed a hand over his face, leaning against the door frame of the library, where Rowan had been just a few moments before. Watching as Liv and Rowan chatted effortlessly as they carried the pizzas through to the kitchen. He couldn't remember the last time he'd spoken to anyone with the ease that he saw in their friendship. No, that wasn't true. He remembered exactly when he'd last had a conversation like that. With Rowan. Right before he'd ruined it.

She was beautiful, sitting across the table from him, her body all long lines and hard-won muscle. She moved with intention, like she was aware of every single fibre of her limbs, placing her feet deliberately as she walked. Crossing her ankles and tucking her feet under her chair. He wanted to hook them with his own. Pull them out where he could accidentally knock against them and get her attention.

They passed the pizza boxes around while the other three chatted and he knew that he should make conversation, but he couldn't think of what to say that wouldn't make things worse.

He shouldn't be thinking about Rowan. He should be thinking about work. He had told himself that he didn't have time to stop for dinner, and here he was, away from his desk, all because she was here. He didn't know how he was going to pay his employees next month, and he was wasting time eating pizza, all because he couldn't bear the thought that Rowan was so close and he couldn't see her.

He couldn't afford to be distracted like this. His parents and then his grandparents had made the business and the family his responsibility. And he couldn't put it all at risk again. It was the reason that he had had to push Rowan away that night.

He had spent days expending his mental energy on how to pay his staff's wages and his suppliers from a pot of money that did not equal the sum of those numbers. He had to be one hundred percent focused.

That was why he had always kept his relationships brief, casual and with like-minded people who were no more interested in commitment than he was. It could never be like that with Rowan. One of his fundamental rules in his love life was that he could walk away with no one hurt any time the business or the family demanded more of him. Even before anything had started, he knew that a relationship with Rowan could never end that way. She simply wasn't someone he could walk away from.

He glanced up at Rowan listening with interest to Caleb talking about his work, and he couldn't take his eyes off her, licking her fingers when they got greasy from the pizza. He didn't realise Liv was trying to get his attention until she waved her hand in front of his face.

'You spaced out,' she said, as he raised an eyebrow in her direction.

'Sorry. Was just thinking about work,' he lied, hoping that no one at the table realised the true direction his thoughts had taken. The last thing he needed was Liv knowing that he was crushing on her friend. Wait, was that what he was doing? He froze, with a slice of pizza halfway to his mouth. Was that what was going on here? Because he had spent years telling himself that he missed their friendship. But he was distinctly aware that he had just thought the word 'crush.' He glanced at Rowan, a little panicked, and felt a tug in his chest as she laughed, doing battle with a long thread of melted mozzarella.

Was this a crush? The way that he felt when he looked at Rowan? He tried to think about it logically. He had been surprised to see her here, but undoubtedly pleased, once the initial shock had burned away. His stomach had fallen when he'd realised how their conversation was getting away from him. How he'd thought of her just now when he'd been thinking about relationships. He felt suddenly cold. Because it seemed so obvious that he had a crush on Rowan. Somehow he couldn't understand how it had taken him so long to realise it. Of course you didn't keep thinking of someone for years since you'd last seen them just because she was your sister's friend who you'd kissed one time. She was special to him. Always had been.

He had to deal with this. Right, like it was that simple. It *had* to be that simple. Now that he had recognised these feelings for what they were, he would be better prepared to deal with them. He would keep his distance from her, bury this…interest…in her deep down and get through this week.

From the look on her face when he glanced up at her

just now, she wasn't exactly glad to be in his company. All he had to do was stay out of her way.

'I want to explore some more tomorrow,' Rowan said, trying to bring him into the conversation. 'I'm going to see if the maze is still navigable. What are you planning on doing with your day?'

'I need to work,' he said, reflexively, knowing that the less time he spent with her the better for his peace of mind. He had spoken to her for barely ten minutes in total today, and he was already stopping work to have dinner and spacing out thinking about her. 'Any spare time I get needs to be spent sorting through Grandmother's study before we hand over the keys to the estate agent. I was going to ask Liv to do it, but I guess I'll have to now. There might be papers in there that need sending to the archives. I don't want to lose anything important.'

'Then don't sell the house?' Liv suggested from the other side of the table, with her eyes narrowed at him.

He tried not to let his irritation show. Liv had been pissed off with him since he had first told her that he was selling the manor. She had no idea that it was breaking his heart to do it, but he didn't have the funds to stop the place disintegrating around them. And he had no intention of leaving wages unpaid just so that they could keep hold of their country retreat. He was just glad that he and his siblings had inherited their properties from their grandparents separately. Liv had inherited a London town house and Caleb a villa on Lake Como. This way, he could sell off his assets and generate some cash without them having to know how dire things really were. He had no desire to burden her with that information. But it did make snidey asides like that one difficult to swallow.

Jonathan gritted his teeth. 'It's my house, and I'm selling it, Liv. If there's anything inside that you want to keep, you're welcome to it. But you're not going to change my mind.'

'Cut it out, you two,' Rowan interrupted, drawing both of their attention. 'Liv, I'm sure you didn't invite me here to be stuck in the middle of a family argument so let's change the subject.'

Even Caleb looked up on her, a surprised grin on his face. 'Nice one, Rowan.'

She shrugged. Jonathan knew that he was looking at her still, startled. He had never, ever heard Rowan raise her voice before, and he felt slightly shamed that he was the cause of it, and for squabbling with his little sister, no less.

She shouldn't have snapped at them, but she couldn't help it. They were all so…careless with one another. If she'd had siblings— default playmates and defenders and allies—maybe her childhood would have been easier. But she'd been an only child to quiet parents and hadn't made friends at school. Maybe she wouldn't have seen herself as such an easy target for the bullies if she'd had a sister at school with her; she could have fought back, knowing she would have someone to defend her. She'd mentioned the problems to her parents, her teachers, but they'd brushed it off as 'kids being kids' and she hadn't wanted to cause a fuss.

Her height had made her a visible target—she'd been six feet tall by the time she was fifteen—and her loneliness had made her vulnerable. When she had arrived at university, still alone, terrified that her school experience was about to repeat itself, it was pure luck that she found herself sharing a flat with Liv, who turned out to be her platonic soulmate, looking for people to love in the absence of her parents, recently departed for South America. They'd both been studying at the business school—accountancy for Rowan, marketing for Liv—and it had been her first true friendship. Gradually, it had transformed her. It had been Liv who had taken her to her first yoga class, where she'd discovered for the first time the wondrous things her body could *do*. That it was so much more than the way it looked. And a friend from yoga who had taken her with her on a run for the first time, which was when she had discovered how it felt to challenge her body, and have it come through for her.

It was a work in progress. Running for half an hour—which had once felt impossible—had proved to her that she shouldn't prejudge what she was capable of. Over the course of the last few years, she'd pushed herself further and further, to the point where she'd finished a marathon and thought to herself, *Why not just keep going?* It was in ultra-endurance running—races of thirty miles, fifty and, in the last year, a hundred—that she had found the strength to still her mind and quiet the critical voices that sounded so much like her childhood tormentors.

But she hadn't had so much resilience the last time that she'd seen Jonathan, when he'd knocked her back and left her feeling like the stupid kid he obviously saw her as.

This wasn't the girl he remembered, Jonathan thought again, the one who had carried herself awkwardly, uncomfortable in her own body, whose voice he had had to strain to hear.

She had a confidence and a sureness that hadn't been there before, and he liked it. It wasn't even a conscious thought. Just something deep inside him that told him that he wanted more of this. More of her. He'd take more of being yelled at by her for squabbling with his sister if that was all she was offering, as long as it was *more*. *Except...* Except then his brain caught up with itself, and he realised his mistake. He couldn't *have* more. He couldn't even want it. There wasn't room in his life for 'more.' If he started something with Rowan, then what was going to slip? Would it be the business? His family? Both of those were only holding together by a thread. The business because he kept throwing his savings at the black hole the bank accounts had become. His family because they didn't know how bad things were.

He couldn't let himself want something that would distract him from keeping it all afloat. He'd been

forced to take responsibility for it all when he was
barely an adult and had been trying to do his best at
it ever since. He'd made it the most important part of
his life since he was twenty-eight, and even that was
never enough.

CHAPTER FIVE

'WHAT THE HELL?' Jonathan muttered, the banging at the front door pulling his thoughts away from next month's financials for the first time in hours. Liv and Rowan had decided to go to the pub hours ago— Rowan had still been talking about getting a train back to London in the morning, and Liv trying to convince her to stay. He'd been at his desk ever since, moving numbers around in his spreadsheet in the hope that they would magically multiply. He glanced at the clock in the corner of the screen—half past eleven—and assumed that it must be Liv and Rowan back from the pub. But why the hell didn't Liv just use her key to get in? At the sound of another crash at the door, he pushed his chair back and walked across the hall to the front door. He opened it wide, and Liv and Rowan practically fell across the threshold.

'What the hell,' he asked again, wedging his shoulder under Liv's arm on instinct, taking her weight as Rowan struggled at her other side. 'What happened?' he asked, as Liv cried out in pain. He had assumed she was just drunk, but her expression was creased and tense, rather than the dreamy vacancy she got after a drink too many.

'Twisted my ankle,' Liv said through another hiss.

'She's broken it, I think,' Rowan said, stopping for a moment to catch her breath. 'We're probably going to have to get it looked at.'

'Are *you* okay?' Jonathan asked Rowan, catching her eye. She was grimacing too, and he knew that with a race coming up an injury would be devastating.

'I'm fine,' she said. 'Have just carried this one the best part of a mile, that's all.'

'Here, I've got her,' Jonathan said, wrapping an arm around Liv's waist and taking all her weight so that Rowan could take a break. Her face was lined around the eyes and she didn't look much better off than his sister did. He kept a watch on her in his peripheral vision, just to be sure that she was okay.

'How did it happen?' he asked, as he lowered Liv onto a bench on the other side of the hall and then looked around for his car keys. He turned to Rowan for an answer, since Liv was currently pressing her hands to her own face.

'We were walking back and she caught her foot in a foxhole,' Rowan said. 'I couldn't get a proper look in the dark, but it seems pretty swollen and she can't put any weight on it.'

'You should have called me,' he snapped, his tone sharper than he'd intended. He regretted it the moment he saw the hurt on Rowan's face. *This* was why he had wanted her to leave. Because it was impossible for him to be around people he cared about without hurting

them. All he wanted to do was protect his family, and
yet doing so left him so strained and stressed that it
came out like *this*, angry and accusatory, when all he
wanted to do was care.

He'd proved that the last time he'd spent any time
with Rowan that he couldn't let his feelings for her
show without hurting her. The last thing he wanted
to do was repeat that.

'No signal,' she told him, sitting beside Liv and
pulling her hands from her face. 'Doing okay under
there?' she asked. Liv replied with a creased brow and
pulled her hands back over her face.

'I'm sorry, I didn't mean to snap,' Jonathan said,
catching Rowan's hand to get her attention, and then
dropping it again when he realised what he'd done.
'I've got my keys,' he said, picking Liv back up. 'Can
you get the doors if I carry her?'

'Rowan, come with us?' Liv asked over his shoulder, and he could hardly argue with his sister when
she was in so much pain. Rowan told Caleb, who had
appeared on the stairs, what was happening, and then
led the way out to the car.

Once Liv had been X-rayed and a broken ankle di-
agnosed, and had been plastered and medicated and
discharged, it was almost light outside. He'd driven
home along the winding lanes, got his sister settled in
bed and then found himself alongside Rowan in the
kitchen, in the small hours of the morning, in a house
that was silent apart from the distant rattle of water
pipes as he filled the kettle.

'Tea?' Jonathan asked, because although what he really wanted was a whisky, he didn't trust himself to give up even a smidge of self-control around Rowan, not when he had hurt her before, and knew he could again. It had been a very long night with very little sleep, and he knew better than to test his self-control. He wondered what she'd been thinking that night, when he'd come so close to forgetting all of the reasons why he couldn't give in to everything that he wanted and kiss her like he did when he was dreaming, when he played out everything in his sleep that he couldn't have in his waking hours.

'Chamomile, if you have any,' Rowan asked with a sigh, dropping onto the bench by the oak table in the centre of the room and bringing him back to his senses. 'I don't want anything that's going to keep me awake.'

'Are you sure you're not hurt too? I wish you'd let the doctors check you over, especially with your race coming up,' Jonathan said, watching her with concern as he placed the kettle on the range, only dragging his eyes away from her to hunt for the tea she wanted. He didn't know how to care for her without hurting her, so he concentrated on making her tea, wishing she would read into it how much she and their friendship had meant to him, and how sorry he was that he had spoilt what they had by hurting her, even though he was hurting himself more.

He placed the mug in front of her, and hesitated, before she moved along the bench to make room for him. 'I'm fine, just tired.'

'Thank you,' he said, 'for helping her. You must be exhausted.'

'She's my friend,' Rowan said. 'Of course I was going to help her.' Well, that put him in his place. Reminding him that it didn't matter how grateful he was to her, none of this had been for him. It didn't tell him anything about what she felt for him. Or what she had felt for him once.

'You know she'll hate having to let me look after her,' Jonathan added, which was true. And also the perfect excuse for Rowan to have to stay, because despite her mentioning the first train back to London earlier, he couldn't imagine her leaving now, not when Liv was going to be off her feet for days, at least.

'You're probably right,' she said, with a despondent look that could only mean that she was thinking the same thing. 'The more you tell her to take it easy the more she'll want to resist.' Rowan smiled. 'I think you two bring out the worst in each other.'

Jonathan gave a sad, helpless laugh at Rowan's assessment of his relationship with his sister, the one that he'd worked so hard at for so long, and only seemed to make worse. 'I only ever want what's best for her,' he said, trying to keep the pain out of his voice.

Rowan shocked him, reaching out and touching his hand. 'I know,' she said, her voice soft. 'I know Liv doesn't always appreciate you looking out for her, but I can see that you do it because you care. She's lucky to have you.'

He snorted. It was a kind thought, but he knew his

sister didn't consider herself lucky. And why should she, when she had lost their parents and been left with a clueless brother who only seemed capable of making her hate him. Did Rowan see that he had been protecting her too, when he'd stopped her from kissing him back? Or had she only resented his overprotectiveness, as Liv always had?

Rowan must have only just realised what she had done with her hand, because she looked at it as if it belonged to someone else, before snatching it away and tucking it under her thigh, where neither of them could see it. He could see as she realised that she had let her guard down and needed to raise her defences. He wished there was something he could do to stop the stiffening of her shoulders, the blankness that she painted over her face.

'Rowan,' he said at last. 'I think maybe we should talk properly about the last time that we saw one another. I'm afraid that I may have given you the impression that—'

'I thought there was an attraction there,' Rowan said, cutting him off gently. 'I was young and maybe I misread the signals. I don't think we need to go over it all again.'

'Rowan, you weren't wrong,' Jonathan said, his voice low.

She held his gaze while she tried to understand his meaning. She hadn't *imagined* that he was attracted to her. Then why had he—?

'It just wasn't a good—' he started again, and this time she held up a hand to stop him finishing his sentence. She didn't need to know which part of it was bad. The fact that she'd kissed him or the kiss itself, or perhaps just her. She'd had enough voices in her head over the years telling her which parts of herself she should hate, and she didn't want to add his into the mix. She'd worked hard over the years to resist the worst thoughts that she had about herself. To retrain her brain not to believe the insults that had been hurled her way through her adolescence and were so resistant to being unstuck.

She was meant to be trying to make him want to kiss her again, not reminding herself of all the ways she had been hurt before. This wasn't going to help her get over him. To stop thinking about him. To stop judging every man she met against how much she had wanted him. How good it had felt to be close to him.

His long fingers wrapped around her wrist, and he lowered her hand, slowly, until he was holding it between them. Jonathan's words had hit somewhere deep and painful. He was attracted to her, then, but hadn't *wanted* her. It hadn't been enough. *She* hadn't been enough.

If she was going to change what those voices said, to move on from what had happened that night, she needed for them to stop talking about the past. See what there was between them now, if anything, and how she could use that to get on with her life. He let out a sigh that made her nervous, pulling her spine a little straighter to counter the deepest habit of trying to make herself disappear. 'I just want…' Jonathan said, glancing down at their joined hands, and only now seeming to realise what he had done. He took a deep breath. 'I would really like it if we could get back to how we were before. When we were friends.'

She forced herself to smile…because she could take that, for now. It was somewhere to start from. They *had* been friends, once. They had been easy with each other. And he hadn't denied that he had been attracted to her. She hadn't been wrong.

Whatever had gone wrong that night, it hadn't been because he didn't want her. The knowledge that she had been right about that settled something deep inside her. That even at twenty-one with no experience and eyes for only this man, she'd been right when she'd known how he looked at her.

With that knowledge, her instincts for how Jonathan might feel about her now suddenly felt that little bit surer. Her plan to kiss him and move on that little bit more achievable.

'I'd like that,' she said. 'I hate how awkward things have been. I miss how it used to be.'

She pulled her hand gently away from him and then looked up to meet his eye. 'Okay,' he said, his expression warm, reminding her of when they'd been friends and she'd managed to convince herself that he wanted more. 'Friends.'

She wondered if he could hear all the things she was trying so hard not to say. Whatever else had gone wrong that night, she clung to that grain of certainty that Jonathan had given her. Because she wanted to know that she could trust her judgement. That when she caught him looking at her the way he had been tonight, she wasn't imagining the heat she saw in his eyes.

He had used the past tense before: *'Rowan, you weren't wrong.'* Did that translate into the present? Did he still find her attractive? Would he kiss her again?

She watched him watching her. His eyes rested on her face now, but she'd seen the way that they'd swept up and then down her body, lingering, before he'd realised she was watching him. She couldn't seem to shake the idea that she'd had in the garden earlier: what if she had the opportunity to finish what they'd started. Then could she stop carrying round this embarrassing torch for him? The one that seemed to get in the way of her forming something meaningful with anyone who wasn't him.

They were going to be thrown together more than ever now that Liv was stuck in bed with her ankle in plaster. And there wasn't any possibility of her going back to London tomorrow, as she'd thought about doing when she'd realised that Jonathan was at the manor.

'It's late,' she said, picking up her mug of tea and standing, knowing that she should at least sleep on this idea of hers before she did something that couldn't be taken back. 'Or early. Either way I should get to bed.'

Jonathan smiled, stood up at the same time as she did. 'So, I'll see you in the morning? Later in the morning, I mean.'

'Yeah. I'll be here. Liv will need me,' she said simply. Jonathan breathed a sigh.

'Then I'll see you later,' he said to her back as she walked from the room.

CHAPTER SIX

'How's Liv?' Jonathan asked Rowan as she walked into the kitchen after she'd finally managed a few hours of sleep. He was sitting at the table, laptop in front of him, and looking like he hadn't slept at all. She resisted the urge to pull the computer from him and send him off to bed.

Rowan gave him a grim smile. 'She's a trooper but needs some more pain meds. I'll make her some lunch to have with them. Do you want anything?'

'How about I make the bagels and you make the coffee,' Jonathan said, stretching his arms over his head as he got up from the table and then holding his hand out for the bread knife she'd picked up. Rowan looked down at his palm for a moment, enjoying the way he was reaching out for her. And handed over the knife, shivering when her fingers brushed against his. He glanced up at her, met her eye for a fraction of a second. Was that…something? He'd certainly seemed affected by it. But it was impossible to know whether it was in a good way or bad. She was careful how she moved around him as they buttered bagels and frothed milk and brewed coffee. Eventually, she had a tray heavily laden for her and Liv, and Jonathan leaned back against the worktop.

'You're sure you don't want me to carry that upstairs for you?' he asked. She knew Liv would have rolled her eyes and sighed, unable to see his desire to help as anything other than a desire to control her.

'It's fine,' she said with a careful smile. 'I've got it.' Jonathan nodded, and she knew that he was reining in his habitual need to insist, something he seemed quite capable of doing with her, but found impossible with his little sister.

She climbed the stairs easily, passed the click-clack sound of a keyboard coming from Caleb's room and pushed the door to her and Liv's room open with her shoulder. Only to be greeted by the sound of Liv's deep, resonant snores. Rowan had been grateful, in the end, to escape that sound by getting a couple of hours' sleep on the sofa in the family room—the only option left to her given that all the other bedrooms were damp and leaking. Even so, it had been draughty in there with the fire burned out, and the antique couch not exactly comfortable.

She left the tray on a side table, picked up her mug and plate and tiptoed out of the room. Liv had slept badly last night, and all her energy was going into healing her ankle. She'd wake when she needed her meds—there was no reason to disturb her before then. Rowan headed downstairs, wondering whether she would find the kitchen empty. But Jonathan was still in there, his long, lean form leaning against the counter with an ease she was sure she'd never achieve, re-gardless of how much yoga she did. She pulled herself up and reminded herself of the principle of non-vio-lence—which applied just as much to oneself as it did to others. She needed to remember that accepting her body was an active choice; it would be all too easy to fall back into old habits.

Jonathan raised an eyebrow—presumably at her being back so soon.

'Liv was asleep,' she explained, taking a seat at the kitchen table and sipping her coffee. 'Noisily,' she added with a smile. 'There's no way I'm sharing a bed with her tonight.'

Jonathan choked briefly on his bagel. 'You're still planning on leaving?' he asked, banging his chest with a fist to dislodge the bagel.

Rowan narrowed her eyes at him. 'I only meant our room. I don't know if it was the meds or what but her snoring was ridiculous. I only managed to drop off once I gave up and moved to the family room for a couple of hours.'

'But you can't sleep there all night,' Jonathan de-clared in an authoritative tone that made her bristle. She didn't need to be made to feel like a stupid kid. Least of all by him.

'Why not?' she asked, folding her arms across her chest and glaring at him.

'Because it can't possibly be comfortable, for a start,' Jonathan said. 'Perhaps if you were Liv's height.'

She glared harder. 'Well, there's not much I can do about that.'

Jonathan looked a little surprised by her tone and held out his hands in a gesture of conciliation. 'I just meant you can't be comfortable there.'

'Well, I'm not sharing with Liv, and all the other rooms are taken. It's only a few days,' she said with a shrug.

'Take my bed,' Jonathan said, and she could see that he had surprised himself. Well, as if he was surprised, then remembered the way that he thought everyone's problems were his to solve and refused to accept that he didn't have to take responsibility for every single person he met.

'You don't need to worry about this, Jonathan. About me, I mean. If there aren't enough beds to go around, then someone has to take the sofa and I don't mind. I'm not taking your bed.'

'I can share with Caleb,' Jonathan countered, a hand rubbing at the back of his neck, and she wondered if he was regretting his offer already. And then she reached for her bagel and her back twinged, reminding her that he'd been entirely right—as annoying as that may be—and as long as he wasn't proposing to be in the bed himself, she had no real reason to turn down his suggestion. She only wished that he could see that not every problem was his to solve. He'd demanded that he be allowed to rescue her, without any thought about himself—not the first time over the years that she had noticed this tendency. It didn't take a genius to know that that wasn't the sort of thing you could keep up for ever. Sooner or later, you had to take care of yourself if you didn't want to burn out.

'I'm not sure about this,' she said gently. 'Why don't you think about it. I won't be upset if you change your mind.' But she knew there was little chance of that. Once Jonathan had decided you needed his protection, there was very little you could do about it.

'I absolutely insist,' he said, proving her point.

'Then I suppose I accept,' Rowan said, thinking of her plan to make him want her, and that this wasn't exactly how she had hoped to end up in his bed. But if she was going to be there, maybe it could work in her favour, somehow. This week was the longest time that she had spent with him for years. But all things considered it still wasn't actually all that long. If she was going to make him want her, she had to make a start soon.

And that start really had to be not leaving a room every time that Jonathan walked into one, so she fought down her instinct to go hide somewhere, and instead sipped her coffee as if she was perfectly at ease in his presence. The friends that they had decided to be, but which didn't seem quite natural yet.

'I need to make a start sorting through the papers in the library,' Jonathan said when he finished his tea, rinsing out his cup and leaving it on the draining board. 'There are decades' worth of loose sheets shoved into boxes and no one's looked at them for years. I'd like to be sure we're not throwing away anything that should be in an archive somewhere before we get rid of it all. Liv was going to help but...'

'Well, let me,' Rowan said, thinking that this was the perfect opportunity to be close to him for a while.

'You really don't have to,' Jonathan said with a frown.

'I've genuinely got nothing else to do,' she said. 'I'm meant to be taking things easy, hanging out with Liv and resting up before Saturday. But if this morning is anything to go by she's going to be sleeping for most of the next few days. It'll be good to have something to do.'

He looked at her carefully, the narrowing of his eyes giving away his discomfort at the thought. But eventually he agreed, and she tried to hide how pleased she was.

So, they spent the morning together in the musty-smelling library, the French doors flung open to let in the sunshine and fresh air. The stacked cardboard boxes were treasure troves of ephemera, receipts and sketches and invoices going back to the thirties. She organised them by decade, first, holding up anything that she found interesting so that she and Jonathan could look at it together.

'You know you really don't have to do this,' Jonathan said from behind the desk, after they'd been working solidly for a couple of hours. He scratched his hands through his hair while his attention moved between the pile of papers in front of him and the laptop perched on a larger pile to one side.

'I already told you. I'm happy doing it,' Rowan told him. 'There's so much interesting stuff in here. It's like a puzzle. You know accountants love boxes of old receipts.'

He smiled, and she considered that a small victory. 'We should at least make Caleb help, though,' he added.

She shrugged, because she was happy that it was just the two of them in there. Somehow, sitting in silence had brought back some ease into their relationship, and she didn't want to risk the tiny steps they had taken back to normality, and towards whatever might come after that. 'Caleb seems pretty happy upstairs. And I like that there's someone near to Liv in case I don't hear her when she wakes.'

Jonathan smiled at that. 'I thought I was the one who was meant to be overprotective.'

She gave him a searching look. 'You don't get a monopoly over caring for her,' Rowan said, coming to stand by the desk, leaning and resting a hip against it. 'You don't have to be the only one who's allowed to.'

'She's my sister,' he pointed out, as if that explained everything.

Rowan thought for a moment, trying to understand the things that he wasn't saying, as well as the things that he was. She'd always loved that about him. How deeply he thought. How deeply he felt. Jonathan didn't know how to take things lightly, and that was a gift, and also—she imagined—deeply painful at times. 'I know that,' she told him. 'And you had to be more than a brother to her when you were way too young for that sort of responsibility. I'm not pretending to know how hard that must have been for you. But I wanted you to know you're not the only one who loves her. It's not all on you, you know.'

Jonathan sighed, as if he'd worked out where this was going, and didn't want to hear the rest of it. 'Thank you for saying that. It's not the same, but I appreciate it anyway.'

She looked at him for a few long moments, wondering whether to let him off the hook. Why it was so important to her that she made him understand that he wasn't alone in this one thing. 'Okay. Whatever you say,' she conceded at last. 'But let me carry on helping in here, at least,' she added. Jonathan nodded and shifted his laptop further to the side, scooting his chair back.

'Are you quite sure that the business doesn't explode when you do that?' Rowan asked with a grin.

He frowned, and she felt a twist of anxiety. She tried to laugh it off, but she couldn't help but feel like she'd touched something raw.

'It's okay, I'm just teasing. You deserve a break. When *was* the last time that you had a day off?' She saw his expression close off and reached out a hand to touch him gently on the shoulder. 'I'm not criticising,' she said, because he seemed not to believe her. 'I'm just concerned. Who worries about you while you're looking after everyone else?'

'I don't need worrying about,' he said, turning away from the desk and walking over to the pile of papers she'd been sorting through. She took that as a less than subtle hint that she wasn't going to get any further asking him about that. The last thing that he needed was to start worrying about the fact that Rowan might be worrying about him.

'So, how have you organised these?' he asked, looking through the boxes she'd made a start on.

'I've started chronologically,' Rowan said, flicking through the pile of papers closest to her. 'I don't understand why these aren't already in an archive somewhere,' she added.

'Because ever since I took over the business, I've been more interested in Kinley surviving the year than looking at cuttings from a century ago,' Jonathan said sharply.

'Hey, it wasn't a criticism,' she said, taken aback by his tone. She'd thought that Kinley's financial problems were all in the past. But the way that Jonathan phrased that made it sound very much like they were ongoing. That would go some way to explaining why it looked like Jonathan hadn't had a good night's sleep in months, if not years. 'Jonathan, are things…okay? With the business, I mean.'

'Of course. They're fine,' he said, before letting out a sigh that told her way more than those four words could.

'Because you know that I can help, don't you? Accountant, remember. If you want me to, you only have to ask.'

'You can't tell Liv,' Jonathan said, the words bursting out of him, seemingly against his will. Rowan sat back on her heels and looked at him closely. So, there was something to tell. She thought for a moment about her friendship with Liv, which had never had any secrets…other than the fairly whopping matter of having nearly slept with Jonathan all those years ago. Compared to that, helping him with his finances didn't seem so bad.

'I won't tell her if you don't want me to,' Rowan reassured him. 'Just tell me what's going on. Please. I want to help if I can.'

Jonathan rubbed his face in both his hands, and for a moment she wasn't sure if he was even going to look up again. Eventually, though, he dragged his gaze to meet hers, and her heart ached for the sorrow that she saw in his expression.

'There's no money, Rowan. None. That's what's going on. There has never been any money. And I've been trying to keep the business afloat by papering over the cracks and using my own savings and inheritance to fill the gaps. But now that's all gone and the accounts are still a black hole. I'm looking at a bill for a supplier that is already a month overdue and wondering how I can pay that and the wages and how a fashion house can survive with either no fabric or no staff. Is that the sort of thing you can help me with?'

Rowan took a deep breath and forced herself not to show on her face how much she agreed with him that actually that did sound pretty awful. She would get to that.

'Right…that's a lot. Jonathan. And don't snap at me for asking, but…why aren't we telling Liv about this? You all have shares in the business, right?'

But Jonathan shook his head, his face haunted. 'It's my responsibility to fix this. She shouldn't have to worry about this mess.'

Rowan frowned, her heart feeling soft around the

edges. She forced herself to toughen it up. This wasn't about her feelings for Jonathan. She would look at the business side of things objectively in a minute. But she hated seeing him like this, like he had dug this hole himself and wasn't allowed to ask for help to get out. He wasn't responsible for the financial mess that they were in. That had been dumped on his shoulders with far too many other responsibilities when he was too young to be expected to carry it.

She could murder his parents for what they'd put him through. What they'd put them all through.

'You don't have to do it all alone, Jonathan. It's too much for one person. And, you know, Liv's a grown-up. She doesn't need you to be her dad. She could be on your side if you let her.'

'Please don't tell me what my sister needs. It's my job to worry about this.'

Rowan reached for his hands, because it seemed like nothing short of physical touch was going to get him to pay attention to what she was saying. And for reasons that she probably shouldn't examine too closely, it was suddenly imperative that she make him feel better. 'It's only your job because your parents left and heaped everything on your shoulders while the others were just kids. But they're as old now as you were then. Perhaps it's time to stop insisting on doing this all by yourself.'

The silence stretched out into long seconds, long enough that she wondered whether she might actually have got through to him. That he might be coming around to what she was saying. But then his face shuttered, and she knew that she'd failed. 'I'm not discussing this, Rowan. If you're going to help me, I need to know that I can trust you not to tell Livia.'

Rowan sighed, because she really did hate keeping secrets. But she could see from the expression on Jonathan's face how serious this was. There was really never any doubt that she would help him if he asked, regardless of what conditions he put on accepting her help.

'Okay, I'll help, and I won't say anything to Liv. If you'll promise me you'll think about sharing this with your family. Letting them help you with something for a change.'

'Fine. I'll think about it,' he said, though she suspected that he had no intention of changing his mind. She could work with that.

'Let's pack away some of these boxes and make some space at the desk. Maybe Liv can go through the boxes for archiving if she's up to it later,' Rowan said. 'Then we can go through your financials together and see where we are.'

Once the desk was clear, she pulled Jonathan's laptop in front of them both, and asked him to walk her through the most recent years' financial statements. Afterwards, she whistled through her teeth, not sure what she could say that wouldn't sound dramatic. 'You're right. It's not…good.' She heard a snort beside her, and when she looked round, couldn't believe what she was seeing. Jonathan was laughing. *Laughing!*

She hit him playfully on the arm. 'Don't laugh at me.'

'I'm not laughing *at* you,' he said, laughing so hard she was sure that she could see tears about to fall from his blond eyelashes. 'My brain is just… I'm fairly sure that I'm exhausted. "Not good" just pushed me over the edge.'

'Have you had a break at all today?' she asked, trying to give him a stern look. 'Have you even stepped foot outside?'

'I'm fine,' he told her, while refusing to make eye contact.

But he wasn't. That was clear to anyone remotely interested in looking. His face was pale, there were black bags under his eyes and creases at the corners where he'd been squinting too long at the screen. 'Come on, that's it,' she declared. 'I'm staging an intervention. You need fresh air and vitamin D.'

'I'm too busy,' Jonathan said, reaching for his laptop again before she caught him by the wrist.

'You're busy being a bore.'

That got a smile out of him, though he tried to hide it. 'Go outside yourself,' he said, his voice gruff.

Rowan hid a smile. 'You're aware that I'm the one helping you, yes?'

He sighed, pinched the bridge of his nose, and she was almost tempted to laugh in relief at the sight of that familiar gesture from him. 'Very aware,' he said, with something of a despairing tone.

'Seriously, though, it's so lovely out there. I know that there are some beautiful walks around here. Show me one of them. Show me the maze.'

He snorted. 'You don't need a chaperone.'

She tried not to let him see the moment when her face fell, before she hid the expression with her usual smile.

'Well, don't complain later that I didn't try and save you from your sedentary lifestyle,' she said with a careful shrug, straightening up some pages on the desk to cover her embarrassment. Jonathan sighed, and Rowan looked over at him.

'I'll come,' he said.

She was torn between wrapping her arms round him and stomping off in a huff at how pained he seemed to find the idea of both an hour off work and an hour spent with her. In the end, she decided that the middle ground was probably safest and only nodded.

'Great. Will you check in on Liv for me before we go? She'll snap at you because she's grouchy when she's in pain but she won't mean it.'

The warmth of the sun was so beautiful on her shoulders when she stepped outside that she worked her way through a couple of salutations, feeling them warm her body and giving her legs a gentle stretch. She turned when she heard Jonathan's footsteps on the gravel path that circled the house.

'Which way do you want to go?' he asked, and she wasn't sure if it was just an effect of the golden sunshine reflecting off the honeyed stone of the manor house, but he had lost some of his pallor already. His skin looked warm and golden, and he had lost that grey tone that had worried her in the library.

'Can we explore the maze?' Rowan asked. The path loped through the formal gardens behind the house, through a little overgrown thicket of trees and into a glade where the sunlight pricked sweat on her skin and made her wish she'd put on sunglasses before she'd left. She stopped to take a drink from the water bottle she'd thrown into her backpack.

'It's so pretty out here,' she said, as Jonathan stretched his arms above his head, no doubt pulling out all the knots that were inevitable if you spent sixteen hours a day in front of a computer. It made it difficult not to objectify him in a way that she knew was frankly rude—history or no history. That being said, she had rather been hoping that he might be looking at her in a similar way. He had said, out loud with no obfuscations, that he had been attracted to her. Though they had been talking very much about the past and not the present. But she really, really wanted not to think about him any more. Not without it leading anywhere. And the only way that she could think that she could possibly move on from him would be to do what they had stopped at the last moment. The only problem was, she had no idea how to get them from this point to there.

'Aren't you going for a run today?' Jonathan asked as they approached the old entrance to the maze, which had grown high and unruly above the once carefully tended yew trees. 'I assumed you went out every day.'

'Usually I do,' Rowan agreed. 'But not the week before a race.' She pushed aside the branches to reveal what remained of the path into the maze. It looked a little spooky in there, and all of a sudden she wasn't sure that this had been a good idea. 'I'll probably only do one short run this week. I want my legs fresh for Saturday,' she said in a carefully even voice, not wanting to let her hesitation show.

'Changed your mind about exploring?' Jonathan asked from close behind her. Far closer than she'd realised that he was standing. His breath tickled the hairs on the back of her neck, and she turned her head suddenly, only to find his face a scant inch or so from her own.

'No,' she said on impulse, because she didn't want him to think that she was so easily spooked. She was an adult. Something that he had somehow failed to recognise before, and she was going to make sure that he knew it now. Anyway, she wasn't sure *exactly* how abandoned mazes fit into planned seductions—having never been in one, or indeed seduced anyone before. But it didn't seem like a bad place to start.

She pushed aside the branches again and squeezed into the maze.

The interior was less overgrown, the height of the trees blocking out most of the sunlight. But it was still narrow enough that they had to walk single file and when she stopped abruptly for Jonathan's chest to hit her back before he had a chance to stop himself.

'Sorry,' he said, jumping back. She wondered whether she was supposed to tell him he had nothing to apologise for. That she didn't mind having his body pressed against hers. But they hadn't even made their first turn in the maze yet, and she didn't fancy being trapped in here if such an obvious come-on resulted in him rejecting her. Again. She'd wait until they were in the open before she offered her heart—no, her ego—up to be broken.

She remembered the thought that had made her stop so suddenly.

'Do you know the route to the centre?' she asked.

'That would be telling,' Jonathan replied, and even without looking round at him she knew that he was smiling.

'That was rather the point of me asking.'

He laughed, a sound that she took as a personal victory. 'There's no fun if I tell you the way,' he said.

'Aha! So you *do* know.'

'I've been coming here since before I can remember. Of course I know the way.'

'Won't you miss it?' Rowan asked, and even before Jonathan's hissed-in breath knew that she'd said the wrong thing.

'Of course I'll miss it,' Jonathan said, his voice low and creaky. She felt his sadness in her chest. 'This whole place feels like a part of me,' he went on. 'Like I'm a part of it. But there's not enough money to even stop it falling down, never mind do anything else with it. And I don't know if you realise this but I do actually need the money from selling this place to stop the Kinley business from completely imploding.'

They stood in silence for a moment, Rowan holding her breath, cursing herself for having said something so insensitive.

'I'm sorry—' they both said at once, and Rowan turned on the spot. It didn't matter how close they were standing, only that Jonathan knew that she hadn't meant to hurt him, or mock him, or taunt him. Or the hundred other ways that she knew her words could have hurt him.

'No, I'm sorry,' Jonathan said. 'I shouldn't have snapped. None of this is your fault.'

She watched as he reached and plucked something from her hair.

'Leaf?' she asked, glancing upward.

'Cobweb.'

She squealed so loudly that she slammed a hand across her mouth to stifle the sound.

'Oh my God,' she said at last, still through her fingers. 'I didn't think this through.'

Jonathan smiled but resisted the obvious urge to laugh at her.

'It was only a very small one. I didn't imagine you'd be afraid of spiders.'

'No? What have you been imagining about me?' she asked. It was only once the words were out that she realised how suggestive they might have sounded. And she could have rushed to take them back, but instead she let them settle into the trees around them. Felt the heavy charge in the atmosphere, the sudden awareness of how her body seemed to be able to feel how close they were together. How easily they would be able to touch, if only one or the other of them would take that last, tiny step.

She really, really wanted to know if Jonathan had ever fantasised about her. What he thought of. What he might be tempted to play out in real life. But she was also aware that they were standing in the middle of what was most likely a spider-infested maze and with the best will in the world she probably wasn't going to be able to push that entirely from her mind.

'Turn back or keep going?' Jonathan asked, and she wondered if he had intended for that to be so obviously loaded with double meaning. She wasn't going to take any chances.

'Keep going.'

She tore her gaze away from his, turned and kept walking, taking first a right and then a left, meeting one dead end after another. After so many about turns that she couldn't be entirely sure they were even in the same county any more, never mind the same maze, she finally gave in and asked the question that she'd been fighting back.

'Okay, I give up. Can you lead the way to the centre?'

Jonathan laughed, giving her a slightly bemused look. 'I know the way from the *start*. I'm sorry to tell you that I have absolutely no idea where we are, never mind how to get to the middle from here.'

She glanced around them, feeling the branches of the trees closing in on them. 'Maybe we should head back to the entrance, then?'

Jonathan lifted his hands up in apology.

'I've got no better chance of finding that than I have of finding the centre. We could try and retrace our steps. Make all our mistakes in reverse.'

She made herself laugh, because she was certain that he was talking about the maze, but it wasn't a bad idea for the entirety of their relationship, if she thought about it. They twisted and turned through the passageways, Rowan jumping every time a leaf brushed against her neck. Eventually, she saw sunlight up ahead and breathed a sigh of relief. She'd started to wonder if she was going to be sleeping in the maze tonight.

But when they reached the opening in the trees, she hesitated.

'Oh, right, I'd started to suspect as much...' Jonathan said behind her.

Because they weren't back at the entrance. They had found the centre of the maze. It was bathed in sunshine so bright that Rowan had to shield her eyes—which had grown used to the gloom—with her hand. She stepped out of the shade of the maze towards the love seat at the centre of the clearing. Climbing roses had been left to creep around the archway over it, and it was covered in enormous white, pink and yellow blooms.

She couldn't help herself. She walked towards it and sat, swinging slightly back and forth, her long legs easily reaching the ground.

'You look like a painting.'

Jonathan's voice took her by surprise. She hadn't realised that he had followed her over, and she looked up. And she'd never heard him sound quite like that before either. His voice was still low, but it was softer now, intimate. The sun was behind him, casting him in silhouette, all tall and slim, his body long flowing lines and easy grace.

'Room for two?' he asked, and she shifted over

without a word, not quite trusting herself to speak. They swung in silence for a while, enjoying the sunshine, Rowan turning her face up to soak in the warmth.

'Thank you,' Jonathan said at last, and Rowan turned to look at him.

'What for?'

'For helping. For understanding when I asked you not to tell Liv. For making me get out for a bit. I can't remember the last time I just sat and did nothing.'

She smiled back at him, a little cautiously, surprised that he was opening up to her. 'You're welcome. On all counts. I'm glad that I can help. It...hurt, to see you that way this morning. I only wish I could do more.'

She held her breath, not sure whether she had said too much, given away too much about how she still felt for him. But she had been hiding her feelings for so long, and hadn't got over him even a little. If she wanted things to change, she had to change the patterns of behaviour that she'd clung to all that time. If she wanted him to come to her, she was going to have to make herself vulnerable, at least just a little.

'I... Do you really think I should tell Liv? And Caleb?' Jonathan asked.

Rowan took a deep breath, aware of the trust that Jonathan was placing in her to ask this. How easily he might close off again if she misstepped.

'I suppose...' she started. 'I suppose I'm less focused on you actually telling her than on the fact that you feel that you can't. Liv is tough, you know. Resilient.'

'I know that,' Jonathan said, and Rowan couldn't mistake the feeling of pride she saw on his face when he spoke about his sister. 'It's not that I think she *couldn't* deal with it. It's that I don't want her to have to.'

Rowan nodded, understanding him a little better. But she couldn't agree with him. 'I'm sure that if she did know what was going on, she wouldn't want you to have to deal with it either, never mind dealing with it completely alone. She cares about you as much as you care about her.'

He huffed something that she thought was probably intended to be a laugh but came out as something much sadder.

'Oh, Jonathan.' She reached for his hand and squeezed, because she could see that he was hurting, and she couldn't help herself. 'I hope you know that she cares about you.'

'She hates me, Rowan. You don't have to sugar-coat it. Our relationship was never going to be the same after Mum and Dad left and I had to be responsible for them. I came to terms with it a long time ago.'

'But it doesn't have to stay that way,' she said gently. 'You're *not* responsible for them any more, or at least no more responsible for them than they are for you. Why don't you share the burden? Tell them what's going on and see if they can help. They can offer their support, even if there's nothing practical they can do.'

He didn't say no immediately, and she supposed she would have to leave it at that. She knew him well enough to know that he would need to mull it over. Jonathan had never been one for snap decisions.

They swung back and forth a couple more times, and Rowan looked up at the flowers above her head, marvelling at how nature had created something so beautiful left entirely to her own devices.

'I think it might be magic in here,' she said, not thinking before she spoke. 'It's so beautiful it doesn't feel real.'

'I think you're right,' Jonathan said, shifting round slightly to look at her. 'I think the whole world could disappear while we were in here and we wouldn't know. Or care.'

She allowed herself a small, hopeful smile, turning her face towards him.

'You know, I quite like the sound of that.'

He reached for her hair again, and she gritted her teeth. 'Another cobweb?' she asked, frozen in place.

'No. Just…you,' he replied, twisting the lock of hair around his finger. 'Is that okay?'

'Yeah,' Rowan breathed, afraid that anything else would break the spell of this fairy-tale place. Perhaps they could just stay, she thought.

And then Jonathan's hand slid more firmly into her hair and she stopped thinking at all.

He was going to kiss her. She had never been more certain of anything in her life. She had been here before, and he had no reason now to think that she didn't know what she was doing. He was taking his time about it, and she knew that he was thinking, over-thinking. But she could be patient, give him the time that he needed to know that he wanted this.

His head dipped, his gaze fixed on her lips, and she held her breath.

But as he leaned in, her phone started to buzz, and she resisted the urge to groan out loud.

'Is that you?' Jonathan asked, an edge of frustration in his voice.

'My alarm,' she replied, real life breaking through the trees into their hideaway. 'For Liv's pain meds.'

'I'm sure that Caleb…' Jonathan started to suggest, but the spell had been broken and they both knew it.

'We should probably get back,' Rowan said, trying to hide how desperately disappointed she was.

'Right, yes, of course. I know the way out from here,' Jonathan said, in a distracted tone that betrayed how thoroughly the atmosphere between them had shattered.

She followed him back out and up to the house, watching his long legs in his slim-cut jeans while trying to see in her peripheral vision whether he was watching her too.

When they were alone, when they caught each other's eyes, something changed about the air, making it harder to pull it into her chest, so she could feel herself struggling to keep it even, to keep her body from arching towards his, following some deeply held impulse to be close to him.

'I should…' Jonathan said, moving towards the door.

'Yes. Of course. I'll see you later, I suppose.'

She was standing in front of the door, she realised, when Jonathan didn't leave the room. She took a step to her left as Jonathan moved in the same direction, and she found herself chest to chest with him. His hands came to her upper arms and she was sure he was going to move her to the side, but then didn't. Instead, his thumbs were skimming over the smooth skin along her arm, making her shiver and want to press closer to him, and she might have done so if it wasn't for the sound of shoes on the flagstones behind her.

She spun around at the same moment that Jonathan stepped back and dropped her arms, the flaming red of her face meaning that they weren't exactly the picture of innocence. Luckily, Caleb had his eyes on his phone and by the time he looked up they were decent.

'Liv's awake,' he said, grinning at them. 'I'm going to make sandwiches for lunch.'

'Great. Thanks,' Rowan said, finding it impossible to get her voice to its usual pitch. 'I'll check on her.'

They were all at the table, passing Caleb's impressive doorstop sandwiches around, Rowan desperately trying to avoid meeting Jonathan's eye and give away what had happened—what had almost happened—in the maze when Liv gasped in shock and slapped her forehead with her hand.

'Oh, God, I've only just thought about your race!' Liv declared, startling them all. 'How the bloody hell am I going to do it on crutches? Caleb, do you think you could drive—?'

'I'm really sorry but I have a thing on Saturday. I can't back out now,' he said, around a mouthful of cheese and pickle.

'It's fine,' Rowan said, putting her hand over Liv's. 'There's a bag drop. I'll prep all my stuff before I leave and they'll make sure it's waiting for me at the aid stations.'

'But you need me there!' Liv insisted. 'To remind you to eat and to change the batteries in your torch and to put on fresh clothes when you're gross.'

Rowan laughed at her friend's assessment of their friendship. She wasn't far wrong. 'And I love having you on my team,' she told her truthfully, because Liv had been there at every one of her ultras, and she had no doubt that she wouldn't have finished them without her. 'But you're injured, so you're going to sit this one out. You would tell me just the same if things were the other way around. You know you would.'

'I'll do it,' Jonathan said. She whipped her head around and stared at him, realising as she did that Liv and Caleb were doing the same. He shifted a little uncomfortably under their combined scrutiny. 'You don't all need to look so surprised.'

'Jonathan,' Rowan said softly, trying not to give anything away with her voice. 'That's really generous but it's a long race. I'll be happy if I manage it in twenty-four hours. I can't ask that of you.'

'You didn't ask,' he said, his voice terse. There was no sign of the softness that she'd heard in the maze. 'I'm insisting. You need a support crew and I'm happy to do it. So, I'm not sure that there's anything more to talk about.'

She gaped at him. There was no way that she could

let Jonathan do that for her. But he didn't seem to be listening.

'Anyway, I suspect that if I don't do it then Liv will insist on hobbling after you on crutches. This way I know that she's resting her ankle.'

Rowan stared at him, sure that if she could make him blink that he would change his mind. But the longer she looked, the longer he looked back, until she felt heat rising in her cheeks. 'Jonathan, I… I…'

'Good. Thank you. Let's not talk about this any more, shall we?'

She opened her mouth to do just that, but Jonathan's hand landed on hers, and she was so shocked she couldn't speak.

'Did you find anything interesting in the boxes we brought through from the library?' Jonathan asked Liv, withdrawing his hand from Rowan's as he turned away.

Fortunately, Caleb was focused on his lunch, but her glance across at Liv confirmed that her friend had seen *something*, even if she didn't know what it was.

'I don't know,' Liv said. 'Maybe. Did you know that Great-grandmother was going to launch a perfume line before the war? I've found minutes from meetings that suggest they had formulations, bottles, packaging, everything ready to go. Then the paper trail just ends and I don't know what happened.'

'That sounds interesting,' Rowan said, jumping on the change of subject. 'And they didn't go back to it after the war was over?'

'Not as far as I can see. Jonathan, do you know anything about it?'

He shook his head. 'First I've heard of it. As far as I'm aware we've never branched out into fragrance or cosmetics.'

'Well, maybe we should,' Liv said, and then immediately blanched.

'Well, there's an idea,' Rowan said thoughtfully. 'Multibillion-pound industry. Decent margins. You've got an established prestige brand. There are far worse moves you could make.' Rowan glanced at Jonathan, wondering how he was taking this. She hadn't given away anything that he'd asked her not to, but she wasn't going to let an opportunity to help Jonathan talk to Liv pass without making the most of it.

'I've offered you a job before, Liv. You've never shown any interest in taking an active role in the family business. This sounds like it would require a lot of investment,' Jonathan observed in a carefully neutral voice. 'I'm not sure that now would be the time.'

Liv narrowed her eyes at him. 'Why? Is there a problem with the business?'

Jonathan shook his head and Rowan resisted the urge to sigh.

'It just sounds like a risk.'

'Well,' Rowan said, cutting in before Liv and Jonathan could return to their well-worn path of sniping at each other. 'It's an idea. Maybe you should both think it over. See if anything else turns up in those boxes. We can work through some more in the library this afternoon and we'll send stuff through to you if it looks like it might be relevant.'

When she walked through to the library with Jonathan after lunch, she wasn't sure what sort of reception to expect.

'That was promising,' she commented, picking up a pile of papers and sorting them, half an eye out for anything to do with perfumes or fragrance. But Jonathan stayed quiet for so long that she had to give in and look up at him.

'I don't disagree,' he said, his expression a little defensive.

'And is that the same as you agreeing?' Rowan asked, softening the remark with a smile.

'It would require a lot of investment.' Jonathan leaned back in his chair, his fingertips going to massage the orbits of his eye sockets in a way that felt endearingly familiar.

'You mentioned that already. But it could generate a lot of income as well. A whole new revenue stream. Surely it's worth investigating.'

'I just don't know when…or how…or…' He trailed off, his forehead creasing.

'So delegate it,' she suggested with a shrug, wondering whether she would have to explain the word to him.

'To Liv?'

'It's worth asking, surely?'

Jonathan shook his head. 'I can't see how I could

do that without telling her about the problems with the business.'

'That's up to you. It's all up to you, of course. I just want you to see that you have the option there, if you want it. Liv is talented. She's freelanced product launches for a dozen companies. She's more than qualified.'

'That's not in doubt,' Jonathan replied dryly. Rowan came to stand beside him and resisted the urge to reach out and smooth the tension she could see pulling at his features. 'But there's no way in hell she would come and work for me. I've asked her before, when she left university. She said she didn't want me trying to control her at work as well as at home.' Rowan winced, remembering that particular episode. 'How have I messed things up so badly with her? I only ever wanted to protect her, and now we can barely have a civil conversation. I can't imagine any situation where she would want to work for me.'

Rowan's heart clenched, and this time she couldn't not reach out and put a hand on his shoulder. 'Liv doesn't hate you.' She would normally hesitate to speak for her friend. It wasn't her place to get in the middle of a family argument. But she couldn't leave Jonathan with the pain of believing that his sister hated him when Rowan knew it was so much more complicated than that, and probably not really about him at all.

'She doesn't,' she said again, squeezing his shoulder.

He huffed, and she wasn't sure if it was a laugh. 'She does a good impression of it.'

'I know. But it's not really you she's angry at.' Because she wasn't blind to her friend's faults, and she had been aware for a long time of how much animosity and anger was there. But she had enough objectivity to know that that didn't mean Liv hated him.

'She's always deserved so much better than I've been able to give her.'

'Jonathan,' Rowan said, her hand coming to cup his cheek this time, and tilting his face up so that he would look at her. 'All you've ever done, as far as I have seen, is try and take care of her.'

'And all that's done is drive her further and further away.'

Rowan gave him a grim smile, wishing she could do more. 'That's not your fault. I wish you could give yourself a break and see what I see.'

He smiled, and the shift of muscles under her palm reminded her of how close they had moved. Reminded her that she was supposed to be getting close. But she hadn't done this to be calculating. All she wanted was to ease the pain that she saw around his eyes. To comfort someone who was trying their hardest under difficult circumstances.

'You can't expect to find yourself at the head of a family and the head of a business when you're only in your twenties and get everything exactly right every time.'

Jonathan frowned. 'Ah, well, that's the thing, isn't it? Because when you have those responsibilities, getting it wrong isn't an option. The consequences are too dire. Mum and Dad left, and my grandparents were already in a care home and not in good enough health to take on their responsibilities. If I hadn't spent so much time looking after the business, then we would have lost everything. I couldn't have afforded Cal's school fees, or the care home fees, or Liv's student accommodation. They were already surviving the trauma of my parents leaving and I wasn't going to add to that with complete financial collapse or having to live with me full-time as well. I was so focused on saving the business that I didn't realise that I was getting things so wrong with Liv.'

'You did what you had to,' Rowan reminded him. 'You've been fighting on God knows how many fronts, trying to fix problems that you didn't cause. No one can blame you for not being perfect. Not even you. I won't allow it.'

Rowan couldn't believe that he had taken all this on himself, when he had been the same age as she was now. She couldn't imagine what that sort of pressure did to a person.

'You were angry with me,' he reminded her, and she wasn't sure where that change of subject had come from. 'When I tried to stop you…making a mistake. With me.'

'You want to talk about that now?' she asked, raising an eyebrow, frustrated with him for changing the subject. 'I think we can do without rehashing my most embarrassing moments.'

'Embarrassing? What reason have you got to be

embarrassed?' he asked. 'We never really talked about what happened, and now I'm thinking perhaps we should have done.'

'It's ancient history,' Rowan told him, not sure whether she wanted to hear his thoughts now that it came down to it.

'It wasn't that I didn't want—' he started, and she decided that maybe she would hear him out after all, because all these years she'd been haunted by the memory of him saying no, and if that hadn't come to him quite as easily it had seemed to, then her ego could do with hearing it. 'You were so young,' he finished, and Rowan snorted.

'I was twenty-one. An adult,' she reminded him, in no uncertain terms. 'There's only seven years between us. Not that that stopped you calling me a kid.'

'I was trying to help! To point out that you'd get over it soon enough. Anyway, by the time I was twenty-eight I had parental responsibility for a girl the same age as you were then. I had responsibility for Cal— who was still at school, if you remember. That makes for a hell of a lot more difference than seven years does. Not to mention the fact that you'd been drinking. You weren't thinking straight.'

She racked her brains, trying to remember. Yes, they'd shared a bottle of wine, but she had been a student for three years and could drink a couple of glasses without her judgement being terminally affected. She'd known exactly what she was doing, and the fact that Jonathan thought she wasn't capable of judging that for herself—wasn't capable of *asking*, instead of assuming—was enraging. 'I'd had a couple of glasses of wine. I knew exactly what I was doing.'

'I know what you look like when you're tipsy. I spent enough time watching you that summer.'

Which was quite the admission, Rowan thought, watching how his cheeks pinked as he realised what he'd said.

She was twenty-one and had barely been kissed, never mind had someone fall in love with her. Unless she thought about those times where it felt like her and Jonathan were two sides of the same coin. When they laughed at the same obscure jokes, or caught one another's eyes across the room, and she felt that warm swell of intimacy between them.

So when she'd found them alone, enjoying one another's company, the evening feeling so *right*—she'd taken her chance to prove her bullies wrong. Only she hadn't. She'd shown herself that they had it right. If not even Jonathan—who she connected with on every other level—wanted to kiss her, then what hope did she have of ever finding someone who would think she was anything other than a freak?

'I couldn't kiss you when I didn't know if you were doing it because you really wanted to or because there was something else going on. I'm sorry. We really should have talked about this at the time.'

Jonathan was right. They should have talked about this before now.

'I should get back to work,' Jonathan said, pushing back his chair and standing up. 'If you… If you wanted to spend some more time in the library this afternoon—' he looked up and caught her eye '—I'd like that very much.'

CHAPTER SEVEN

IN THE END, she had spent most of the afternoon in the library, looking for any signs of the long-forgotten fragrances in the older papers, and any sign of how the company had got into its current financial difficulty in the present. The former she'd given to Liv, who had taken up residence in the family room, and the latter she'd pored over herself, talking with Jonathan in quiet tones so that they wouldn't be overheard. They'd eaten dinner in there too—Liv had fallen asleep while watching a movie and they hadn't wanted to disturb her, and Cal was up in his room.

The whole evening had such an air of intimacy, as they had worked, and eaten, and— when she could tease one from Jonathan—laughed together, that the prospect of sleeping in Jonathan's bed come nightfall felt a little more loaded than it had when they'd agreed to it that morning.

She hesitated outside of his bedroom door, aware of the sound of him moving round inside. It was one thing telling herself that morning that sleeping in Jonathan's bed wouldn't mean anything, but it was quite another to be standing on his threshold, listening to him in his room and building up the courage to knock. Especially after all they had been through today. Not least that moment in the maze when she had been sure that he was going to kiss her—which had been playing on a loop in the back of her mind, even as she worked through his accounts.

It was only the sound of footsteps moving towards her from inside the room that prompted her into action. The only thing worse than lifting her hand to knock at this point would be being discovered lurking here like some kind of blushing schoolgirl.

She knocked quickly, and Jonathan opened the door a fraction of a second later, and almost barrelled into her. She lifted her hands instinctively and found herself stumbling backwards until Jonathan's arm reached around her waist and stopped her falling.

'Rowan!' Jonathan exclaimed as they tried to find their balance, reclaim their hands and pretend that their bodies weren't touching from chest to knee. 'I'm sorry, I wasn't expecting you to be there,' he said, stating the obvious while refusing to make eye contact.

'You said I could sleep in here so I don't have to spend the night on the sofa,' she reminded him. 'If you've changed your mind, it's fine. I can—'

'Of course. I hadn't forgotten,' Jonathan said, taking a step backwards so he was firmly in the landing while she hovered in the doorway, not sure which direction she should be moving in. The movement had brought their bodies close together, and there was a hum of awareness all over her skin as she waited for him to move away. Was she brave enough to ask him to stay? Yesterday, she wouldn't have been. But yesterday felt like a different world. One where he hadn't told her that he was attracted to her, and that the only reason he had pushed her away that first time was to try and protect her. She looked up and met his eye just as he took a half step backwards, and she lost her nerve.

'Make yourself at home,' Jonathan said in a low gravelly voice, gesturing into the room. 'There are clean sheets on the bed, and there's extra firewood in the basket by the hearth if you want it. That door leads into the bathroom but remember to lock the door to the hallway.'

She didn't think that she could blush any harder than she already was—until, that was, she pictured herself in the huge copper free-standing bathtub, surrounded by bubbles and lit by endlessly flattering candles. Her eyes closed until she was startled by a sound in the doorway, and opened them to find Jonathan watching her, an interested look on his face.

'Rowan?' Real Jonathan said, sadly distracting her from the far more easily seduced fantasy version.

'Bathroom door,' she said, remembering the last thing that he had told her and hoping her thoughts weren't showing too obviously on her face. 'Got it.'

Then they ran out of conversation and were both just staring at each other. 'I'll, um. I'll leave you to it,' Jonathan said awkwardly, trying to pretend that they weren't both standing there thinking about her climbing into his bed, sinking into his mattress. When he walked away, she stood at the door for a moment watching him retreat. Wondering what it would have taken to be closing the door on the world *together*. Locking themselves in with the fire and the sweet-smelling sheets and the drapes pulled across the curtains and around the bed. Creating a space for them to…be.

She'd let herself imagine scenes like that once. When she had first nurtured and nursed her crush on him. When she thought that the looks that they exchanged and jokes that they shared were building towards something. It would be easy to fall back into thinking like that, she acknowledged. To remember how easy things had felt between them once. But that only led her thoughts back to how he had rejected her, which was very much not where she wanted them to be just now.

She got ready for bed with resolute determination to pretend that everything was perfectly normal, and that sleeping in the bed of the person she'd been crushing on her whole adult life was completely unremarkable to her. It was only as she slid into the sheets and found herself engulfed by Jonathan's familiar scent that she realised how much trouble she was in. It shouldn't smell of him because the sheets were fresh, she told herself. Which did absolutely nothing to dampen the physical reaction she was having to finding herself in a veritable cloud of Jonathan. But imagined or not, it was going to make it impossible to convince herself that she was in anyone else's bed but his.

When sleep eventually took her, her unforgiving subconscious whisked her straight back to that copper bathtub, Jonathan watching her from the doorway, looking as if he were waiting for the nod to climb in there with her and grant her every wish. Her hands followed where his eyes roamed. Bold with her body in fantasy in a way she hadn't yet learned to be in reality, her palms slicked through the mounds of bubbles on her breasts, her mouth ticking up on a smile at the sight of what that did to Jonathan's expression as he stood in the doorway, watching, with a look of fierce possessiveness she'd pay all her worldly goods to see on him in real life.

Her hands sank into the hot water as they spread over her stomach, and she gave Jonathan a smile that she hoped he realised meant, *Get yourself over here and do this for me*. Dream Jonathan didn't need telling twice and was on his knees beside the tub before she could form another thought.

His hand threaded into the artfully undone bun at the back of her head, of the sort that only existed in dreams, tilting her face towards him while the other sank below the water to do things with her body she'd only attempted solo.

Jonathan was a quick study and had her breathless and in danger of splashing all of the water out of the tub in outrageously short order. Because of course he was as wordlessly competent at this as he was at everything else he set his mind to. It was just at the point that she grabbed him by the shirt and pulled him into the tub on top of her, causing a tidal wave of ceiling-destroying proportions, that she woke with a start, panting into the cold air, sweat cooling on her skin.

A door had slammed somewhere in the house, and if she ever found out who had disturbed her dream at the crucial moment, she would slam *them* into a door.

She turned her face into the pillow, and would have screamed out her frustration, if she hadn't got a faceful of Jonathan's scent. Really, how did he do that? She was tempted to just finish the job herself. But making herself come in Jonathan's bed was probably taking his offer of hospitality a step too far. Not to mention the fact that DIY was a lot less appealing when a moment ago she'd had a skilled craftsman applying himself to the job.

Thinking that way wasn't going to get her back to sleep, she acknowledged after tossing and turning for another half an hour. She needed to get up, make herself a cup of soothing tea and find something extremely dull to read to bore herself to sleep. She remembered the bookshelf of pulpy thrillers in the family room as she set the kettle on the range to boil and then crossed the hall to go and choose one.

She flicked on the light in the family room and let out a scream as a body rose from the sofa in the middle of the room and bellowed.

'Jonathan!' she called out, as she realised who was there. He was wearing a cotton T-shirt and tight black boxers, cut high over long thighs. She pulled her own hoodie down lower over her sleep shorts, wishing she'd taken the time to pull on joggers as well. Though by the way Jonathan's gaze seemed to have fixed on her legs he didn't seem to mind.

'Rowan, what are you doing in here?' Jonathan said,

asking the obvious question that at least one of them needed to.

'I couldn't sleep,' she said in a rush. 'There was… I had a dream.' She stopped herself, hoping Jonathan wouldn't guess that she had been dreaming about him. And then realised none of that explained why she was there.

'Did you want to talk about it?' he asked, sitting back down on the couch. She winced in sympathy, remembering how uncomfortable she had been the night before.

'I was looking for something to read,' she blurted out, stepping into the room and crossing to the bookshelf. 'I couldn't get back to sleep.'

'Me neither,' Jonathan said with a wry grin, that she couldn't help but return. They were interrupted by the whistle of the kettle, making Rowan jump.

'I was making tea,' she said, stating the obvious, delaying the moment they would say goodnight.

'I wouldn't say no to a cup,' Jonathan said, standing again and stretching. 'Might help this torture device seem less offensive.'

'What are you doing down here anyway?' Rowan asked in a low voice as they walked through to the kitchen. She grabbed a tea towel and pulled the kettle off the hot plate and Jonathan rummaged in a cupboard for mugs and teabags. 'I thought that you were sharing with Caleb.'

'Chamomile?' he asked her, dropping a bag into a cup, and she smiled, embarrassingly pleased that he remembered her favourite.

'Ah, well…' Jonathan looked uncomfortable, and Rowan gave him a questioning look.

'What?'

'I didn't exactly check with Caleb that he didn't mind me sharing his room before I offered you mine. He was very much against the idea. And, well, the sofa was the only other option.'

'The sofa is a terrible option,' Rowan said, sighing. 'I would never have accepted your room if I'd known you would end up sleeping there. I'll swap with you. Or go back in with Liv,' she said, as Jonathan carried the tea to the table. She sat beside him on the bench, tucking one foot underneath her and propping her chin on her knee as she wrapped her hands around the steaming mug.

'No,' Jonathan objected. 'Don't disturb Liv. She needs to rest.'

'Then I'll take the sofa,' Rowan countered. 'I won't sleep knowing that I've kicked you out of your bed.'

'Absolutely not,' Jonathan declared. 'I offered you my room. What sort of person would I be if I changed my mind now, in the middle of the night?'

Rowan groaned, because really she was too tired and too frustrated to get into an argument with Stubborn Jonathan just now. 'You'd be a reasonable person making life easier for a very tired person. I know what that sofa's like, remember? You've already spent half the night on there. It's only fair that we swap. Why can't you just agree that it's fair and let it drop?'

'Because fairness has nothing to do with it,' he said,

catching her eye and holding her there. 'I gave you my word.'

Rowan rolled her eyes, trying to shake off his intensity. 'And your word is law? You said I could have your room because you thought you would be in Caleb's room. It didn't work out. This doesn't have to be a big drama.'

But Jonathan's expression didn't budge and he shook his head as he crossed his arms. 'And whose fault is it that I didn't check it was okay with Cal first? If you've any doubts, I'm sure that he or Livia would be pleased to enlighten you.'

Rowan groaned, because they were back here again when all she wanted to do was get to sleep. 'New rule,' she declared. 'You don't talk to me about Liv. No more talking to her about you. We build a wall. It's the only way I'm going to survive this.'

A hint of a smile ticked up the corner of his mouth and she narrowed her eyes at him, convinced in that moment she'd missed something. 'What?' she asked, suspicious about his abrupt change in mood.

'You talk to Liv about me?'

Damn. Walked straight into that one.

'Liv talks to me about you,' she amended, her head resting on her crossed arms on the table. '*Complains* to me about you. One-way traffic.'

'So you never told her about our...' She looked up, interested, as he trailed off, and wondered if he planned on finishing his sentence.

'I didn't think there was anything to tell,' she said carefully. Perhaps if he hadn't made it so clear that nothing like it was ever going to happen again, she would have felt like there was something to say. And since they'd been here? Nothing had happened, and Liv wouldn't thank her for sharing the things she'd been imagining might happen. If anything ever did… well, she'd worry about it then.

'No. Well,' Jonathan said, his cheeks a little pink, and she realised that she liked him a little bit embarrassed. When he lost his air of certainty and let her see the human being underneath.

'I really need to get some sleep,' she said, letting her head rest back on her arms and wondering if it would be so bad to sleep here at the table.

'Of course. You go up, I'll turn the lights out in a minute,' Jonathan said, taking their mugs over to the sink.

'I thought I was taking the sofa,' Rowan murmured into her forearm.

'I thought I had made it clear that I had no intention of letting a guest in my home sleep on a sofa. It's bad enough that you slept there last night.'

Rowan pushed herself upright and gave him the sternest look she could manage while being really quite bleary-eyed. 'I'm perfectly capable of deciding for myself where I'm happy to sleep.'

Jonathan rested his hands on the table and leaned in. 'You're spending the rest of the night in my bed if I have to carry you there myself. Now would you please stop arguing and let me take care of you?'

Rowan let her mouth fall open and stared at him, shocked by the strength of feeling in his outburst. And then her brain helpfully hijacked her with a slideshow of Jonathan sweeping her up in his arms and carrying her up to bed and taking care of her in a variety of different ways. She was too shocked to even say anything, and stood looking at him, waiting for the penny to drop.

'Rowan, I'm sorry,' he said, starting to look awkward. 'I didn't mean to imply...'

'No, it's fine,' she said, reaching out to him, an idea occurring to her. 'You know, the bed is plenty big enough for the both of us, just for one night. Only half a night now. We can sort something else for tomorrow.' And, well, if she wanted him to kiss her again, there were worse ways to make that happen than to share a bed and see if it led anywhere.

'I don't know...' he said, the conflict on his face easy enough to read. He didn't want to spend the rest of the night on the sofa any more than she did, but he didn't want to overstep either.

'We don't need to make a big thing of it,' she said, not wanting him to get the wrong idea. 'I was sharing with Liv before and none of us thought anything of that.' Because there was no way that she was going to make a move on him—plan or no plan. If she was suggesting sharing his bed, she was also going to wait for him to make the first move.

He gave her a fierce, heated look that told her this was different, and she was perfectly aware why.

'I don't want to take advantage,' he said gruffly.

'You're not. I'm insisting,' she told him, holding out a hand for him to pull her up from the bench.

'If you insist, then I suppose I don't have a choice,' he said, taking her hand and pulling until she was standing in front of him. So close they were almost touching. They were being so careful with one another, and she didn't know how to stop.

Rowan had never felt more aware of her body than she did in those moments when she was climbing the stairs with Jonathan behind her, knowing that they were about to go to bed together. Jonathan hadn't stopped by the library to pick up any more clothes, and she realised she was happier being the one with legs on show, instead of having to try and keep her eyes off Jonathan's backside in those boxers. At least under his heavy duvet, he would be safely out of view and she wouldn't have to rely on her self-control. But then again, she wasn't sure that being tucked under the covers with Jonathan was going to be enormously helpful when it came to making good decisions. 'Are you sure about this?' Jonathan asked by the door to his bedroom, so seriously that you could have believed she had suggested an amateur appendectomy, rather than two old friends sharing a bed for a few hours. She reached past him to open the door.

'Come on. It's late. I want to get *some* sleep tonight.'

She slid under the duvet and pulled off her hoodie, turning her back and trying not to imagine what Jonathan looked like as he slid into bed behind her. She allowed herself to imagine his arm coming around her waist, pulling her against him, her back to his chest, their bodies matched inch for inch right down to their ankles. Eventually, she felt him climb in beside her, felt the dip of the mattress and held her breath, wondering if either of them was going to break this stalemate. But soon she heard his breaths slow into the gentle, rhythmic sound of sleep, and she closed her eyes tight and tried every trick she knew to make oblivion come.

CHAPTER EIGHT

WHEN JONATHAN WOKE the next morning, it was to arm-
fuls of Rowan. Her chest against his and the smooth
skin of her legs tangled with his own. He should move
away from her. He had known even as he had climbed
into bed with her last night that this was a hopeless
idea. He'd known that his self-control wouldn't be able
to hold with her this close. He still remembered all the
reasons why this was a bad idea. Why letting himself
fall for Rowan could never work. He couldn't take
care of his family and keep the business afloat *and*
be a good partner to someone else. He already had
more responsibilities than he could handle, and the
very last thing he should be thinking about was adding more to his life.

But at the same time, he couldn't make any of that
matter.

He still hadn't been able to gather the strength to do
what he knew he had to when her eyes blinked open,
millimetres from his. They widened, startled, as she
realised where she was, and he tightened his arms
around her waist instinctively.

'You're in my bed,' he whispered, stating the painfully obvious. He expected her to jump from him as soon as she realised how close they had moved in the night. One of Rowan's thighs was already trapped between his legs, and he couldn't think of a single thing on earth that would make him want to move away. By some apparent miracle, it seemed Rowan must feel the same. Because instead of scrabbling away from him as he feared she would do after he'd pointed out where they both found themselves, she gave a contented sigh and lay warm and relaxed in his arms, her nose practically brushing against his.

Her tongue darted out to wet her lower lip. She was so close that he could only just see it in his peripheral vision. He closed his eyes, tightened his arms around her waist again and refused to think of all the reasons he shouldn't be doing this as he closed the distance between them and brushed his lips against hers. He sighed into the kiss as Rowan's hands crept up to his shoulders, her legs tangling even more tightly with his own.

As she moved against him, he became aware of just how long he had been waiting to do this. How long he had been denying himself even the knowledge of what he wanted. For the longest time, Rowan's infrequent and unannounced visits to the home that he had shared with Livia and Caleb during the holidays had been the highlight of a period of his life that had been characterised by unlooked-for responsibilities and unparalleled stress.

He'd realised too late after he'd rejected her without properly explaining himself and the reasons he couldn't allow himself the luxury of falling in love with her—because he couldn't imagine indulging this need for her leading anywhere else. He loosened an arm from around her waist and felt a shiver of possessiveness and desire at her groaned dissent, which was only quelled when he tangled his fingers into her hair and angled her mouth so that he could plunder it more thoroughly.

It was just as he was wondering how efficiently he could get them both naked, desperate to have her closer, that the door to his bedroom swung open, and he and Rowan sprang apart, like magnets repelling one another.

'Rowan, could you give me a hand with—? Bloody hell!' Liv cried from the doorway, slamming her hands over her eyes and turning away. 'Sorry, I didn't realise... When you said you were sleeping in here, Row... Never mind, I'm going, I'm gone, I didn't see anything.'

Rowan jumped from the bed, revealing acres of leg that he really should have averted his eyes from. But that ship had well and truly sailed. 'Liv, hold up, it's not what you think,' Rowan said as she reached her friend, where Liv was struggling down the hallway on her crutches.

He wanted to call out to Rowan to come back. To leave Liv and get back in his bed where she belonged. But he couldn't ask that of her, not in front of his sister, at least. So he threw himself back on the pillow as Rowan talked to Liv in a low voice so he couldn't make out what she was saying. With an arm across his face for good measure, he tried in vain to remember why he had spent the past seven years trying not to think about kissing Rowan and could come up with nothing.

Rowan lingered over her shower, letting the hot water obliterate her senses, trying not to think about how it had felt that morning waking up with Jonathan and failing miserably. She tried focusing on the simplicity of sensation, the hot water on her skin, the steam she was breathing in. But all she could feel were Jonathan's hands on her sides and in her hair. Jonathan's mouth on hers and his breath in her lungs. It was only when the hot water tank gave out that she decided it would be childish to risk hypothermia by staying in the shower just because she was afraid of seeing the man she'd been kissing not an hour ago. It wasn't as if she regularly went round kissing people and then having breakfast with them as if nothing had happened.

This was what she had wanted to happen. A kiss that didn't end with him rejecting her, and then…the rest of her life. Without him in it.

When Liv had appeared in the doorway, expecting to find Rowan alone and looking for help with taking a shower, Rowan had let herself follow her instinct to chase after her and try and explain, and ignore the tug in her chest that was telling her to go back to Jonathan and pick up where they left off.

Liv had taken it well, all things considered. Rowan had told her what she knew, which wasn't much. That she and Jonathan had shared a bed because Caleb had kicked Jonathan out, and that the kiss wasn't planned and she didn't expect it to happen again.

Did she *want* it to happen again? Every part of her body was screaming yes, of course. She'd wanted this to happen pretty much since she'd arrived at the manor. She knew that Jonathan wouldn't hurt her on purpose. He knew now how much he'd hurt her the first time, and she didn't think he would be deliberately careless with her feelings. She had to keep reminding herself that all she wanted was a kiss that didn't end up with her heart being stamped on. A chance to move on with her life and get over him. And she'd had that. But they had a few more days in this house. A few more days when she could—if she had the courage—let herself feel desirable. Desired.

But she would have to be careful, she thought as she towelled herself dry. She'd been careless with her feelings around Jonathan once before, and she wouldn't make the same mistake again. She needed to get out for a run. Even if it was just a couple of miles to clear her head.

Fifteen minutes later she was pounding along one of the woodland paths, striving with every pace to find the flow that usually came to her so easily. But every metre felt like a struggle in a way she didn't recognise.

She consciously took stock of her body, trying to pinpoint the source of the problem. Her shoulders were tense and her fingers rigid, so she took a deep breath, trying to let go of the tension in her upper body, making herself more efficient. She concentrated on her affirmation, which always helped to quieten her thoughts and allow her first to exist in the moment. But today its magic seemed to have worn thin. Because the moments it most wanted to live in were the ones from early that morning, when she had been in Jonathan's bed, with the man she'd fantasised about for so long kissing her hard and exploring beneath her clothes before they'd been so abruptly interrupted. Instead of achieving zen and flow, her brain wanted her to consider all the possible places that kiss could have gone if they hadn't been disturbed, and whether she was ever going to get a chance to find out.

She'd chased after Liv so quickly that she'd not had a chance to see how Jonathan was feeling about what they'd done. Whether he regretted it. Again. She'd been so focused ever since on not letting him have a chance to reject her that she hadn't stopped to look and see how he was feeling about what had happened. She tried to concentrate on her stride but she was so in her head that she stumbled over a tree root and had to break her fall with her hands before she went face first into a patch of nettles.

She scrambled out of the stingers, her legs burning, wishing she'd worn her full-length tights, and sat at the foot of the tree, rubbing at her burning skin with a dock leaf.

It could be worse, she told herself, as a fiery rash bloomed and she squeezed her eyes shut to stop the tears. A broken ankle like Livia's would have had her out of training for more than a month. Her only real injury was to her pride. She mashed another dock leaf in her palm and rubbed it on her leg, her teeth cutting deep into her lip as she winced with every stroke over her skin. She pushed herself up from the ground and forced herself to jog back to the manor, knowing that she had to wash the sting off before it would get better. Even stopping for every good patch of dock leaves she saw wasn't going to be enough to calm her angry, inflamed skin.

By the time she reached the back door of the manor, her legs were bright red, streaked with green and covered in welts. Her hands were still stinging and stained green from dock leaves and her face was streaked from the tears she'd given up fighting back for the last half mile. She needed a cool flannel and a vat of lotion and somewhere dark and quiet to nurse her wounds.

'Oh, my God, what happened to you?'

Rowan barely stopped herself from falling and bashing her head on the flagstone floor at the sound of Jonathan's voice. Because of course today would be the day he took actual breaks from the library to do frivolous things like visit the kitchen and hydrate.

'It's not as bad as it looks,' she said, turning away from him to try and hide the worst of it because she knew full well that she looked a fright and she wasn't sure that she could cope with him seeing her like this on top of all the other knocks she had just endured. But Jonathan wasn't letting her get away with that. He took her by the shoulders and steered her into a chair and pulled her feet up onto the bench. 'Nettles?' he asked, running a gentle finger down the front of her shin, making her shiver and wince at once.

'Yes,' she gasped, fighting the urge to scratch at the burning sensation that followed.

'Wait here,' he instructed, and Rowan found that she didn't have the strength to argue. She dropped her face into her hands and scrubbed at the tear tracks on her cheeks.

'Are your legs the worst of it?' he asked, returning with a bowl of water and a cloth.

'And my hands,' Rowan said with a little sniff, holding them out for him to inspect.

'You poor thing,' he said, pressing a kiss to first one muddy palm and then the other, leaving Rowan stunned into speechlessness. She hadn't known what to expect from him today: whether he would be cool and distant, whether he would push her away as firmly as he had the first time that they had kissed. Never in her wildest imaginations had she envisaged this, Jonathan being soft with her. And so tender. She watched as he dipped the cloth into the water and wiped at her grazed, blistered skin, and let out a groan of satisfaction as the cool water soothed the burning.

'Better?' he asked, inspecting her palm intently as he cleaned each graze, only looking up once it was done.

'Much,' she croaked, not trusting herself to say more than that. He left her hand in the bowl of cool water as he methodically worked on the other, and if it hadn't been for the trail of fire ants that felt like they were crawling up her shins, she could have lost herself in the pleasure of it.

'What's wrong?' he asked, his face tilting up with concern when she shifted her legs uncomfortably.

'I think my hands are okay now,' she said.

'Your shins?' Jonathan asked, reading her mind. She bit down hard on her lip and nodded, resisting the urge to claw at her skin.

The first swipe of the cool cloth, from her knee down to her ankle, was a crashing wave of relief so strong that it brought a tear to her eyes. Jonathan followed that up with another cool slide of the cloth on her other leg, and she let her head fall back against the chair and her eyes shut as he took care of her.

'I didn't know that the countryside was so dangerous,' he observed, drawing a laugh from her, even though she kept her eyes shut. 'You and Liv are making it an art form.'

She hissed as he cleaned a graze on her knee, and she smiled as he mumbled some comforting nonsense as he did the other.

'I should know better than to run unfamiliar trails when I'm distracted,' she said as he worked. He looked up at her words, her admission.

'Why were you distracted?' he asked, all innocence, and she let out a breathy laugh. As if he didn't know. 'Do you want to talk about what happened?' he asked.

'Do *you* want to talk about it?' she shot back. After all, he was the one who had had plenty to say after the first time that they had kissed. Very strong opinions.

She should be breaking this off now. Wasn't that what she had wanted? Had planned? This was meant to have been a second chance at a kiss. A chance to leave things on her own terms this time so that she could stop asking herself 'what if' and finally move on. But…being interrupted hadn't been a part of her plan. To have it end like that, with her chasing Liv down the hallway trying to explain what she'd just seen. That wasn't the ending that she deserved, after all this time. She'd come into this looking for closure, and instead now all she had were more questions.

'I wouldn't say that talking is top of my to-do list,' she answered at last, catching Jonathan's eye and trying to look suggestive. She couldn't tell from his expression whether she had hit her mark. He was holding something back, that much was clear. But whether he was resisting telling her that he wanted her or he was going to knock her back again, she couldn't be sure. A sensible woman would bolt before he had a chance to reject her again. There was no way that a sensible woman would risk being rejected again. But he was kneeling at her feet, with her hands in his, and she didn't know how to make herself not want more of that.

'I think I want to hear that list,' he replied with a small smile. Small enough that it told her that he was fighting something bigger. But he was letting her have this, now, and she was going to take whatever was on offer.

'Hey, Rowan,' she heard Liv shout from the family room. 'Is that you? Can you come in here?'

When Liv had called her away, she'd assumed it was something to do with her broken ankle. She doubted she would have let anything other than a broken bone tear her away from Jonathan at that moment. But it turned out all she wanted was to ask whether Rowan wanted to watch a movie when she and Jonathan were finished in the library.

Sitting at one end of the back-breaking sofa later that night, with Jonathan mirroring her body language next to her, she was certain that saying yes had been a terrible idea. She had assumed that Jonathan would carry on working in the library, but to her and everyone else's surprise, he had shut his laptop not long after seven and come to find them all in the family room.

Did this mean that he thought last night had been the start of something, rather than the end? She'd spent all day hoping that it was, even if it was a something that would only last a few days. All she knew was that she wanted more of the kisses that they had shared that morning. More of the way that she had felt when she was in his bed and in his arms. The only thing was, she wasn't entirely sure how to get there from here, trying to sneak sideways glances at Jonathan from her side of the sofa.

She scratched absently at her shin, the nettle rash starting to bother her again. Until she found her fingers gently pulled away and trapped in Jonathan's palm, and looked up at him in surprise. 'It'll make it worse,' he said in a low voice so that the others didn't hear. 'Do you want me to fetch you something for it?' he asked, and she wanted to melt under his kindness.

'It's fine,' she whispered, not pulling away. Maybe this was how they got there, she thought to herself. With tiny moves towards each other in the dark.

Jonathan didn't move away either, other than to give her hand a quick squeeze back. And so they sat holding hands, Rowan feeling positively adolescent—if her adolescence had involved such things as holding hands with boys, rather than trying to make herself as small and unnoticeable as possible in the hope of avoiding her bullies. Or, at least, not offering them further ammunition.

When she started to scratch at her other leg, Jonathan drew her closer, his arm around her shoulders this time, and he ran his palm slowly up her shin. Sensation enough to distract her from the stings. She held her breath, not sure that she could take this intimacy from him when both of his siblings were in the room.

'Right,' Liv said, as soon as the movie finished. 'I'm going to bed.'

'Do you need me to hel—?' Jonathan started to offer, half rising from his seat before he was interrupted.

'No, I've got it,' Caleb said, jumping up and passing Liv her crutches, before helping her out of her chair. 'I think I'll turn in as well,' he said to no one in particular, even though it was barely past ten o'clock.

Jonathan watched them leave before he turned to her. 'So, Caleb knows too?' he asked with a resigned sigh.

'Liv must had told him something,' Rowan said, shrugging as she watched Liv reach the top step and hop out of sight.

'I didn't realise we were so newsworthy,' Jonathan observed dryly, turning to look at her.

Rowan felt her cheeks warm under his attention. 'Newsworthy is a bit strong,' she said with a smile. 'Nothing really happened. It was just a kiss,' she added, not sure whether she wanted him to agree with that sentiment or not.

It would have been more straightforward, she supposed, to simply ask him what he thought about the kiss that they had shared. But she couldn't quite bear risking his answer feeling like another rejection. 'I wouldn't call it nothing,' Jonathan contradicted her, taking her hand and using it to bring her closer, which lit a warm glow deep in her belly and gave her the confidence to ask her next question.

'What *would* you call it?' she asked.

'Well,' Jonathan said, once she was pulled back against his side. 'I suppose in simplest terms we *could* call it just a kiss,' he observed, picking up her hand, examining the palm, pressing a kiss there and then dropping their linked hands into his lap.

'And in more complicated terms?' she ventured, feeling brave.

'Then I suppose it's something that we started, and that I've been thinking about all day.'

'Thinking about…finishing?' she asked, the double meaning very much intended. She'd been thinking about it all day too, not even her nettle stings distracting her from her daydreams. Jonathan coughed in surprise and Rowan chuckled gently. She had always loved throwing him off guard, and this time was no exception.

'You don't want to know the things I've been imagining.'

Oh, now, that was where he was wrong. She wanted to know every single thing that he had imagined, and then make them come true. Until he decided to share, though, she had her own fantasies to work with. Taking a deep breath, she decided now was the time to start, and climbed into Jonathan's lap, her knees straddling his thighs, her hands coming to rest on top of his when they came naturally to her hips, leaving things entirely in her court when it came to what happened next.

She flushed with the knowledge of that power and shifted forward, threading her fingers into his hair and taking her time, watching his face as she shifted her hips to get comfortable, using her hands to tilt Jonathan's face, deciding on what she wanted first and the best way for her to take it. And all through it, Jonathan's hands were still on her hips, holding her close but not directing her movement, as if he was as intrigued by her suddenly taking control as she was.

She rubbed a thumb across his lips and followed the touch with her lips, so fleeting that it was gone before she had a chance to take in Jonathan's gasp, and the quick grasp of his hands on her hips.

'Taking your time?' he asked, his voice strained.

'We have all night,' Rowan replied, hoping very much that they did. Jonathan's hands dropped from her hips to the curve of her backside, gently tipping her towards him. An invitation, not an instruction. It was too tempting an invitation to ignore, and so she leaned in and kissed him again, more slowly this time, letting herself revel in the unhurried glide of her lips over his. The hint of salt from the popcorn they had shared, the red wine that he had been sipping throughout the night.

His arms wrapped tight around her waist, a double brace of hard muscle across her back, pinning her to his front and taking her weight, leaving her free to explore, to play and to test his resolve. He opened his mouth beneath hers, and she sought out his tongue with her own, and groaned when he licked into her mouth, her resolve to take control faltering when her entire body seemed to dissolve into jelly.

But Jonathan was there, right when she needed him, his hands on both sides of her face, angling her so that he could kiss her deeper and harder, until her hips were rocking against him of their own accord, and she was pulling at the hem of his T-shirt, desperate to get at what was underneath. When Jonathan broke suddenly away, she looked down at him in shock, her breath coming quickly and her hair around her shoulders, her clothes creased where they had been caught in the tight press of their bodies.

She might have been embarrassed if it wasn't for the sight of Jonathan looking thoroughly debauched below her. His cheeks were flushed and his hair messy where she had run her hands through it. And his lips were red and swollen—she couldn't be sure why that made her want to bite them, only that it absolutely did.

'Are you okay?' he asked, and she had to laugh because she felt better than she had in her entire life.

Not that she planned on being quite that effusive with her praise.

'I'm good,' she said simply. 'Are you?' she asked as well, it suddenly dawning on her that he had been the one who had put the brakes on. Doubt flooded through her in an instant and she glanced towards the door, wondering if there was a way to make a quick yet elegant exit from a man's lap, and if the technique still worked if one had the legs of a newborn foal.

Her face must have fallen, because Jonathan was suddenly alert, lifting her off him and putting her down on the sofa beside him. 'Are you okay?' he asked again, brushing hair back from her face and looking at her with genuine concern.

'I'm fine,' she said quickly. 'But if you don't want to… You stopped us,' she pointed out, waiting for the blow of his rejection.

'Oh, Rowan,' Jonathan said with a pained groan. 'I didn't do that because I wanted to stop. I just…' He glanced around him at the family room. 'I need to be sure that this is what you want. I don't know what I have to offer you. I don't know what we can make of this. I like you so much, Rowan, and I would never hurt you on purpose, but I have so much—'

'Shh,' Rowan said gently, her fingers finding his bottom lip. 'It doesn't have to be anything you don't want it to be. I'm not thinking past this minute,' she told him.

He stared up at her for several long seconds, and for a moment she thought that he was going to change his mind. But then his hands found her hair again, and he was murmuring in her ear as he dropped kisses along her jaw. 'Then let's take this somewhere with a lock on the door. I don't really want to be interrupted again.'

'Oh.' Rowan sighed, realising probably far later than she should have that both Liv and Caleb had gone to their respective rooms with no mention of sharing with either of them. It seemed that everyone else in the family was expecting her to share Jonathan's bed that night, even if they themselves hadn't talked about it. 'I'm still not entirely convinced that this is really happening.'

The corners of his mouth turned up and he pulled her into a gentle kiss, one hand warm and comforting against her cheek.

'Definitely feels real,' he said, kissing her a second time, and then a third.

'You were thinking of moving this upstairs,' she reminded him, as his other hand slid under her and lifted her up and across, so that she was on top of him again.

'I have the best ideas,' Jonathan said, standing suddenly, so that she had to clutch at him with her arms around his neck and her legs locked around his waist as he carried her up the stairs, into his room, and kicked the door closed behind him.

CHAPTER NINE

SHE KEPT HER arms tight round his neck as he lowered her gently onto his bed, and the smell and feel of the sheets summoned memories of waking up wrapped around him that morning.

His long legs had been wrapped around hers, and she wanted to feel her skin on his like that again.

She tried to get a hand between them to make that happen, but he was too close, and so she contented herself with running a hand up his back under his T-shirt, pulling at the waistband of his jeans so that he could be in no doubt about what she wanted and how. He broke away, panting, and before she could lose her nerve, she threw off her T-shirt and pulled him back down, hiding her body from him before she had a chance to be self-conscious.

She reached for the hem of his shirt too, wanting to level the playing field. Because she couldn't be embarrassed about her state of undress if she got him naked too. The next minutes were a blur of kisses broken only by clothes being pulled off and sharp intakes of breath and long, muffled groans. Of doing battle with stubborn buttons and zips, until somehow, she was breathless and desperate for him, and Jonathan was above her, his weight on his elbows as he ravished her with kiss after kiss after kiss.

'Jonathan,' Rowan said, her hand on his chest holding him back, just for a moment as he scrabbled in his bedside drawer for a condom.

'What is it?' he asked, dropping his forehead to rest against hers. 'Do you want to stop?'

'No, God, no,' Rowan said, which produced a satisfied grin from Jonathan. 'It's just…' She hesitated, because this was putting it all on the line. She didn't have to tell him, but she wanted to. Wanted him to know what this was for her.

'I haven't done this before,' she said in a rush, before she could change her mind. Jonathan stilled instantly and she groaned, thinking that he was about to pull away. Her hands found the small of his back and held him close.

This was her first time? For a second, the pressure of knowing that was overwhelming, before he realised that it didn't change anything, not really. He wanted her first time to be perfect for her. But he'd want that for her second and third and every time after that. She deserved nothing less. And if she was sure that she wanted this, then who was he to second-guess that.

He rested his forehead against hers a moment longer, and she watched him bite his bottom lip before he spoke.

'You want to?' he asked. 'You're sure?'

'I'm so sure,' she said in a rush, reaching up to kiss him, a hand cupping the back of his neck. 'I want to. I want *you*. Please?'

Her words hit him straight in the chest. Because they were so close to the rhythm that his heart was pounding out. He wanted her. He needed her. He had not a single doubt about this, despite every reason he knew that he should be thinking better of this.

He groaned. 'If you're going to ask so nicely...'

He took his weight on his elbows, moving his face back so that she could see every line of concentration around his eyes, the tick of a muscle in his jaw as he held himself so tightly in check. She moved her hand from his nape to his jaw, stroking the muscle there.

'Hey,' she murmured in a low voice. 'It's okay, I'm not going to break.'

She followed her thumb with her lips, kissing along his jaw until she reached his mouth.

'I don't want to hurt you.'

'I know. And you won't,' she said on a breath. 'You can trust me. Trust yourself.'

Jonathan made a noise that was somewhere between a groan and a laugh as he buried his face in her neck. Her skin tasted so good. He wanted to kiss every inch of it, but he wasn't going to rush this. Wasn't going to waste this chance to know her, in case it was the last one that he had. He took his time getting to know her body, what made her gasp, what made her moan, what made her grab his shoulders and urge him on.

When there was no part of her that he hadn't kissed or touched, whispered to or stifled a groan on. When she had begged, and asked nicely, and then given a growl of frustration and taken things into her own hands, he sank so slowly inside her that she had to clutch at his shoulders and pull him into a deep kiss.

She gasped aloud at the unfamiliar sensations, and bracketed Jonathan's face with her palms, kissing and kissing with a desperate urgency she hadn't realised she was capable of. When Jonathan broke their kiss, it was only to brush her hair back from her face and stare at her, as if she was something rare and precious. And he had never before wanted anything this much.

It was so much more intense than he had ever allowed himself to imagine. He suspected that he had always known that it would be like this. That they moved together, spoke to one another, *knew* each other in a way that he hadn't known existed, before tonight. That being with her felt like every broken part of him had found where it fit with a part of her. That together they were so much more than two stupid people who had stumbled around one another for too long. And he knew, with a certainty that terrified him, that he would never have this with another person. That whatever it was he had discovered here with Rowan tonight was unique to them.

Afterwards, when she lay in his arms, her skin damp and cooling, her limbs soft and spent, he refused to let himself think about what came next. Because in this moment of calm and quiet, she was perfect, and so was he.

CHAPTER TEN

JONATHAN WAS STILL sleeping when Rowan woke the next morning, and she permitted herself the indulgence of watching him for a few minutes. Last night had been everything that she had dreamed and hoped that it would be. It had been perfect, and the shadow of that hung over her now. Because where did one go from perfect? The only possible direction was down, and she wasn't sure that she had the heart to let anything taint her memories of the night before. She wanted to preserve it complete and unspoiled. If she let this play out without taking control now, she was going to get hurt. She was suddenly struck with the certainty of it, and the certainty of how devastating it would be for this to go wrong.

She rested her head against Jonathan's chest, a consolation prize for what she knew she would have to do next. She was going to have to get up, out of this bed, and tell him that this couldn't happen again. It would take every ounce of her resolve to drag herself into the shower and wash his scent off her skin, and the fact that she was even thinking that should have been enough to prove to her that she was making the right decision. Because how much worse would it be to walk away after two nights like this one? Three? She wouldn't want to do it, which would mean that Jonathan would have to be the one to end things. To reject her. And she wasn't sure that she could do that to herself again. No.

Right now, the most important thing was to remember what her priorities were: fixing the holes in her self-esteem that had resulted from Jonathan walking away from their kiss all these years ago. Getting over him. Moving on.

Well. Job done. Very well and thoroughly done, as it happened. She slipped from the bed and pulled on some clothes, and then headed straight for the bathroom before she could talk herself out of it.

Jonathan's door was still shut when she was showered and dressed and she headed down the stairs and into the kitchen for breakfast, not allowing herself to think about whether she wanted him to be in there or not. Of course she wanted him, but what she didn't want, couldn't bear, was the thought of being rejected by him. She had to quit before she got hurt, however much she might be tempted to wish for more.

'Hey,' Jonathan said as she walked into the kitchen, and she squealed, jumping out of her skin. She hadn't heard anyone moving about the house, and had just assumed that Jonathan was still in bed where she'd left him.

'Hey,' Rowan replied quietly, feeling surprisingly tongue-tied. 'I didn't realise you were up.'

'I woke and you weren't there.'

Rowan shifted a little uncomfortably under his intense gaze. 'It was early. I didn't want to disturb you,' she lied, hoping that he would take her excuse at face value.

'Right,' Jonathan replied, his inflection free from emotion. He moved closer, and for a moment she thought that he was going to kiss her, but something must have made him change his mind, because he took a step away from her.

'So…you're okay, then?' he asked. 'After last night?'

'Of course,' Rowan admitted. 'I'm fine. Are you?'

He stared at her, and she would have given anything for him to smile at her just then.

'So you didn't leave because something was wrong?' he asked. 'I didn't… I wasn't…'

'You were perfect,' she said, suddenly realising how he had interpreted her early departure that morning. She couldn't leave him thinking that, but she also knew what she had to do.

She took a deep breath and forced out what she needed to say. 'It was fun, Jonathan, and really, really…' She searched for the right word, but knew that she couldn't do justice to what it had meant to her without giving away too much about what she felt for him. 'It was lovely. I'm glad that we're friends, but I think anything more than that would be too complicated, what with Liv and family stuff… You know?'

'Oh.' Jonathan's face fell, and for a moment she wondered whether she had actually hurt him. Before she remembered that this hadn't meant the same thing to him as it did to her. It was surprise, and nothing more, that had put that expression on his face. 'Yes. Right. You're probably right,' Jonathan said, rubbing at the back of his neck with an expression that made her wonder if they should have talked about expectations before they slept together, rather than waiting for the morning after.

But that was absurd. Even the idea that she could hurt Jonathan was ridiculous. He frowned at her, and asked again, 'And you're sure that last night was... okay?'

'It was perfect, Jonathan, honestly. I just don't think we need to make a big deal out of this.' She made herself turn her mouth up in a smile, even though it was the last thing that she felt like doing.

'I just need... I need to move on,' she said at last.

It was perfect.

Jonathan replayed the words over and over in his head as Rowan took her plate of toast and her coffee and went off to find Liv. He sat back at the table and reran the whole night in his head. It had been...dreamlike. Or it had been for him, at least. He had thought that Rowan had enjoyed it every bit as much as he had but... Well, he must have done something wrong, or she wouldn't have snuck out at dawn and then made clear at the earliest opportunity that she never wanted it to happen again. He felt an uncomfortable pang of conscience.

He shouldn't have just rushed in yesterday without thinking through the consequences. Without weighing up what he and Rowan meant to one another. Without talking carefully about what this meant for Rowan's friendship with Liv, never mind his own relationship with his sister. Because, despite her assurances that everything was fine, there was no hiding from the fact that Rowan had been strange and awkward with him, and he had the distinct feeling that he had hurt her without knowing how.

He got to work in the library and looked up in surprise when he heard Rowan clear her throat behind him later that afternoon. She was standing in the doorway, sun streaming through the hall windows backlighting her hair, lending her an almost supernatural glow.

'Hi,' he said, guarding against the leap he felt in his chest and the sudden urge to smile, lest it gave away his feelings about last night and this morning. 'What can I do for you?' Jonathan asked, instantly regretting how stuffy that made him sound.

'I…er, I've been looking at the accounts that you sent me and working through the numbers,' Rowan said. 'I was wondering if you still wanted to talk through it with me. I have a few ideas.'

'Oh, you're here to talk about work.' By the time he realised his face was showing how disappointed he was, it was too late to stop it.

Rowan grimaced, and he guessed that she hated how awkward this was too. 'I understand if you don't want to after last night…'

Had he really thought that she was here to give them another chance after what she had said in the kitchen? After she'd left that morning without a word? Maybe he should have gone to her and asked that they talk this through properly. They'd left things unsaid the first time that they had kissed, and he'd hurt her more than he'd known. He should know better than to avoid important conversations.

But he had gone into this knowing that he didn't have enough of himself to give to a partner to make a relationship work. Rowan deserved better than that. Deserved someone less distracted, less committed elsewhere. It would be too easy to let himself take what he wanted from her and ignore that he couldn't give her what she deserved in return. She had done them both a favour by giving what they had a clean ending. One that didn't hurt either of them.

An hour later, his back was aching from holding himself so straight and still while she talked through the financial options that she'd outlined on his laptop.

'The problem is,' Rowan summarised, reaching the end of her spreadsheet, 'that you can't go on as you are. You've been plugging holes, but you can't do that indefinitely. We need to find you a new source of income but it's not going to be easy to bring an investor on board a business that's failing—I'm sorry to be so blunt. But if we can show that we have viable plans to create the potential for a new revenue stream, we have a much better chance of securing the funds that you're going to need.'

'What are you thinking?' he asked, looking away from the figures on the laptop and meeting her eyes for the first time. She looked unsure of herself since they'd first started talking about the business, and he guessed that that meant he should brace himself for whatever was coming next.

Rowan clasped her hands together and rested her elbows on the desk. Her face had a determination that he hadn't seen before, but which he definitely liked. 'You know that Liv is excited about the research we found on the old fragrance line—well, so am I. That's exactly the sort of thing that could hook an investor. There are PR and publicity opportunities, and you really should consider using Liv's expertise. She's got the experience and the family name, and she's talented. She knows how to build excitement for a new brand. I think you know that this is a good idea. Your competitors are already doing this and making a lot of money from it.'

Jonathan nodded. He agreed with everything she had said. And if they were talking about anyone else's business, he would be telling them to start it yesterday. But this wasn't just business—he couldn't do this without getting Liv and Caleb involved, and he'd promised himself that he wouldn't do that. That he wouldn't burden them with the knowledge that they might lose the family business on top of everything else until it was inevitable. 'I know it's a good plan,' he told her. 'I trust you—I trust your judgement and your numbers—but I can't do this without telling Liv and Cal about the trouble that the business is in. I don't want to do that. They shouldn't have to worry about that. They've been through enough.'

Rowan gave him a sympathetic smile. He didn't

deserve her pity. 'You shouldn't have to worry either,' she told him. 'But you do. And you shouldn't have to do this alone. Let them help you. Let them be a part of it. If this was someone else's business, you know what you'd be telling them.'

'Of course I would.' He'd had the same thought himself moments ago, and felt like a hypocrite arguing with Rowan about it now. 'I'd be telling them to take a risk, that they had no other choice. But *I'm* the one that would be looking their staff in the eye and telling them that they didn't have a job if all this goes wrong. I'd be the one telling my brother and sister that the family business went down on my watch, after more than a hundred years. We could lose everything.'

'Jonathan,' Rowan said gently, 'that's what's going to happen if you don't do anything.'

He shook his head, because surely there had to be some other way. 'But if I just—'

'What, find some more money from somewhere? It might help for a few months, and then you'll be right back here again.' She smiled, sympathetically, trying to soften the blow. He appreciated the gesture, but it didn't help, because he knew that she was right. She rested a hand on his shoulder, and he let himself draw comfort from it, even though he knew that he didn't deserve it. He couldn't keep taking from her like this when he had nothing to reciprocate with.

'So I should go down fighting?' he asked, his voice near to breaking.

'You should make sure you've considered all the options before you make a decision one way or another,' she told him firmly.

'Did you do that with us? Consider all the options before you decided whether you wanted out?' He didn't know why he had said it. Why he had brought the conversation back to the topic that they'd been studiously ignoring for the past two hours. But the weight of all the things that they weren't saying—all the questions he had about why she had put an end to things that morning when they still had days and nights here that they could be enjoying together—was suddenly unbearable.

Rowan was evidently so shocked that she couldn't speak for a few moments.

'I... That's completely different,' she said. 'We were talking about work.'

He shook his head, not sure if he was apologising. 'I can't concentrate on work when I keep thinking about last night.' The words settled into the room around them, and he wasn't sure where they went from here. 'Look,' he said at last. 'Why don't we get out of here for a bit. I'm sick of these four walls, there's too much going on in my head to make sense of any of it and I can't talk to you properly when my brother or sister might walk in at any moment.'

She stared at him for a minute before nodding. 'Okay, I guess we've earned a break,' she said at last. 'Liv mentioned that there's a market in the town today. I wouldn't mind going for a look.'

'That sounds perfect.' Jonathan said, closing his laptop. 'I'll meet you in the hallway in five minutes.'

CHAPTER ELEVEN

THIS WAS SUCH a stupid idea. Her whole plan was to get over Jonathan. To kiss him, take what she needed from him. And then *move on with her life*. Because he was never going to be the one. Or, to be more specific, she was never going to be the one for him. He'd had every opportunity to fall in love with her and never once decided to take her up on it. Falling for him would be utterly reckless, and she knew it. She shouldn't have gone to bed with him last night.

But she couldn't make herself regret something so perfect. Something that had felt so right in the moment, and even now, knowing that it was a bad idea, *still* felt so right.

And instead of keeping her distance from him, like she had told herself this morning that she must, she had spent the morning poring over his company accounts to try and distract herself while Liv slept, two more hours talking through what she had found with him, and now she was picking up her backpack and slicking on some tinted lip balm so that they could go look at antiques and artisanal cheeses and local handicrafts.

They walked down the long, gravelled driveway towards the town, and Rowan had never been so aware of her own hands before. They seemed to swing at her side like great weighted balloons. This was stupid. If she wanted to hold his hand, she could just do it, but she knew deep down that she wouldn't. The only way that she could avoid getting her heart thoroughly trodden on was to try and forget that last night had ever happened. She had been perfectly clear with Jonathan that they were better off as just friends.

They were enveloped by an uncomfortable quiet as they walked, with just the wind-rustled leaves and tweeting birds interrupting the silence. She glanced across at Jonathan, only to find him looking back at her, and she blushed, fiercely, as she looked away again.

'Look,' Jonathan said at last as they reached the first houses on the edge of the town. 'Tell me if you don't want to have this conversation. But last night being a one-off…is it really because of Liv? Or is it me? Is it something I've done?' he asked.

'What? No!' Rowan replied, genuinely surprised that he could think that this was anything that he had *done*. 'I just think it would be too complicated.'

It seemed easier to say than, *We both know that you're going to tap out of this first, and I don't think I can handle that again.* She was meant to be moving on, and she couldn't do that off the back of a heart broken for the second time.

'But you knew it was complicated yesterday,' he pointed out, not unreasonably. 'I'm not disagreeing with you or trying to change your mind. I'm just trying to understand what has changed since then.'

For the first time she felt ashamed of the fact that she had gone into this knowing that this was temporary for her, but without asking whether that was what Jonathan wanted too. He had made clear the first time they kissed that his interest in her had its limits—it was attraction, not something deeper. She hadn't even known that she had the power to hurt him. How could she know that, when up until now he had been the one doing the hurting.

It was just hurt pride that he was feeling, she told herself as they crossed a bridge over a small brook. Not a real wound. Not like he had hurt her. He would have forgotten about her in a matter of days. Not carry these memories round with him for years, until he had to take drastic action to get over it. So why did she feel guilty?

They'd reached the marketplace, the stone cross at its centre weathered with centuries of exposure to the elements. The steps at its base smoothed with use. The stalls were all covered with blue-and-white-striped awnings, customers crowding round each one. The smell of coffee from a tiny three-wheeled truck competed for her attention with the pop of a Prosecco bottle from a temporary bar in the centre of the square.

She turned to face Jonathan. 'I just think it's best if we forget about it.' He stared and stared at her, until she had to ask, 'What?'

'This isn't how I thought today was going to be,' he said at last, pinching the bridge of his nose.

'Oh? And how did you expect it to be?' She gathered her courage and decided to call his bluff. 'Were you planning on asking me to be your girlfriend?'

'We… I— No. Um… I thought that I'd made clear…' Jonathan spluttered, and Rowan gave him a sympathetic smile as she pushed him towards one of the stalls. *See?* she reassured herself. His ego might be bruised that he didn't get in there first, but he hadn't wanted this to be more than casual any more than she did.

Except, oh, it hurt to lie to herself. And just because she wouldn't let herself want any more than he was willing to give, that didn't mean that she wouldn't have wanted it if things had been different.

'Come on,' she said, pretending that it wasn't breaking her inside to have to be the one pushing him away. 'Let's not argue. There's tons here to explore. Where do you want to start?'

The stall behind them was loaded with mountains of olives in every variety she could think of, and more besides. The next was stacked with wheels of cheese, and the one after that with sausage rolls and Scotch eggs the size of her fist. By the time that they reached the antique stall at the end of the row, they were both toting little paper bags of goodies to take back to the house with them. And Rowan briefly allowed herself to entertain the thought that she could happily come back to this town, this market, every week for the rest of her life and be perfectly contented. And then tried to shake away the thought because that picture didn't make any sense without Jonathan in it, and she'd just told him that there was no way that was ever going to happen.

She did her best to shake off the melancholy and look properly at the antiques, because if you weren't going to do that when you were in the Cotswolds, when would you?

She gasped when the decorative glass bottles at the far end of the stall caught her eye.

'Oh, my goodness, are those—?'

'Perfume bottles?' Jonathan finished for her, following the line of her gaze.

He checked with the stallholder and then picked one up, handing it to her. She lifted the stopper and inhaled, hoping to catch a hint of the scent that it had once held. There were half a dozen of them in different styles. Some cut glass, some coloured. One was decorated with a crown of tiny ceramic flowers.

'They're so beautiful,' she said with a smile. 'Do you think that this is a sign?'

Jonathan smiled at her, and she got the feeling he was indulging her a little. 'Maybe. We should take them home for Liv. Except for this one,' he said, taking the one that she was still holding, and passing it to the stallholder. 'This one's for you.' She smiled, wide and unabashed, and didn't care that her whole heart was on show. It was too tempting, being cherished by this man. He was too good at it. Making her feel like she mattered. She had to keep reminding herself that she would only get hurt if she let herself think like that. Eventually, he would push her away, and she knew that she couldn't survive that again.

They wandered among the other stalls, searching out their treasures, and when the sun reached the top of the roof of the pub at the other side of the market, Rowan sighed and suggested that they walk home.

'Tell me more about your race,' Jonathan said, as they retraced their steps over the bridge and out of the centre of the town.

Rowan grinned, still more excited than nervous at the thought of her ultramarathon. The nerves would come later, when she was tossing and turning and struggling to sleep the night before. Counting down the hours before her alarm went off at five in the morning.

'It's an early start,' she warned him. 'And a long event. I'm not going to hold you to doing it if you've changed your mind. If you didn't really understand what you were volunteering for.'

'No, shush,' he said, a gentle hand at her elbow. 'I just want to know more about it. Why you love it. It sounds like torture to me: I didn't know that you were into that,' he added with a smile.

'Oh, I don't know, I've never really experimented,' she replied with a gleam in her eye that made him blush and then laugh. He nudged her with his shoulder, so she carried on talking.

'It's a hundred miles. Will probably take me about twenty-four hours. I've only done two before so it's sort of hard to judge. This will probably be the furthest I walk between now and the start line. I'll have to park myself in a chair for a couple of days. Conserve energy.'

'So you run through the night?' he asked.

'Yep. With a head torch and a map. And a compass. It can get a bit hairy, but I've always managed to find the finish line eventually.'

'And you run the whole way?'

She shrugged. 'It depends how I'm feeling. I might walk some of the bigger hills to save my legs. The important thing is to keep moving.'

'And what do you need me to do? Hand out energy bars and water bottles?'

Rowan nodded. 'And change batteries and make sure my phone is charged and find me dry socks. But…' She hesitated. 'Liv knows when to push me and when to listen and…she knows my limits. Knows what I can do.'

'I don't know you as well as she does,' Jonathan said, sounding worried for the first time.

'No,' Rowan agreed. 'But… We have a connection, right? I've not imagined that? I trust you to know what I will need.'

The words struck him right in the chest.

She trusted him to know what she needed from him. She might need him to make a call for her that she couldn't make for herself.

The thought of that should have filled him with dread. He should have been turning on the spot and walking away from a woman who was being completely open about the fact that she needed something from him. On paper, it looked like an obligation. A burden. But it didn't *feel* like that. It felt like something that he would willingly give—let her take—because they would be a team and he knew that she would do the same for him. Was this what she had been talking about? That he was the one who kept his relationships so one-sided. How he kept secrets from Liv to protect her, and in the process cut off his family, who should have been his greatest source of support over the last years.

They walked the rest of the way back to the house in silence as he thought over everything that Rowan had said, and the different paths for his future that she'd shined a light on.

'So you'll trust me with that but not with…' He let his voice trail off, but she knew exactly what he was talking about. He couldn't blame her for wanting to make her boundaries clear, but he couldn't shake the deep sadness that he felt at the idea that the night before might be a one-off. He wanted more of her. It had felt like the beginning of something, not the end.

But the beginning of something didn't have to mean the beginning of for ever, he reasoned. They were only here for a few more days. There was a natural end point built into this little rural idyll, so why didn't they make the most of it?

'Come on, out with it,' she said, looking across at him. 'What are you thinking?'

'Just that…we're leaving in a few days. So, anything that we start would naturally—'

'Come to an end,' she finished for him.

He nodded, glad that they were on the same page. Because suddenly the thought that everything he had shared with Rowan was in the past, that they were destined now to just grow further and further apart filled him with sadness. 'That's right,' he said. 'So we could…enjoy one another and then draw a line under it. If that's what we both wanted.'

He watched her carefully as a small smile crept from the corner of her mouth and he felt something in his chest ease, like he had staved off a heart attack.

'And that's what you want?' she said. 'Something temporary. Something we can draw a line under.'

No. He had to force himself not to say the word out loud. Because it wasn't what he wanted but it was all that he could risk. All that he could justify taking for himself. So he nodded.

'Yes. We enjoy ourselves while we're here, and then we go back to being friends.'

Rowan thought for a few minutes more. 'Define enjoy one another,' she said at last, with a defiant look in her eye.

He took a step towards her and trapped her chin between his thumb and forefinger, making sure she was looking him right in the eye. 'You look flushed,' he said, with a deadly serious tone of voice. 'Tell me what you were thinking just then.'

The corner of her mouth ticked up again. 'I wasn't thinking anything. If I'm flushed it's because it's so warm out,' she said, turning her face up to the sun before he brought her gaze back to his. 'I think I need to cool off a bit. Maybe I'll take a shower when we get back.'

His brain conjured the whole scene in the space between one heartbeat and the next. Water pounding on her shoulders, running over her breasts, sluicing down her belly. The click of the door and the slide of a shower screen. She'd keep her back turned, her eyes closed, as she waited for his arms around her waist pulling her back to him. He could feel the cold tile and hot water, her soft skin and the smooth slide of soapsuds.

He grabbed her hand and pulled, thankful that she was every inch as tall as him and could keep up with the near sprint as he dragged her up the drive.

'What are you doing?' she asked, laughing.

'Getting you home for that shower,' he replied, deadly serious. She gave him a self-satisfied grin, and he guessed that every thought he'd just had had shown on his face.

'I'll leave the door unlocked.'

CHAPTER TWELVE

THEY'D NEVER QUITE made it downstairs after the shower. God knew what Liv and Caleb thought was going on, Rowan considered as she got dressed the next morning. Actually, they probably knew exactly what was going on and that was why no one had asked. At least she could trust Liv not to ask questions she didn't want the answer to. Still, she supposed at some point she was going to have to talk to her best friend and figure out how their friendship worked now that she was sleeping with Liv's brother.

'Sleeping with' in the present tense, she acknowledged to herself, because any pretence she'd managed to maintain that she would be able to move on once she'd got Jonathan out of her system was long gone. But he'd pointed out that this week had a natural end point, and she was not going to argue with him. It was no different from a holiday romance, she reasoned to herself. She was going to enjoy him while they were here and then go back to her normal life, all sun-kissed and satisfied, warm with memories.

Lying in bed that morning, she and Jonathan had

come up with a plan to tell his siblings about the problems with the business, and the possible solutions that were on the table. Jonathan was going to explain the financial difficulties the business was facing.

'So, what's this all about?' Liv said, cringing slightly as they all sat around the kitchen table. 'Is this all to tell me I'm getting a new sister?' she said, trying to force a laugh, and wincing as if she was preparing to hear something gruesome. Jonathan blushed and glanced at Rowan, who rolled her eyes.

'This is about Kinley,' Jonathan said, cutting straight to it. 'About your idea for the perfume. I want to explore the idea further and I want you to do it. I think we should give it a try, but there are some things that you need to know first.'

'About perfume?' Cal asked, looking dubious, as if he wished he could be back in his room rather than being dragged into family business.

'About the business. There are some things going on that I haven't told you about, and I should have done. The long and short of it is, there's no money to do this. There's no money for anything. If we want to launch a new product line, we're going to have to get finance from somewhere, and that's not going to be easy, considering the mess that the company is in.'

'How big a mess?' Liv asked, narrowing her eyes. Rowan just hoped that she could hold off her interrogation long enough for Jonathan to tell his side of the story.

'Very big,' Jonathan said with a sigh.

'And you've been trying to handle it all by yourself,

which is why this is the first that we're hearing about it?' Liv guessed out loud, which showed she knew her brother better than he thought she did.

Jonathan nodded. 'I've been using my savings to keep us afloat but that's not an option any more.'

Understanding dawned in Liv's expression. 'So that's why you're selling the house,' she said. 'Because you need the cash.'

'I can't afford to keep it. And any profits from the sale I can use in the business. It's not what I want either, but there really isn't any other way.'

'Cal and I have savings,' Liv interjected. 'Why don't we use those, and keep the house?'

'And, you know, I have some bitcoin I invested in a while back,' Caleb added.

They all stared at him with wide eyes for a few moments before Jonathan brought the conversation back on track, shaking his head as he spoke. 'I can't let you sink your inheritances into the business.'

'Why not?' Liv asked, a little more heat in her voice. 'It's what you did with yours. Do you think that we don't care as much about the business as you do?'

'That money is for your futures,' Jonathan said firmly, and Rowan could see what direction this conversation was about to take and wasn't quite sure how to stop it, or if she should.

'The money was left to us to decide what we want to do with it,' Liv pointed out. 'I don't think that it's fair of you to tell me that I can't invest it in the family business. *Our* family business. The fragrance line was my idea. The least you can do is let me put my own money on the line.'

'What if you lose it all? I'm trying to protect you,' Jonathan told his sister gently, before Rowan laid a hand over his.

'Okay, let's take a breather,' Rowan said, looking at each of the siblings in turn. 'Jonathan, I don't think that you can tell your siblings what they can do with their money. If they want to invest it in the business, what better investors do you think you're going to find? Let's treat this like any other business decision. We'll write a business plan and see where we get to. Be as objective about this as we can. If you decide to look for investors, you should give Liv and Cal the chance if they want it,' she said.

And then she held her breath to see how her words landed. Whether Jonathan was going to give the people he loved the chance to support him for once, rather than pushing them away. Suddenly, the outcome of this felt much more pertinent to her future than she had ever wanted it to.

'Okay,' Jonathan said. 'Okay. Let's do the numbers and come up with a proper plan, and if you really want to take the risk, then I'm not going to stop you,' he said, sounding resigned. Rowan let out her breath. So he was going to try. It was a start.

Cal and Liv headed upstairs, muttering between themselves, leaving Jonathan and Rowan alone at the kitchen table. Rowan wanted to slide her hands into Jonathan's hair, turn his face up to hers and kiss away that despairing expression on his face. But she knew from the stiff line of his shoulders that that wasn't what he needed right now.

'I think that went well,' she suggested gently, wincing slightly when Jonathan snapped his gaze up to hers, making it clear that he didn't agree.

'I had no intention of them losing their own money in this,' he said, a sharp edge to his voice.

'You didn't think that they would want to help?' she asked. How could he not have seen that the suggestion might come up?

'I don't want them to lose their inheritance. I would never have suggested it if I'd known that this was how it was going to go.'

She sighed, because he might be showing some outward signs of growing out of this martyr complex, but right now he was showing who he was deep inside, and that person didn't seem to be open to change at all. 'At some point, Jonathan,' she told him sharply, 'you're going to have to accept that they are adults who are allowed to make their own decisions and take their own risks. Cal has a secret stash of bitcoin none of us knew about, for goodness' sake. Surely you should be happy to have willing investors, ones with as big an emotional stake in the company as you have? You couldn't ask for better partners. You don't have a monopoly on caring about the business or your family's legacy.'

'They're not my partners!' he said, standing and coming round to her side of the table. 'They're my...'

'Your what, Jonathan?' she prompted when he didn't finish his sentence. 'They're not your kids. They're not even your responsibility any more, at least no more than you are theirs. Why is it so impossible to accept that they're capable of making their own decisions? To let them help you, for once. Do you have such a God complex that you can't even let them stop your business from going under? You just expect all the people who love you to stand by and watch while you stress yourself into a heart attack because you're too proud to let anyone help you? We're here, Jonathan. I'm here. For you. We love you—I love you—and I want to help you and you won't let me. You're allowed to accept help. You're allowed to *ask* for it. You're allowed to let people love you and it doesn't make you a failure.'

That was it, everything she'd always wanted to say to him and more. She'd told him that she loved him. She hadn't even admitted that to herself until the words had been spilling from her mouth in a desperate attempt to get him to help himself.

'But I don't want that, Rowan,' Jonathan said, his voice broken. 'I can't let you love me, and I don't want to love you back, because you'd be just one more person I'd be letting down when this all falls apart.'

It wasn't how this was supposed to go. He was meant to protect his family. Protect his business. Protect Rowan by staying the hell away from her. And somehow in the space of a few days he'd managed to make everything so much worse on all three fronts. If he'd thought he had too much at stake before, it was nothing to where he found himself now, after his siblings and Rowan had conspired to convince him to take a risk that he almost certainly couldn't afford.

This was why he'd made the choices he had. The sacrifices he had. This was why he had torn himself away from Rowan the first time that he had kissed her and kicked himself until he remembered exactly why he wasn't allowed to have this.

And then he'd been stupid enough to forget. To convince himself while he was here, away from his real life, that this was something that he was allowed to have. He'd held Rowan close and refused to acknowledge the fact that it was never going to work out. That it could never last once they were away from this place.

He'd not even been able to keep it that long without messing up. Without dragging his family and his business into things as well until it was all so tangled that he didn't know how to fix one thing without something else unravelling.

And the worst of it all was that she was in love with him. Or believed that she was. When he'd thought that he was the only one with their heart on the line, it had been bad enough. He didn't think that he'd be able to hurt Rowan so badly so soon. Which had been entirely his mistake, of course. He should never underestimate the harm that he can do to the people closest to him.

'I'm sorry, Rowan. I know that we said that we could enjoy this while it lasts, while we're here, but this has just proved everything I thought before we started. It was never going to work. I was never going to have space in my life to give you what you deserve, and it was foolish of me to even try.'

CHAPTER THIRTEEN

I DON'T WANT to love you back.

It shouldn't have felt like such a shock. She'd known, always known, that what she and Jonathan had was temporary. She'd managed to convince herself that *this* was who she was now. Someone Jonathan would never want to walk away from. And she'd been so distracted by that, so tempted by the thought that she might be someone he could want more than once, that she'd missed her opportunity to walk away before he could hurt her.

But she had told him that she loved him, and that hadn't even registered. Hadn't moved him one bit—and that utterly broke her.

The worst of it was, she couldn't even be angry with him. She'd known well enough that this would happen. She'd been relying on the fact that she was going into this thinking that she knew what she was doing. That she'd be able to keep her head and make rational decisions and… Oh. She had been completely deluded.

'You know what, it's fine,' she lied. 'We both knew that this was only going to last a few days so let's just forget it ever happened. Leave the whole thing behind us.'

'Don't pretend with me,' Jonathan said, sounding defeated. 'You just told me that you love me. Don't pretend that you're not hurt for my sake.'

'For God's sake, Jonathan. Stop trying to fix it! You don't want me. Fine. All I wanted was the chance to finally move on and forget that kiss. Well, I've got plenty of new mistakes to ruminate over now. Job done.'

He stared at her in a way that made her want to run, fast, but she fought the urge down, because she had been running and hiding from him for years, and she was tired of it now. They were going to have this conversation all the way to the bitter, inevitable end.

'That's what this was about for you? A chance to reject me and get your own back?' he asked, his voice as hard as she had ever heard it. Which wasn't entirely fair. She was under no illusions over the mistakes that she had made. But she hadn't broken this…fling, relationship, whatever…up on her own. In fact, in the end, she hadn't done it at all. 'Then I really don't see how I am the villain here if this was never real for you.'

'I never said it wasn't real,' she objected. Certainly the pain that she felt in her chest right that moment felt as real as any other. 'For me, anyway. I never expected you to feel the same way.'

'Good, because I don't feel the same way. I hate the way I feel when we are together,' Jonathan said, as if he had deliberately chosen the most devastating comeback.

Rowan felt herself physically flinch. She took a step

away, glancing over her shoulder at the doorway and wondering whether she should have just left the question unanswered. She should have walked away and left herself in her blissful, blissful ignorance.

'I wish that I could love you the way that you deserve to be loved. But I can't. There's not enough of me left to give, not without breaking me completely. I could never ask you to settle for so little.'

She huffed through her nose. Because, just once, couldn't he actually speak to her about what she wanted rather than just deciding for her? 'Ask me?' she said derisively. 'I don't remember you asking me anything. I remember you making an awful lot of assumptions about what I might or might not want.'

Jonathan stared at her for a moment, and she wondered which of her words he was struggling to process. In the end, he sat down, leaning back against the side of the table.

'What, and you're saying you did anything different when you walked out the morning after we slept together?'

She felt that one hit home, and when her cheeks burned this time, it was with shame. Had she been the one who had ruined this? Because she didn't trust him not to reject her again?

'I'm sorry, Rowan. You don't know how much I wish that things were different.'

'So do I,' she said sadly. 'I wish that you could understand that loving someone means letting them look after you too. I wish you knew how good we could have made this if you were willing to take a chance on it. On me.'

She felt her heart throb for him. For this kind, loving man who thought that he wasn't enough. Who gave so much of himself that he didn't realise that he could take as well. And then her heart broke, because she had put everything on the line here, to give herself a chance to move on. To think that one day she would let herself fall in love without her whole heart belonging to Jonathan, and she knew now that that would be impossible.

CHAPTER FOURTEEN

ROWAN WAS AVOIDING him and he should allow her that
space, Jonathan told himself the next morning. He
couldn't blame her, not after everything he had said
the day before. He'd seen the look on her face when his
words had landed, and he knew that he'd hurt her, even
when he was trying to save her from himself. And he
knew that he should leave her alone. He couldn't offer
her what she wanted—what they both wanted—and it
could only make things worse to keep prodding that
wound. But he couldn't bear the thought that they were
under the same roof and not speaking either.

He only had a few days with her, and even if they
weren't spending them in bed, as he'd allowed himself to hope they might, that didn't mean that he didn't
want to see her at all.

Perhaps it was selfish—probably, it was selfish—
to go to her room just to see her, speak to her, given
that he wasn't going to change his mind. But he found
himself outside her door anyway, because it took
more strength than he had to be where she wasn't.

* * *

Rowan supposed she should feel better now that she and Jonathan had been completely honest with each other at last. She looked over her drop bags for the ultramarathon, spread out on her bed. At least she knew now with absolute certainty that they didn't have a future. Jonathan didn't even *want* to fall in love with her, because he saw love as nothing more than a burden. If he fell for her, she'd just be someone else who he'd have to take care of, and hadn't ever considered that in loving him back she'd maybe give as much as she took.

Shouldn't she feel…better than this, now that she knew everything? She looked at the bags that she had spread over Liv's bed, individual bags full of snacks, spare clothes, blister plasters and batteries, one for each of the seven stops on her route. It would be the first race that she'd run without a crew—she hadn't asked Jonathan whether he had changed his mind. He'd made it clear that he didn't want anyone else to look after, and she couldn't see him spending a full day in a field somewhere after the argument that they'd just had.

It was essential that she didn't miss anything. She lined up all the bags and dug around for the laminated checklist that she always put together before a race, but every time that she tried to concentrate on it, her mind wandered.

She hadn't known that it was possible to go from feeling so hopeful to so broken in the space of a day. God, she was going to need so much therapy when she got back to London, she groaned to herself.

After all, when left to her own devices, how had she done trying to fix her battered and broken self-esteem—she'd thrown herself into bed with a man who had already rejected her once, didn't want her now, made all their relationships endlessly more complicated, and then fallen in love with him. It was hard to imagine any therapist doing a worse job than that.

She heard footsteps in the corridor and looked up to see Jonathan in the doorway. They'd been studiously avoiding each other since their argument earlier, and she still couldn't bring herself to meet his eyes. He seemed just as awkward, hesitating on the threshold for a few moments, and she wondered if he was going to bring up everything they had said to one another. 'Checking your kit?' he asked, and she felt disappointed all over again.

'Big day tomorrow,' she said with a false smile. She wouldn't let him see how much she was hurting. It was the only control she had left. He came over and took the checklist from her hands, gently prising it from her fingers and ignoring her quiet protests.

'You've already done this,' he said, looking down at the careful rows of check marks. 'It looks like you have everything you need,' he said.

She nodded. They could do this. She could talk about running. That was safer than talking about... anything else, really. 'I think so,' Rowan replied. 'I just need to make sure I know where everything is. If I can't find what I need tomorrow—'

'Then I'll find it for you,' he said, frowning. 'Isn't

that what I'm there for? Unless you're saying that you don't want me to be, after—'

'I just assumed you wouldn't want to,' she interrupted, so taken aback that he was still planning on giving up his Saturday for her, after everything that had happened. She knew that her hurt was showing in her voice. Well, fine. She wasn't going to pretend not to be. She had offered Jonathan everything that she had to give, and he'd been too scared to take it. To even let himself want it. She was allowed to be hurt.

'Rowan, we're still friends,' he said, though the past day hadn't exactly felt very friendly. 'I want to be there for you.'

She had to force herself not to snort at that. 'But I'm not allowed to be there for you?' she asked. 'It's too unreasonable to think that this could be reciprocal, that we could be a team?' She looked him straight in the eye, refusing to back down. Because she'd decided that this mattered. Once upon a time, she'd hidden her feelings from him, and it had led to years of misunderstandings and embarrassment. She wasn't doing that this time.

And, well, maybe it was working. Because she heard what he was saying, that he didn't want her. But any idiot could say that he did. This wasn't about her and whether she was enough for him. This was about his issues and the way that he was letting them stand in between them and something that could be really good. Well, fine. But she wasn't going to pretend that she agreed with him.

'I can't go over this again,' he said. 'I'm coming

with you tomorrow. Concentrate on your race. If you want to talk more when you're done, we can do it then.'

She stared him down, and realised she wasn't going to get more than that from him today. He looked utterly drained.

'Okay,' she agreed. And it irritated her that he was right. Tomorrow's race was as much a test of her mind as it was her body. She should be taking tonight to meditate. To rest. To see herself crossing that finish line over and over again so by the time that she set off tomorrow the race was half done.

Rowan nodded and did what he suggested, moving the bag from the bed to the floor and sitting in the divot it left in the duvet.

'Are you nervous?' he asked, coming to sit beside her.

She let herself have a sigh of relief. This felt…almost normal. 'I always am the day before. Can you please remind me why I'm doing this?'

He laughed, sudden and startling in the quiet house.

'Why you're running a hundred miles in a day? I wish I knew.'

'I know, I know.' She dropped her head into her hands. 'I don't have to do it,' she said, as she usually did around this point pre-race. 'I can just not go. No one would know. No one would care.'

'True,' Jonathan acknowledged, and she looked up. She'd been expecting him to just tell her to stop being silly, but he was actually thinking about what she'd said. 'What if you'd done that before the last one,' he asked at last. 'Do you regret running that race?'

Rowan groaned, because she knew that she wasn't going to be able to argue. 'No. You know that I don't. If I did I wouldn't have entered this one.'

'Well then.'

He nudged his arm against hers, before realising what he had done and practically jumping away, putting space between them.

'You give quite the pep talk,' she added. 'Thank you.'

'You didn't need a pep talk. Just someone to listen, and I'll always do that.'

She forced herself to smile and wished that they were back in that place where it felt natural to do so, rather than strained. 'Thanks.'

When Jonathan left—she guessed he was sharing Cal's room—she set her alarm for five a.m., which would give her enough time to fret over the checklists in her drop bags one last time before she headed to the start line.

She was still staring at the ceiling when her alarm bleeped the next morning, and she swung her legs over the side of the bed, as if her phone had given her the permission she'd been waiting for to finally admit that sleep wasn't going to come. It could be worse. She'd had sleepless nights before races before. She pulled on her kit, trying to mentally prepare herself for the day to come. Reminding herself of the reasons she was doing this. To test herself. To find the limits of her body and her mind and push herself through them step after step after step. To prove to herself that whatever else it might be, her body was strong and capable and would not let her down, regardless of what she threw at it. She had followed her training schedule. She had nourished her body. She had prepared in every way that she could to get as far as she could today.

Her kit consisted of comfortable old tights that had run hundreds of miles with her. A lightweight jersey with smooth flat seams. Every detail considered, so that when she was eighty miles in and convinced that she couldn't make another step, she'd done everything in her power to keep herself going. She looked up at the sound of a soft knock.

'Ready?' Jonathan asked, his head appearing around the door.

'No,' she confessed.

'Yes, you are,' Jonathan replied. 'And you know you are. Now come on. Breakfast.'

When she got downstairs, she was surprised to find Liv and Caleb already in the kitchen.

'This is for you,' Liv said, holding out a bar of home-made granola, and a handful of Ziploc bags with extra portions. She pulled her friend into a hug and squeezed her tight.

'You're going to be amazing,' Liv told her, pushing her away so she could get a good look at her. 'Enjoy it. Soak it in. You're ready for this.'

'I will. I will,' Rowan replied, feeling a little tearful. 'I'll be back here tomorrow with a shiny new medal.'

She gave Liv one last squeeze and then turned to go.

CHAPTER FIFTEEN

At the starting line

SOMETIME BEFORE THE starting gun fired he lost her. He had watched her check her pack, double knot her shoelaces and choose a playlist, and although she was standing only a few feet from him, she was already gone. Out running the race already, and all he could do was watch and wait.

Except, well, none of that was true, was it. He'd actually lost her yesterday, when he'd snapped and told her that he couldn't let himself love her. He tried not to remember the look on her face when he'd said that, like he'd stuck his hand right inside her chest and twisted her heart. But it was still dark out and her face was all he could seem to see.

He watched as the light from her head torch shrank smaller and smaller as she ran from him, and he shivered. He had been so certain in the moment when he had told her that he couldn't love her. But now he was alone, and cold, and just as certain that he *did* love her, whether he wanted to let himself do it or not. She was a part of him. He could feel it as she moved further and further away from him. He glanced at his watch and tried to calculate how long it would be before he saw her again, before he could lay his hands on her shoulders and look in her eyes and know that she was okay.

Checkpoint One

Jonathan looked at his watch and then checked against the lists of expected times at the aid stations that Rowan had given him that morning. He wouldn't worry for another quarter of an hour, he told himself, even though it was fifteen minutes past the time that he'd been expecting Rowan to appear in the distance, running towards him. That was the deal that he had made with himself. When he finally saw her turn the corner, running down the track towards the aid station, he couldn't deny the flood of relief he felt. Or then the pride that immediately followed it.

She looked strong, her head high and her chest out. He was by her side before she pulled to a stop, offering her a drink and a granola bar. She took both, with a breathless word of thanks, and he walked with her towards the exit of the aid station, guessing that she wouldn't want to stop and lose her momentum at this early stage. He couldn't resist wrapping an arm around her shoulders, just to feel that she was really there, solid and present. To soak her up as much as possible before they reached the gates out of the station and he would be left waiting. Again. 'You're doing so great,' he told her as they approached the volunteer checking race numbers. 'Just keep doing what you're doing and I'll see you at the next one,' he told her as she ran through the exit of the station and back out onto the course.

It had all happened so fast that he was still a little dazed as he watched her run off down the road, wondering whether he'd even helped at all. She'd barely needed him—and he suspected that that wasn't what he wanted at all.

Checkpoint Two

Three hours later, he watched Rowan hobbling up the track towards the second checkpoint and felt a clutch of concern in his stomach. It had been thirty minutes since he'd fixed his eyes firmly on the track and refused to move until he had seen that she was okay.

And she wasn't. There was something wrong. She was only a quarter of the way through the race distance and yet she was limping and grimacing.

'What's wrong?' he asked, rushing up to her, wrapping an arm around her waist and helping her to a chair. 'Feet,' she said simply. 'Hurt.'

He unlaced her shoes, pulled off her socks and found the problem quickly. A seam had rubbed a blister on the side of her little toe, and Rowan hissed as he wrapped a plaster around it, replaced her socks with a seamless pair from her drop bag and retied her shoes.

'Have you eaten since the last stop?' he asked, and when she shook her head he tutted gently and held up a sandwich so she could have a couple of bites. He tucked a couple of snacks into the right pocket of her pack and pulled out her phone.

'Music or talking,' he asked.

When she didn't reply, he made an executive decision and cued up some Beyoncé, thinking that she needed the boost. And then there was nothing more he could do. He pushed her to one of the Portaloos, then to the exit of the station, and watched as she ran along the track, wishing he could be out there with her and resigning himself to another few hours of watching and waiting. This was exactly why he didn't want to love her. Because he had spent most of his adult life feeling like this about Liv and Caleb, about his business and employees. Every moment that they were out of his sight he was worrying about them. Whether he was going to be able to pay the wages bill. Whether he was doing a good enough job with Liv and Caleb.

He didn't want to have to feel that way about Rowan as well. But it wasn't like he didn't think about her already. Like he hadn't played that night they had kissed over and over in his head, wondering if there was anything that he could have done differently to avoid hurting her. Surely that would only get worse the more he let himself love her. He didn't have a choice with Liv and Cal. The responsibility that he felt for them had been dumped on him and he'd had no say in it. But with Rowan, it would be different. He would be *choosing* to feel like this, and he wasn't sure if he had the strength, regardless of how much he wanted it.

Checkpoint Three

Rowan had been in such bad shape the last time that he had seen her that Jonathan was almost dreading her arrival at the halfway marker, with hours to indulge his worst fears about her in physical and mental pain. So when she appeared at the end of the track looking strong and fresh and not in the least like a woman who had just run two marathons back to back, he didn't know quite what to make of her. He had the contents of her drop bag laid out on a towel, sweet and savoury snacks, water and energy drinks and energy gels, plasters and painkillers and a change of clothes. But all she did when she saw him was wrap her arms around his neck and hug him tight.

'Thanks for the soundtrack,' she said between deep, gasping breaths. 'It was just what I needed.'

'My pleasure,' he said honestly, taking a step away so that he could get a proper look at her and see if he could work out what she needed. He couldn't stop staring. She was radiating energy, her long, lean limbs shining with perspiration, her face flushed. He was so intensely proud of her, he wanted to look around and make sure that everyone knew how amazingly she was doing. How incredible she was.

'I need sugar and salt and then carbs. A lot,' Rowan declared, looking to him to find them for her. He handed over the food he had ready for her, and asked if she wanted to sit.

'Need to keep moving.'

He walked with her through another enclosure, adding bits and pieces to her pack, fitting her head torch and swapping out her phone and headphones for ones with fresh batteries, all while she got some calories and hydration inside her.

When they reached the exit of the aid station, he squeezed her shoulder and she turned to him with a huge grin on her face. 'We're smashing this,' she told him. 'Absolutely smashing it.' And he felt himself nearly burst with pride that she was letting him do this, to be a part of it, trusting him. She didn't *need* him. She could be out doing this on her own, and he would have missed out on being a small part of her huge achievement. It was an absolute privilege to be here for her, he realised. To feed her and make sure she was drinking and to remind her to put on dry socks. It wasn't a burden to take care of someone who needed you. It was an honour. And in that light, the last ten years of his life, the last few days of his life, looked entirely different. If he let himself love her—well, it was too late for that. If he let himself believe that they could be together, to try and make this work—is that what it would look like? That loving someone would bring joy, alongside its responsibilities. That the responsibilities that he carried would feel lighter if he had someone to bear them with him. That he and Rowan as a team could be as unstoppable every day as he felt today.

Checkpoint Four

The glare of the sun had started to fade when Rowan hobbled into the station just five minutes past the goal time on his laminated card, but Jonathan could tell that she had not seen him.

He half expected her to be disorientated and confused but when he approached her and asked her what she needed, what he saw in her face was focus and determination. 'Bathroom, then…food, something to drink,' she said, faltering slightly before making herself move again. While she was in the bathroom, he got her food and snacks and tried to anticipate anything else she might need.

She appeared back where he had laid out her gear and refilled her drinks bottles while she grabbed food and walked towards the exit. He watched her carefully and—remembering something he'd read on an ultra-running blog—produced a can of Coke. She looked up as he opened the ring pull with a satisfying hiss of gas, and she stopped abruptly. With absolutely nothing to warn him of what she was about to do, she grabbed him, a hand on each side of his face, and kissed him hard on the mouth. 'This is the best idea anyone's ever had,' she told him, taking three long swigs of the drink. Then she handed the can back to him as they reached the exit of the aid station and headed back out on the course.

He stood and watched for a long time as she grew smaller and smaller, moving further and further away in the distance. She hadn't *needed* him. If he hadn't been here she could have grabbed what she needed without his help. But it brought him so much joy to be the one who could give it to her. That's what he wanted to do: bring her happiness. With cans of Coke and comfortable beds and by being someone who always, always listened when she told him what she wanted, and who worked it out for himself when she couldn't. He had never seen someone as focused and determined as she had been when she had headed back onto the route.

He'd given up hours ago trying to pretend that he didn't love her. He was only now starting to realise all the different ways that he did—he loved the way that she could fix her eye on a goal and push herself beyond what most people could endure to achieve it. She set superhuman goals and worked and trained and then simply endured until she had achieved them. And with that remarkable capacity for endurance, he wondered, could he possibly hope that whatever feelings she had for him might have endured his rejections and his stupidity? Might he still have a chance with her when all this was over?

He packed up their gear and headed to the final checkpoint with the embers of this hope burning warm in his chest, and he determined to feed them, just little by little. But first, he had a more important job to do, and that was to be and do whatever Rowan needed of him to get her through the rest of this night and the rest of this race. All he could do after that would be to tell her how he felt and hope for the best.

And then he had to watch her run off into the setting sun, and shivered, not sure what the night would bring.

Checkpoint Five

Jonathan was braced for another whirlwind stop at mile eighty, the last aid station before the end of the race, so as he watched the time on his phone tick further and further into the predicted window for the stop he grew more and more concerned.

What if something had happened to her out there? She had changed her emergency contact details to his mobile when Liv had hurt her ankle. But what if there was a mix-up? What if they couldn't reach him, or if Rowan was hurt by the side of a road somewhere and no one knew about it?

Then, just seconds before he had decided he would have to find a race organiser to ask, there she was, walking up the track, her shoulders rounded and her face wet with tears, reflecting the light from his head torch. He jogged to her and wrapped his arms around her on instinct, squeezing her tighter when she burst into fresh tears.

'What is it? What happened?' he asked, pushing her into a folding chair and forcing a hot cup of tea into her hands.

'I can't do it,' she said, sniffing back tears and wiping her face with the back of her hands. 'I can't do it.'

'Okay, okay,' Jonathan said, holding the hand that wasn't wrapped around her mug and pressing a kiss to the back of it.

He tried to think fast, wishing they had covered what to do in this situation—he didn't want to second-guess what she wanted. But he didn't want to let her down if all she needed was someone to tell her to get back out there. She had been so focused at the last checkpoint that he had never anticipated this.

'Tell me why you started,' he said, asking the first question that came to mind. 'Tell me why you run.'

'To see if I can,' she replied in a small voice, and he nodded. 'What a stupid bloody reason.'

'It's not stupid. And you can. You've run eighty miles already. That's more than most people can even imagine. A *regular* marathon is more than most people can imagine running. So why a hundred?'

She sat up a little straighter as she considered the question.

'Because I wanted to prove to myself my body wouldn't let me down. Even if I threw the hardest races in the world at it.'

He couldn't help but smile at that.

'And has it let you down?' he asked.

He couldn't tell her what to do—only she could decide that. All he could do was ask questions so he could try and understand her. Try and understand how to support her. She shook her head.

'Everything hurts,' she sniffed, and her voice was so small that something inside him broke. He pulled her to him for another hug.

'Does it always hurt after eighty miles?' he asked, tipping her face up and brushing the hair back from her face, clipping it back with the grips that it had escaped.

'Of course it does. But…'

'But?' he asked.

Rowan grimaced, like she didn't want to hear her own answer. 'But sometimes I run through it. Sometimes it doesn't matter that it hurts—I just do it anyway and then it's over.'

He thought about that for a moment. 'Do you want to run through it tonight?' he asked.

Rowan shook her head. 'I don't know. I don't know if I can.'

'You don't have to know,' he told her gently. 'You don't have to think too far ahead. Can you do another step, another mile?'

She nodded.

'Do you want to?'

She hesitated, and for a moment he thought that that was it, they were done. But then she got a look in her eye that was unmistakeably Rowan—battle ready— and nodded again and finished her tea.

'You can do this,' he told her earnestly. 'I've never seen something as incredible as you have been today. You endure like no one I've ever met before. You're strong and you're capable and you're amazing. You've been preparing for this for months and months and all you have to do is trust in yourself. Trust your body to do what you know it can do. I believe you can do it.'

She nodded again, eyes fixed now. Barely seeing him. He couldn't have cared less. Not a single moment of this was about him, no matter how his feelings for her had changed through the day, and the night. This was about Rowan. About helping her to be everything that she could be.

'I can. I can do it. I'm going to do it. I have to do it.'

She stood abruptly, knocking over the flask of tea and making him laugh. 'Steady on, sweetheart. Take a breath.'

He stuffed spare batteries, gels and blister plasters

in her backpack and unscrewed the lids on her drinks bottles so the volunteers could fill them without costing her any more time. 'Your feet okay?' he asked, and she nodded, her eyes and her mind, he guessed, already back on the route. He pushed her towards the bathroom, forced a few spoonfuls of food into her and then pushed her back out into the dark night hoping that he had done the right thing.

The finish line

By the time the sun had started to rise, he'd managed a few hours' sleep in twenty-minute bursts, folded uncomfortably into a plastic chair, close to one of the small fires they'd lit for a little light and warmth. The festival atmosphere had quieted, and the time between runners arriving in the camp had stretched out, until each one was an event in itself, and they all pitched in to try and keep them running. He watched the sun come over the horizon, unable to think of anything but Rowan.

His alarm went off to alert him that they were approaching the finishing window. Given the state that Rowan had been in at the last checkpoint, he'd been expecting a call to say she was at the side of the road somewhere and would he come pick her up. But he had to assume that no news was good news and started to pull together what she might need when she was done.

And then he joined the small crowd still waiting and watching the approach to the finish line. Twenty-four hours ago, he had sent Rowan out into the unknown, with no clue that he would have fallen heart over gut in love with her by the time she was back.

But now wasn't the time to be thinking about his feelings for her. The only thing that mattered right now was getting her back safe and well. He checked his watch against the timecard. Still plenty of time. He abandoned his post just for a couple of minutes to get a fresh flask of tea from the van. His last twenty-four hours had nothing on Rowan's, but they hadn't exactly been the most restful or comfortable either, and both a little warmth and a lot of caffeine were needed right now.

And just as he was about to drop into his seat to resume his vigil, there she was, turning the corner of the lane. Her feet were barely leaving the ground as she took short, shuffling steps towards him, but she was still moving, still running, and he was still falling harder and harder for her by the second, seconds which seemed to crawl by as he waited by the finish line, cheering and whooping and clapping and desperate to have her back whole and safe.

She staggered straight into him across the finish line and he clutched her so tight that he lost his balance, and her legs gave out at the same time he was trying to find his centre of gravity. Without him knowing exactly how it happened they were in a heap on the floor with Rowan sprawled on top of him.

While he was still clutching for something to say, Rowan burst into both tears and laughter simultaneously, leaving him flailing for how to react.

Eventually, when helpful volunteers appeared in

his peripheral vision to help them up from the ground, he managed to wave them off, roll her to the side of him, prop himself up on his elbow and look her over and make sure that she was all in one piece and that the tears were of relief and of nothing more serious. He brushed her hair back from her face, and she managed a weak smile, though she looked dazed and not entirely present.

'You did it,' he said, bursting with pride.

Rowan laughed aloud. 'I did it. At least I think I did. If I'm not hallucinating. Is this real?'

'Very real,' he said, wiping away more tears that she seemed to be unaware of. 'You really, really did it.'

And with that, she grabbed him by the hair and kissed him hard. He couldn't help but laugh against her lips as a couple of wolf whistles sounded behind him. He eased her hands from behind his head and knelt up on the ground, pulling Rowan upright.

'You need to drink something, sweetheart,' he told her. 'And then eat something, and then sleep for a week,' he told her firmly.

He looped her arm around his shoulders and walked her to his camping chair, where he could take care of her properly. After twenty-four hours of not knowing where she was, how she was, he just wanted to soak in the fact that he had her in his sight for the next twenty minutes, or twenty days, or however long she'd let him be there. Because there was no way that he was walking away from her. He loved her—nothing had ever been more obvious. And nothing could be clearer to him than that being allowed to love her and care for her and take care of her was a privilege—one that he could never tire of. He had seen her strength over the course of the past twenty-four hours, but even if she didn't have apparently superhuman strength and endurance, he knew that they were stronger together. That he wanted to face his future with Rowan in his life, and for him to be in hers.

Now he just had to try and convince her that he knew what an idiot he had been, that he was sorry and beg her to give him another chance.

But that could wait. Right now all he wanted to do was take care of her, so he fed her and hydrated her and helped her into warm clothes and was content to just watch her rest for a while until she started nodding and the cup of tea in her hand tipped precariously towards her lap. 'That's it,' he said with finality. 'I'm taking you home: you need to sleep.'

In her exhausted state she let him half carry her to the car, and she made soft, appreciative noises as he opened the door and helped her into the seat. She was snoring before they even reached the road.

CHAPTER SIXTEEN

ROWAN WOKE TO the sound of a creaking floorboard.

'Hello?' she called out, not quite up to opening her eyes yet. She wasn't on the back-breaker, that much was clear. But this didn't smell quite like Liv's room either. Which meant... She opened her eyes, and found Jonathan watching her from the doorway of his own bedroom.

'I'm sorry, I didn't mean to wake you,' he said.

She shook her head, because honestly she wasn't sure that he had. Truth be told, she wasn't even sure that she was awake or not. She had a horrible feeling that her memories of kissing Jonathan hard, even after they had talked endlessly of all the reasons he didn't want to be with her, weren't a dream. Something inside her chest threatened to curl up and die, but she forced herself not to show it on her face. Hopefully Jonathan could write it off as some sort of exhaustion-induced delirium.

'You've been out for a while,' he said now, leaning against the door frame. 'I just wanted to check you were okay.'

'I'm fine,' she said, and then tried to sit. At which point every single muscle in her body protested, and she decided that she was probably okay lying down a little longer. 'Maybe not completely fine,' she conceded. 'I'm in your bed again,' she said, realising that she had no memory of how she got there.

Jonathan nodded. 'You fell asleep in the car. I did try and wake you but you were insistent that you weren't moving and I couldn't let you stay out there after everything that you've been through. So. Here you are.'

'You carried me?' Rowan asked. She risked the pain of throwing her arm up to cover her face, because she couldn't bear the thought of him being that close to her while she looked, and smelled, like this. 'I'm disgusting.'

'No, you're lovely. I'm in love with you.'

At that she sat bolt upright, aching muscles be damned, and then groaned, loudly, as every single one of her abdominal muscles punished her for it.

Jonathan's hand was over his mouth, as if he couldn't quite believe what he'd just said. 'I— I'm so sorry,' he stuttered, crossing the room and sitting on the edge of the bed. 'I didn't mean to say that.'

'You didn't mean it?' she asked, terrified that he was about to take the words back, because she had been waiting to hear them for so, so long, and she wasn't sure she had the energy for mental gymnastics today.

'No! I mean, yes. I just mean…this isn't about me,'

Jonathan said. 'This is your day. It shouldn't be about my feelings. I was going to say that I'd run you a bath.'

She laughed, a little weakly. 'Honestly, Jonathan. As delicious as a bath sounds, I think I'd rather know whether you're in love with me. And, if you are, what you're planning on doing about it.'

He hesitated, and then reached for her hand. She didn't even know whether she wanted to let herself hope. She was too tired, too drained. But apparently no one had told her heart, which had kicked back into race pace, and was waiting eagerly to hear where this was going. 'I... I am. I'm in love with you. I'm sorry.'

And as much as she wanted to let her heart sing and clouds to part, and angels descend, she couldn't quite get there. 'Why do you keep apologising?' she asked, and she could hear the tension in her own voice. 'Why do you have to be sorry that you love me? Why does it have to be so hard, Jonathan?' Maybe she would have guarded her words better if she hadn't been utterly wracked with exhaustion. Or maybe she should have all her conversations when she was too tired to filter. Too tired to lie.

'Because I've already told you how impossible I am,' Jonathan said, with a touch more regret in his voice than she wanted to hear. 'How difficult I'm going to make this.'

She stopped him with a hand on his arm and opened her eyes wider. 'This?' she asked, because she had to know what he was talking about. What he was offering, if he was offering anything beyond the knowledge that he loved her.

'This. Us. If you'll have me,' he said, and that sounded so much like everything that she had ever wanted that she still couldn't let herself believe it. 'I love you, Rowan. I have for such a long time. And in the past few days I have seen over and over again how strong you are and how capable, and I can't believe I ever tried to take a decision out of your hands. So if you'll have me, I'll try. Because I think that all I want is to be there for you, for your whole life, and to let you be there for me too. If you want to, that is.'

She stared at him, still not quite sure that she was really awake. That she wasn't still out there at mile ninety-two, hallucinating. Because this was everything that she had ever wanted. Everything she was afraid that she would never have—it had seemed so close a few days ago, and then further away than ever. And she still couldn't quite trust that it wouldn't be snatched away the minute that she admitted how much she wanted it to be true.

'And you realised all this…when I look like this?' she asked at last. Which wasn't exactly the most important part of this whole scenario, but it made it all so much less believable that she couldn't not address it directly. She looked down at herself, not quite sure what she was going to see. She was still in the soft sweats that he'd coaxed onto her when she'd finished the race, her medal still around her neck.

'You wouldn't let me take it off,' he said with a soft chuckle.

She stroked it. If the medal was real, then she really had finished the race. Which meant that she was really here, and… 'You love me?' she asked, just wanting to be really very doubly sure that she hadn't got that part wrong. 'And you're just going to…let yourself love me?'

'I love you,' he said, and his voice was surer now. 'And I'm not saying that I'm not terrified, but I'm much more scared of a life without you in it.'

She groaned, and even in her state she was sure that that wasn't the right reaction. 'I love you too, Jonathan, you know that I do,' she said from behind the hands she appeared to be covering her face with.

Until Jonathan pulled them gently away and met her eyes.

'Then why does that sound like a no?' he asked.

'It's not a no. It's just… Let's think about this, logically, I mean. Yesterday…the day before… I've lost track. But you were very clear that a relationship wasn't what you wanted. And you've just been more than twenty-four hours without sleep and accidentally told me that you loved me instead of telling me that you were running me a bath. It's just hard for me to trust that this is really what you want. What if I *do* say yes and then you get a good night's sleep and realise you've made a huge mistake?'

He nodded, and she could tell that he understood why she was holding back. 'I know what it looks like, sounds like. And I know that I've messed you around, Rowan. I absolutely do not deserve another chance and I completely understand if you don't want to give me one. But it's true, Rowan. Every word of it. I want this. I want you, more than anything I've ever wanted in my whole life. And I'm not pretending that I'm not utterly terrified at the thought of how we're going to make this work. I just know that I want to make it work with you, rather than without you.'

'I *want* to believe you,' Rowan said. More than she'd wanted just about anything else.

'You were right,' Jonathan went on. And okay, maybe she'd just keep letting him talk while she rested her eyes. 'Everything you said the other day when I was being a complete idiot and a coward. I don't give Liv and Cal enough credit. I've never seen my position as something that I'm blessed with, rather than something that I'm encumbered with, and I'm a complete idiot for insisting on doing things on my own for so long.

'It shouldn't have had to take watching you put yourself through what you did yesterday to make me realise it. But I was so proud of you. So grateful that you let me be even a small part of it. I like being a team with you, Rowan. I want to spend the rest of my life being a team with you.'

She watched him, the man she loved, as the torrent of words flowed from him. It all came down to one thing, really, and that was whether she could trust him. He had given her every reason before today not to. He had hidden his feelings and fudged his words and avoided her. But if she wanted proof that things were going to be different now, here it was, right in front of her. Telling her exactly how he felt, and how hard he was going to try. She would be a fool if she walked away now.

'I should have realised a long time ago that my life is so much richer and kinder and stronger with you in it and I can only hope that you can let me prove to you how much I love you and how much I want to be there for you. Whatever we're doing. Whether it's business or running or family, I want to do it all together, Rowan. I can't imagine doing any of it without you. Except no, I can. Because that's what I've been doing all these years and it's been miserable. And I've been happier this week with you than I've ever been before in my life and I can't believe that I was stupid enough to think that I could just walk away from that.'

Jonathan carried on talking, because he had no idea she'd already decided there was no way that she was letting him go. 'I'm sorry,' he added, when Rowan eventually put her hands to his face and kissed him, if only to make the words stop coming.

'You can stop,' she told him gently. 'I believe you. I believe that you love me, and that you want to make this happen.'

He nodded, his turn to be open-mouthed and speechless now.

'I'm… This is a lot to take in,' Rowan said, though she twisted away when his kisses trailed down to her neck. 'And I feel disgusting. Just…let me think? Give me a little time?'

'Of course,' Jonathan said into her collarbone, before looking up at her. 'Would it help if I actually ran you that bath?' he asked, and Rowan all but whimpered with anticipated pleasure.

'Run me a bath and I might marry you,' she said,

her voice a little dazed. She winced—she had meant it as a joke, but maybe it was too soon for those sorts of throwaway comments. But Jonathan didn't even flinch and Rowan widened her eyes. Was that…on the cards? He just smiled and asked her something about bubbles in her bath as he crossed to the bathroom door and she desperately tried to struggle out of bed, her brain still trying to process everything that he had just told her.

She hadn't even thought beyond the bath that she could hear running in the next room, never mind where she and Jonathan might be a week or a month from now. But with that last smile of his, she realised that this actually had a future. They could start thinking about what they wanted their life together to look like and then just…make that happen.

CHAPTER SEVENTEEN

ROWAN LET OUT a long, low sigh as she leaned back in the tub, letting the water take the weight of her limbs and finally feeling some of the ache draw out of them.

'I'm in here,' Rowan called when she heard Jonathan walk back into his bedroom. She glanced down to check that the thick, foamy bubbles were protecting her modesty—which was maybe a bit horse and stable door et cetera—and then saw Jonathan appear and then hesitate in the doorway.

'It's fine,' she told him. 'I'm decent, you can come in.'

His eyes widened, so perhaps her idea of decent and his weren't quite meeting in the middle. But, honestly, she could look at that expression on his face all day— as long as she was the one putting it there.

'I made you a cup of tea,' he said. 'I was going to leave it in the other room.'

'It's okay. Stay, sit if you like,' she said.

So he did, on the floor, leaning against a vanity cabinet, his head level with hers, the rim of the tub hiding her body from his eyes, so that he finally looked like he might be able to have a conversation without being fatally distracted.

'I've been thinking about what you said,' she told him. Because how was she meant to think about anything other than him declaring his love for her. Especially when she was in the most delicious bath of her life—that he had run for her—just minutes after declaring his love. She let out an involuntary sigh of pleasure. If things didn't work out, would she be able to keep him just for this? But no, that would never be enough for her. She wanted him, all of him, and she wanted to keep him for ever.

'I knew I was in love with you before the race,' she told him. 'And even when you said that you didn't want to try, I knew that it wasn't about me.'

'Of course it wasn't—'

'No, wait, will you let me say this please?' Rowan said. They'd spent years not talking about the way that they felt about one another, and it had hurt them both. She wasn't going to go into this with anything left unsaid. 'I've felt that way about you for a long time. At least since we kissed that first time, and probably before that. And I never in my wildest, most fanciful dreams thought that you would ever feel the same way about me.'

He opened his mouth to protest, but she leaned forward, resting her forearms and her chin on the edge of the bath, anything to be closer to him. 'I just looked at myself, and I heard everything that my bullies had ever told me, and I looked at *you* and I thought—of course he's not going to want me back. When you pushed me away that first time, it proved every bad thought I'd ever had about myself.

'And then any time I tried to be with someone else, they…they weren't you. So they were never what I wanted.

'Being here with you this week, I saw something in you that I'd never let myself see before. I saw how deeply you were hurting, and that your issues weren't with me at all—it was all about you trusting yourself to be able to do this. So I need to tell you this, and I need you to believe me if we're going to work: I know you, Jonathan Kinley. I know that you are kind, and thoughtful, and you care about me, and you know *me*. Yesterday wouldn't have worked if you didn't. And so I'm going to believe you when you say you love me. I'm going to trust you when you say that you mean it. And I'm going to do everything I can, for as long as you'll let me, to make sure you know I feel the same way. And if you start doubting yourself, and thinking you need to carry the whole world on your shoulders, and thinking that you're not good for me, or that *we're* not good for you, then you have to promise to talk to me about it.'

Jonathan rose to his knees in front of her, and she suddenly felt incredibly naked in a way that had absolutely nothing to do with the fact that she was in the bath.

'I promise. I meant every word I said,' he said, slightly breathless. 'I love you. I'm going to tell you again and again and again. Until you're sick of hearing it. And while I'm at it I'm going to tell you that you're brilliant and beautiful and so strong. And I'm thinking that I'll tell you that for ever, if that's okay.' He leaned forward, through the steam spiralling up from her bath, smoothed damp tendrils of hair from her cheeks and brushed the softest of kisses to her lips.

'I'm not sure for ever will be long enough,' she whispered between kisses, her hands curling into the front of his T-shirt. And then she pulled him into the tub, clothes and all, and squealed as a wave of water cascaded over the side.

He blinked down at her, his face a picture of surprise. His lips a soft O, his eyes wide and startled.

'Will you marry me?' he asked, still with that dazed expression.

Rowan managed to get her arms round his waist, her hands to the hem of his T-shirt, the sopping wet fabric somehow over his head and onto the floor.

'I think I asked first,' she reminded him as she pushed her hands into his hair and pulled him down for a kiss.

When their skin was wrinkled and the hot water tank empty, they admitted defeat and reluctantly left the bath. And then when they had towelled themselves, and each other and the bathroom floor, dry, they found themselves back on Jonathan's bed, on crisp clean sheets, curled around one another in the warm sunlight that found its way in through the diamond-patterned windows.

'So, we should probably tell Liv about this,' Jonathan said.

'Oh.' Rowan looked up at him from where she had tucked herself under his arm. 'You're right. Just as soon as I'm ready to leave this bed I'll talk to her.'

'I don't even want to think about what her reaction to me asking you to marry me is going to be.'

'Uh… I'll be telling her that *I* asked *you*,' Rowan corrected him, because she didn't want him thinking that this had happened all on his terms. 'And you still haven't answered, by the way. I proposed to you and you left me hanging.'

Jonathan turned on his side and propped himself on his elbow, his hand stroking a long line up her side. She blushed under his scrutiny but didn't look away. 'No, I didn't,' he said. 'I proposed back.'

Rowan rolled her eyes. 'That is absolutely not the same thing as accepting.'

He stared down at her and she grinned.

'Ask me again,' he said, brushing his knuckles across her cheek, letting his hand drop to her shoulder, nudging at the strap of her tank top. She bit her lip, not quite able to believe that she was doing this. That it was real.

'Jonathan, will you marry me?' she asked, her voice no more than a whisper. She reached for him, her arms around his waist, as she waited for his answer.

'Yes, I'll marry you,' he whispered in her ear, before kissing her on the sensitive skin just behind. 'I'd do it over and over and over again if I could.'

Rowan laughed into his neck. 'I think just the once will do it.'

'Okay, then,' he said, pressing her onto her back,

holding her to the mattress with his body and kissing her hard. 'This. I want to do this every day of my life. Would that be okay?'

'I think I can probably live with that,' Rowan conceded with a sigh.

'Good.'

M. O'Keefe

Inc. muscle, but it was a weak, lift their words surely
confess. Then I would regret heavily was all of my life.
Rowan tried a slowly of force? I thought someone in
when I saw somebody I met with taunter, was not
under it like a minor and.
Come

CHAPTER EIGHTEEN

THEY WALKED OUT to the maze that afternoon in a weak effort to make her legs move again, strolling slowly in the last warmth of the day, their fingers intertwined and swinging between them.

'Tell me you were going to kiss me in there or I'll always wonder,' Rowan demanded as she pulled him towards the entrance, untangling their fingers so that she could wrap her arm around his waist and lean into him.

Jonathan sighed and squeezed her side. 'Of course I was going to kiss you,' he said, leaning in and doing it now, slowly, until she was ready to drag him somewhere secluded. 'I feel like I've been about to kiss you since you appeared in my hallway,' he said. 'I've thought about you so often that for a minute I thought that I'd imagined you.'

'Mmm, I like hearing you confess things like that,' she said. 'Though it makes me sad that we didn't figure all this out sooner.'

Jonathan shrugged. 'We had to wait until we were ready,' he said, turning her face to him for another kiss. 'And we can make up for lost time now. I hope you don't want a long engagement.'

She broke away with a smile and pulled him into the maze. 'Maybe we should get married in here,' she said, walking backwards and pulling him by both hands. 'I think I was right when I said it was magical. And it feels like our place now.'

Jonathan smiled ruefully. 'Well, I don't know how much longer we're going to be able to. The estate agents are coming next week to take photos for the listings.'

'That's still happening?' she asked gently.

His eyebrows pulled together, and she rubbed away the creases between them with her thumb. 'I really don't think I have a choice.'

'Caleb can't buy it off you with his mystery bit-coins?'

Jonathan laughed. 'I'm really going to have to ask him some questions about that, aren't I?'

'If you don't, I will. You never told me your brother has hidden depths. And he's cute too.'

Jonathan shoved her gently. 'Don't joke. It's bad enough that Liv gets first dibs on you.'

'Yeah, well, it's not my fault it took you so long to realise you were in love with me.'

He groaned, pulling her in tight to him and tweaking her ponytail. 'Don't remind me how much time I've wasted,' he said into her hair.

Rowan leaned back and kissed him on the lips. 'I'll forgive you if you promise there will be no nonsense about taking money from your siblings—because if you put the house on the open market they could just buy it off you with a lot more hassle if you really wanted to be mean about it.'

He nodded, and looked her in the eyes. He wasn't messing around, and she had never been so glad to see him so serious. 'I'll hear them out. I promise. The three of us—the four of us—will make a decision together. I've got no plans of being more of an idiot with my family, or with you, than I already have been. And if it helps, I fully expect you to take Liv's side if I'm causing problems.'

She smiled, because she hadn't quite got her head around how this was going to work yet, her best friend and her...fiancé, competing for her affection. 'Oh, that was never in question,' she told him. She could foresee a long night with Liv and several bottles of wine in her near future, just as soon as she could stand up from a sofa without groaning, and could go more than ten minutes without feeling she needed a full plate of carbs and two pints of water.

Jonathan led her through the maze easily this time, and they were soon in the sunlit clearing in the centre, the rose-covered love seat exactly as she remembered it.

'You're right. This place is ours now,' he said, wrapping his arms about her waist and resting his chin on her shoulder. 'I don't think I can let it go.'

'Because we didn't kiss here?' she asked, turning her head to give him a kiss and a wry smile.

'Well, we can put that right now,' he said, dragging her over to the love seat. 'Hand me your phone?'

Rowan hesitated. 'What, why? Are you planning on documenting this?'

'No,' he said, taking it from her and turning it off before wrapping his arms around her again. 'Because I'm not taking any chances of being disturbed this time. I want you all to myself.' He pulled her into his lap on the swing and she let out a long, contented sigh, relaxing her body into his chest. She let her eyes drift closed and turned slowly in his arms, tipping her face up to his with a certainty and confidence she hadn't believed that she was ever going to find. And his lips met hers with an honesty that she was sure he'd never allowed himself before.

It was a kiss that told her everything about how he felt about her. How hard they'd fought to get here, to find one another. To overcome all the fears that had told them to walk away. It was a kiss that promised a lifetime together, and she was going to spend every day of that lifetime grateful for this man.

* * * * *

COMING SOON!

We really hope you enjoyed reading this book. If you're looking for more romance, be sure to head to the shops when new books are available on

Thursday 14th April

To see which titles are coming soon, please visit

millsandboon.co.uk/nextmonth

MILLS & BOON ®

Coming next month

SECRETS BEHIND THE BILLIONAIRE'S RETURN
Rachael Stewart

'Why have you come home? Now, after all this time?'

Felicity felt Sebastian's gaze on her, burning into her, and for one silly moment, she wondered: was he going to tell her he was here for her?

Like some fairy-tale romance where the hero made his fortune and returned to sweep the heroine off her feet...

As if. She almost laughed aloud at the ridiculous notion and choked on her drink in the process.

'Steady.' He placed a hand on her back, the innocent touch reverberating right through her. 'You okay?'

She hurried to recover, to break the electrifying contact. 'You avoiding the question?'

He gave her a slight smile. 'No. Truth is, now my grandfather's gone, my brother and I can do what we like with the estate. We toyed with letting it go but I figure the old man will turn in his grave to see us return to it.'

She could hear the bitterness, see the smile still playing about his lips adding to the chill of his hatred, and fought back a shudder. She'd never known Sebastian to be cold, stripped of his good humour, his care, his passion.

Was this more the man he was now? A cold-hearted business mogul?

She wanted to ask, but she was only putting off the inevitable, the all-important conversation that they had to have and that wasn't fair...on any of them.

'Sebastian?'

His eyes wavered over her face, his brows drawing together. 'Yes.'

'There's something I need to tell you...'

'I figured as much.'

She wet her lips. 'You did?'

'You look like you're about to confess to some heinous crime.'

'No.' She gave a tight laugh. 'No crime. Only...'

'Only?'

'I'm—I'm a mum.'

'I know.' His smile softened, his eyes, too, something akin to regret lingering there. 'I gathered that earlier. Is—is her father around? I notice you don't wear a...'

He gestured to her ring finger and she snatched it back self-consciously, twisting her hands together. 'No, he is— wasn't.'

Oh, God, why couldn't she just say it? Why was it so hard?

'Can't have been easy bringing her up alone, looking after your gran, especially when she got sick, and then there's this place...' He gestured around him and she couldn't even nod, couldn't even blink.

His eyes narrowed as the silence extended...a beat, two, three. 'Flick?'

Continue reading
SECRETS BEHIND THE BILLIONAIRE'S RETURN
Rachael Stewart

Available next month
www.millsandboon.co.uk

JOIN US ON SOCIAL MEDIA!

Stay up to date with our latest releases, author news and gossip, special offers and discounts, and all the behind-the-scenes action from Mills & Boon...

 millsandboon

 millsandboonuk

 millsandboon

It might just be true love...